# THE DAUGHTER OF ZION

## The Soul Summoner Series Book 9

## ELICIA HYDER

## CHARACTER LIST

**MAIN CHARACTERS:**

**Warren Parish**
the Archangel of Death. Father of Iliana. Son of Azrael and Nadine.

**Iliana Parish**
The Vitamorte, an Angel of Life and Dead. Daughter of Warren and Sloan.

**Nathan McNamara**
Warren's best friend. Married to Sloan Jordan. Commander of SF-12.

**Sloan Jordan**
Mother of Iliana. Married to Nathan McNamara. Daughter of fallen Angel of Life Kasyade.

**Azrael**

Former Archangel of Death. Father of Warren. Love interest of Adrianne Marx. Owner of Claymore Worldwide Security.

**Fury (Allison)**

Member of SF-12. Human daughter of Abaddon, the Destroyer. Twin sister of Anya. Former girlfriend of Warren.

**The Morning Star**

Fallen Angel of Life and Angel of Knowledge.

## SUPPORTING CHARACTERS (ALPHABETICAL)

**Abaddon "The Destroyer"**
(Deceased)
Father of Fury and Anya. Former guardian of Nulterra, and former Archangel of Protection.

**Adrianne Marx**

Sloan's best friend. Love interest of Azrael.

**Alice**
(Deceased)
Childhood best friend of Warren.

**Anya**

Angel of Protection. Twin sister of Fury. Daughter of Abaddon, the Destroyer.

**Ariel**

The Archangel of Life. Lives in Eden.

**Audrey Jordan**
(Deceased) Adoptive mother of Sloan.

**Chimera**
Seramorta of Knowledge. Hacker, security specialist. Newest member of SF-12.

**Enzo**
Special Operations Director of SF-12.

**The Father**
The creator of Eden and Earth. Masquerades on Earth as "Father John."

**Flint McGrath**
(Deceased)
Adoptive human father of Fury and Anya.

**Huffman**
Claymore operative. Works at the armory at Claymore Headquarters in New Hope, NC.

**Ionis**
Messenger Angel.

**Jett/Malak**
Angel of Protection born to Fury. Friend of Rogan.

**Johnny McNamara**
Uncle of Nathan McNamara. Former love interest of Fury.

**Kane**
SF-12 Operator.

**Kasyade**
(Deceased)
Biological mother of Sloan. Fallen Angel of Life.

**Metatron**
Angel of Life and Ministry (Born on Earth).

**Nadine**
(Deceased)
Mother of Warren.

**Phenex**
(Deceased)
Mother of Alice. Fallen Angel of Life.

**Reuel**
Angel of Protection. (aka Guardian).

**Robert Jordan**
Adoptive father of Sloan.

**Rogan (Nico)**
Angel of Protection born to Shannon Green. Friend of Jett.

**Shannon Green-Reese**
Nathan's former girlfriend. Mother of the angel Rogan (Nico)
Married to Tyrell Reese.

**Samael**
Angel of Death who guards the spirit line.

**Sandalphon**
Angel of Prophecy and Knowledge (Born on Earth)

**Taiya**
Seramorta Angel of Life. Daughter of Ysha and Melinda Harmon.

**Theta**
The Archangel of Prophecy.

**Torman**
Fallen Angel of Knowledge. Father of Chimera. Helped Warren and Fury escape from Nulterra.

**Tyrell Reese**
Married to Shannon Green. Friend of Nathan McNamara.

**Ysha**
(Deceased) Father of Taiya. Fallen Angel of Life.

**Members of Sf-12 (*denotes ability to see angels):**
1. Enzo*
2. Kane*
3. Cooper
4. NAG* (Mandi) - pilot
5. Lex
6. Doc*
7. Wings - pilot
8. Cruz
9. Pirez
10. Justice
11. Dalton
12. Chimera
*Fury* (Retired)*

# The Soul Summoner Series Order

Book 1 - **The Soul Summoner**
Book 2 - **The Siren**
Book 3 - **The Angel of Death**
Book 4 - **The Taken**
Book 5 - **The Sacrifice**
Book 6 - **The Regular Guy**
Book 7 - **The Soul Destroyer**
Book 8 - **The Guardian**
Book 9 - **The Daughter of Zion**

**Standalones:**
**The Detective**
**The Mercenary**
**The Archangel**

*This book is for Hydernation.*

*I make shit up and write it down.*
*It's YOU who give these characters life.*

*Thank you for believing in them.*
*And for believing in me.*

*Many more adventures await.*

# THE PROPHECY

I saw the great sword come down from Eden,
having the key to the bottomless pit.
And he laid hold of the dragon
when a thousand years had expired.
The devil that deceived them
was cast into his lake of fire
and tormented day and night for ever and ever.

# CHAPTER ONE

"Hi, Appa."

My daughter's words drove me to my knees. I looked down at her from the top of the hill. Dark hair, same as her mother's. Black eyes, same as mine.

I sat back on my heels, my heart throbbing in my chest. "What...how?" I swallowed, and my throat was coated with sandpaper. "How did I not see this?"

We'd been in Nulterra for two days. *Two* days. But somehow, seventeen years had passed on Earth. Iliana, who'd only just had her first birthday when I left, was now an adult standing before me.

Someone retched.

I turned and saw Fury spewing water and bile over our "graves." Her sister, Anya, was holding Fury's hair back.

Iliana started toward us cautiously. When she reached the hilltop, she knelt down in front of me. "I knew you weren't dead." She put her arms around my neck and hugged me.

My stunned arms finally wrapped around her. "Is it really you?"

"It's really me."

I held the back of her head against my shoulder. Her hair was silky and smooth, just like Sloan's. I closed my eyes. "You led us out."

I felt her nod.

She pulled back. "You'd been gone so long. None of us could see you or feel your spirit, but I knew. You promised me you'd come back."

Tears brimmed my eyes. "You remember that?"

"I remember everything." She hugged me again. "I knew you'd keep your word."

"I always will." The tears erupted then. My god. I'd missed *everything*. All I'd wanted was to get the sanctonite stone so I could be with her. So I could be part of her life. So I could watch her grow up.

Now I had the stone, but suddenly, Iliana was a woman. No longer the baby I'd just kissed goodbye. And it had happened overnight—for me, anyway.

She stood, pulling me up with her.

I took a step back and dried my eyes. "Well, let me have a look at you."

Iliana was taller than Sloan, the extra height in her long, lean legs. She wore a pale-pink T-shirt and athletic shorts with hiking boots.

The hair was the reason I'd mistaken her for her mother. It was almost the same length as Sloan's the first time I'd seen her, a memory that would be eternally burned into my mind. It was long and wavy, a dark river perfectly framing her slender face.

Unlike Sloan, Iliana had the faintest of freckles across the bridge of her small nose. And she had my mother's smile.

I hugged her again, unable to stop myself.

"What about the others?" Fury asked, her voice raspy and shaking.

Iliana stepped back, then extended her hand toward Fury. "You're Jett's mom, aren't you?"

A puff of air squeezed from Fury's chest. "You know him?"

"Sure I do." Iliana jerked her thumb over her shoulder. "He's here."

Behind her, a few more bodies emerged from the jungle's tree line. Two angels and three humans.

"I asked them to let me come out first," she said. "They allowed me to have my moment."

Of course they did. She *commanded* them, or at the very least, she commanded the angels. And I suspected the humans were under her as well, as part of her personal protection detail, SF-12. Almost all of them were armed, but from our distance, none of them, I recognized.

And how could I after seventeen years?

Seventeen years.

Acid burned in my stomach.

The two angels were both male. They were about the same height. Both young, around Iliana's age. One had straight blond hair sweeping his forehead. The other's was dark, nearly black, and unruly.

His eyes and Fury's were locked on each other.

Jett.

I touched Fury's arm. She was trembling.

"You can go see him if you'd like," Iliana said.

I stroked Fury's wrist with my thumb. "Want us to go with you?"

Fury shook her head, then reached back for her sister. I nodded, and she started down the hill first with Anya right behind her.

Reuel and Samael stayed with me. Reuel was still holding

Hannah's hand, the little girl we'd rescued from Nulterra. She was, for lack of a better word, a ghost.

Iliana bent in front of the child. "*Salak*," she said, greeting her in *Katavukai*, the language of the angels.

Hannah beamed, then hid sheepishly behind Reuel's big hand.

Iliana straightened, looking up—way up—at Reuel, a giant guardian angel and one of my closest friends. "Hi, Reuel. Good to see you again."

The guardian angel looked as bewildered as I felt, and I swear, tears sparkled in his eyes. "*Salak*, Iliana." He knelt on one knee at her feet, bowing his head. "The Daughter of Zion," he said in perfect English.

With a laugh, she touched his hair. "No need for all that." He looked up, and she opened her arms. "I will take a hug though."

He stood and pulled her against his massive chest.

When Reuel released her, Iliana raised a finger, pointing beyond him. "Who's he?"

I looked over. "Oh, that's Torman. One of the fallen who—"

Iliana's hand shot forward, and Torman was ripped off the ground. The demon screamed, suspended in the air. Her other hand touched her ear. "Rogan, we've got one."

"Whoa, whoa, whoa." I put my hands up. "This *one* is with us."

Iliana looked at me, confused.

"In exchange for safe passage out of Nulterra, Torman helped us escape." I stepped toward her. "I gave him my word, Iliana."

She held my gaze until the angel with blond hair joined her, passing Fury and her sister beside the entrance to Nulterra. It had returned to its closed state: a giant salt mirror in the middle of the Island of Fire.

The angel—I assumed he was the guardian Rogan I'd heard so much about—exchanged a nod with Reuel when he reached us.

"Who did you say this is?" Iliana asked me.

"Torman."

Iliana looked at Rogan, then flashed her eyes toward Torman. "What can you tell me?"

"Torman is Chimera's father," Rogan said, a muscle twitching in his jaw.

Iliana seemed to squeeze Torman tighter. Then she pulled him through the air to us and set him down in front of her. "Seize him."

Rogan grabbed Torman's forearms and clapped what looked like two metal slap bracelets onto his wrists.

I took a step, but Iliana turned her hand toward me. She cut me off before I could speak. "*You* made a deal with him. I did not."

Well.

A shocking thought detonated in my mind. Iliana was now of age. She commanded not only her entourage, but all the angels in Eden.

*Iliana commands me too.*

My mouth parted.

Torman caught my eye as Rogan led him away. "Warren! Warren, you promised!"

I shrugged. What else could I do?

"You've been gone a long time, Appa. A lot has changed while you've been away."

"Apparently."

"All angels suspected of being fallen are now taken into custody," the Angel of Death Samael explained.

"Taken where?"

"Back to headquarters." Iliana watched Torman and Rogan

go down the hill. "We've been looking for this one for quite a while."

"Torman, why?"

Her eyes widened a bit. "We have a *lot* to catch up on."

Yeah. Seventeen years' worth of information, apparently.

Rogan pulled some jungle-camouflage netting off a four-wheeler I hadn't seen disguised in the trees. He forced Torman onto the back of it and secured him to it with his powers as a guardian.

"Why don't you come back to the resort with us?" Iliana nudged my side. "We can discuss everything there. Mom will want to see you."

"Mom?" Every nerve ending inside me stood at attention. "Sloan's here?"

Iliana smiled. "Yeah. About twenty minutes away by ATV. She and Da—" Her lips snapped shut.

"It's OK. Nathan's your dad too," I said gently.

"They came over with me when we got word you and Fury were still alive."

"When was that?" Reuel asked.

Iliana thought for a moment. "Ten, eleven months ago, I think. Cassiel came from Eden to tell us just before…"

"Before what?"

"Before the spirit line was destroyed," Samael said, his voice tight with emotion.

I raked my fingers through my hair. "I can't believe it."

There were only a handful of angels powerful enough to destroy the spirit line. The Morning Star—the angel who'd created it—was one of them. After he was thrown out of Eden, a powerful veil kept the spirit line hidden from him—a veil I'd unintentionally destroyed when we were in Nulterra.

"That's only the beginning of it, I'm afraid." Samael gripped my shoulder. "The Father, too, was outside Eden when the bridge between worlds collapsed."

"Shit. The Father's on Earth?" In his human form, outside Eden, the Father was almost as limited as a mortal. I didn't have to ask to know we'd be screwed without him in Eden.

Samael nodded sadly. "Yes, but I'm not sure where he is at the moment. He came to help during the fever and has been traveling to take care of the sick."

"Fever?"

Samael's face fell. "There's so much to tell you."

"Cassiel is here as well," Iliana said.

I pointed to my feet. "Like *here,* here?"

"At the resort," she said.

There were bigger problems to worry about, but my brain quickly did the math on the situation. *Every* woman I'd ever had any real relationship with was on la Isla del Fuego, the Island of Fire.

Hell of a way to begin the apocalypse.

"Is Azrael at the resort too?" I asked.

Samael and Iliana exchanged a loaded glance. Neither of them answered.

My stomach twisted. "What?"

"Azrael's at Claymore in New Hope," Samael said.

I relaxed.

Iliana's head tilted toward her group. "Come on. Let's go see Mom."

"Warren?" Reuel held up Hannah's ethereal hand.

"Oh." I looked at Samael. "Without the spirit line, human souls are stuck here, aren't they?"

He nodded slowly, his eyes dim with concern. "It's been a problem."

"I bet."

"But her father's soul is still here." Samael looked around, like Hannah's dad might be standing behind us.

"He's dead, you mean?"

"Yes. A few months ago."

"Well…" A worried sigh puffed out my cheeks. "Think you and Reuel can find Hannah's father?"

"Of course," Samael said, bowing his head. "Then I can bring Reuel to the resort to meet you."

"Excellent. Thank you, Samael."

"It's really the least I can do." He turned to Reuel. "Ready?"

Reuel looked down the hill to where Fury was crying and hugging the boy she'd given birth to, the boy who was now a grown man.

"I'll take care of her," I told him.

With a heavy sigh, he nodded.

"We won't be long," Samael added.

When they turned to leave, Hannah broke free of Reuel's hand and ran back to me. I bent and caught her in a hug, and for a brief second, my heart was full. Like the whole dangerous trip, which had stolen the best parts of my life, wasn't for nothing.

I wished I could go with them to shake her father's hand when I delivered my promise of returning her. But there was too much else to be done, and I'd only just gotten my own daughter back. As a father, I was sure Hannah's would understand.

I stroked her hair. "I'll see you and your papa again."

I hoped that would be true, that someday I'd see them both in Eden. But unless we found a way to recreate the spirit line, Hannah would never go there.

Neither would I. I'd be locked out of my heavenly home forever.

Hannah scampered back to Reuel, and the three of them walked toward the mirrored Nulterra Gate.

"You all right?" Iliana asked gently.

"My brain hurts." I turned toward her. "So much to process."

"I'm sure." She slipped her hand into mine. "We'll have plenty of time to catch you up."

I forced a smile, and we started down the hill. My eyes were on Fury and her son. "He calls himself Jett?"

"Yeah. He also answers to Malak."

I stopped and spotted Rogan near the trees. "And Rogan, he's…" I couldn't remember the ridiculous name his biological mother, Shannon, had come up with. He looked a lot like her. Same peachy skin, same blonde hair.

"Nico," Iliana said with a knowing grin. "But he prefers Rogan."

"What's his full name?" I asked, unable to remember.

Iliana snickered. "Reginald Nicolas Green-Reese, the Fourth. His mother calls him Nico."

"Oh god, that's right. Still, so funny." I laughed, and it felt good. Felt good to think about anything other than reality at that moment.

Seventeen years.

As we neared, the other faces in the group finally came into focus. I blinked. Cruz was there, grayer now. Slimmer too. And Kane was more salt than pepper, but mostly unchanged. Still strong. Still intimidating. Another man was with them I didn't recognize. I looked around for Enzo and didn't see him anywhere.

They walked over to greet me.

"Welcome back, brother," Kane said, first offering me his hand and then pulling me into a hug.

I hugged Cruz next. "God, it's good to see you," he said, slapping me on the back.

"Where's Enzo?" I asked.

"Washington probably," Kane answered, resting his bulky arms over his rifle.

"Washington?"

"Works at the Pentagon, last we heard," he said.

"Damn." As I turned to introduce myself to the new guy, I caught sight of Fury's face. She was wiping her eyes as she took a step back from Jett, and she looked like she might faint.

The new guy would have to wait.

I touched the small of her back, and she sniffed. "Jett, this is Warren. Warren, this is—" She swallowed.

I stretched out my hand. "Nice to see you again, Jett. Or should I call you Malak?"

Jett looked at my hand for a second before he accepted it—a forced human gesture if ever I'd seen one. "Jett is fine. It's nice to finally meet you, Warren."

When he released me, he turned to Iliana who was standing behind him. I put my hand on Fury's waist. "You OK?"

She nodded, but it was a clear *no* as she turned into me, burying her face in my chest. I guided her away from the group and let her cry.

"I know exactly how you feel," I whispered against her hair.

Her nails dug into my sides.

I anticipated there would be a lot of this in the coming days. First Flint, Fury's father, sacrificing himself to get us out of Nulterra alive—now this. It was too much, even for me.

"How did no one know this?" she asked.

"I should have. I should've put it together, but I didn't."

"You couldn't have."

"We knew the Morning Star created Nulterra in the image of Eden. We also knew he did it in direct response to the

Thousand Year Prophecy. Now it's so clear. I should've seen it."

"There's no way, Warren. If the Father himself didn't know, how could you?"

My mind drifted back to my last time in Eden. I'd seen the Father in the Throne Room where he waited for news about our journey. His words floated to my memory: *I'm sorry for all this trip is costing you, but you'll have plenty of time with your daughter when you get back.*

My jaw tightened. The Father *had* known. He'd known all along.

Fury rested her forehead against my breastbone. "What do we do now?"

I kissed the top of her head. "One day at a time. Or hell, maybe we're taking it minute by minute at the moment."

That, at least, got her to look up and crack a smile.

She relaxed into me again, turning her face toward Jett. The boy who was never really her son. "He's a man."

"Well, technically, he's an angel."

"You know what I mean." She let out a slow breath. "John raised him."

Before we'd left, her ex, John McNamara, had found out he wasn't Jett's biological father as he'd thought. Fury hadn't cheated on him—as an angel, Jett had no biological father—but she hadn't told John the truth either.

He'd threatened to leave Jett at the front gate of the Claymore compound if we were gone more than two weeks. With the time jump, we'd missed the deadline—by a lot.

"John's a hothead, but he's a decent man," I said.

"He's still alive. Living off the grid now, sort of close to Claymore."

"Not in Raleigh anymore?"

She shook her head. "Jett said most people evacuated the

major cities. There was some kind of disease outbreak a few years ago."

"Samael called it a fever."

"Didn't you and Sloan discover that the Morning Star was developing some kind of weaponized virus at a lab in Chicago?"

"Yeah, but if he's responsible for the disease, then Azrael wasn't successful in locking him up," I said, staring out over the Nulterra Gate.

She shuddered against me. "I can't even think about that right now."

I pushed her back to arm's length, holding onto her shoulders. "Let's get out of here. I don't know about you, but I could use a really strong drink."

"Amen."

Her sister, Anya, joined us. "Where's Reuel?"

"He and Samael took Hannah to find her father, probably at their village nearby. I'm sure he won't be gone long."

"Their village?" Fury asked.

"The spirit line is gone. There's no way to take human souls to Eden now."

"So dead people are stuck here?" Fury asked.

Anya's eyes widened. "Like ghosts?"

"Like ghosts," I confirmed.

"Whoa," the two sisters said together.

I looked at the bandage around Anya's throat. "How's your neck?"

"Hurts. I need to see a doctor soon."

I blinked. "Oh shit."

"What?" she asked, alarmed.

"You don't need a doctor." I turned toward my daughter, who was talking with Kane. "Iliana?"

"That's right. Iliana's an Angel of Death *and* Life."

I watched her walk across the grass. "The most powerful being in all of existence."

"What's up?" Iliana asked when she was close enough.

"This is Fury's sister, Anya." The two girls—shit, I mean, *women*—shook hands. I put my hand under Anya's chin, and when I tilted her head up to display the gauze surrounding her neck, she winced. "Think you can help her?"

"Heal her, you mean?"

I nodded.

"Of course. Can you take off the bandage?"

As gently as I could, I helped Anya peel off the tape and gauze. The tendons strained in her neck as we pulled the gauze away. Charred flesh pulled away with it, and blood and water drizzled down her skin. Anya cried out in pain.

"Stop," Iliana said. "Sorry, I didn't realize it was so fresh." She curled her hands over the top of what remained of the gauze. Then she closed her eyes, and the brightest light I'd ever seen outside Eden shrouded them both.

I shielded my eyes with my forearm and backed up. Everyone was watching. All of SF-12 was smiling.

The light dissipated, and Anya gasped for air as she grabbed her throat. She pulled away what remained of the bandages.

There wasn't so much as a scar left behind.

"Wow!" Laughing, I clapped my hands. "That's my girl right there! Hey, Kane, did you see that?"

He smiled and nodded his head. "I did, sir. She's quite impressive."

"Yes, she is." I grabbed Iliana and wrapped my arms around her again.

She gave my chest a patronizing pat. "Welcome home, Appa."

I kissed her forehead.

Over her head, my eyes caught the glint of the sun off the

silver case we'd carried the blood-stone cuffs in. "I need to finish something."

"What?" Iliana asked.

"I swore I was going to seal the gate for good. I know Nulterra is gone, but what lies beneath that mirror is a shrine. An altar of worship for the Morning Star. I want to make sure no one ever happens upon it again."

"How will you do that?"

"Come on."

She walked with me to the case at the gate's edge. The rest of our group followed. I knelt down and opened the case. Inside were the sanguinite cuffs we'd used to take Fury into Nulterra.

I pulled them out, and one by one, tossed them toward the center of the circle. The entire surface rippled with a supernatural wave. I spread my wings and lifted into the air.

Iliana joined me.

Stunned, I dropped a few feet. "But..." I flew in a circle around her. "You don't have wings."

She smiled. "I don't need wings."

"Can you do this?" I opened my hands and stretched my fingers as wide as I could spread them. Then I bent my knuckles till my hands became strained claws. Fire sparked and sizzled, then danced in my palms.

Iliana's eyes widened. "Whoa. That's cool. Can you teach me?"

There was something wildly comforting about the fact there was still a thing or two her old dad might teach her. Something told me she'd pick up the skill faster than I had.

I extinguished the fire in one hand and held the other in front of my face. "Fire is nothing but energy, oxygen, and fuel. This air has the oxygen. I create the energy."

"And the fuel?"

"Hydrogen." I tapped my knuckles against my chest. "Our bodies have a higher concentration of it than average humans." I let the fire go out and showed her the empty palm of my hand. "The hard part is drawing the hydrogen to the surface of—"

"Like this?" She focused hard on her hand, and in a few seconds, sparks ignited in her palm.

I laughed. "Yeah. Something like that." I shook my head. "It took me years to learn that."

She held up the flame and looked through it. "Now what?"

"Now we burn the blood-stone cuffs," I said, looking down at the salt mirror.

I lowered until I was a few feet above the surface. I aimed my hands at the scattered pieces of blood stone. Fire shot like a blowtorch from my palms.

At first, not much happened, but it was widely known that sanguinite had an incredibly high melting point.

Iliana's flame joined mine.

The stone changed from its reddish-black to bright red. Then from red to orange. Orange to yellow. Then, finally, from yellow to blue.

It began to lose its form, and the sanguinite melted in a wide puddle as it mixed with the salt of the mirror. It spread... and spread...until it finally spread across the surface.

"What now?" Iliana asked over the noise of the fire.

"Cassiel says once it's thoroughly boiled, it will harden into a—"

The center of the boiling mirror gave way, and the ground started rumbling and shaking. Fury and the others below steadied themselves on the trembling earth. The hole at the center of the gate widened, thick steam and smoke rising out of it.

I dropped my hands, letting the fire go out. So did Iliana.

We both rose higher into the air. Looking down into the hole, I saw liquid fire churning toward the surface.

I spun toward Fury. "Get back! Get up the hill!"

Our friends on the ground ran to the highest point away from the mirror. I hoped it would be enough. The hole continued spreading, the entire surface now cracking and crumbling and falling to the depths below.

The noise was deafening. Rocks crashing against rocks. *Hissing. Popping.*

I grabbed Iliana's hand, pulling her to the side as smoke billowed up from the depths. Hot smoke that smelled like rotten eggs.

Liquid fire, like boiling magma, roiled and bubbled its way to the surface until the giant crater was filled to the rim. The hot lava-like substance sloshing onto the grass.

Iliana and I settled on the ground at the top of the hill with our friends.

"Is it a volcano?" Iliana asked.

"I don't think so." I reached for Fury, and she took my hand. "I believe that's the lake of fire."

"What's the difference?" Cruz asked.

"Magma comes from the Earth's core." Anya nodded at the fiery pool. "This came from Nulterra."

"But how, if the gate was destroyed? Nulterra wasn't *underground*." Fury looked confused.

"I have no idea." I carefully scanned the surface to make sure any demons didn't bubble to the top.

Anya stepped forward and pointed. "Warren, what's that?"

I followed the direction of her finger, straining my eyes as they snagged on something dark in the lava. It looked like a stick, but there was no way a stick could—

*Oh shit.*

"My sword." The handle was bobbing up and down in the lava.

"Shut up," Fury said.

I flew over the lake again. Heat radiated from the surface. I extended my hands and used my power to lift the sword. As it rose from the fire, something else came with it.

The blade was still buried in the stone Fury and Anya's father, Flint, had stayed behind to destroy. It had cost him his eternal soul to save us all.

Rather than hardening around it, the fire completely dripped off the sword and stone as I hovered over the lake. When the last drop hit the liquid-fire surface below, the ground shook once again.

I returned to the hilltop.

"Warren, man, I think you made it angry," Kane said, taking a few steps back from the edge.

Huge bubbles ballooned across the surface, churning the lava over the edges of the circle. The surrounding earth cracked, and lava rushed through the fissures as they fractured the ground.

While the lake spread, its center thickened and compounded, quickly growing higher and higher. Lava spewed it in every direction, first like a fountain, then like a fire hose.

"He's right. It's gonna blow!" I shouted over the roar. "Everybody, run!"

I dropped the sword on the ground, grabbed the back of Fury's shirt, and yanked her against me. Hooking my arm across her chest and under her armpits, I launched off the hillside away from the fire. Jett grabbed Anya, and they and Iliana caught up with us in the air.

Kane, Cruz, and the new guy ran down the shaking hill toward the trees. I touched my ear and called out to Samael. "The lake of fire is erupting. Evacuate everyone who's close!"

"What?" he shouted back.

"Evacuate! Get in the air!"

*Kaboom!*

Lava blasted into the air. We were above it, but the guys on the ground were directly in its trajectory.

Iliana dove.

My first instinct was to follow her, but Fury would never survive it. I rose higher and watched in horror as my daughter rocketed through the fiery spray.

In a blink, an invisible shield ballooned out against the fire, like an umbrella opening against sheets of rain. Iliana stood on the other side of it, her arms stretched toward the wave of lava.

The fire oozed off the force field and puddled beneath it. The guys reached the tree line and jumped on their waiting ATVs.

I exhaled for what felt like the first time in my life. The supernatural volcano calmed, but the lava didn't cool. It burned everything it touched, sending black smoke billowing into the sky.

"Holy shit," I said, panting against Fury's back.

Her arms covered mine as she coughed in the smoke.

On the ground, Iliana reached toward the sky.

"What's she doing?" Anya called to us.

I had no idea.

Puffs of white began materializing and thickening in the blue sky above us.

My lower jaw dropped as I looked up. "My god."

"What?" Fury asked, coughing some more.

"She's creating rain."

The white clouds turned dark as they swelled, and a large drop of water splashed square in the middle of my forehead. I laughed as I wiped it with my fingertips.

Rain poured down, extinguishing the flames in the trees.

Jett and I lowered to the earth, settling on the ground with Fury and Anya. I released Fury and slowly clapped my hands as I walked toward my daughter. "Nicely done."

Steam rose off the jungle as the flames died, but the liquid fire that had splashed onto the ground remained. It was unaffected by the water.

Fury knelt down beside a puddle of it. "It's going to relight once the ground dries up!" she called over the rain.

I looked at my daughter. "I think you're going to have to put it back."

Iliana looked around the clearing. The fire had spread like finger paint blasted from a cannon. It was a mess.

Kane came and stood beside me. "She's impressive, isn't she?"

"She's extraordinary."

"Hard to believe she came from you," Cruz said, walking up on my other side.

I shot him the bird, but he wasn't wrong.

Iliana stretched her hand toward the puddle in front of Fury's boots. It rose off the ground in a blob. Fury stood and stepped back by me as Iliana gathered all the lava around us and between where we stood and the original circle.

We followed her as she walked in the rain, as she moved the hovering and growing glob toward its original boundary. She lowered the fire back down into the lake, then released it with a splash.

Iliana shook out her hands as she looked around at all the other puddles. "This is going to take a while."

"Come on. I'll help you," I said.

She smiled.

"So will I," Jett added. Then he turned back toward the tree line. "Rogan!" He gestured him forward.

"I'll man the prisoner," Cruz said, heading back toward the

ATVs.

I needed to call Samael. I touched my ear. "Samael, you guys whole?"

"We're fine. What happened?"

"I'm not sure. Iliana put out the fire."

"Is that why it's raining?"

"Yep."

"OK. We're at Hannah's village. We'll see you guys later."

Jett and Rogan took the right side of the lake. Iliana and I took the left. A half hour later, the four of us had wrangled all the eternal fire back into the pit. When we were finished, Iliana looked up. The rain stopped like she'd turned off a faucet.

"That's so damn cool," I said with my hands on my hips.

Fury and Anya had walked back up to the top of the hill. "Warren!" Fury called. "Come here!"

Iliana and Jett followed me.

Anya was sitting on the wet ground. Fury got on both knees beside her. Between them was the sword, stuck inside the stone.

Fury crooked her finger to beckon me forward. "Look at this."

I bent between her and Anya. Fury was pointing to the hilt. The glowing impression of a hand was still wrapped around it.

Flint's hand.

Anya put her arm around Fury's shoulders, and they both cried. I walked back to Iliana and Jett to give the two sisters some privacy.

"What happened down there?" Iliana asked quietly.

"We learned the meaning of the word hero." I took a deep breath and let it out slowly. "Someday, I'll tell you all about it."

She smiled up at me. "I already know the meaning of the word. Mom has told me everything you did for me, and for her."

My eyes tingled. "I'd do it all again."

When Fury and Anya had regained their composure, Jett walked over for a closer look at the sword. "Seems like it would have melted."

"The sword's made of helkrymite and was forged in Nulterra, so I doubt the hellfire would be able to destroy it," I said, joining him.

"Helkrymite?" he asked.

"It's a metal foreign to Earth." I leaned down and grabbed the hilt. "Jett, can you hold the stone?"

He grabbed the dark oval rock with both hands. I pulled until the sword broke free. I carefully dusted off the blade with my hand, then stuck it into the scabbard strapped across my back.

"What do we do with this?" Jett asked, holding up the stone.

I looked down toward the lake. "Return it to where it came from?"

Jett handed it to me.

Iliana came and stood beside me. "Maybe you should let me."

I offered it to her. "Talk about heroes," I said with a wink.

She smiled, took the rock, and hurled it into the lake.

It bobbed at the surface for a moment, then disappeared with a *hiss.*

The sound of engines rumbled through the jungle behind us. We turned as another four-wheeler tore through the trees like someone had set the woods on fire.

It emerged from a path that hadn't existed when I first came to the gate. The driver removed their helmet.

Nathan McNamara.

His passenger did the same.

Sloan.

# CHAPTER TWO

"Oh my god!" Sloan threw her arms around my neck when I was close enough. She cried. I was trying hard not to. "We thought you were dead."

"I told you, I'm immortal." I pulled back and smiled.

One whole patch on the side of her long bangs had turned white. There were crinkles around her eyes, and she had laugh lines, hopefully from years of happiness with our daughter.

"Is everybody OK?" Nathan looked panicked. The blast had been loud with lots of smoke, so they'd probably heard and seen it from wherever they'd been on the island.

"Everyone's fine," Iliana announced as she walked up beside me with Jett. Her face was streaked with soot and rain.

Nathan carefully looked her over. "We heard an explosion."

"That would be my fault. The gate's more of a volcano now." I turned toward him and opened my arms. "Nate."

With his hair now more silver than blond, he looked so much like his dad. He greeted me with a strong hug. "Damn, it's good to see you."

Sloan still cried beside us. "It's been so long."

"For me, not so much."

She gripped my arms, and her eyes sobered as she studied me. "You haven't aged at all."

I took a deep breath. "Because I've only been gone two days."

She blinked.

"Two days?" Nathan asked.

"We figured out how the Morning Star escaped the Thousand Year Prophecy. He all but stopped time in Nulterra. We only spent one night there."

Sloan covered her mouth with her hand. "Then this has been more of a shock than a happy reunion."

"It's been both, but yes. An unbelievably huge shock." I looked at our daughter. "She's all grown-up." I could hardly believe it. We were all silent for a moment. Sloan wiped away more tears.

Nathan put his hand on my shoulder. "On the bright side, you can finally be together."

"True." I reached into my pocket. "And to think, an hour ago I was really excited about having these." I let both sanctonite stones, the Father's blood stones, dangle from my fingertips.

Sloan grasped them. "You found them."

"A lot of good they'll do." They should have allowed me to help raise Iliana, but now…

When Sloan finished looking at them, I offered one to Iliana.

"For me?" she asked.

"It was meant for you all along. It'll still help with headaches when you're away from other angels."

"I'm *never* away from other angels, but thank you." She smiled as she took it. Her eyes doubled when her hand closed around the stone. "Whoa." She almost dropped it.

"Everything OK?" Nathan asked, alarmed.

Iliana clasped the chain around her neck. "It's zingy."

"It's a powerful stone," I said.

"I can tell."

Nathan craned his neck to look past me. "What the hell happened here?"

"The gate?" I asked.

"The lake of fire," he said.

"I'm not really sure. We tried to seal it."

"Looks like you boiled it instead."

Iliana shrugged. "We kinda did."

"The explosion set everything on fire and nearly killed us, but someone"—I looked at Iliana—"saved the day."

"She's pretty good at doing that," Sloan said.

Nathan touched my shoulder. "She gets it from her dad."

I smiled, and he hugged me again.

Fury and Anya joined us. All emotion had left Fury's face. Not surprising since her entire life had been one long exercise in hiding her feelings. Ironically, it was probably the only thing holding her together while the reality of our current situation sank in.

"Fury," Sloan said with a tearful smile. She approached her with open arms, and Fury embraced her. It was weird. And wonderful. "I'm so glad you're OK."

"You are?" Fury asked with a forced, dry smile.

"Of course." Sloan glanced at Jett before taking Fury's hand. "You must be as shocked as Warren by all this."

"Shocked doesn't scratch the surface of what I'm feeling."

"I really can't imagine." Sloan tugged on Jett's sleeve. "But we like this son of yours. He's a good man."

For a second, Fury looked ready to vomit again, but it passed quickly.

Jett—*Malak*—stood close behind Iliana, quite obviously

ready to spring into action at any threat. He smiled gratefully. "Sloan and Nathan helped John a lot when I was younger."

"Thank you," Fury told Sloan, her voice cracking with emotion.

"No need for thanks. You'd have done the same for me."

"Uhh." Nathan's head tilted. "Would she though?"

The anguish engulfing us all broke, and we laughed. Sloan shoved Nathan's shoulder and rolled her eyes. For the briefest moment, it was just like old times.

And yet, *nothing* like them.

"This must be your sister. The resemblance is uncanny." Sloan stuck out her hand toward Anya. "I'm Sloan."

"Anya. It's nice to meet you, Sloan."

"You as well. This is my very inappropriate husband, Nathan."

Nathan and Anya shook hands. "Welcome home," Nathan said.

"What a strange new home it is," Anya said, dropping his hand. "What year is it?"

Nathan hesitated. "Today is Wednesday, August 15, 2032."

Hearing the number took my breath. "Shit. Seriously?"

"Afraid so," he said.

"Do we have flying cars now?" Anya asked.

"No, but we do have self-driving ones," Sloan said.

Anya's mouth gaped. "Really?"

"Not a hundred percent automated, but yeah. And most cars are battery powered with solar-paneled exteriors," Nathan said. "We haven't seen many on this island, but back in the States, they're everywhere."

"Have you really been here for eleven months?" I asked, remembering Iliana had said they'd come over when they found out we were alive.

"We've been here in shifts. Iliana's been here the whole

time, but Nathan and I have taken turns between here and Asheville." Sloan and Nathan exchanged a curious glance. "Our son just started his senior year of high school back at home."

"Your *son*?" The question was louder than I intended. When Iliana was born, Sloan's ruptured uterus had been removed. More children shouldn't have been possible. My eyes darted to Iliana. "Did you heal your mother?"

Iliana looked confused. "What?"

"No, no," Sloan said. "We adopted Luca after we couldn't find any family members of his in Italy."

My brain was having a hard time connecting the dots.

"Luca is the son of the woman Azrael kept alive at Echo-10 in New Hope," Nathan said.

My head snapped back. "Oh."

When Cassiel and I had been in Venice—only a few months prior, for me—we'd been hunting an undead serial killer that had been set free from Nulterra. Vito Saez preyed on humans with the ability to see angels. He'd been in the process of murdering his last victim when we found him—a pregnant woman in Venice, Italy.

Days before the trip to Nulterra, Azrael had shown Fury and me his wild and dangerous plan. He was keeping the woman on life support at Claymore headquarters to swap her baby with the Morning Star once Adrianne gave birth.

I turned to Nathan. "But if you have Luca, what happened to the Morning Star?"

Nathan flashed a worried look at Iliana. "You didn't tell him anything?"

"I didn't want to overwhelm them. I thought I'd wait until we got back to the resort."

"Tell me what?" I remembered the hesitation surrounding the questions about my father, Azrael. "What happened?"

Sloan was bordering on tears again. Nathan looked every-where except at me.

I clenched my jaw. "Someone needs to start talking fast."

"Azrael's blood stone." Nathan's voice cracked a bit. "You've had it this whole time."

I actually had two of them. One around my neck. The other in my pocket. I assumed they were the same stone, magically duplicated somehow in Nulterra. It had been inside Azrael's safe at the Claymore base that had been part of Fury's waking nightmare in *Ket Nhila*, the Bad Lands. The base had vanished, but the second stone had survived.

"What are you saying?" Fury asked.

Sloan visibly swallowed. "Without the stone, Azrael's memories of the supernatural world faded in the first year you were gone. He lost everything, including his memories of the Morning Star."

I ran both hands down my face.

"It started before Adrianne gave birth," Nathan said. "I told Sloan everything I knew about Adrianne and her baby. Around the same time, the nurse at Claymore..." He looked at Sloan. "What was her name?"

Sloan lifted both shoulders. "That was too many years ago to remember."

"Dana. Her name was Dana," I said.

They both stared at me. One more reminder of how much time I'd lost. For me and Fury, it had been less than a week since we'd met Nurse Dana at Claymore Worldwide's head-quarters in New Hope, North Carolina.

"Yes. Dana," Nathan said. "Azrael had instructed her to contact me and tell me everything if anything ever happened to him—"

"Az had a backup plan? That's a miracle," Fury said.

"I know. Thank God he did. Dana worried about Azrael's

strange behavior, but she didn't know about the blood stone or how he would be affected by its absence. She told us about the pregnant woman at Echo-10."

I looked at Fury. "I knew that plan would never work."

"Was he really going to swap Adrianne's baby with the ICU woman's kid?" Nathan asked.

Fury sighed. "He was going to try."

"Sounds like something Azrael would do," Jett said.

Fury and I both turned to look at him. It was weird to think this man-child, a stranger essentially to us both, had more history with my father than either of us combined and multiplied exponentially. Azrael and Jett would have existed together since the beginning of time.

My head ached from information overload. "Does Azrael remember me? The last time he lost his memories, he didn't know me at all."

"This is very different from the last time," Nathan said. "When he lost his memory before, he was a blank slate when he was found. This was gradual. Painful to watch."

"My dad says it resembled the decline of dementia and Alzheimer patients. That part of his brain just faded away," Sloan said.

"Cassiel says his exposure to the Morning Star and Iliana may have slowed the progression of the condition," Nathan added.

"But you'd supposedly died before that happened." Sloan's eyes saddened. "It was really hard for him, and to be honest, his memories fading eased that pain. When we were still in contact, he remembered you in theory, but probably only because Adrianne helped him hold on to some information," Sloan said.

"Where is he?"

"The last we knew, he and Adrianne lived at the beach

house in Kill Devil Hills. Across the bay from Claymore in the Outer Banks," Nathan said.

"So he's still running the company?" Anya asked.

"For now. We heard he has plans to transfer ownership to his son." Nathan looked like he might vomit. "His *other* son."

"The Morning Star." I was so horrified, my voice didn't even sound like my own.

"More commonly known on Earth as Michael Claymore," Nathan said.

My stomach turned.

"Azrael and Adrianne named him after you." Sloan's chin quivered as she fought back tears.

A devastating thought occurred to me. "Oh god, Sloan. What happened with you and Adrianne?" They'd been best friends since they were kids.

"I told her the baby was the Morning Star, but she didn't want to believe it. What mother would? Deep down, I think she knew the truth, but the baby was so normal when he was born. Tiny. Cute. Pooped a lot. Even we questioned for a while that Michael was really the Morning Star."

"Didn't he have migraines after being around Iliana?" I asked.

She shook her head. "We found out later, Chimera had given the boy her sanctonite stone. He and Iliana were immune to each other."

My fists clenched at my sides. "Chimera gave the Morning Star her stone?"

"Warren, Chimera was in on it from the beginning," Nathan said.

"I knew I didn't trust that bitch," Fury hissed.

"She's been helping the Morning Star develop weapons against humans and angels," Sloan said.

Nathan lowered his voice, and pointed to where Torman

was being guarded at the four-wheeler. "They had Rogan for a while. Took him right out of his bed while their family was on vacation. Chimera and her minions tortured him for almost a year before we found him."

"Tortured?" I asked.

"Tested their weapons on him," Nathan clarified.

Iliana nudged me with her elbow. "Now do you understand why I detained her father?"

"Yeah, I do. Want me to kill him for you?"

The corner of her mouth twitched up.

"Chimera convinced Azrael to move to the beach house permanently about a year after the baby was born. Adrianne, of course, went with him. They had two more kids together. A girl and another boy," Nathan said.

"Human kids?" I asked, surprised.

"As far as we know," Sloan said.

"Do you still talk to her?" I asked.

"Not in years. We think Michael came of age and understood his identity when he was really young. Nine, wasn't it?" Sloan looked at Nathan.

He thought for a second. "Eight."

"You're right. He and Luca were the same age. We went to visit them around the holidays, and it was obvious the boy wasn't normal."

"How so?" Anya asked.

Sloan's eyes widened like she was unsure of where to begin. "He spoke with the vocabulary of an adult, though he tried to hide it."

"Yeah. What kid from North Carolina uses *whom* correctly in a sentence?" Nathan asked with a smirk.

I smiled, but there was little amusement behind it.

"The boy had zero emotion. A lot like Azrael could be sometimes, you know?" Sloan asked me.

I nodded.

"But it was infinitely worse," Nathan said.

Iliana crossed her arms. "And he had no interest in playing with me or my brother. I remember that clearly."

"It was unsettling," Sloan agreed. "He just stared at Iliana like he was memorizing every little detail."

"It was so uncomfortable, we left early," Nathan said.

"Did you talk to them about it?" I asked.

Nathan frowned. "Talking to Azrael about any of it was pointless. He literally has no memory of the supernatural."

"None of it," Jett echoed, sadly shaking his head.

"I mentioned it to Adrianne privately a few days later, but she blew me off," Sloan said. "I didn't bring it up again until Adrianne's mom got sick the following year. She was diagnosed with stage-three liver cancer, so they came back to Asheville."

"Let me guess. The Morning Star healed Adrianne's mom?" Fury asked.

"Correct. I tried to tell Adrianne again that the Morning Star had the power to heal." Sloan's whole body slumped. "She cussed me out, and we haven't really spoken since. That was…" She thought about it. "God, that was about eight years ago."

"Eight years?" I asked in disbelief.

"Nobody holds a grudge like Adrianne," Sloan said.

Nathan grinned. "Remember how she was with Shannon?"

"Yeah." My head dropped. "I'm so sorry, Sloan."

She forced a strained smile. "Like I said, I think Adrianne knows. Logically, she has to. I just hope she doesn't get caught in the crossfire of everything."

"Sounds like there might be a literal crossfire if the Morning Star's in charge of Claymore now," Anya said.

A chill rippled my spine.

"He's not in charge of it yet," Nathan said.

"Technically, I guess, he's too young," Sloan added. "He's younger than Iliana. Seventeen."

"I thought you had a controlling interest in the company," I said to her.

"I did, but they pushed me out a long time ago. We were given a lump-sum payment and the Wolf Gap property to go quietly."

Nathan glowered. "A lot of good it does us, when Chimera knows the security system of Echo-5 in and out."

"Is Echo-5 still connected to Claymore's servers?" I asked.

"No. We had it rewired, but I don't completely trust it," Nathan said.

"What happened to SF-12?" Fury asked.

"No longer employed by Claymore. Enzo was recruited by the NSA before we broke ties with Claymore. He's some hotshot up in Washington now," Nathan answered.

"That's what Kane told me," I said.

Nathan looked beyond us, and I followed his eyes to where the group was talking by the lake. "A few of the guys stuck around though. A while back, Kane, Cruz, Lex, and Cooper started a firearms-training company for police special-ops units. They were based in Asheville, so they could still keep an eye on all of us. It went really well until the fever hit. It killed Cooper before we could get Iliana to him."

"What fever?" Anya asked.

"Blackmouth Fever," Iliana answered.

Fury shook her head. "Never heard of it."

"You wouldn't have," Sloan said. "It didn't exist before a few years ago. It was like airborne Ebola. Highly contagious. Extremely deadly."

"It was a weaponized virus," Nathan added.

Fury caught my eye and held my gaze for a second.

My jaw clenched. "Weaponized by?"

"The official answer is no one knows." Nathan crossed his arms. "It's called Blackmouth Fever because it killed *everyone* in the town of Blackmouth, North Carolina, just forty-seven miles north of New Hope."

I swore.

"They found the first dead rats there that carried the virus. Lab rats," Nathan said.

"By then, it had already started popping up in the demons' favorite cities." Sloan started counting on her fingers. "Chicago, Los Angeles, New York, and San Antonio."

I pulled both hands through my hair.

"All those are international hubs," Iliana said.

"So the virus jumped continents." Anya pinched the bridge of her nose. "Wow."

Nathan grimaced. "Unfortunately, that isn't the worst of it. Some of the earliest and hardest-hit places were the major military installations in the US. Even the US government, who has been wildly in denial that this was domestic bioterrorism, agrees that the bases were deliberately targeted. Fort Bragg and Camp Lejeune, both in North Carolina, were the first to fall. Followed soon after by Fort Benning, Fort Campbell, Fort Lewis, and Fort Hood."

"What do you mean by 'fall'?" I asked.

"The disease spread like wildfire. Almost three-quarters of the bases' populations were infected, and the mortality rate is ninety to ninety-five percent."

"The population at Fort Bragg alone went from almost three hundred thousand to seventy-five thousand in a month," Jett added.

"Within eighteen months, the US military lost more than half its members. The majority who survived were reservists," Nathan said.

"And guess who filled the gap?" Sloan asked.

My heart sank. "Claymore."

They all nodded.

I felt sick. "I almost don't want to know, but what was the death toll?"

No one spoke for the longest time. Finally, Nathan shifted uneasily on his feet. "Over two billion dead worldwide."

"Shut up," Fury said, her mouth gaping.

Anya hugged herself and closed her eyes.

I just stood there, staring.

"It did the most damage in China and India, and it decimated the most densely populated cities around the world. I doubt any family on Earth was left untouched by it," Sloan said.

"Who that we know?" I asked.

"Cooper and Wings from SF-12. Both of Kayleigh Neeland's grandparents. She stayed with us some while she finished college. My mom's sister, Joan. She died before we even knew she was sick." Sloan tapped her fingers on her lips.

"Taiya's mom," Iliana said.

"That's right. Melinda Harmon died trying to get to Asheville. Almost made it too. Warren, you remember Taiya?" Sloan asked.

"How could I forget?"

Taiya, the Seramorta daughter of the demon Ysha, had lived with us for a wild few months when Sloan was pregnant with Iliana. Taiya had been raised by her father, and the prolonged exposure to him from such a young age had fried her brain. She was Sloan's age with the mental capacity of a six-year-old.

"She's living with us again."

"No kidding?" I asked.

Nathan chuckled. "Definitely not kidding. She'll be *very* excited to see you."

I touched my chest. "Me?"

"Oh yeah. She's still very much in love with you," Sloan said.

"She has your picture framed in her bedroom," Iliana said. "It was almost the only thing she brought from New York when she came to live with us."

"Is she here too?" I asked.

"No. She's back at home with my dad and the others," Sloan said.

"How is your dad?"

Sloan's happy expression faltered.

"What?" I asked.

"He retired last year, sold his house, and moved in to help us manage Wolf Gap. I think he got lonely. Anyway, we found out he had pancreatic cancer after Cassiel told us you were alive—"

"He got sick around you?" I asked Iliana.

She looked away.

"When she came of age, her powers balanced each other out." Nathan put his arm around Sloan's shoulders. "Iliana can heal, and she can kill, but it's only intentional now."

"She wanted to heal her papa, but he asked her not to." Sloan reached for Iliana's hand. "He said he wanted to go to Eden and be with my mom. He'd been ready for a while. Even when the virus swept through, he refused to let Iliana protect him. He died peacefully with us at home."

My head tilted. "But you said he's with Taiya at—" I swore. "The spirit line was destroyed. He's stuck here."

She nodded. "He passed right before we got word."

I gripped my temples.

"But he's OK. He's not sick anymore, and he's still with us. Iliana can communicate with him." Tears were sparkling in Sloan's eyes again. "He sends his love."

I looked up at the sky. "Damn."

"Everything has changed since the fever. Lots of others got sick, including Nathan's whole family." Sloan gestured toward our daughter. "But Iliana saved them."

"She did more than that," Nathan said. "This girl projected a whole damn healing force field. That sickness didn't come within thirty miles of Asheville."

Iliana's cheeks were tinged with pink. I put my arm around her and kissed the side of her head. "I'm so proud of you."

"Asheville is the only city in the US that's *grown* through the epidemic," Jett said.

I squeezed Iliana's arm. "I bet."

"Have they gotten it under control now?" Fury asked.

Sloan tilted her head from side to side. "For the most part. The World Health Organization implemented really strict quarantine laws that helped, and we did receive some assistance from the Father and the Angels of Life."

"Really? The Angels of Life?" I asked, surprised.

"I'm sure he had to force them to come, but yes," Iliana said.

"Did Azrael have a hand in spreading the virus?" I asked, terrified to hear the answer.

"Knowingly? No," Nathan said with so much conviction that the tension building across my shoulders immediately eased.

"But we do have reason to believe that the Morning Star is only getting started." Jett's tone was ominous. "Now that the spirit line is gone, nothing will stop him from trying to annihilate the human race."

Fury looked at me. "I wouldn't say *nothing.*"

Her confidence lifted my spirits.

"What assets do we have?" I asked Nathan.

"Angels or human?"

"Both."

Sloan and Nathan looked at Jett. "Cassiel can give you exact figures"—*of course she can,* I thought—"but a rough estimate would be a few thousand Angels of Ministry, a couple of Angels of Knowledge, and a few prophets, including Sandalphon."

"Sandalphon, really?" I asked, surprised because Sandalphon rarely left Eden.

He was an angel, a bit like Iliana, born on Earth with two angel spirits and no human soul at all. He was an Angel of Knowledge and Prophecy, and his physical body was a few hundred years old. Because he was some kind of angel/human hybrid, the power of Eden couldn't restore his youth as it did with humans.

In Eden, he was known as the *Oragnosi,* which loosely translated to "old wise dude."

"Cassiel asked him to come before the spirit line went down," Iliana said.

"That's good for us, I guess."

Jett grimaced. "Not as good as it should be. Without the auranos, prophecy is extinct."

"Who else is here?" I asked.

"About a thousand Angels of Death, and about a third of the guardians," Jett said.

"Reuel will be happy about that," Fury said.

"I assume the Angels of Life and the messengers hightailed it back to Eden?" I asked.

Jett nodded. "As soon as the veil tore apart, exposing the spirit line."

"But Ionis and a few others are here," Nathan said. "And Gabriel. Iliana is our only Angel of Life—"

"Don't forget about Mom." Iliana pointed at Sloan.

Sloan rolled her eyes. "Yes, please forget about Mom. The help I can offer won't amount to anything."

Iliana looked up at me. "Don't let her fool you. She's more powerful than she thinks."

"Some things never change," I said, holding Sloan's gaze. "Any other Archangels? Me, Gabriel, Cassiel, Anya."

Anya's face whipped toward me. "Me?"

"You will be once we restore the spirit line." I looked at Jett for confirmation.

"*If* we restore the spirit line, yes," he said.

"What does that even mean that I'll be an Archangel?" she asked me.

"For starters, it means you'll become immortal. And I'd imagine, that, like me, as long as you stay in Eden, your body won't age anymore."

"And you'll be able to fly," Jett added.

"Cassiel says restoring the spirit line can't be done," Sloan said.

"Did she say why?"

Sloan scrunched her nose. "She did, but to be honest, it didn't make a whole lot of sense to me."

"I know that feeling. I'll talk to her," I said.

"Wait." Fury's brow pinched. "Cassiel is *here*?"

"She came to Asheville to tell us you both were alive," Sloan said.

"And she's been here on the island with us since we came," Iliana added.

"Huh." Fury crossed her arms. She was more than intrigued. She was worried. Maybe even jealous.

"Looks like you'll finally get to meet her." I couldn't squash the smile that was fighting its way to my face.

"Great," Fury said, completely unamused.

Sloan's eyes narrowed, and her finger slowly moved between me and Fury. "What happened down in that pit?"

I reached for Fury, and she stared at my hand a second

before reluctantly accepting it. She had never been one for public displays of affection. Still, I pulled her to my side and slid my arm around her waist.

"Really?" Sloan's jaw dropped slightly.

"You and Fury?" Nathan blinked a few times. "You and Fury are together, and Cassiel is back at the hotel waiting for you?" His head fell back, and he laughed—howled, really—toward the sky.

I was confused. Nothing about this was funny.

Sloan nudged his ribs. "What's the matter with you?"

He laughed even harder and pointed at me. "Holy shit! He's finally in a love triangle I'm not part of!"

At that, I chuckled. "Fair enough, asshole."

Fury rolled her eyes.

"Nathan," Sloan scolded.

"This is amazing." He put his arm around my neck. "Warren, I never thought I'd say this, but I'm so damn glad you're back."

"Me too, you jerk." I pushed him away.

His laughter died on a melodic wane. Then he touched his finger behind his earlobe. "This is Nathan," he said, taking a step away from us.

My head snapped back. I pointed at him and looked at Sloan. "Is he talking to someone?"

"Huh?" Sloan seemed confused. "Oh yeah. He's on the phone." She reached into her own ear, then showed us her finger. On it was a tiny chip about the size of a pencil eraser. It was flesh colored and had a small clear wire about an eighth of an inch long.

Fury and Anya came closer. "That's your phone?" Anya asked.

"Yeah. Part of it, anyway. It has a screen too, but you don't have to carry it. I never do, but Nathan wouldn't be able to go to the bathroom without funny cat videos or basketball recaps."

Hands-free devices were nothing new, even before I left the planet, but Nathan appeared to be talking to himself. It reminded me of how angels looked when we communicated with each other.

"Uh oh," I said.

"What's wrong?" Fury asked.

I touched my own ear. "I won't be able to communicate with Eden anymore."

Iliana shook her head. "You can communicate with those of us on Earth though."

No more Eden. The prospect of the separation being permanent was almost too much to process. And I'm sure I'd only considered a tiny portion of the consequences. I really couldn't wait to talk to Cassiel—as awkward as that was bound to be.

Nathan walked back to our group. "We've got to go."

"What's up?" Iliana asked.

"That was Cassiel. Azrael got in touch. He knows Warren is back."

"How?" The question came from everyone.

Nathan shrugged. "I didn't ask."

Sloan's eyes bugged out. "Nathan!"

"Sorry. I've had a lot of information to process today!"

"What did Azrael say?" I asked calmly.

"He wants to see you."

# CHAPTER THREE

For the eleven months they'd been on the island, Iliana had made the team leave an extra ATV at the gate in anticipation of our return. Kane had even started it every week to keep the battery alive.

I drove Fury. Anya rode with Cruz.

The terrain out of the jungle was almost as we'd left it, except the trail was wider and worn with tire tracks. And this time, Fury's arms were around me.

And my daughter was in front of me, riding with Jett.

My brain needed to catch up to speed on so much.

I slowed the four-wheeler as we passed Cambugahay Falls. Unlike the last time we'd visited, the parking lot and trailhead were nearly deserted. The welcome sign was faded and dangling from one corner.

If the fever had wrecked this remote island, where hadn't it touched? La Isla del Fuego was as far off the beaten path as one could go. It wasn't even accessible by air travel.

*Shit. Air travel.*

Without the spirit line, I'd be limited to my wings and

human forms of transportation. The only way back to the States would be by airplane—which had proven problematic—or by boat, which might take another seventeen years.

And where would we go? Asheville, I'd guess, but did they even live at Wolf Gap anymore with its vulnerabilities? And no matter where we went, neither Fury, Anya, nor I had *anything* left on the Earth.

Nothing.

Even my Challenger, if it still existed, would be a thing of the past. Vintage. Antique. That depressed me more than the thought of not having a bed to sleep in.

The ATVs in front of us turned off the road sooner than I'd expected. I followed them up a steep and winding rough-gravel road until we reached the top of a ridge. A sign at the end of the drive said, "High Vista Resort and Villas."

A bamboo privacy fence enclosed the property. Our group, seven ATVs total, rolled through the gate and up to a building surrounded by thatch-roof huts built into the ridgeline. There was a large infinity pool with a view of the distant ocean.

I killed the engine when we parked next to Iliana and Jett. "Wow. This place is nice."

Sloan and Nathan had parked on our other side. "And it's a steal. Less than twenty dollars a night for an entire villa," Nathan said. "We've been here for the past six months, and we've only seen one tourist."

"I knew the island was empty when we passed the falls. That place was packed when we were here a couple of days—" I stopped myself.

Nathan sadly shook his head. "I'm sorry, man."

"I still don't believe it."

"I can't imagine."

Jett and Rogan led a handcuffed and gagged Torman toward the huts. The rest of our group moved to the main building, but I hung back and watched Torman being led away. Nathan stayed with me.

"Where are they taking him?" I asked.

"They'll keep him locked up in one of the villas until he's been thoroughly questioned by Iliana and Cassiel. Then they'll probably kill him before we leave. That's always been the plan if they ever found him."

"Why kill him?"

"To cripple Chimera. If Torman is dead, her Angel of Knowledge side will die with him. It might even kill her too, which Rogan would love after what she did to him. She's Azrael's top advisor and the chief lackey of the Morning Star."

"How did she fool all of us?"

He shrugged. "We've been asking that question for seventeen years. There's no good answer except she's smart, and she'd been planning this for a long time."

"No doubt with help from her father." I watched Rogan drag Torman through one of the far villa's front doors. "If Iliana needs help killing him, I'll be happy to oblige."

Nathan smiled like a proud dad. "Iliana doesn't need much help with anything."

I gripped his shoulder. "Thank you, Nathan."

He shook his head. "The gratitude is mine, man. I really hate you had to miss so much."

"Me too."

"Come on. You'll feel better after you've had a good meal and some rest. Looks like you went through hell or something." He grinned as we walked to the building.

I was exhausted. I'd dozed off a couple of times the night before, but Fury had been in my bed, so sleep hadn't been a priority. Not that I was complaining.

Inside was a restaurant. One whole wall was sliding doors open to the view. A small Filipino woman walked in from the kitchen. "You're back!" she said with a bright smile. "And you brought friends." Her smile faded when she saw me. A reaction I expected as the Archangel of Death.

Humans didn't need to know what I was to fear me.

"Angel, these are the friends we've been waiting for," Sloan told the woman.

I leaned toward Nathan and lowered my voice to a whisper. "Her name's Angel? Seriously?"

He snickered.

Sloan continued her introduction. "This is Anya and Fury." She pointed at me. "And this is Warren."

The woman's brow tightened with confusion. "But I thought Warren was Iliana's father."

*Oh, this is going to be fun.* It was going to be like telling people Azrael and I were brothers all over again.

"He is," Nathan announced with a smile as he plucked a banana from a fruit basket. "Sloan liked 'em young."

Sloan put a hand on her hip. "So I guess I settled for an old man like you."

Nathan paused with the banana halfway to his mouth and laughed. "My dear, I do believe your wit is getting quicker with age."

She ignored him. "Angel, can we get a couple more rooms made up?"

"Of course. Are you hungry?"

Fury and I answered yes in unison. "Starving," she added.

"Dinner should be ready in a half hour, but I can have the kitchen prepare you a snack," Angel said.

"Half an hour is fine." Fury turned to me. "I'd like to get cleaned up. I certainly feel like I haven't showered in seventeen years."

"Me too," Anya said.

"We can find you all something to wear," Sloan offered.

Nathan nodded. "And we can go into town later to get whatever supplies you need."

"Sounds good," I said.

Nathan leaned against the counter. "Hey, Angel, can we get a round of beers to celebrate?"

"Coming right up."

Angel disappeared into the kitchen, and I walked over to Kane and Cruz. I still didn't know the third man with them. "Thank you, guys, for looking after my family."

"We've always known what we were protecting. Welcome home, brother," Kane said with a smile. "It's sure as hell good to have you back though. To have all of you back." He looked over my shoulder.

I turned as Fury and Anya joined us. They'd been part of Claymore and SF-12 before I ever knew it existed. That history was reflected in the reunion; Kane hugged Anya so tight I thought her head might pop off.

I turned toward the third man and offered my hand. "Hi, I'm Warren."

"We've met," he said.

He was younger than Kane and Cruz. Closer to my age; maybe a little older. His eyes were both brown, but something in them felt familiar.

"Nash," he said. "Nash Wright."

I took a full step back. "Damn."

"The kid from Azrael's beach house?" Fury asked.

He chuckled. "That was a long time ago, ma'am."

Not for me and Fury.

The last time I'd seen Nash, the day I'd met him, he couldn't have been more than twenty. Now, in less than a week on my time, he was older than me. I shouldn't have been so shocked, considering the changes in everyone else, but I still hadn't adjusted to this new reality.

Part of me wondered if I ever would.

"You're part of SF-12 now?" I asked.

"More like SF-4. We're a little understaffed," Kane said.

I frowned. "I heard about Cooper and Wings. I'm sorry."

Kane and Cruz both nodded sadly.

"What happened to the others?" Fury asked.

Kane crossed his arm. "Well, you heard about Enzo."

"You ever hear from him?" Anya asked.

"Not ever, but I'm sure he stays busy, especially since the military fell apart."

"Doc?" I asked.

"Doc retired. NAG got married and moved to Boston. Lex is still with us, back at Echo-5, keeping watch there. The rest of the team sought out other employment when we were cut off from Claymore," Kane said.

I crossed my arms. "I can't wrap my head around it."

"Honestly, neither can we," Kane admitted. "Az completely checked out. Nothing helped. Not even Iliana. Eventually, he didn't remember her at all, except for what he'd been told."

"I wonder how much of that was the Morning Star's doing," Fury said.

"Probably a lot," Cruz said.

"And then there's Chimera. She's had more influence on him than anyone except the Morning Star," Kane added.

Fury made a low growling sound. "I can't wait to get my hands on that bitch."

"Get in line," Kane said. "Unfortunately, she's very well protected. Since Claymore was the only military, private or otherwise, completely left untouched by the virus, their size has doubled. They've taken over most of North Carolina's east coast, all the way down to Camp Lejeune."

"The government even gave them Cherry Point and the Croatan National Forest," Cruz said.

"Geez. How much land is that?" Anya asked.

"About a hundred and eighty thousand acres," Kane said.

I gave a long low whistle. "Do we have anyone left on the inside?"

"Huffman still runs the armory." Kane tilted his head toward Nash. "But he's kept pretty silent since Nash got booted out."

"Booted out?" Fury asked.

Nash's shoulders went rigid. "Chimera found out I was communicating with Nate and Kane. Michael—sorry, *the Morning Star*—questioned me about it and knew I was lying, of course. I'm lucky I wasn't killed."

"Lucky indeed." Kane looked at me. "We've got to get that necklace back to Azrael."

"God, I wish I'd refused to take it."

"You couldn't have known. None of us had any idea," Kane said.

Cruz nodded. "We're just glad you're alive."

"Warren?" a woman said behind me.

I knew it was Cassiel before I even turned around. I felt her presence as clearly as I saw my friends standing in front of me. I turned and saw her silhouetted in the doorway, the sunlight sparkling through her golden hair. "Cassiel."

She met me halfway across the dining room and threw her arms around my neck. "You're alive," she breathed over my shoulder.

"Thanks to you." I stepped back. "You got us out of Nulterra."

Cassiel had sent a memory stone with Flint into Nulterra. She and Theta, the Archangel of Prophecy, had figured out that in order for us to destroy Nulterra, we had to destroy the three sanctonite stones that held it together. The largest stone gave Nulterra its power. A second stone powered the gateway to the spirit line. The third powered the gate to Earth.

Tears spilled down her cheeks. "I thought you'd have to stay behind to destroy the last stone."

"Someone did."

"Flint." Cassiel's eyes drifted past me. "Fury, I'm so sorry."

Fury walked up beside me.

"He was one of the bravest humans I've ever met," Cassiel added.

"He was. Thank you." Fury offered a weak smile. "And thanks for your help. I would have died without the crystal water."

Cassiel straightened, obviously surprised. "*You* drank the crystal water."

"It saved my life."

In her eyes, it was clear this was new information for Cassiel. When she'd given me the crystal water, she'd done so under strict instructions that it be used under life-or-death peril only. She'd said it was forbidden to use outside Eden. That her disobedience could cost her everything.

As it turned out, neither of us had any idea what it would actually cost us all.

Using the crystal water—the life water of Eden—in Nulterra was not only powerful enough to destroy the veil that kept Nulterra hidden from Eden's watchful eye...it was also powerful enough to destroy the veil that kept the spirit line hidden from the Morning Star.

She hadn't anticipated that so much time would have passed on Earth that he would be old enough, mature enough, to take advantage of his sudden ability to use it—and destroy it.

It suddenly occurred to me, Cassiel had meant the crystal

water for me. To save *my* life if there'd been a need. She'd never considered that it might be used to save Fury.

Now the spirit line was gone, and it had cost Cassiel everything. Everything, including me.

I was truly sorry for her.

Cassiel's eyes blinked furiously as they fought back more tears.

"Here you are!" Angel announced, returning with a tray of bottled beers.

"Celebration time," Fury said with a tired smile as she walked backward to rejoin our group.

I caught Cassiel's lifeless gaze. "We'll talk later, OK?"

"Of course. We need to talk about your father, but for now, go celebrate. You deserve it."

I wasn't so sure about that. We'd survived, but at what price? I started toward the group, and when I looked back to see if Cassiel was coming, she was gone.

Nathan thrust a frosty beer into my hand, and I rejoined the group.

Iliana raised her bottle of soda into the air. "I'd like to make my very first toast."

The room fell silent as everyone else gathered close. Fury put her arm around my waist, holding her own beer to her chest.

"Everyone told me to give up hope. That they couldn't have survived. That they had to be dead. That they would never return." Iliana looked at me. "But my father swore he'd always come back for me, and I knew, no matter what happened, he'd keep his word."

My eyes teared up.

She tilted her soda toward me. "So this is for Warren. My promise-keeper. My appa. My angel. Welcome home." Everyone cheered, and heat rushed to my cheeks. "And to everyone else!" Iliana shouted over the applause. They quieted back down. "I told you so!"

The room erupted into laughter. I stepped away from Fury to hug Iliana. I kissed the side of her head. "I'll always keep my word."

She rested her head against my chest. "I know."

Then I took a long slow drink of ice-cold beer.

When we finished, everyone dispersed to get ready for dinner. Fury and Anya went to the first villa available, and I walked outside to try to find Cassiel.

As I stood on the grass, I closed my eyes until I sensed the pull of the supernatural to my left. I followed the feeling to a garden past the pool. There was a small gate. I opened it and walked inside, inhaling sweet jasmine.

I heard her voice before I saw her. She and Sandalphon came around a bend in the path. The old angel was holding onto her arm and using a cane. Cassiel was smiling until she looked up and saw me.

"Warren," Sandalphon said, straightening his hunched back as much as possible.

I had no idea how old Sandalphon actually was, but his face was wrinkled and droopy, like a wax mask that had sat too long in the sun. Shockingly, he'd cut his long gray beard and had trimmed his hair. And instead of wearing his favored wizard-like Eden robes, he was dressed like an island civilian. He wore a wide-brim hat, khaki pants, and a white button-up with the sleeves rolled up his thin forearms.

The sight was jarring.

I met them halfway across the garden. "Sandalphon."

"Please, my son, call me Elijah, or Eli, here on Earth." He lowered his voice to a whisper. "It's much easier for the humans to spell."

I smiled. "It's surprising to see you here, Eli."

He looked up at Cassiel. "She asked me to come. How could I say no?"

"I had hoped he might be able to help me figure out a way to restore the darkness veil around the spirit line." Cassiel's expression wilted even more. "Then the spirit line went down, and he was stuck here with me."

Sandalphon patted her hand. "Never *stuck* with you, my dear."

"When was the spirit line destroyed?" I asked.

Cassiel didn't have to think about it. "Two hundred and ninety-three days ago, about a week after it was exposed."

"About a week after we used the crystal water," I said, the guilt settling around my shoulders like a pillory.

"It's my fault, Warren, not yours. You had no idea the consequence of using crystal water, but I did. When I gave it to you, I knew I'd have to take full responsibility for my actions."

"You couldn't have known how much time would pass or that the Morning Star would be old enough to be a threat," Sandalphon argued.

"I'm not sure that will matter to the Council," Cassiel said.

Sandalphon lifted his bony shoulders. "Well, the bright side is you have a reprieve from their judgment. Possibly a permanent one."

"You really don't think the spirit line can be repaired?" I asked.

Cassiel sighed. "There's nothing to repair. The spirit line is gone."

"Recreated then? If the Morning Star was strong enough to create it, surely Iliana can do it too."

"Iliana is strong enough, but she doesn't know how." Cassiel gestured between herself and Sandalphon. "We don't even know how."

Sandalphon held up a hand. "Can we take this conversation

to a park bench or a table? My old joints can't stay vertical much longer."

"Of course," Cassiel said, gripping his arm as they walked toward the gate. "Warren, you coming?"

I followed. "What about the Father? Does he know?"

"He does, but not while he's on Earth in the form of Father John," she said as we exited the garden.

"What if we kill him?"

Cassiel stopped and looked back so quickly Sandalphon almost fell down.

"Not *kill* him, but what if I dispatch him from his earthly body?" I asked.

She continued on toward a thatch-roof gazebo near the pool. "It's not only his body that limits him. It's this realm. In order to access his full powers, he must return to Eden."

My head dropped back in frustration. "And he can't return without the spirit line."

"Bingo." She led Sandalphon into the gazebo. There was a table and chairs inside it. "I've almost wondered if the Morning Star's intention behind the virus wasn't twofold. One reason being to kill humans, but also to ensure the Father would be on Earth. Before that, he stayed in Zion almost the entire time you were gone."

"Really?"

She pulled out a chair for Sandalphon, and he sat down. "Yes. He never gave up hope that you were alive."

I walked over. "I saw him there just before I left for Nulterra. He told me he sent Rogan and Jett to protect Iliana."

"Your tone sounds as if you doubt the Father," Sandalphon said as he eased onto the chair.

"Not exactly, but it's clear we can't be too careful."

"I agree," Cassiel said. "So I checked them out myself. Their motives are pure."

As an Angel of Knowledge, Cassiel could extract information with a touch from angels or humans. It was impossible to lie to her. Impossible to keep secrets.

"Good. Thank you."

She gestured toward the chair beside her. "Come sit. We have much to discuss. We've just spoken with Torman."

I pulled out the chair and sat down. "Did he tell you how this happened?"

"Which part?"

"How did I lose seventeen years? We were only there two days."

"You were only there for what *felt* like two days. As I understand it, you spent most of your visit to Nulterra in the land of Ket Nhila. Torman tells us Ket Nhila is an illusion subjective to the human souls present. I would guess your experience there was very much like Earth."

"That's right. We spent our first night on the military base where I was stationed in Iraq. It was almost exactly the same." Realization hit me. "It mimicked the days and nights of Earth."

"I believe so," Cassiel said.

"The next morning, we awoke to a wasteland with no sun. It was dark, except for the glow of the lake of fire." I closed my eyes. "That was the real Nulterra. I'm sure we were there a long time, but we had no way to measure it."

"Torman said the days there were equal to almost a decade in this realm," she said quietly. "Thus extending the Thousand Year Prophecy, as it was relevant to the Morning Star's existence—not Earth's time clock. In spirit form, he could travel through the gate without it being open."

I pinched the bridge of my nose. "And while I was caught up there, things went all to hell here."

Neither of them spoke.

"What about Flint? Why didn't he tell us how much time had passed?" I asked.

"He didn't know. Samael had taken him to Zion to wait for news with the Father, and we didn't tell him."

Inside Eden, humans had no concept of time. Nor did they have any connection with the things of Earth outside what they were told by the angels.

Cassiel looked mildly guilty. "We decided you all knowing would be counterproductive to getting you out."

She was probably right, but I couldn't help but feel a little pissed off about it. I'd never been blindsided like I was by Iliana showing up at the gate.

Sandalphon steepled his fingers, studying me carefully. "Perhaps we should focus on what's ahead, rather than what's in the past."

With a heavy sigh, I nodded and sat back in my chair. "Who else might know about the spirit line? Surely the Morning Star and the Father aren't the only ones."

"You're correct. Someone else was present for the spirit line's creation," Cassiel said.

I leaned in.

"Azrael."

"And he has no memory of it, I'm sure," I said.

Cassiel's eyes fell to the lump beneath my shirt. "You don't have the memory either." It wasn't a question. It was a statement. A fact she was certain of without even asking.

I pulled out Azrael's blood stone and clenched it in my palm. "I don't. I've never seen anything in the blood stone about the creation of the spirit line."

"I told you Azrael would take off the necklace when there was information he didn't want anyone else to know," Cassiel said to Sandalphon.

I could attest to that. I'd found the stone locked away in his safe during the time he'd employed Fury to *distract* me.

Sandalphon closed his eyes.

I looked at Cassiel. "Nathan said you talked to Azrael."

"I did. He got the number for the resort from someone at Wolf Gap. He didn't want to talk to me, however. He wants to talk to you."

"OK. Give me a phone."

"First, we need to come up with a plan." Cassiel tapped her finger on the tabletop. "Azrael is on his way here."

"He is?"

She nodded. "Yes, and we need to be prepared."

"What's to prepare? When he gets here, I'll put the necklace on him. Boom. He'll have his memories back."

Cassiel looked confused. "You think it's that simple?"

"Why do you think it's so complicated?"

"Warren, this isn't like the last time where Azrael suddenly lost his memories when he came through the spirit line. He hasn't been fumbling around a few days not knowing who he is. He isn't desperate to remember like he was before."

"I don't understand."

"Everyone thought you were dead. He mourned your death at the same time his memories of the supernatural world were fading away. Not only did stories of angels and demons and Heaven and Hell become fiction to him, they became synonymous with the most painful experience of his mortal life."

She touched my forearm. "It's more than a memory problem. Azrael doesn't want anything to do with the supernatural."

"So I'll hold him down and put the necklace on him if I have to," I said.

"That may have worked before, when Azrael's mind was a clean slate, but Cassiel is right. This is very different."

Sandalphon's cool-blue eyes drifted toward the horizon. "Azrael would no longer be searching for truth in the blood stone. That's the only way those memories are accessed."

Cassiel sat back and put her hands in her lap. "And if the Morning Star gets ahold of the necklace instead, the memories are as good as gone."

"So what do you suggest I do?" I asked.

"You must get close to him. Gain Azrael's trust. Only then might he be willing to seek out the truth."

"And accept the truth," Sandalphon added.

"If he gets his memories back from the blood stone, do you think he'll remember how the Morning Star built the spirit line?" I asked.

Cassiel shrugged. "We can only hope."

"When's he coming?"

"As soon as they can ready a plane," Cassiel said.

"So two days, at least, including flight time. I'm sure I'll talk to him before then."

"When you do, tread lightly on the supernatural," she warned.

"What does he think happened to me if not that I died in Nulterra?"

"He believes you died here on the island, on a rescue mission to find Fury's sister."

"So he remembers Anya?" I asked.

Because Anya was an angel, he shouldn't remember her either.

Cassiel shook her head. "He remembers Fury."

I raked a hand back through my hair. "What a mess."

"I'm sorry, Warren."

"Don't be. The crystal water saved Fury's life down there, and it allowed you, Theta, and Flint to help us get out. We wouldn't have survived without it."

Cassiel's eye glistened. "And for your safety, I'm grateful. That's all I ever wanted."

My heart tugged. "Cassiel, I—"

"There you are." Fury came up the stone path from one of the huts. Her damp hair hung loose around her shoulders, and she wore a short tank-top dress, unlike *anything* I'd ever seen her in before. "The shower's free if you want to clean up before dinner."

I was torn. There was so much I wanted to say to Cassiel.

"Go shower," Cassiel said with a pained smile. "We can talk later."

"You sure?"

"Positive." She leaned toward Sandalphon. "Would you like to secure a nice table in the dining room?"

Fury offered me her hand. I took it and stood. "We'll see you in there then," I said to them.

Neither responded nor looked at me as we left.

Fury led me down the path along the ridgeline. "What was that about?"

"They were filling me on Azrael's situation and the destruction of the spirit line." I tugged on her hand. "Why? Worried?"

She laughed sarcastically. "No." She pulled me to a stop. "Should I be?"

I turned toward her, closing the space between us with a step. I curled my hand behind her neck and pulled her lips up to meet mine. My kiss was hard and greedy, and when I broke it, I dragged my teeth across her bottom lip.

She smiled. "Guess not."

"You look hot in that dress."

"It's your daughter's."

I groaned up toward the sky. "Shit, don't tell me that."

"It's messed up, right?" She continued down the path, towing me behind her. "We missed everything."

I followed her up the steps around to the back of the first villa we reached. "I feel like I'm stuck in a dream I can't wake up from."

"Me too." She walked through the unlocked door. "This is us."

Inside, a queen-sized bed faced a wall of windows and a balcony looking out over the jungle toward the ocean. "Wow. This is nice." I walked to the window. The sun was low in the sky, and there was nothing as far as I could see across the water in the distance.

Fury stood behind me and rested her head on my shoulder. I took her hand, pulling it around to my chest. I tilted my face toward her. "How are you handling everything?"

She shook her head.

I exhaled slowly. "Same."

After a moment, she pulled away. "You should shower. Dinner is supposed to be soon."

"I'm so hungry."

"I know." She picked up a bag off the floor, and the cotton dress strained across her butt. She straightened and handed me a bag. "This is from Kane. He's the only one here about your size." Her head tilted. "What?"

I realized I was smiling. "You could've waited for me to shower."

"We'd never eat." She stretched on her toes and kissed me. "Hurry up. Everything you need is in there."

The hot water didn't last long, which was probably a good thing, knowing Fury was in the next room. Cold showers were necessary if I wanted to get anything done around her.

After drying off, I stepped out and wrapped the towel around my waist. In the mirror, my gaze fell on the stone resting between my pecs. I touched it, remembering what Cassiel had said. *You don't have the memory either.*

It was such an odd statement. A declaration, really. It stuck with me, but I couldn't figure out why.

There was a light tap on the bathroom door. I twisted the handle and opened it a crack.

"I thought I might blow-dry my hair while I wait for you." Fury's eyes drifted the length of my damp torso, and when they settled on the towel, her lips parted with a small breath.

I opened the door wider. "Help yourself."

She came inside, and I stood behind her as she bent to look in the cabinet beneath the sink. Unable to stop myself, I slid my hand around her hipbone and squeezed.

The smile she flashed over her shoulder was all the encouragement I needed. I grabbed the hem of the dress and pulled it up over her hips.

She wore nothing underneath it.

A deep groan rolled up my throat.

Fury grasped the fabric bunched around her waist, and in one seamless motion, pulled it over her head and dropped it onto the floor.

Letting the towel fall to my feet, I pulled her bare back against my chest. She reached back, tangling her fingers in my wet hair, and all my blood rushed south so fast it made me dizzy.

When Fury arched her spine, my mind went blank.

A blank slate.

There was nothing between us but the blood stone.

*"You don't have the memory either."*

Cassiel could extract information with a touch. A similar scene with her had given her full access to Azrael's blood stone through me.

*Holy shit.* My eyes popped open. *Cassiel had been spying on me the whole damn time.*

# CHAPTER FOUR

*I* yawned all through dinner.

It wasn't really a surprise, as my body had been going for days—or years, depending on which clock you used—with barely any sleep. The exhaustion got the better of my emotions while we ate.

The tables in the dining room had been pushed together to form three long tables. Fury and I sat at the center one with Iliana, Sloan, Nathan, Anya, Jett, and Reuel. Our friends gathered at the surrounding tables.

Cassiel sat facing me with Sandalphon one table away. Each time we made awkward eye contact during dinner, my jaw clenched.

We needed to talk, but I needed a good night's sleep first.

For dinner, we were served the best slab of meat I'd eaten in ages. Steak marinated in soy sauce, testosterone, and happiness. It was topped with caramelized onions and shrimp.

Sloan eyed my cleaned plate with a grin. "Good to be back?"

I leaned back in my chair and rubbed my full stomach. "We haven't eaten since we left."

At the end of the table, Reuel made a whiny sound of rebuttal.

"Cheetos and granola bars don't count," I told him.

Nathan chuckled. "I was going to say, Reuel went two whole days without food, and you guys made it back alive?"

The whole table laughed. Reuel just shrugged and ate the leftover steak off Anya's plate.

"What was it like down there?" Sloan asked, putting her hands in her lap.

I pushed my plate forward and leaned my elbows on the table. "I don't mind telling you about it, but I'd rather hear about everything I missed." I looked at Iliana. "What's your life been like?"

"You want me to ruin the play-by-play interactive documentary Mom has kept of the past seventeen years?" Iliana asked, flashing a teasing smile at Sloan.

I looked at Sloan. "You have?"

Sloan's cheeks flushed. "I may have been a little overly sentimental."

"A little?" Iliana laughed. "You saved my first training bra."

Nathan covered his ears. "We don't need to hear about that at the dinner table."

"And nobody needs to see it either," I said, shaking my head.

Everyone laughed.

I looked at Iliana again. "But yes, I would love for you to spoil the play-by-play just a little. I'll settle for the highlights."

She crossed her arms on the tabletop. "Well, I was homeschooled until the third grade. Then everyone decided Asheville was safe enough for me to attend public school. I was the only kid who had a security detail working just off the property, but it was an uneventful few years."

"Uneventful is always good in our world," I said.

"Amen to that," Sloan agreed.

"I never had a dramatic coming-of-age moment like Jett or Rogan did, but by the time I was fourteen, I could control my powers fairly well. Mom practiced with me, and so did Kane and Samael."

"You practiced with her?" I asked Sloan.

She held her hands in the prayer position in front of her, then she opened them slowly. White light danced in her palms.

"You still have your powers." I clapped my hands.

She hid her hands beneath the table again. "They never came back like they were before Iliana was born, but yes. I've been able to strengthen them over the years."

"She healed a lot of people, too, during the virus," Nathan said, draping his arm across the back of her chair.

Of course she had. "I'm so proud of you."

"Be proud of her." Sloan pointed at our daughter. "She's been putting me to shame since she was a kid."

I was proud of her. And I couldn't wait to see what else she could do.

"Tell Warren about the Christmas cookies incident," Sloan said to Nathan.

Nathan burst out laughing.

"Christmas cookies?" Fury asked.

Iliana groaned. "They love to tell this story."

"And it's my right as a father to tell it the rest of your life." Nathan took a drink of his beer, then put the bottle down. "So every Christmas, Sloan and the kids make a bunch of Christmas cookies to hand out to teachers and leave out for Santa. And every Christmas, Iliana and Luca get in big trouble for sneaking the cookies out of the pantry."

"They aren't the only ones," Sloan said, glaring at her husband.

"Hey, this story isn't about me."

She laughed.

"Childproofing shit did nothing with a Houdini baby in the house." He pointed at Iliana. "So Sloan decided to start hiding the cookies in the panic room."

"You have a panic room in your house?" Anya asked.

"Do you remember the material, high-Z, that lined the walls of Echo-10?" Fury asked her.

"The angelproofing stuff?"

"Yeah. The panic room was made from it," Fury said.

"It was put in for emergencies, but we hadn't used it in years, so Sloan started hiding things in there. As for high-Z being angelproof, it's not if Iliana really makes her mind up about getting through it," Nathan said.

I sat back and covered my mouth. "Oh no."

"This kid pulverized the panic-room door. I mean, a billion tiny shards of metal embedded in the drywall."

"It was a wonder she didn't kill herself," Sloan added.

"She almost killed her brother. He was an accomplice, and he got caught in the explosion," Nathan said.

"Luca was fine," Iliana argued.

Sloan's mouth dropped open. "Only because you healed him."

The whole table erupted into laughter, drawing stares from the rest of the room. Cassiel and I locked eyes before I quickly darted mine away.

"You blew up the door?" Anya asked Iliana.

"I was hungry! They never fed me!"

"Yes, we did," Sloan argued. "Why do you think we had to lock everything up? If something had sugar in it, it wasn't safe around you."

Fury chuckled. "Wonder where she got that, *Nathan*."

He put his hands up in defense. "Hey, I never tried explosives to get to the snacks."

"Hmm." Reuel looked guilty. He inched his hand up in the

air, and everyone laughed again.

"How old were you?" Anya asked.

Iliana shrugged. "Maybe twelve. I dunno."

"After that," Nathan continued, "Iliana was forbidden from using superpowers inside the house."

"Did you at least find the cookies?" Fury asked Iliana.

"Yeah, but most of them didn't survive the explosion. Santa didn't get any cookies that year."

"And Santa was *pissed*," Nathan said.

"I hate I missed it." My laughter faded into sadness. I'd missed everything. All the stories. All the milestones. Her whole childhood and then some.

Static crackled in my ears. "Appa, don't be sad," a gentle voice, inaudible to the others, said. Iliana was smiling at me. "And if you have to be sad, I'll be happy enough for both of us because you're home."

I smiled and blinked hard to keep the tears at bay. I reached across the table for her hand and squeezed it.

Beside her, Jett's face snapped up. Someone, I suspected Rogan, was communicating silently with him too. He turned to Iliana and kept his voice low. "We need to deal with the prisoner."

"Now?" She released my hand.

Jett whispered something in her ear even my keen ears couldn't hear. Iliana pushed back her chair. "I'm sorry, but I need to excuse myself. Drama calls."

"What's the matter?" I asked.

She and Jett stood. "Your Nulterra guide has decided he's done cooperating." Iliana searched the room until she spotted Cassiel. "It's time."

Cassiel offered Sandalphon a hand up.

"I'll come too," I said.

I expected Fury would want to go, but she didn't budge. I

put my hand on her thigh under the table. "You coming?"

"No, unless you really want me to." She let out a slow, tired sigh. "I've had enough of demons and destruction for a while. I'd kinda like to spend some time with my sister tonight, if that's OK with you."

It was interesting she'd rather spend time with Anya than go with me and Jett. But then again, Jett was a painful subject at the moment. And would probably be one for a while.

"Of course." I leaned over and planted a kiss on her forehead. "I'll meet you in the room later?"

"Wake me if I'm asleep," she whispered.

The mention of sleep triggered another yawn.

"You gonna make it?" she asked with a smile.

"I'm gonna try." I stood. "Reuel, you coming?"

His brow scrunched together as he shook his head. Not surprising. This situation had a high probability of turning violent, and Reuel was a pacifist in most situations if he could manage it.

Also, dessert hadn't yet been served.

I turned to Sloan and Nathan. "Thank you, guys, for a wonderful welcome home. Sorry we have to cut this short."

Nathan waved his hand. "Go handle your angel business. We're not going anywhere."

I smiled, and Iliana and Jett met me around the table. Cassiel and Sandalphon were moving slowly toward the door. We easily beat them there, saving me from an uncomfortable walk with Cassiel.

Arguing voices floated on the night breeze when the three of us walked outside. The noise was coming from the villa where Torman was being held.

"Are you really going to kill him?" I asked Iliana as we crossed the lawn beneath the stars.

She was between me and Jett, and she looked over at me in

the moonlight. "Why? You don't want me to?"

"I didn't say that. I'm just curious if there's a protocol for this. Is he given a trial, or what?"

"We need to question him about his involvement in what's happened recently. And find out if he has any knowledge of the Morning Star's future plans. Cassiel and Sandalphon will determine if he lying, and then I'll make my decision."

"What decisions have you made in the past?"

"Are you asking me how many times I've inflicted a death sentence?" She stared straight ahead.

"Yes."

With humans, death leaves tally marks on the soul, and my whole life—human and otherwise—I'd been able to count those tally marks with a glance. But angels were different.

And Iliana was different from all angels.

It was a strange thing for me to wonder. And an even stranger thing for me to ask my child.

"I've destroyed four of the fallen."

Her tone brought me some relief. The thought of my daughter as an executioner wasn't exactly a pleasant one, but it was clear she didn't enjoy it. Her eyes were on the ground.

"That's four fewer demons we'll have to worry about if this comes to war," Jett said, putting his hand on the back of her neck.

"*When* this comes to war, don't you mean?" I asked.

His head tilted to the side. "Perhaps."

"Do you really think we can take on the Morning Star and win?" Iliana asked.

I stopped walking and turned toward her. "Iliana, since before you were born, the angels have marveled at and *feared* just the possibility of what you'd be capable of. Angels don't fear anything, but I have literally had to fight to convince them that you wouldn't be a threat to Eden."

I bent to look her in the eye and put both hands on her small shoulders. "And don't ever forget, even though you were conceived in love, by the demon's own design, you were created to be the most dangerous weapon to ever exist. So do I think we can beat the Morning Star?" I leaned closer. "Hell yeah, I do."

With a smile, she wrapped her arms around my neck. "I'm so glad you're back."

"Me too, sweetheart. Me too."

Something crashed inside the villa. I released her, and the three of us ran the rest of the way. Jett threw open the door, and Rogan was using his power to hold Torman on the ground. A chair had been thrown through the sliding-glass door out to the deck.

"Warren…you're here," Torman choked out.

"Let him up," Iliana said to Rogan.

Reluctantly, Rogan dropped the hand that was aimed at Torman. The Angel of Knowledge gasped for air. Torman rolled onto his back, wheezing like his trachea had been crushed. Perhaps it had been.

Jett walked over and picked up the chair. Then Rogan used his power again to lift Torman off the floor and put him in it.

Iliana walked over and stood in front of him. "Decided to get rowdy, did we?"

"I'm being held here unjustly," Torman said, his voice pained and raspy. Around his wrists were the silver cuffs Rogan had clamped on him earlier. I assumed they somehow limited the demon's power.

"You think we're holding you here without cause?" Iliana asked, crossing her arms over her chest.

"You know you are. Warren, tell them."

I stood behind Iliana. "We know nothing of the sort."

"I've been imprisoned in Nulterra most of your life. There's no way I could have possibly done anything to offend you. Whatever has happened here in the last seventeen years has been done without my knowledge or involvement."

Cassiel and Sandalphon walked in the door behind us.

"We'll see about that." Iliana looked back at Cassiel. "Are you ready to get the truth out of him?"

Cassiel bowed her head. "Gladly." She walked behind Torman's chair and put both her hands on the sides of his head. "I'm ready when you are."

"Torman, I shouldn't have to explain to you what Cassiel's purpose is here, but I will so there's absolutely no confusion as to what the consequences will be if you don't cooperate.

"We are going to ask you a series of questions. As an Angel of Knowledge, like you, Cassiel has the ability to tell us if you're lying. If you refuse to answer, she will extract the information from your mind and tell us anyway. Should we need her services, you will be punished." Iliana turned her right palm over, and electric blue energy sizzled to life above it.

It was the same power the Angels of Death could use to kill a human. It wouldn't be strong enough to kill Torman, though she had that ability too, but it wouldn't be pleasant for him. His widened eyes told us he knew that.

"I have nothing to hide from you."

"I hope, for your sake, that is the case," Iliana said, letting the energy fizzle out.

I fought to suppress a smile. My kid was a badass.

Iliana widened her stance and kept her arms crossed in front of her. "When was the last time you spoke to the Morning Star?"

"I haven't spoken to the Morning Star since he came to Earth and implanted himself into the womb of Azrael's human."

"Not at all?" Iliana asked.

"I've been in prison. Our chains there cut off all communication with other angels."

We all looked at Cassiel for confirmation. She nodded that he was telling the truth.

"Demons can communicate with each other?" Iliana asked.

"Of course."

"Mind if I ask a question?" I asked Iliana.

"Sure."

I stepped up beside her and looked at Torman. "Abaddon, the Destroyer, told me it was his idea for the Morning Star to be born to Adrianne, 'Azrael's human' as you call her. He said it was his plan for the Morning Star to be born into his own prison. Is that the truth?"

"Yes, it was the Destroyer's idea. However, you would be stupid to believe that the Morning Star hadn't worked out every possible scenario before making the decision to put himself into such a potentially precarious situation. I have no doubt he carefully considered the implications of being born so close to the Vitamorte." Torman looked at Iliana.

"But you don't know for sure?" I asked.

"I do not. The Morning Star kept his own counsel. He would not have shared such vital information with anyone else. And shortly after he put the plan into motion, I was arrested by the Destroyer and locked in a cell."

Again, Cassiel nodded.

"How long has Chimera been working for the Morning Star?" Iliana asked.

Torman was hesitant to answer. Cassiel's knuckles turned white as she tightened her grip on his head. He winced. "I don't know when she got directly involved with the Morning Star, but I convinced Chimera to join us when I found her living in Ukraine in 2012."

I gritted my teeth. "Chimera told us she met you in 2013,

the year I met Sloan. So she lied to me about absolutely everything."

"We told you she was good at it," Iliana said.

"What can you tell us about the spirit line?" Rogan asked.

Torman shrugged. "It's gone, so I've been told. I haven't had access to the spirit line since Chimera was born. And as I've already said—"

"You've been locked up in Nulterra. Yeah, we know." Jett shook his head and looked at Iliana. "He's of no use to us."

"Do you know how the Morning Star created it? Or how he created the second spirit line into Nulterra?" I asked.

"Of course I don't. The only angels who could tell you are the Morning Star and Azrael. Why don't you ask him? Oh, that's right. Azrael has rejoined the fallen. Old habits, you know."

My fists clenched.

"I overheard you talking at the gate," he continued. "Sounds like things turned out far better for the Morning Star than even he had planned. The world's largest army at his disposal and a quarter of all humans dead? And he's just getting started."

Iliana's expression was pained.

"What do you know about the virus?" Jett asked.

"I know nothing about a virus, but the Morning Star has researched biological weapons for centuries. He always dreamed of being able to pick and choose the humans he wanted to live and die."

Iliana looked up at me. "We believe he vaccinated all the employees and operators at Claymore. There weren't any reports from anyone at the company getting sick."

"And no one found that suspicious?" I asked.

"There was so much chaos when the virus hit, no one was paying attention," Rogan said.

"Did the Morning Star have any other schemes in development?" Jett asked.

Torman pointed. "Only the Vitamorte."

The Morning Star had carefully planned to bring Sloan and I together so we might breed the Vitamorte—a powerful angel of both life and death. He'd wanted to use our child's power to forever separate Earth from Eden.

"But I don't see how that's relevant now. The plan was to use Iliana to destroy the spirit line, but he's already done that." Torman eyeballed Cassiel. "Thanks to someone."

She stiffened.

"What about after he used her to destroy the spirit line? There must have been a plan for Iliana after that," Jett said.

Torman looked Iliana up and down. "He would have raised her to be one of us. And if she didn't conform, he would have killed her."

Rogan and Jett, Iliana's protectors, exchanged a loaded glance. "Kill her how?" Rogan asked.

My brow lifted. "Helkrymite." Everyone looked at me as I pulled the sword from the scabbard on my back. "The swords have the power to kill angels."

Cassiel looked up. "They were created to kill the Vitamorte."

My stomach turned. Something about holding a weapon specifically made to destroy my daughter made me want to drop it.

"True?" Jett asked Torman.

"She pulled that information out of my brain, didn't she?" Torman asked with an annoyed glare. "The Morning Star's plan had always been to breed the Vitamorte, but he was well aware of the risks. Before he ever set Iliana's birth into motion, he protected himself if the plan were to go wrong."

"Then why did guards in Nulterra have them?" I asked.

"Why do you think? The swords may have been created to kill her, but their use has obviously spread beyond that now. Abaddon was executing angels in Nulterra. I've watched the demise of many of my friends by the swords' blades."

"How many swords are there?" Rogan asked.

"The Morning Star had enough of the Father's sanctonite to forge seven swords."

"You're sure?" Jett asked.

"Positive. At one time, I was responsible for keeping up with them."

We waited for Cassiel to confirm.

"He's telling the truth. Only seven swords exist."

"If you were tasked with keeping up with them, then where would we find them now?" Iliana asked.

"You have two." Torman gestured toward me. "Warren has one. Reuel has Etred's."

"Where did you get yours?" Jett asked me.

I returned the sword to its scabbard. "From the demon Uko."

"Who has the others?" Iliana asked Torman.

Torman hesitated again. This time, Cassiel squeezed, and he still didn't answer.

Iliana raised her palm and let the electricity sizzle to life again.

When she took a step toward him, Torman leaned back as far as he could. "OK. OK." He held his hands up in surrender.

Iliana didn't let the spark die out.

Torman's fearful eyes fixed on it. "Three swords were in Nulterra. Etred's, we know, made it out with Reuel, but the others would have been consumed by the pit. Those guards were running in the opposite direction of the exit when you destroyed the spirit line."

Cassiel confirmed his statement with a nod.

"And the rest?" I asked.

"Moloch, and the angels who left with him, had four swords among them when they brought a few human souls back to Earth."

The memory of that mission still stirred anger inside me. Cassiel and I had traveled the world trying to stop an African famine and a serial killer because of it. In it was the roots of Cassiel's first betrayal of me—or, at least, the first betrayal I'd discovered.

She'd been spying on me for members of the Council who were plotting with the demons to harm Iliana. Cassiel had given them the access information to Echo-5, Iliana's supernaturally secured home. She'd plucked the information from my brain under the guise of lovemaking. I should have wondered then what other secrets she'd stolen...

Iliana nudged me with her elbow.

Everyone was staring at me.

I blinked. "Sorry. Tuned out for a second."

"He said Moloch had swords. Did you see any when you fought him in Malab?" Iliana asked.

I thought back to the day Cassiel, Reuel, and I had battled Moloch, the now-permanently deceased Archangel of Knowledge. "We didn't see much of the palace, but I would have remembered seeing a sword. Cassiel?"

"There were plenty of guns. No swords," she confirmed, her face sour. She still hadn't gotten over how many times we had been shot.

"I know he had them when he left Nulterra," Torman said.

"Moloch didn't take them with him from Malab. When I destroyed his body, his spirit went directly across the spirit line to attack Echo-5," I said.

"Should we go back to Malab and look for them?" Cassiel asked.

Rogan grimaced. "It's going to be hard to travel."

"You must find the swords," a voice said behind us. I turned and saw Sandalphon. He'd been so quiet, I'd almost forgotten he was there. "They are the only true weapon the Morning Star has against us."

"He has an army," Iliana said.

"Yes, but no human army can stand against an angel, my child." He looked at me. "Even if you succeed in destroying the Morning Star, we will all be watching over our shoulders for the rest of eternity as long as the swords exist. You must find them."

He was right, but without the spirit line, traveling would be difficult, to say the least.

"Who had the other swords?" I asked.

"Uko, Orin, and Saraiah. Uko is dead, and Orin and Saraiah will be close to the Morning Star," Torman answered.

"Who are they?" Iliana asked.

"Saraiah is a prophet, and Orin is a messenger," Sandalphon said. "Torman is correct. They would be very useful servants."

I didn't know either of them, but I'd heard stories about Orin all over Eden. He was the messenger who'd spread the Morning Star's propaganda throughout the angelic choirs. He'd also challenged the Archangel Gabriel during the First Angel War. Gabriel had won, but the fight had become legendary. Orin was, apparently, *very* good with a sword.

Jett held up three fingers. "So we need to find three swords. Orin's, Saraiah's, and Moloch's."

"Yes," Torman said.

"Does anyone have any more questions?" Iliana asked, looking around our group. After a moment, when no one had spoken, the white light in her hand grew and had flickers of purple.

I'd seen a similar light before. From Sloan, when she was

pregnant with Iliana. It was the power to destroy angels.

The fear in Torman's eyes told me he knew it too. "Wait. This wasn't part of our agreement."

Iliana shook her head and slowly walked toward him. "We didn't have an agreement."

Torman's eyes flashed to me. "Warren! Warren, please help me."

I swallowed.

His whole body vibrated with fear. "Consider your actions carefully. If you kill me, Chimera will be crippled, and the Morning Star will know why. You'll start this war before you're ready and give the advantage to your enemy."

"Wait." Jett walked toward Iliana. "Maybe he's right. If you kill him, it will be an act of war."

"Who cares? Kill him," Rogan said.

Cassiel lifted her hand. "But our only advantage at this point, Iliana excluded, would be surprise. We don't want to give the largest army on Earth a chance to prepare if we don't have to."

"And you don't want to start a war before all the swords have been found, if you can help it," Sandalphon added.

Iliana was still for a moment, and then she turned toward me. The sparkling light reflected in her dark eyes. "What do you think?"

She wanted my opinion. I wasn't sure anything on Earth could feel so good. Such a shame it had to be about execution.

"They're right. At the moment, they don't know we have him—"

"That's not true," Cassiel said. "Before Rogan cuffed him, he made contact with the Morning Star."

"Damn it, Torman." I shook my head and closed my eyes. "How do you expect me to help you when you pull shit like that?"

"Archangel, it is no different from what you would've done."

True.

I looked at Cassiel. "Did he tell the Morning Star we're all here?"

"I didn't!" he shouted

Cassiel shook her head. "He only told the Morning Star that Nulterra was destroyed and that he had returned with you, Fury, Reuel, and Anya. He did not tell the Morning Star that Iliana is here."

Jett touched the small of Iliana's back. "That gives us an advantage for now. Wouldn't you agree, Warren?"

I was staring at his hand on Iliana.

He quickly pulled it back.

"I think it's too soon," I agreed. "Even if we had all the swords, we're still not ready. We're exhausted. We're distracted. If you kill him now, none of us will be ready for the consequences. You should let him live."

Iliana closed her fist, quenching the killing force. "Very well."

Torman whimpered. "Oh, thank you, thank you, thank—"

"For now," I snapped. Horror filled his eyes. I unsheathed my sword again as I walked toward him. Then I lowered the blade until its point touched the center of his chest. "If I so much as hear a squeak from you, I'll end you myself."

His chin quivered. "Yes, sir."

I looked at Rogan. "But we shouldn't keep him here, not if Azrael is really on his way."

"You don't trust Azrael?" Iliana asked.

"I don't trust the Morning Star. If he knows we have Torman, he'll want him back. He's too great a liability for Chimera."

"Right." Iliana put her hands on her hips. "But what will we do with him?"

"Can we send him back to headquarters?" Jett asked.

She shook her head. "Not without travel paperwork."

"Travel paperwork?" I asked her.

"If you thought international travel was strict when you were here before, just wait. You'll all need passports and medical records," Iliana said.

"How will we get those?" Torman asked.

"I'm not sure, but we won't get back to the States without them." Iliana thought for a moment. "Rogan, take him to Manila. Maybe you can find a document forger there."

"Yes, ma'am."

"Maybe Jett should go with them," I suggested.

Iliana shook her head. "Jett stays with me."

"You sure?" I shrugged my shoulders. "Can't be too careful."

"I'm positive," she insisted.

"All right." Before putting the sword away, I stared at Jett. His mismatched eyes drifted to the blade. *That's right, kid. Keep your hands off my little girl.*

As if reading my mind, he took a small step back.

Behind me, Cassiel snickered.

I put the sword in its scabbard and yawned. "If that's all, I'd really like to go sleep for about a year."

With a smile, Iliana stretched on her toes to kiss my cheek. "Get some rest. You've earned it."

I hugged her. "I love you."

"I love you too."

I released her. As I turned to leave, Cassiel caught my eye. Nothing in me wanted to talk to her right then. I wanted a bed. And sleep. And maybe a snack.

She moved like she was going to start toward me, but I turned and walked out the door.

# CHAPTER FIVE

The hair on the back of my neck stood on end.

When I opened my eyes, the bedroom was dark, lit only by the slivers of moonlight slipping in through the cracks in the curtains.

The bedside lamps flickered again. I hadn't been dreaming. The quiet crackle of electricity echoed around the silent room.

Fury and I hadn't talked much when I got back to our villa after questioning Torman. I'd been so tired I hadn't even tried anything when I crawled into our bed and found her nearly naked.

I'd fallen asleep hard, melded against her back. My left arm was curled around her waist, and my right seemed to be missing completely. It had fallen asleep stretched beneath her pillow. As I carefully inched it out from under her, my fingers began to tingle.

I winced as the prickling pain spread through my hand.

The lamps flickered again, and the tingling told me I was *definitely* awake. I pumped my fist as I rolled onto my back. Then I propped up on my elbows.

Blinking a few times, my eyes went in and out of focus.

Then I saw it.

The silhouette of a man standing at the end of our bed.

Startled, my heels dug into the mattress, pushing me backward and knocking my skull against the headboard.

I grabbed my chest to make sure my heart was still inside it, then sat up.

Immortal or not, a soul watching me as I slept was some freaky shit. I rubbed my eyes and looked again, letting my eyes adjust to the dark.

It was a man—or what used to be a man.

A hand waved beside him. I looked down and recognized Hannah as she peeked around him. I raked both hands back through my hair and steadied my breathing.

When I finally remembered I was immortal *and* had superpowers, I held my finger over my lips. "Shh."

Fury hadn't stirred.

The digital clock on the nightstand said 1:39 a.m.

I wore only a pair of my Eden-made boxer briefs, so I gathered the sheet around my waist before swinging my legs off the side of the bed. My foot groped the floor for the pair of gym shorts I'd borrowed from Kane. I hooked them around my toes and lifted them high enough to reach. Then I shimmied into them under the covers before standing up.

I started toward the door and motioned for them to follow. I slowly and quietly twisted the lock to open it, but when I turned back to look for the ghosts, they were gone.

*Well, damn.*

I opened the door and found them waiting on the path outside. He was holding her hand.

Everything in me wanted to launch into a lecture about ghosts sneaking up on people when they were asleep, but Hannah's father grabbed me and pulled me in for a hug. He was crying, happy tears because sadness wouldn't exist for him as a spirit. His soul was pure, and his heart was good.

"Thank you," he said over my shoulder.

I patted his ethereal back. "I'm sorry it took me so long, and I'm sorry I couldn't bring her back alive."

He stepped back, wiping tears of light that had dribbled down his cheeks. He cupped the back of Hannah's head and pulled her against his side. "But you brought her back. That is all that matters to me. I'm sure you saved her from a terrible fate."

He was right. We had saved her kidnapped soul from being completely obliterated by the lake of fire. "I kept my word. That is all."

"That is enough." He smiled, and the seventeen years it had been since he'd last seen me showed on the spiritual projection of his face.

When humans die, their souls resemble their bodies as they had left them. It's not until they cross through the Eden Gate that their souls are returned to perfect youthfulness. This man looked like a shadow (pun intended) of the man I'd just met a few days before.

He would remain an aged ghost until we restored the spirit line to Eden. *If* we restored the spirit line to Eden.

"What's your name?" I asked him.

"John Mark."

"I'm Warren."

"I know. Your friends have told me about you."

"Well, don't believe everything you hear." I smiled. "Where will you go now?"

He shrugged. "We will stay here until we can no longer. Your friend, Samael, tells me this is not all there is."

I shook my head. "Not even close."

"He says your home is a land of wonders."

My eyes narrowed. This ghost was incredibly astute. Typically, they're disjointed from reality. The only exception I'd ever seen on Earth was Flint, but he'd been able to see angels his whole life, so that wasn't much of a surprise.

John Mark was different.

"Will we get to go there?" he asked.

"I'm going to do everything in my power to make that happen."

He looked down at his daughter. "And I know you are a man of your word."

The door to the villa creaked open behind me. "Warren?" Fury peeked her head through the crack in the doorway. "Who are you talking to?"

I flashed a sleepy smile back at her. "Hannah and her dad."

Fury's eyes doubled, suddenly awake. "They're here now?" She wouldn't be able to see them. Fury could only see angels, not human souls.

"Yeah. I'll be back inside in a second." I turned back to Hannah and John Mark. The door closed, and I heard the light switch flip on inside.

I knelt down in front of Hannah. "Are you happy?"

Her head bounced up and down, and she smiled up at her dad. I ran my fingers through her shiny black hair. "I hope this isn't the last time we'll see each other."

She put her tiny arms around my neck. "I will miss you, angel man."

I chuckled, and when she pulled back, I pinched the tip of her nose. "I'll miss you too, kiddo." I stood and shook her father's hand.

"Hopefully the next time we see each other, we will be in paradise," he said.

"Paradise, indeed."

"Goodbye."

"Take care of yourself," I said out of habit as they walked down the path.

Nothing on this Earth could harm them now. Nothing except for me, anyway. I wasn't even sure the sword could kill them if the Morning Star wanted to.

And I was sure he probably wanted to.

When they were gone, I walked back inside and found Fury sitting on the edge of the bed. All the lights in the room were on.

I cracked a smile as I locked the door behind me. "Scared of ghosts?"

Her face was pale. She pointed at the door. "That was some creepy shit, Warren Parrish."

I stood in front of her and pushed her long black hair back off her bare shoulders. She wore a tiny pink tank top and black boy shorts. They likely belonged to my daughter, but I refused to dwell on that.

"Would it make you feel any better if I told you I almost screamed and woke you up when I saw them standing in our room?"

She pointed to the floor. "They were standing in our room?"

I nodded.

"Like watching us sleep?"

I laughed softly. "They're gone now, and I doubt they'll be coming back."

"But how did they get in—"

"Shh." I slid my basketball shorts down off my hips and let them fall to the floor. Then I pressed the base of her throat and gently pushed her back onto the mattress.

"Want me to distract you from it?" I hooked my fingers in the waistband of her panties.

She shimmied out of them. "You'd better because there's no

way in hell I'm going back to sleep."

I slid my hand up between her thighs. "The legendary Fury is afraid of ghosts."

She pointed at me. "And if you tell anyone, I'll kill you."

---

I stretched my arm across the sheets, my fingers finding a whole lot of nothing. The light of the sunrise burned my eyes when I pried them open. It was rare that anyone beat me out of bed, but Fury was sipping coffee on our deck.

I rolled over and pushed myself up. Then I stood and tugged on my shorts. I padded barefoot across the bedroom to the doorway.

Fury sniffed and dried her eyes on the back of her hand.

I knelt down behind her and ran my hand down her bare arm. "You're up early," I said softly. "And I thought I'd worn you out last night."

"You did, but I woke up around dawn and couldn't go back to sleep. Must be the crystal water still in my system."

Crystal water didn't explain the tears.

"Can I help?" I pressed my lips against her shoulder.

Staring straight ahead, she nodded. "You already are."

It didn't seem like I was helping, but I was smart enough to realize neither of us would get over all we'd been through easily. Sure, we'd rescued Anya, but the cost was steep.

Flint was gone. There would be no seeing him again in Eden. No happy reunion on *the other side.* His death was permanent. Eternal. Even I, the keeper of death, couldn't comprehend such loss.

What I did understand, all too well, was the seventeen years we'd lost with our children. I'd been *so close* to being able to help raise Iliana. The sanctonite that would allow it was mine. Now? Those years were stolen in a blink.

At least Sloan and Nathan had apparently kept a detailed record of her life. Probably pictures, scrapbooks, and video. Had John done the same for Jett? The boy who wasn't his son? I doubted it.

And I'd have a relationship with Iliana. Our father-daughter bond had outlasted our years apart. She might outrank me, and she might be infinitely more powerful—but part of her still needed her dad.

But Jett? He was no longer the son Fury had given birth to. He was Malak, an angel who'd existed since the beginning of time. Thankfully, he was kind to her, and his insistence that we call him Jett was but one example of his best attempt at sympathy—not an easy emotion for an angel. But Malak had no need of a relationship with a human. No need of a mother. No need for Fury.

And she knew it.

She offered me her coffee, and I took a long drink as I walked around to the other chair. "You seemed angry last night at dinner," she said, staring out over the horizon. "What's up?"

It was clear she wanted to change the subject.

"I'm not angry, but I need to have a very uncomfortable conversation with Cassiel that I'm not looking forward to."

"I bet. She's in love with you."

That was debatable.

"Cassiel has strong feelings, but I'm not sure she even understands what love is," I said, returning her coffee.

"She risked everything on just the possibility that it might save your life. Sounds like love to me."

I looked at Fury.

She lifted the mug to her lips. "Don't think I didn't notice how bummed she was when she realized it was my life that was saved."

Couldn't argue that.

"What are you going to say to her?"

"I'm not sure." I leaned forward, balancing my elbows on my knees. "We still need her help."

"You're going to lead her on?"

"Me? Really?"

She smiled behind her cup. "Forgot who I was talking to."

Even with all the trauma, Fury was more relaxed than I'd ever seen her. In all the time we'd been together, it was the first time I'd seen her in pajamas. Her bare feet were propped up on the railing with her toned legs crossed at the ankles. A messy knot of black hair crowned her head, and her eyes were soft, wet, and sleepy.

It was like all the weight she'd carried for years had been burned up with Nulterra. In a way, I guess it had. All the pretense. The lies. The shame. For the first time in years, Fury was free.

She lifted an eyebrow. "Why are you looking at me weird?"

"I'm just happy."

She put her coffee on the table between us and pushed herself out of her chair. I sat back, and she eased down sideways on my lap and put her arms around my neck. "On the bright side of all this, we don't have to worry about you being around Jett anymore. So you can drop all that nonsense about me making a life without you."

I ran my hand up her smooth thigh. "I only ever wanted what was best for you."

"You are what's best for me, Warren." She leaned her forehead against mine. "I love you."

I closed my eyes and smiled. "Say it again."

She lowered her lips to my ear. "I love you," she whispered softly.

A bolt of energy sizzled through my nerve endings. Smiling, I angled my face to meet her lips and kissed her.

Someone whistled down the path.

Fury pulled away, and we both looked through the deck railing. A wide smile erupted on my face when I saw Iliana. It faltered when I saw Jett walking with her. They were heading toward our villa.

"Hello," I said.

"Morning!" Iliana waved. "Hi, Fury."

Fury waved back.

Jett watched Fury. "Good morning." He sounded a bit like a robot.

"Hi." Fury forced a smile.

"Mom sent me to find you."

My head snapped back with surprise. "Your mom's awake?"

"I know, right? She wants you to join us for breakfast. She stayed up last night pulling together pictures and journals for you to look through."

"I'd love that," I said.

Fury pushed herself up.

"After we eat, we might head into town if you want to join us," Iliana said.

I leaned forward. "Absolutely."

"We'll see you up there?" she asked.

I gave her a thumbs-up, and they continued past our deck. Before Fury got too far, I reached back and grabbed the tail of her shirt. "Where are you going?"

"To shower," she said, her whole body slumped.

I pulled her back in front of me and guided her back down onto my lap. "Two more minutes."

She tried to smile.

"It's really hard for you." I picked up her hand and slipped my fingers between hers. "I'm sorry."

She let her head flop to the side. "I'm not ready to do another meal with him. Mind if I skip it?"

"Why don't we both skip it? I can get something to go, and we can have breakfast in bed."

"Absolutely not."

"Why?"

Her free hand slipped behind my neck. "I appreciate the gesture, but there's no way I'm going to keep you away from breakfast with them. They're your family."

"Fury, so are you."

Her smile was grateful. "I know. And I'll be here when you get back."

"You're sure?"

"Positive." She pressed a kiss to my forehead then stood. "Maybe bring me something back to eat."

---

Iliana wasn't joking.

Sloan had created a play-by-play of Iliana's entire life. She had literally kept record of *everything*.

We spent two straight hours after breakfast looking through photos and videos and reading through a digital journal they'd kept for me. Iliana had taken over the journal when she was old enough, and there were entries from almost every day I was gone.

I got to see it all.

Her first lost tooth.

The time she'd cut her own hair.

Learning to ride a bike.

Pictures from her first high-school dance.

We laughed and cried. And I sat there quietly, soaking it all in. I forced myself to focus more on the sweet than on the bitter. Nothing could be done about the past, but at least we had a future together. My daughter's life had been full, happy, and *safe*.

I intended to help keep it that way.

"Thank you all for this." I nodded toward Sloan's fancy tablet that held all the photos and videos.

"That's just the digital stuff," Sloan said. "The rest is back at home."

"What else is there?" I asked.

"Mom wouldn't throw anything away. Everything from my first lost tooth to my tricycle are in the garage attic," Iliana said.

Nathan leaned toward me. "And your car."

"Shut up. Are you serious?" I asked.

He smiled. "Dad helped me and Iliana rebuild the engine over the last few years."

"It still runs?"

"Almost like brand new now. Lex was given strict orders to start it every few days while we were here."

"Damn. That's awesome," I said.

"It was supposed to be my first car, but *someone* won't let me drive it." Iliana was staring at Nathan.

"You learn how to drive like you're not in a bumper car, and we'll talk about it," he said.

She laughed and threw a balled-up napkin at him.

Sloan looked past Nathan. "There's Fury and Anya."

I'd taken breakfast to Fury before our jaunt down memory lane, and I'd asked her one more time if she'd like to join us. She didn't. Not because she wasn't happy for me, but I think she knew there would be no hiding the pain it would bring her. And she didn't want that for me.

She spent the morning with her sister instead. They'd gone for a run down to the beach and back.

Fury was smiling and breathing hard as they approached our table out on the lawn. Anya was right behind her.

"You look like you feel better," I said when they were close enough.

"I do." Fury wiped her face with the front of her tank top.

"Feel *better*?" Sloan asked skeptically. "I'd die if I had to run up that hill."

I expected Fury to say something snarky, as had always been the dynamic between her and Sloan.

"It's actually not that difficult when you think there are ghosts behind you," she said instead.

"There probably are," Iliana said.

Sloan grimaced. "Yeah. Better get used to it. The death rate is still pretty high after the virus, and now there's nowhere for them to go."

"We're learning. Did Warren tell you there was a ghost in our room last night?" Fury asked.

"No." Sloan's mouth dropped open.

"It wasn't anything sinister. We saved a little girl from Nulterra, and her father came to thank us," I said.

Sloan frowned. "We heard about her from Reuel after you guys left dinner last night."

"Yeah." My head tilted. "But even I didn't expect them to show up in our bedroom." I got up and dragged two chairs over from the next table for Fury and Anya.

"I was going to go take a shower, but this is way too interesting," Anya said as they sat down.

"Where's Jett?" Fury asked.

"He and Reuel took Rogan and Torman to catch the ferry to Dumaguete," Iliana said.

Fury visibly relaxed. I reached over and took her hand. Across the table, Sloan was watching us, and she smiled.

She'd asked about my relationship with Fury over breakfast. I'd told her the truth, that a part of me had always loved Fury, that I'd never really gotten over her. Sloan had laughed and said, "Warren, you were the only one who didn't know." Perhaps she was right.

Sloan and Nathan were both happy for us though, which meant the world to me.

"You can kill the dangerous ones, right?" Nathan asked, snapping me back to the conversation.

"The dangerous what?"

"The dangerous souls."

My brow crumpled. "Souls aren't dangerous. They're dead."

Nathan smirked. "Oh, you say that. Wait till they're throwing shit at you, and then we'll talk."

Anya looked doubtful. "Really? Throwing stuff?"

Worry flashed across Fury's face, but it disappeared before anyone else but me saw it.

Nathan straightened in his chair. "Oh yeah. We can't see them, but we can sure as shit feel them, and they can disrupt the hell out of our lives."

"How so?" Anya asked.

"You can feel them watching you," Sloan said. "I'd had that feeling several times before the spirit line went down, but it happens a lot now."

"How do you know it's ghosts watching you if you can't see them?" Fury asked.

Sloan pointed at Iliana. "She's confirmed it whenever she's been with me and I felt it. Now that I know what causes that sensation, I realize all those times before, I was probably encountering a ghost that hadn't been sent across the spirit line yet. It makes sense because I've spent a lot of time in hospitals throughout my life. And my father worked with the elderly."

"Goes with his job more than others, I guess," I said.

She nodded. "Sometimes when they get close enough, you can feel a draft. And sometimes the electricity gets crazy."

I thought of the lights flickering in our room the night before.

"All ghosts do that?" I asked.

"Yeah. Most of them are pretty docile," Iliana answered.

Nathan held up a finger. "But the bad ones, the ones you have to watch out for, they smell."

"Smell?" Anya asked.

Nathan nodded. "Like sulfur. It's faint, but it's there."

Fury and Anya both looked at me.

The others noticed.

"What does sulfur mean?" Iliana asked.

"Nulterra smelled like sulfur. I thought it was because of the fires," I said.

"Were the fires burning up the souls?" Nathan asked.

"Yeah," Fury answered.

Nathan turned his palms up. "There you go then."

The thought was a little sickening. "What else do they do?"

"Sometimes they get violent," he said.

Fury's eyes widened. "Really?"

"There's a man in the market who's been terrorized by his dead wife." Nathan laced his fingers behind his head. "But we hear he deserves it."

"What does she do?" Fury asked.

"Apparently, she set his bed on fire while he was asleep in it," Sloan said.

I blinked. "Damn. How'd she manage that?"

Nathan shrugged. "They say she also leaked carbon monoxide from their water heater."

"Have you seen this soul?" I asked Iliana.

"No. Mom doesn't want me adding ghost hunting to my resume," she said, smiling at Sloan.

"Not if you can't kill them," Sloan said.

"Why can't she kill them?" Anya asked. "Warren can, and she's clearly more powerful than him."

I frowned. "Thanks a lot."

Anya shrugged. "I'm right though."

She was.

"Cassiel warned that it can be dangerous to inflict the final death outside of…" Nathan snapped his fingers. "Someplace in Eden."

"Reclusion," I said. It was the home of the Angels of Death in Eden. I pointed at the purple sanctonite stone dangling around Iliana's neck. "But maybe now that you've got that, you can do anything you want."

Nathan's hand shot forward. "Hey, hey, not *anything* she wants."

I chuckled. "Let me rephrase. I believe your body and mind will be protected from any supernatural consequences if you inflict the final death here on Earth. Hell, you were destroying angels just fine without it. You might not even need it."

Iliana smiled and leaned back in her chair, folding her hands over her stomach. "Cool. Let's go find some ghosts."

"We are going into town today, right?" I asked.

Nathan nodded. "Whenever you're ready."

"I might sit out the ghost hunt," Sloan told him.

"I'm in, but only because I need clothes." It was the closest thing to an admission of fear I was sure Fury would ever say. She flattened her palms on the table and pushed herself up. "But before we go anywhere, I have to shower."

Anya stood as well. "Me too."

We all started toward the villas. "I wonder why the souls are so active now."

Iliana double-stepped to walk beside me and Fury. "Sandalphon thinks they're evolving from being trapped here in spirit form."

"That makes sense. The guy I talked to last night, John Mark, he was much more *aware* than any other human soul I'd ever seen outside Eden."

"It seems the longer the souls are here, the more *known* they can make themselves to other humans," she said.

Anya groaned behind us. "Don't tell me that."

Iliana looked at her. "It's not as bad when we're at home. They can't walk through high-Z."

"We're moving into Echo-5, right?" Fury whispered to me.

I smiled. "Maybe if they have room." I dialed up my volume. "Do you guys have room for a few more bodies at Wolf Gap?"

Nathan smiled back over his shoulder. "Oh, we have plenty of room."

---

Reuel made it back in time for lunch, of course.

We drove to the village near where he, Fury, and I had stayed when we'd first shown up on the island. By comparison, it was now a ghost town—in the metaphorical sense, at least. It seemed the population had been halved.

We ate lunch at a small fish shop, where I made the owner nervous with my sword, and Reuel frightened the shit out of her with his size. Her fear faded by the time he ordered a third round of grilled fish and lumpias stuffed with pork and fresh vegetables.

One thing about the locals, they could cook.

Nathan paid the bill.

"I'll pay you back," I said as we waited for his change.

"Small price to have you here. I'm buying clothes and stuff today too, so don't worry about it."

"Not to get all in your business, but I assume you're funding everything these days." I gestured toward Kane, the only member of SF-12 who'd come into town with us. "And running payroll. Did you really get that much out of Claymore?"

The restaurant's owner brought Nathan his change. "We're not flying in private jets anymore, but we walked away with enough to keep us all comfortable for a while."

"How long has it been since you guys separated from Claymore?" I asked, splitting a glance between him and Kane.

They looked at each other.

"Five-ish years ago," Kane answered.

"That's about right," Nathan said. "It was around the time Iliana started high school."

"You must be getting pretty bored," Anya said to Kane. Before working exclusively with Iliana, Kane had been a full-time warrior. He and I had spent time in Iraq and Somalia together, and he'd done countless missions without me.

Kane shook his head. "Not at all. I'm getting older. My joints hurt, and I'm tired. Besides, when we're back in the States, the boys and I pick up a few private gigs here and there. It's not Afghanistan, but it's also *not Afghanistan*."

Anya, Fury, and I all laughed. "Completely understood," I said.

Nathan left some of his change on the table. "What shall we do first, ghost hunting or shopping?"

"Neither sound like much fun," Anya said.

Iliana waved her finger between me and herself. "We could go ghost hunting, and the rest of you could get the shopping done."

*"Onra appa makai tanam,"* Reuel said with a smile.

I scowled. "No, not like a daddy-daughter date. She's an adult now." On the inside, though, I was smiling at the thought of a date with my daughter. I looked at Fury. "Do you mind?"

Her head pulled back. "Do I mind not going hunting for evil ghosts? Absolutely not." As soon as the words had left her mouth, her ears realized she'd said them. Her eyes widened.

Nathan crossed his arms. "So we've finally found something the badass Fury is afraid of."

She held up her middle finger. "I'll still kick your ass, Nate."

We all laughed.

On the back of our check, I wrote out a short list of the necessities I needed. "Anybody know how long we'll be on this island?"

"I'm not really sure," Nathan said. "We have to figure out a way to get passports and paperwork for you all before we can go anywhere."

"Rogan is going to work on it while he's in Manila." Iliana's face didn't show much hope. "But it's a lot harder these days to forge documents than it used to be."

"Forged a lot of documents in your day, have you?" Kane teased.

"So I've heard," she replied with an eyeroll.

I finished the list and handed it to Fury.

"So we'll all reconvene back at the resort?" Nathan asked.

Iliana stood. "Sounds good to me."

"How will you get back?" Anya asked.

Iliana and I exchanged a smile and answered at the same time.

"We'll fly."

# CHAPTER SIX

The shop of the man with the evil-ghost wife was closed that day, and we had to ask around to find out exactly where he lived. It took over an hour wandering around the village to learn the address and the man's name: Ronald Navarro.

Then we had to walk, as flying angels in town would probably start some rumors. It was a nice hike, however, and even nicer to spend some uninterrupted time with my daughter. She used the GPS on her fancy phone to guide us to the man's house.

"How much farther?" I asked.

She touched her ear. "Estimated time to destination," she said to the digital listener in her ear. After a moment, she replied, "About five minutes."

"It's a little weird, isn't it?" I asked. "Humans now communicating like angels."

"I'll give you three guesses as to why that is. You should only need one."

I thought for a moment. "The Morning Star is in the cell-phone business?"

"You could say that. Apparently, he helped create the technology. Claymore has been using it for a few years. I heard they sold the patented design, and now here we are."

I shook my head in disbelief. "He really does have his tentacles everywhere."

"Wait till we get back to the States."

"Does everyone live at Wolf Gap now?"

"Yeah. Dad wasn't kidding when he said we have a lot of space. You haven't seen the underground bunker yet, have you?"

"It was a big hole in the ground the last time I was in Asheville."

"It's really nice."

"Most things your grandfather builds are."

Staring up the road ahead, I realized how much I missed Azrael. Even though it had only been a handful of days since I'd seen him, the years I'd missed were becoming more and more real to me. He was on his way to the island, but how much of my father would remain?

I couldn't think about that now. "So Jett lives at Wolf Gap too?"

She dropped her head back and groaned toward the sky. "Don't get started on Jett again."

"That's not where I was going with the question." That was only half-true. "I'm just worried about Fury."

"It's hard for her to be around him, isn't it?"

"Very. When we left, I feel like she had just gotten excited about being a mother. And in two days, it was all taken away from her."

Iliana looked at the ground. "It's really sad. Jett doesn't know how to handle it either. He's spent enough time with humans to have a better grasp on empathy than most angels, but he's still not human."

"I've heard he worked at the Pentagon in his last life here."

"Both he and Rogan did."

"That was before the ban on angels speaking English was lifted. How did he manage it?"

"He was sent to the Pentagon by direct order from the Father himself. They both had special exceptions to the law."

"I'll bet that drove Cassiel nuts," I said almost to myself.

"She's quite a stickler for rules."

"You have no idea."

"When the Father came to Wolf Gap, the night Mom got some of her powers back, he stayed on for a few days, then went to Washington and asked Jett and Rogan to return to Eden. The Father wanted them to grow up with me, so they were both reborn in North Carolina."

"Reborn to Fury and Shannon." My head swiveled toward her. "How has that gone? Your mom and Shannon hated each other."

Iliana chuckled. "It can still be pretty tense at times. Shannon has her good qualities, but she drives us all nuts. No one more so than Rogan. Can you imagine a guardian with an overprotective mother?"

The thought made me laugh really hard.

"She was always clingy, but since Rogan was kidnapped, she hardly lets him out of her sight."

"So you see her a lot?"

"We see *the sun* a lot. We see Shannon infinitely more. It was the number one reason Rogan wanted to come to the island."

I laughed again and shook my head.

"What?"

"You've got Nathan's sense of humor."

She nodded. "Nana says the same thing, but she doesn't think it's nearly so funny."

"Nana?"

"Dad's mom."

"Kathy?"

"Yeah. Nana and Poppie are staying at Wolf Gap with Luca until we get back."

My eyes widened. "Does she cook?"

"Oh yeah."

I rubbed my palms together. "It's been seventeen years since I've had a home-cooked meal."

Iliana laughed. After a few more steps, she pointed toward an orange house up ahead. "I think that's it."

Evil shrouded the house like a cloud. Death ached in my bones. "Something is very wrong here."

"Lots of death," she said, surprising me.

It was weird, but the comment made me smile. Not since Azrael was the Archangel had anyone on Earth shared my gift. And sensing death everywhere can make for a lonely existence.

When we reached the door, I knocked. "There is a spirit here," I said quietly. My eyes narrowed. "And lots of bodies."

"There's a human too. He's home," she said.

I knocked again.

After a moment, the door swung open. A Filipino man, easily a foot shorter than me, stood on the other side. Evil was confirmed on his spirit, and I suddenly felt better about the fact he was being haunted.

This man was a killer, responsible for three human deaths.

Iliana tensed beside me. "No wonder it's so creepy around here."

The smell of rotten eggs permeated the air.

"Yes?" the man asked.

"Hi. Are you Ronald Navarro?" Iliana asked. The man

looked stunned. "We understand you have a problem with a spirit."

My brow rose with surprise. The last time I'd been on Earth, we never talked about such things with humans.

"Who are you?" the man asked, leaning against the door.

"We've come to help you." I realized that had been true on our walk to the house. Now, my intentions were very different.

He looked up at me, hesitated for a moment, then opened the door wider. "Come in. What is your name?"

"Warren. This is my daughter, Iliana. Who's your wife?"

"Her name was Althea."

We walked inside. "Her name *is* Althea. She's still very much here."

I looked around the modest living room. The furniture, now vintage I was sure, was held over from my era on Earth. Dishes were piled high in the sink, and every surface was cluttered with papers, books, and trash. The sulfur was so thick inside it nearly burned my eyes.

The lights flickered over our heads.

Death radiated from beneath the floorboards. There were bodies buried down there; I was certain of it.

"How did Althea die?" I asked, no longer buying the rumors in the village.

"Blackmouth Fever," he said. "It took her late. About six months ago."

I didn't need to be an Angel of Knowledge to know the man was lying.

"But you believe her spirit is here?" Iliana asked.

Ronald's face shifted to an expression I was all too familiar with. He might've been a murderer, but in that second, he worried we might think he was crazy. "Everyone talks about the strange things that happen now. The smell. Things moving without explanation. The lights." He looked up as they flick-ered again. "I believe what they say. Spirits no longer leave."

He was right. There was old death in the ground, but a spirit still resided in the house.

"Mind if we look around?" I asked.

"Why?"

"Because if your wife is here, we are the only ones who can help you."

He hesitated, his eyes darting between me and my daugh-ter. Of course he wouldn't want a search of his house. He had buried people here.

"You want rid of her, don't you?" Iliana asked.

"She tried to burn me alive."

Iliana lifted her shoulders. "So let us help you."

"Okay." His fear for his own safety obviously outweighed his fear of getting caught.

As we walked around the small house, I counted five burial sites in the crawlspace beneath the house. Only three were accounted for on Ronald's soul. If his wife was putting off as much sulfur as we smelled, she must have been responsible for the others. It wouldn't be a friendly ghost we found in the house.

Iliana opened a door.

A spirit charged out and tackled her.

The spirit of a boy, not of a woman, rolled her into the legs of a coffee table. She blasted him off her as quickly as he had tackled her.

I grabbed the soul with my power and pinned him against the wall so hard a picture frame fell and shattered on the ground.

"Are you all right?" I asked my daughter.

Panting, she pushed herself up. "I'm fine."

She looked through the door she had opened, then turned toward the boy. "Who are you?"

The boy had died—or had been murdered—in his early teens. He was shaking with fear against the wall as his eyes darted between me and his father.

And he didn't smell at all.

"What is it? Have you found her?" Ronald asked behind us, his eyes searching for something he couldn't see.

"We haven't found a woman, but we have found a teenage boy," Iliana said, straightening her rumpled clothes.

"Daniel?"

The soul's face whipped toward the man.

"So your name is Daniel," I said to him.

He looked at me but didn't answer.

"Who is he?" Iliana asked.

"Daniel was my son. He died not long after his mother."

Iliana and I exchanged a glance. In the village, we'd heard about the wife but nothing about a son.

"Let me guess," I said. "The virus?"

"Yes."

My eyes narrowed. "You're lying to me."

"I promise I'm not—"

"Let me tell you something about the human soul. When humans are tortured in life, that echoes in their death. Normally, the souls leave this planet and recover, but you were right. Now they're stuck here. This kid is terrified, but not of me. He's terrified of *you*."

I released my grip on the boy and turned toward his father. "I'm going to ask you again. How did he die?"

As I walked slowly toward the man, he shuffled backward, knocking over an end table. "It wasn't me! It was his mother."

"You just said he died after his mother," Iliana said behind me.

"I didn't do it! I didn't kill him!" The man backed into a disheveled bookcase and shielded his head with his arms.

"Wait," Iliana said.

I turned to look, and the man bolted toward the front door. My hand shot toward it, and the lock turned. He fought with it frantically, but could not open it.

The soul of the boy was leading Iliana to the other room. The room he'd run from. Inside was an old rusted bed frame with no mattress and with handcuffs chained to the headboard. The window was covered with paper, with only a corner torn away.

"This is where he died," Iliana said, looking at me.

The boy pointed to the floor, to a spot where I felt the pull of death the strongest in the house. I extended my hand, and the floorboards broke apart and splintered up through the carpet. Dirt from the ground below spun up like a tornado, revealing a large cardboard box, partially rotted away and eaten by bugs.

The corpse inside it was unrecognizable, but chains remained just below the jawbone of the skull.

My stomach turned. In all the wickedness I'd seen, I didn't think I'd ever grow numb to the abuse of children.

"He's so afraid." Iliana walked toward the boy's soul. "I don't think they ever let him leave this house."

I closed my eyes. "It would explain why no one in town mentioned him."

"It would also explain why he doesn't say much." Iliana reached for the soul's face. The boy cowered back from her touch. Then the tips of her fingertips began to glow.

"What are you doing?" I asked.

"This kind of fear is nothing but injury to the soul." She touched his cheek. "And injuries, I can heal."

I watched in awe as the white light spread from the boy's

cheek in glittering tendrils all over his soul until it consumed him. When the white light dissipated, he stumbled forward.

His eyes were clear and peaceful when he looked up again. Joy filled his face. *"Gratalis,"* he said in Katavukai.

I blinked "What did you do?" I'd never heard a human outside those in our group speak Katavukai this side of the spirit line.

Iliana smiled as she shook her head. "I'm not sure."

*"Akai un cel vliye?"* he asked, looking toward the window.

Iliana took both his hands. "Of course you can go outside. You can go anywhere you want."

With an excited leap, the boy ran from the room. We followed him. His father was trying to pry open the front door. I jerked him backward and released the door's lock for Daniel before I realized it wasn't necessary.

Daniel ran right through the front window without breaking it.

"What did you do to him?" Iliana asked angrily as I turned Ronald around to face us.

Ronald was crying, and he had wet himself. "Please. The boy was sick."

"The boy was tortured," she corrected him.

Ronald dropped to his knees as I walked toward him and pulled my sword from its scabbard.

"What are you doing?" Iliana asked.

"Testing a theory." I could have used my power to kill Ronald and inflict the final death, but I wanted to see what effect the sword would have on a human soul.

"Please," Ronald cried, looking up at me. Tears and snot streaked his red face. He trembled all over. "What are you?"

I raised the sword. "The Angel of Death."

"Well, that was dramatic," Iliana said, standing beside me over the bloody corpse.

"It worked though. His soul was obliterated." I wiped the blade on a sofa cushion.

Iliana looked around the room. "We haven't found the wife."

"She isn't far. The smell is still here, and I can sense her presence." The body at my feet flaked away in pieces of black ash that disintegrated into the air.

When the corpse was gone, Iliana and I searched the rest of the house. Frustration set in after clearing the final room. I put my hands on my hips. "I know she's here."

"Where would you hide in a house if you didn't want to be found?" Iliana asked.

My mind flashed back to a story Sloan had once told me. She and Nathan had found kidnapped Kayleigh Neeland stashed in the attic. I looked up. There was definitely someone up there. "Look for access to the attic."

We searched the house again, this time for a pull-down staircase or a covered access hole. There wasn't one. Only mildewed drywall sheets.

Iliana looked at me. "Would she need a door?"

I thought of Daniel running through the window, then of how I'd held him against the wall. "I'm not sure. You've spent more time with ghosts here on Earth than I have. We usually take them straight into the spirit world."

"I've only spent time around Papa, and he didn't leave his room much. When he did, he was walking with me through *open* doors."

"Interesting. Well, I do know one way to get her out of the attic." I walked back to the bedroom where I'd felt the soul's presence the most and the smell had been the strongest.

Standing in the doorway, I reached toward the ceiling. And pulled. The whole thing crashed down.

The startled ghost fell with it, landing on top of the heap of crumbled ceiling between me and the bed. The woman was screaming.

I jerked her up onto her feet. "Althea."

She flinched at the sound of her name.

"You're Daniel's mother," Iliana said, squeezing between my side and the doorframe to enter the room.

"Daniel is dead," the ghost said, her voice raspy and quiet.

"Yeah. We know. Thanks to you and your husband." Iliana crossed her arms. "He's dead too, by the way."

"Good," Althea snapped.

I tapped my boot on the floor. "Who else is buried down here?"

She glared at me, her eyes angry slits. "The children."

"Your children?" Iliana asked.

The ghost nodded.

This bitch had zero remorse.

"Mind if I take care of this one?" Iliana asked, cracking her knuckles.

I worried.

She must have noticed. "I'll be fine. I had no side effects from you destroying Father of the Year earlier."

"In a minute. We need some information first." I held Althea's spirit a few inches off the ground. "How did you get in the attic?"

She spat at me. Ghost spit, but still.

"You know what? Never mind." I stepped out of Iliana's way. "Destroy her."

"Gladly."

Before Iliana could blast her with killing power, the ghost

began to vibrate. I touched Iliana's outstretched arm. "Hang on a second."

The vibration increased until her whole supernatural body shook violently. Smoke began to rise from the rubble beneath her feet. Embers began to glow. Tiny flames began to lick the outsides of her feet.

"Guess we know how she started the fire," Iliana said, staring at flames as they rose around the woman's legs. "Can I kill her now?"

"Be my guest."

Iliana aimed both hands at her, and energy sparkled through her fingers. The bright light blasted toward Althea, and her figure exploded, extinguishing the fire at her feet.

The sun was low in the sky when we walked outside. I pulled her into my arms and kissed the side of her head. "I'm so proud of you, Iliana."

She patted my back. "Thanks."

"You ready to head back?"

"It's still too bright to fly." She looked up the road. "Doesn't look like it's too much farther to the top of this hill. Wanna see if we can watch the sunset over the water?"

I smiled and offered her my hand. "Bet your ass I do."

Around a couple more bends in the road, we reached a clearing near the top of the hill. A boulder near the edge provided seating with a spectacular view of the ocean. We sat down and watched the sun splash the waves with yellow and gold.

She leaned her head against my shoulder. "I'm so glad you're back."

"I won't leave you again." I put my arm around her as the sky faded into twilight.

It was the only time of day where angels on Earth could see the stars on the Eden side of the auranos. I searched the sky for Alice's pink star. She'd made it with her girlfriend, Forfax, not long before I left Eden the last time.

The star was gone, along with all the others.

The loss of Eden tore through me again. My mother. Alice. My dog, Skittles. I took a sharp and painful breath as emotion rose in my throat.

"You all right?" Iliana asked softly.

"I'll be fine."

"Everything changes tomorrow. Azrael will be here."

"You remember him, right?"

She nodded. "I was eleven the last time we saw them, but I can't say I know very much about him. What's he like?"

"He's one of the bravest angels I know."

"But he isn't an angel anymore, is he?"

"No."

"Can he still fly?"

I stared out over the water.

She straightened and looked at me. "What?"

"No one ever talks about Azrael flying," I said with a pained smile.

"They say he's afraid of it."

"He's afraid of airplanes and heights, but there's a difference. He's not afraid of flying."

"How can that be possible? It makes no sense."

I sighed. "Because he used to be able to fly."

"I don't understand."

"Can you keep a secret?"

She held out her pinky finger. I smiled and wrapped mine around hers.

"Azrael was once one of the brightest angels in the sky. He loved to fly, but the day I was born, the Morning Star forced him to join the fallen in order to save my mother's life."

"My grandmother, Nadine."

"That's right."

"Mom told me the story. She was dying because another demon had cut you out of her."

"Yeah, and the Morning Star fulfilled his promise to save her by possessing Nadine's body."

"That's horrible."

"That wasn't all. The Morning Star wanted to shame Azrael. To make sure he knew his place in the fallen's regime. So wearing the face of Azrael's wife, the Morning Star cut off Azrael's wings."

Iliana covered her mouth with her hand.

My stomach bottomed out. "He hasn't spoken of it since. Not even to me. All the angels know—the guardians saw it from the auranos—but nobody talks about it."

"And now the Morning Star has taken everything from him."

I nodded.

She sighed and pulled her knees up to her chest. "I hope he comes tomorrow."

"Azrael?"

"The Morning Star."

I looked over at her as her eyes watched the sun dip below the horizon.

"Because I'm going to kill him."

# CHAPTER SEVEN

A knock on the door woke me the next morning. "Warren?" Samael called.

The sliding-glass door opened, and Fury came in from the deck. "Morning, sleepyhead," she said as she walked by the bed.

I rolled onto my back and tugged the sheet up around my waist.

"Morning, Samael." She pulled the door all the way open and stood back to let him in.

"Sorry to disturb you," he said, entering the room. "You're still sleeping?"

I pointed at Fury. "She kept me up late."

"Nathan kept you up late," she corrected.

I groaned. "That just sounds wrong. We were planning out scenarios for today."

"And drinking bourbon."

My head throbbed. "And drinking lots of bourbon." I piled the pillows behind me and sat up. "What's up, Samael?"

"I thought you'd want to know we just heard from Azrael's pilot. They landed in Palawan just after sunrise."

"How are they getting here?" Fury asked.

"A ferry, I assume."

"Is air travel still suspended over the island?" I asked.

"I believe so."

"Thanks, Samael. We'll get dressed and head up for breakfast in a few minutes," I said.

Samael nodded and backed out of our room.

Fury walked on her knees across the mattress, then straddled my thighs. "Are you ready for this?"

"Nope." I leaned my head against the headboard. "What if he really doesn't remember me at all? What if he only knows me by what other people have told him?"

She raked her nails up and down my bare chest. "That's possible, but if he's coming all this way, it's clear he's missed you. And who knows? You and Az spent a lot of time together when he wasn't wearing the blood stone, right? Maybe some of those memories stuck."

"Maybe." My stomach growled so loud we both heard it.

She chuckled. "Why don't I go get us some breakfast? We can have one last peaceful meal together before shit gets crazy again."

"Mmm, I'd like that." I grabbed her hips, pulling her closer up my lap. "But I'll get breakfast. I know you've been waiting on me to wake up so you can take a shower."

With a smile, she trailed her fingertips along my jugular. "You really do know more about me than I thought you did."

"I'm paying close attention."

Fury had been an enigma since the day I'd met her. Now, after all I'd found out in Nulterra, I understood why. I'd been a job before.

My father had tasked her with recruiting me to Claymore, while keeping my identity a secret—from *me*. She also had another job. A mission so covert even she didn't know about it.

Keeping me away from Sloan.

She'd been successful too, until she found out she was a hired piece of ass to prevent me and Sloan from fulfilling a demon-borne destiny. The day I told Fury I loved her, she quit me and the company with hardly a word. I hadn't gotten an explanation until she ditched her armored cloak of secrecy in Nulterra.

Down in that pit, Fury had come clean about a lot of things. Some that mattered. Some that didn't. She loved me. She had *always* loved me. That was the only information I needed to know.

I slipped my hand behind her head and drew her in for a kiss. She tasted like coffee and coconut.

When she pulled away, she bit her lower lip. "Keep that up, and we'll go hungry today."

As if responding in protest, my stomach growled again.

I laughed. "I'm getting as bad as Reuel."

"Nobody's as bad as Reuel," she said, turning to get up.

She moved to the edge of the bed and stood. Then her eyes snagged on something outside, past our deck. I leaned forward and followed her gaze.

Cassiel was walking toward our villa, probably also on her way to breakfast. She either didn't see us, or she was ignoring us. I suspected it was the latter.

Fury stood. "You haven't talked to her, have you?"

I didn't answer.

"Get dressed and go get it over with." She leaned down and kissed me one more time. "And bring me back some of that sweetened pork if they have any."

Steam was rolling out of the bathroom by the time I was ready to leave the villa. "Sweet pork. Is that all you want?" I called over the sound of the shower.

"Some eggs." I heard the shower hooks slide against the rod. "And mangoes!"

I stuck my head into the bathroom for a peek, but all her best parts were covered as she looked around the curtain. "Pork, eggs, and mangoes. Anything else?"

"Hurry back, and I'll lick the mango juice off your abs," she said.

My whole body quivered. "Hurry? I'll fly."

She laughed, and with a wink, I left the villa.

At the top of the hill, Cassiel sat with Anya at one of the outdoor tables. Anya stood when I was close. "Is my sister coming?"

"No. She's in the shower," I said.

"Cool. I think she grabbed both packs of socks when we got back from the store yesterday."

"Have you heard an ETA for Azrael and his crew?" I asked.

"Not exactly, but the fastest ferry from Dumaguete can make it here in an hour."

That didn't sound right to me. "Is that where they are?"

She shrugged. "That's how Angel, the human hostess, said most people get here."

"OK. Thanks, Anya." When she was gone, I looked down at Cassiel. "Hello."

She wore a white linen sundress, and her long blonde hair was twisted up in a complicated but pretty pattern on her head. She gestured toward the seat Anya had vacated. "Care to join me?"

No.

"Sure." I sat down.

"I was beginning to wonder if you were avoiding me. You said we'd talk, and I've hardly seen you since." She picked up the water in front of her.

"I've been pretty busy."

She stared at me over her glass. "I know when you're lying."

"Was that a lie?"

"It wasn't the whole truth."

"What else did you learn about me, Cassiel?"

"Excuse me?"

"What did you learn about Azrael?"

"What are you talking about?"

I pulled the blood stone from under my shirt. "I'm talking about this." Cassiel's face flooded with guilt. I let the stone thump against my chest. "When you and I were together in Italy, when we kissed, when I was inside you—"

"Warren, stop—"

"You can extract information from skin-on-skin contact. Was all of it a recon job?"

Her lips pressed in a hard line.

"Cassiel?"

"You know it wasn't."

"I *really* don't. I mean, I knew you'd gotten the access code to Echo-5 out of me, but I'd truly believed that information had been taken against your will by the Council."

"It was," she insisted.

"But you didn't stop at searching through my memory. You went through Azrael's as well." I tapped the stone. "You went all the way back to the beginning."

She didn't speak. Or argue.

"What I want to know is why? What were you looking for?" I put the blood stone back under my shirt.

"Azrael was a formidable leader in Eden for a long time. When he fell, he took a lot of valuable and dangerous information with him. I was only trying to keep Eden safe." She couldn't look me directly in the eye.

I wondered if this was what she felt when she knew she was being lied to.

"Or perhaps you were trying to better your position. And hell, I guess it worked. You are the Archangel of Knowledge now."

"The information I gained from Azrael's blood stone in no way helped me become the Archangel," she said, sounding as offended as I'd ever heard her.

"I'm sure it didn't hurt."

Her mouth snapped shut.

"Good morning, Warren!" Angel, our Filipino hostess, was too cheerful, even for me, in the mornings. "Would you like some breakfast?"

"I need two meals to go. Do you have the sweet pork again today?"

"Every day."

"Then I'll take an order of pork, a couple of over-easy eggs, and some fresh mango."

She scribbled the order down in a notebook. "What else?"

"I want you to surprise me." The truth was, I didn't want to have to make a decision about food, and pork—unless it was bacon—wasn't high on my list of favorite breakfast foods. Besides, thanks to this conversation, my stomach was no longer growling. "Bring me whatever is the best breakfast on the menu."

"For you?"

"Yes. And two cups of coffee, please."

"All of it to go?"

Across the table, Cassiel looked away.

"Yes, to go. Thank you."

"Coming right up!"

I refocused on Cassiel. "Where were we?"

"You were accusing me of espionage," she said, staring off the cliff.

I sat forward, leaning my elbows on the table and propping

my hands beneath my chin. "Why were you looking for Azrael's memory of the spirit line's creation?"

She was silent.

"I need an answer."

Crossing her arms, she let out an exaggerated sigh. "Because I knew if the Council failed to bring Iliana to Eden, the spirit line was in serious danger."

"So you didn't trust me to protect her?"

"Are you serious?" She leaned toward me and gripped the side of the table. "You just got back from being gone seventeen years!"

Good point.

I was tempted to present the irony that it was Cassiel's decision that ultimately brought the spirit line down, and that Iliana had nothing to do with it. But I didn't. I took a deep, calming breath instead.

"Cassiel, I will be forever grateful to you for saving Fury's life and for your help in getting us out of Nulterra—"

"But?" she snapped.

"I'll never trust you again. You're such a stickler for truth and honesty, but you used me and kept me in the dark about it. That's not love. It's exploitation. And I'm not sure you would've ever told me had I not found out for myself."

Her gaze drifted away again. "I was only doing what any leader of Eden would do."

"You could have asked me." I glared at her until she finally met my eyes. "I would have told you. I would have given you the blood stone had you asked me for it."

"Are you finished?" Her words had the bite of a viper.

I gave a slight nod, and she stood from the table so quickly that her chair toppled backward. She didn't stop to pick it up before stalking across the yard.

"Whoa." Iliana walked up behind me. "What was all that about?"

My eyes followed Cassiel, but my heart stayed squarely in my chest. "Iliana, don't ever forget, you'll always be different from the angels."

I stretched my hand across the table, focusing on the chair lying on its back. I use my power to pull it upright. "Would you like to sit?"

"I'd love to." Iliana sat down. "Too bad you pissed off Cassiel. I need to talk to her."

"About what?"

"See if she has any genius ideas for us all getting back home. Rogan hasn't found anyone who can forge the documents we need to get us into the US. But don't worry. I'll figure out a way to get us off this island." She waved to someone behind me.

I looked over my shoulder and saw Jett. He was walking up the hill with Reuel. "So you talked to Rogan then?" I asked, turning back around.

"Yeah. He called us this morning."

"Rogan called you and your parents?"

"No, me and Jett."

My brow scrunched together. "You and Jett are very close."

"He came all the way from Eden to protect me. Of course we are."

"Is that all? A guardian-and-charge relationship?"

A thin smile spread across her face. "We're not dating if that's what you're getting at."

"I'm not."

I totally was.

She smirked. "OK."

"But if you were, I'd have to remind you, he's too old for you."

Her head snapped back. "He's almost a year younger than me."

"Correction. He's a bazillion years older than either of us."

She sat back, rolling her eyes.

"Did I just get my first teenage eyeroll?"

"Keep asking dumb questions and you'll get more of them." She laughed and straightened in her chair.

"Where's your mom?" I asked.

Iliana looked at the time on her phone. "Probably asleep. She can't wake up early two days in a row."

I grinned. "Sounds about right."

"Did you hear Azrael is on his way?"

"Yeah, Samael came and told me and Fury this morning."

"May we join you?" a deep voice asked. I knew it was Jett without looking from the way Iliana perked up.

Jett didn't wait for a response. He grabbed a chair from another table and dragged it over beside my daughter. My eyes narrowed. Beyond him, I could see Angel coming with a to-go bag and a drink carrier. I stood. "Reuel, you can have my chair."

"You're not going to eat?" Iliana asked.

I nodded toward Angel, and the guardians looked. "I'm taking breakfast to Fury."

"Ooo," Iliana teased.

It was my turn for eyerolling.

Angel offered me the bag. "Here you are."

"Thank you, Angel." I took the food and the drinks. A strong mix of smells rose from the bag. My stomach rumbled like its name had been called.

Angel smiled. "Go eat. I'll bill your room."

"Thank you." I turned back toward the angels at my table. "We'll all reconvene back here soon, I'm sure. Does anyone know who's meeting the ferry?"

Reuel wasn't listening. He'd pulled open the edge of my bag

to peek inside. I moved it away before he started rummaging through it.

"I believe Nathan and Samael were going," Jett said.

Part of me wanted to tell Jett he should call Nathan "Mr. McNamara." Another part of me wanted to tell him to move away from my daughter. Neither part spoke.

"Can someone come get us if they get here early?" I asked instead.

"Sure thing," Iliana said.

"Reuel, you've got your sword?"

He patted his side.

"Keep it handy. I hate to think we might need it, but we need to be extra cautious today."

"Warren!" a man yelled.

We all looked as Nathan and Sloan walked out of the restaurant. "Found Mom," Iliana said, pointing.

I chuckled. "Smart ass."

"You heading out?" Nathan asked, funneling something with his hand into his mouth. Probably candy.

I raised the bag. "Taking food to Fury in the villa."

Nathan poured another handful of Skittles. "We'll walk with you."

"Didn't you just eat breakfast?" I asked.

Sloan pulled on my arm. "Might as well save your breath, Warren, because like you said, some things never change."

Laughing, I tipped my chin up toward Iliana and the guardians. "I'll see you all later."

"How's your room?" Sloan asked as the three of us started toward the villas along the ridge.

"Really comfortable. I've finally caught up on all the sleep I missed."

"I thought angels didn't need sleep?" Nathan asked.

"We do if we're on Earth, just not as much as humans.

Where's your villa?"

"Same row as yours, a few villas down," Nathan answered.

"We're next to Iliana on the right side, if you know where she and Anya are staying," Sloan said.

"Before we got here was Iliana staying in a villa by herself?"

Sloan looked up at me. "Yeah. Why?"

I walked a few steps, contemplating how to ask what I wanted to ask. "I was just wondering about Iliana's relationship with Jett."

Sloan chuckled. "You think Nathan would let her share a villa with a boy?"

"No. Not at all."

"I put tape on the outside of her door every night to make sure she didn't sneak out and no one else sneaked in," Nathan said.

I looked across Sloan at him. "So you've noticed it too?"

"We're not blind." Sloan smiled. "Jett's a nice boy though. He really cares about her."

"He's not a *boy* at all," I said.

Nathan pointed at me. "See? Warren agrees it's messed up."

I nodded.

"I know, but it feels like he's a kid. We've known him since he was born," Sloan said.

"We've known him since he was *reincarnated*," Nathan insisted.

She stopped walking and crossed her arms. "Would it really matter if he were a human instead?"

Nathan looked caught. His wide eyes searched for an answer. "Yes."

I laughed.

She smirked. "No."

"Are they together?" I asked.

"They both say they are not," Nathan said as we started walking again.

"So you've talked to him?"

"Yeah, but you should give him a good old Angel of Death scare like you used to give me."

"Jett's an angel too. Warren can't hurt him," Sloan said.

Nathan held his hand toward me. "He has the sword."

"I do have the sword," I agreed.

Sloan shrugged. "Remember, she is an adult now."

"The hell she is," Nathan and I both said in unison.

He reached across her to give me a high five.

Sloan laughed and shook her head. "She says there's nothing going on. If you push the subject, or if you forbid it, you're only going to make her want him even more."

"She can't want him if he's dead," Nathan muttered.

"Nathan!" She backhanded his chest.

I laughed and stopped near the steps that led to the front door of my villa. "Nate, are you and Samael going to meet Azrael's ferry?"

"Yeah. You wanna go? We're leaving in about fifteen minutes."

"Yes. Grab me on your way?"

"Will do!"

When I reached the villa, the hair dryer was on in the bathroom. I put the food on the bedside table and walked to the bathroom door. Fury gasped when she saw me in the mirror.

I laughed.

She turned off the dryer. "Don't do that!"

"Breakfast is here. Did your sister find you?"

"Yeah, she came and stole my socks." She put the dryer down and followed me to the bedroom.

I picked up the bag of food. "Wanna eat on the porch?"

"Sure." She opened the glass door and slipped on her new sunglasses. "Did you talk to Cassiel?"

"I did."

"How'd it go?"

"Not well." I opened the bag and the medley of smells hit me in the face again. "What's in here?" I opened the first cardboard clamshell take-out container. Strips of saucy meat, fried rice, and eggs, sunny-side-up, were inside. "This is probably yours." I handed it to her.

"What's that smell?" she asked, sitting down.

I opened the second container and flinched. "Oh." Fish eyes stared up at me. "Oh no." Frowning, I picked one up by the tail and turned its face toward me. "It's crispy."

Fury gagged. "What is it?"

"An anchovy? I'm not sure." I shuddered and dropped it back on the pile. "Why does it have to have eyes?"

"Looks like you're eating rice for breakfast."

"I should have asked for pork."

She skewered a piece and held it toward me.

I bent and ate it. "Thank you."

"What happened with Cassiel?" She ate a wedge of mango.

I handed her a coffee before taking my own. Then I shoveled the fish into the bag and sat down with the rice that was left. "It's over. Whatever *it* was."

"How'd she take it?"

"She's pissed at me."

"Pissed? That's a strong reaction for an angel."

"It's complicated."

"Wanna talk about it?"

"Not really."

"All right." She offered me another bite of pork.

A lot of significant others would have insisted on the details of how the *other* relationship had been ended. Hell, I probably would've wanted to know if the situation were reversed. But not Fury. Unless I was reading her wrong again —something I *was* prone to do—she honestly didn't care.

I ate the pork. "Thank you. Guess who joined me at breakfast?"

"Iliana."

"Yes. And Jett."

She tensed at the mention of his name. He was going to be a sensitive subject for a while. Maybe forever.

"So?"

I scooped up a forkful of rice. "Iliana says nothing's going on, but those two are inseparable. Nate and Sloan agree. What are your thoughts?"

Her expression soured. "I think it's going to be really awkward if we have to explain to people that we're together and our kids are together."

I narrowed my eyes at her. "I'd hate to have to kick your kid's ass if he hurts my daughter."

She chuckled. "OK."

"I don't know why that's funny." I leaned over and skewered another piece of her pork. "Who puts sugar on pork for break-fast? Ham for Christmas, sure, but not breakfast."

"What are we doing today?" Fury asked.

"I told Nathan I'd go with him and Samael to meet—" A distant *whomp whomp whomp* caught my sensitive ears. I searched the sky.

"What is it?"

"A helicopter."

She started looking. "I don't see anything."

"It's coming." A speck dotted the sky. I stood and pointed. "There."

"I guess the airspace isn't closed after all."

"Or Az just doesn't care," I said.

Fury stood beside me. "But he does care. About helicopters, anyway."

"You're right. The flight would be unavoidable, but he'd never willingly choose a chartered helo with an unknown pilot over a ferry. Even if it has been seventeen years."

I watched the helicopter coming closer. It hummed with supernatural energy.

"Unless…" The thought sickened me.

"Unless that fear faded with his supernatural memories?" Fury asked.

"Unless he's not on the helicopter *by choice*."

She swore and turned toward me. "The Morning Star is an Angel of Life. You think he's controlling your father?"

"Azrael is mortal now, and no matter what memories he's lost, there's no way he'd be involved in the things they suspect Claymore of."

"True, and he'd never let anybody else call the shots at Claymore. Not as long as there's breath in his lungs. Hell, he didn't even let you stay in control when he put you in charge of Claymore."

The helicopter was so close now I could see it was a big one. A big army-green one.

Fury took off her sunglasses. "Is that military?"

"If it's not, the charter company has done a really shitty job of branding."

Something else was more worrisome than the paint color.

Fury touched my arm. She sensed it too. "Azrael isn't alone."

"No, he's not."

The Morning Star was with him.

# CHAPTER EIGHT

The helicopter didn't slow as it neared us. It flew over the resort and kept on going. Fury and I had walked outside and up the hill to meet it.

So had everyone else. Nathan and Sloan came over beside us.

"Where's it going?" Sloan asked, shielding her eyes with her hand as she looked up at the sky.

"To check out the gate would be my guess," I said.

"Did you see a flag on it?" Fury asked.

"No. Did you?"

"I got a glimpse of one when it turned." She looked at me. "I think it was American."

I shook my head. "America hasn't had a base in the Philippines since the nineties."

"You know them all?" Nathan asked skeptically.

"No, but I did some research before we headed here, in case we got in trouble."

Sloan grimaced. "That was seventeen years ago."

"True."

I looked around for Kane. He, Cruz, and Nash were all carrying assault rifles across the lawn. I waved him over. "Did you see that helicopter?"

"Not well, sir."

"Was it American?"

"There's a good chance."

"How? We didn't have a base here when I left."

"The US opened a small installation on the island of Palawan about ten years ago," Kane answered.

"Damn." I rubbed a hand down my mouth. "They have a military escort."

"You think it's Azrael?" Nathan asked.

"Probably." I turned toward him and Sloan. "I think it's the Morning Star too."

Nathan closed his eyes. "I was afraid of that." He put an arm around Sloan.

"What's the matter?" Iliana asked, joining us with Jett right behind her.

"You getting any vibes off that helo?" I asked her.

"I was about to ask you the same question. It's him, isn't it?" Iliana looked worried.

I nodded.

"You got your sword?" Nathan asked, leaning to see if it was strapped to my back.

It was.

He lifted an eyebrow. "You ever learn how to fight with that thing?"

*No.* "I can hold my own."

"Don't you dare use it," Cassiel said, a few feet behind us with Sandalphon and Samael.

"If he's got a clear swing, why the hell not?" Nathan asked.

"Because the Morning Star isn't stupid," Kane said.

Sandalphon leaned on his cane. "They're right. The

Morning Star knows what he's walking into. Chimera would have told him Warren had a sword. He'll be protected, one way or another."

"How many people were on that helicopter?" Sloan asked.

I shrugged. "Looked like it could hold six or seven—"

"There were five humans and two angels," Iliana said.

I turned and looked at my daughter. "Impressive."

"Thanks. Who would he have brought?"

"Beats me. I've been gone seventeen years."

"It's coming back," Samael said.

He was right. The *whirr* of the helicopter blades were getting louder again. I looked back at Kane. "Is there enough room here for them to land that thing?" The helicopter was huge.

"If they've got a good pilot," he said.

"Everybody!" Nathan shouted as the helicopter neared the property. "Move up by the dining hall!"

Our group huddled around the restaurant's entrance, scattered among the breakfast tables. Fury stood in front me, stretching on her toes to search the group.

"What's the matter?" I asked.

"Where's my sister?"

I looked and didn't see Anya anywhere. "Reuel's not here either."

"Hey! What's going on out here?" Angel, the resort hostess, called from one of the restaurant's open windows.

"Nash!" Nathan yelled. "Go make sure Angel and the rest of the staff are safe inside!"

"Roger that, sir." Nash left Kane and Cruz to go inside.

The massive helicopter spun up near tornado-speed winds as it slowly lowered above us. Its skids eased onto the ground. Two pilots were up front. Beyond them, I couldn't see the other passengers, but I knew an angel was on the right side closest to us. Behind a door clearly marked with an American flag.

The helicopter's engine died, and the back side doors opened. Two fully armed soldiers got out—guards wearing Claymore black with American flags on their shoulders.

Fury's face turned slightly toward me. "They weren't kidding. They've taken over the military."

An angel I didn't recognize got out next. He was about my size with dark skin and long hair tied back in a thick ponytail. In his hand was a helkrymite sword.

*Orin.*

His eyes carefully scanned the group before he stepped to the side of the door.

Behind him, a brown dress shoe lowered to the ground beneath a khaki pant leg. The angel stepped out in a navy button-up, tucked in with a tan belt. The outfit alone *screamed* this was no seventeen-year-old kid. He wore dark sunglasses and had light-brown ivy-league haircut whipping around in the wind. The boy was tall—*really* tall—just like Adrianne.

Fury's shoulders pulled back, and I felt her draw in a shaky breath against me. I flexed my fingers behind her, ready for war.

Standing beneath the slowing helicopter blades, the Morning Star removed his glasses. Even from our distance I could see his gleaming hazel eyes as they drifted over our group. They were unnatural. Unearthly. And they took a close inventory of us all.

He lingered the longest on the angels, particularly on Sandalphon, as he was almost as powerful as the Morning Star himself. Then he moved on to Cassiel and then Samael before finally seeing Iliana. His gaze fixed on her like he was calculating her position in the crosshairs of his sights.

She was a few feet in front of me, to my left. I stepped

around Fury and reached for Iliana's hand, then pulled her behind me. His eyes rose to mine, and an eerie smile spread across his lips.

He looked back over his shoulder. "Come on out."

My father's head leaned out the doorway, and my breath caught in my chest. We no longer looked like brothers. The creases around his eyes had deepened, and there were faint lines across his forehead. His hair was short and black, though it was nearly white around his sideburns.

He stepped out onto the grass. Still tall. Still broad shouldered with a powerful physique. Unlike his "son," Azrael was in his standard tactical attire: dark cargo pants, a black Claymore shirt, and combat boots.

How anyone would ever believe the two of them were related, much less father and son, was beyond me.

They were light. And dark.

Life. And death.

"You were right," Fury whispered. "The Morning Star has his hooks in Az."

"You can see his power?"

"It's like a leash."

"Fury, show me," Iliana said.

I glanced back as Iliana and Fury locked hands.

When I looked toward my father again, our eyes connected. His face pinged with recognition when he saw me, but there was no joy or even familiarity in his reaction. Sloan had been right. He identified me from pictures, from stories, and from the memories of others, but I was a stranger.

Azrael didn't know me at all.

When he turned to face me, something strange caught my attention. In the center of his torso, deep inside his chest, was a dense blemish, unseen to all the humans—and probably the other angels—around me.

It was death.

At first glance, it looked like cancer, but as Azrael came closer, I realized it was something more. It was round and black, about the size of a paintball, and lodged near his heart. Death swirled inside it, contained by some kind of membrane, like a shrapnel grenade ready to explode.

Panic tickled the back of my neck.

Sandalphon was right. The Morning Star had protected himself. My father was booby trapped.

We should've planned this better. We had known there was a chance the Morning Star would show up, but seeing him in the flesh, I realized how unprepared we were. The gunmen didn't help, their trigger fingers poised and ready should anyone make a move. And Orin, ready to swing his fatal sword of eternal death.

The Morning Star said something to Azrael and Orin, then walked toward me alone. "Well, well." His voice was smooth and melodic. "If it isn't the great Warren Parrish, come back from the dead." He stuck out his hand. "I'm Michael. It's a pleasure to meet you finally."

So this was how it would go.

All of us feigning stupidity. Michael knew who I was, and I sure as shit knew him.

Nevertheless, we would both play our roles. Because as long as we kept up the charade, we'd maintain the peace. The end of the game wouldn't be good for anyone.

I didn't accept his outstretched hand, a lesson learned from my angel comrades. The Morning Star was an Angel of Knowledge. To touch him would be to give him an advantage.

With a knowing smirk, he lowered his hand. "Ah, you're one of those."

I held up my hands and wiggled my fingers. "Germs. I've heard there's a virus going around."

He had a curious smile. "Touché." He crossed his arms. "Warren, where have you been?"

He already knew where I'd been. His flyover of the Nulterra Gate told me that. And why else would we be on this island?

"I've had some business in the area. It looks like you have too." My eyes flashed toward the soldiers behind him.

He glanced back. "Yes. No doubt you've heard that Claymore Worldwide Security has expanded its operations around the globe."

"Yes, I've heard."

"It was a stroke of fortunate luck for us."

"*Fortunate* indeed." I was thinking of the power even more so than the profit. "Too bad over half the American military had to die for you to experience such a windfall."

"It was quite the tragedy, but I'm sure our government is thankful Claymore stepped in to fill the gaps while the rest of the world rebuilds."

"I'm sure they are."

He turned to the side. "I believe you've met my father, Damon Claymore."

"*Our* father, you mean."

"So they say."

My jaw clenched. Technically, Azrael wasn't his father at all. They shared no DNA—human or angelic.

Michael stepped back to allow my father to come forward.

As he walked past the Morning Star, my eyes fell to the spot in Azrael's chest again. Dread pooled in my stomach, and I looked back at Iliana. She was staring at it too.

Azrael scanned the group. He spotted Nathan first and gave a slight nod in greeting. Then he paused by Sloan and squeezed her arm. At least it wasn't a hateful reunion.

                    

When he finally reached me, the muscles tensed in his neck. "Warren."

He, too, extended his hand in greeting. This time, I didn't refuse. I grabbed him and pulled him to me. My arms went around him, but he stood there awkwardly frozen in my embrace.

"Azrael." I fought hard to maintain my emotions.

"Please don't call me that," he said over my shoulder.

My heart wrenched. I almost apologized, but I didn't. He *was* Azrael, and we all needed him to remember it. I stepped back and released him. "Do you remember me at all?"

Azrael tensed, and his eyes fell to the ground.

"He has long-term selective amnesia," Michael answered for him. "It upsets him to be reminded of it." The Morning Star was probably telling the truth, something he couldn't be accused of often.

I nodded and stared at the ground, trying to think of something, anything, else to say that wouldn't upset him. "Where's Adrianne?" was all I came up with.

"She's in New Hope with the children. We left in such a short time we couldn't get a sitter," Azrael said.

"The children?"

"They're fifteen and nine."

"I have siblings younger than my daughter," I said, almost to myself.

"Three of them," Azrael said, looking at Michael.

Nausea turned in my stomach.

"Is this Iliana?" Azrael asked, pointing to her behind me.

"Yes." I turned and gestured her forward. Then I side-stepped to block Michael behind me as she approached. "Damon, this is your granddaughter."

Azrael winced like the words physically harmed him.

"Hi," Iliana said, extending her hand.

He stared at it but didn't accept—or probably *couldn't* accept, I realized. I almost felt Michael's breath on my neck as he watched.

Iliana must have sensed it too because she turned her narrowed eyes toward him. "I know what you're doing."

Michael seemed surprised by her candor. "Do you?"

"Yes." She turned back to Azrael and waved her hand in a wide arc through the air. An invisible wave rippled the space around him, and he suddenly stumbled like he was drunk. I grabbed his arm to steady him.

Michael fell back a few steps, panicked. "What have you done?" He froze, looking at Iliana. Then his nostrils flared, and he started toward her.

Before I could react, movement caught the corner of my eye. The Morning Star must have seen it too, because he did a double take.

Reuel charged up the hill, his sword in hand.

The Morning Star spun toward him instead, with Orin now at his side. Two of the soldiers raised their weapons in Reuel's direction. In turn, Kane and Cruz aimed at the soldiers.

I pushed Iliana out of the way and into Jett's arms, then I ran out in front of the Morning Star. "Reuel, put the sword away."

Reuel looked at me, worry and anger plain on his face.

"Put it away. We're just talking!" I called.

He hesitated, staring at something behind me. Probably Orin and his sword.

I held up both hands. "It's OK. I promise."

Reuel slowly lowered his sword. The guards lowered their rifles. So did Kane and Cruz.

I let out the breath I was holding.

The Morning Star made a skeptical whining noise behind me. "I think I'd rather test out our new toys."

*New toys?*

"Guards!" he shouted. "Fire!"

My sensitive ears heard the click of the safety switches on the sides of the soldiers' rifles as they raised them quickly again. "Stop!"

Suddenly, all the weapons lurched sideways, knocking each man off his feet and onto the ground. My face whipped toward Iliana, but her hands were at her side. She looked as surprised as me.

"That will be enough of that shit!" Anya yelled from the driveway to our right. Her arms were extended. Her fingers were stretched. She wore a tank top and running shorts, and her face glistened with sweat. "What the hell's going on up here?"

On the ground, the two Claymore soldiers were stunned and confused. Cruz rubbed the side of his head. Kane massaged his knuckles.

The Morning Star was pissed. "I should have known."

Anya stormed toward him. "I don't give a damn what you should have known. We have civilians here."

Like he cared.

Orin started toward her, but Michael's arm came across his chest to stop him. Before Anya reached them, Michael's glare turned sinister.

Anya faltered. Her eyes and mouth widened as she grasped at her throat. A squeaking sound escaped as she fought to breathe. She fell to her knees.

"Enough!" I pulled my sword from its scabbard and jumped between them.

Michael's face relaxed, his eyes watching the sword.

I heard Anya finally gasp for air. "Enough," I said again, more calmly. I was breathing hard from the adrenaline flooding my veins.

"Do you even know how to use that thing, Warren?"

"Let's not find out." I was ready to swing.

"Perhaps Orin could give you a lesson."

Orin stepped in front of him, his blade ready to clash with mine. Fear pulsed through me, but my hands were steady as I stared down the messenger. *God, I wish I'd learned how to sword fight.*

Azrael held up his hands. "He's right. That's more than enough. Chapman! Bell! Don't raise your weapons again."

It was nice to see Azrael still in charge, even if he didn't have all his faculties. "We didn't come all this way to fight," he said to the Morning Star.

Michael seemed surprised, but his eyes locked with Orin's as he jerked his head to the right. Orin stepped aside and lowered his sword.

Fury ran to Anya and pulled her back into the group.

"Why have you come?" I asked as I put my sword back in its scabbard. It clearly wasn't because of Azrael's desperation for a reunion.

"I wanted to see you."

I put my hands on my hips and stared at him.

He sighed. "My wife wanted me to come."

"Adrianne?" Sloan asked, speaking for the first time since Azrael landed.

Azrael nodded. "She said I needed to see for myself if you were really alive." His eyes studied me. "I had hoped that if I saw you, it might trigger something…"

"But you don't know me," I said.

"I only know what others have told me about you."

I took a step toward him. "I can help you."

Michael's hand swung up so fast I dodged, thinking he was setting a curse on me. He laughed. "Jumpy, are we?" His hand aimed at Azrael. "I was going to say I think we should take this slowly. We have traveled for almost twenty-four hours. I'm sure my father would like to lie down."

My fists balled at my sides. "*My* father." I didn't bother with niceties a second time.

"I agree," Iliana said. "We all need a break."

Static crackled in my ear. "I can't completely block the Morning Star's control on Azrael," Iliana added silently to me. "I need a minute to think. Regroup."

Michael's face turned slowly toward her, and his wicked smile returned. He had heard her. "Yes. Let's all take a break. Perhaps you can take us to wherever you're holding our friend Torman."

"Torman isn't here," Cassiel said.

Michael spun all the way around on the heel of his loafer. "My, my. What an interesting welcoming party you have here, Warren." He walked slowly toward Cassiel. He looked from her to Sandalphon. "Even the great Elijah has come to welcome you back. Hello, Eli."

"What do you want?" Cassiel snapped.

Michael crossed his arms. "I want Torman. Where is he?"

"I don't know." Cassiel's shoulders were rigid, and her chin high.

"That's not true." Michael reached for her face, but his hand jerked to a stop, like it had hit an invisible wall in the air. His eyes snapped toward Iliana and narrowed. He dropped his hand. "Well, I can see this won't be an informative visit."

"You've got that right," Nathan said.

Michael lurched to grab Nathan, but Iliana shoved him backward with a glance. Jett held her arms to keep her from charging the Morning Star. "Touch my dad, and you'll be regrowing your hands," she warned through clenched teeth.

The Morning Star glared at her for a long time. Judging by

the way Iliana's expression changed from heated to worried, I could tell he was silently communicating with her.

"Michael!" Azrael shouted. "Come here."

The Morning Star blinked, obviously severing his covert connection with Iliana. He straightened the front of his dress shirt, and surprisingly, obeyed and walked toward Azrael.

I backed closer to our group. Iliana walked up behind me and grasped the back of my shirt. She stretched toward my ear. "That spot inside Azrael's chest will kill him if anything happens to the Morning Star," she whispered. "No matter what happens, we can't move against him, or Azrael will die."

Damn it.

Orin stood guard while Azrael and Michael were talking in hushed voices near the helicopter. I closed my eyes and listened. I could only hear Azrael's side of the conversation. "Call this off," was an alarming, perfectly clear phrase.

Beyond them was a quiet roar somewhere in the distance.

"Something's happening," I whispered.

It was the sound of wheels grinding against gravel. A *lot* of wheels.

"What's that noise?" Iliana asked quietly.

"Vehicles. There's a convoy coming up the mountain." No sooner had the words left my mouth did the convoy roll through the bamboo gate. One, two, three…seven vehicles in total. Four minivans and a black SUV, all of them endcapped by armored Humvees in the front and back.

"What is this?" I called to my father and the Morning Star.

Michael walked toward us. "It's your ride home, of course. You didn't think we would leave you all stranded here, did you?"

"Who says we're ready to leave?" I asked.

The Morning Star approached me. "We can do this one of two ways, *brother*."

The sound of the word in his mouth made me queasy.

"We can do it peacefully, where we allow you to gather your belongings and board the vehicles yourselves. Or we can do it by force, stripping you of everything you have on this island and dragging you back to New Hope. Either way, this is happening. Which shall it be?"

More soldiers exited the vehicles. One of them carried over a large armored case and opened it on the ground near the Morning Star. He held out his hand, and the soldier placed two cuffs in his open palm.

They looked a lot like the cuffs Torman had been forced into.

Fingers dug into my sides. Iliana stepped around me. "We'll go peacefully, but you will take nothing from us. Not even our weapons."

Michael spread his arms wide. "I wouldn't dream of taking anything from you."

I very seriously doubted that.

Iliana looked at me and mouthed the words, "Trust me."

With a painful gulp, I nodded. "OK," I forced myself to say.

Michael signaled to the soldiers, and they came toward us in pairs, each stopping at the case to pick up sets of cuffs. "Cuff them. Then take them to pack up their things. Harm no one, or you'll have to deal with me."

Azrael grabbed his arm, his eyes clearly pleading for Michael to stop. Michael argued with him again.

I looked at Iliana. "Are you sure about this?"

"Trust me," she said again.

"Yes," Sandalphon said, catching my eye. "Trust her."

They cuffed Iliana first. Then a young man, maybe nineteen years old, grabbed my left arm. When we touched, I felt the familiar pull of death deep inside him. Like Azrael, this man was rigged. I couldn't *see* it through his body armor, which I assumed was plated with high-Z.

The cuff was made of high-Z too. I recognized its porous metal as he closed it around my wrist. A jolt of electricity shot up my arm to my spine. It traveled all the way down my back. The second cuff did the same, except its energy ran up through my brain.

For a moment, I thought I'd gone deaf. The volume died, like someone had shoved earplugs into my ears. I turned my palms over and tried to conjure my killing power into them; nothing happened. I tried spreading my wings; it was like they didn't exist.

For the first time in a long time, I was reminded of what it felt like to be human. Powerless and fragile.

I looked at my daughter. "I hope you know what you're doing."

We were all escorted to our villas. A guard followed me and Fury, with his rifle ready to fire. She had been cuffed as well. She took my hand as we walked. "What was Iliana thinking? Half our group can fly, so most of us could have escaped."

"I don't know, but we have to start trusting her to lead us. She's the only one more powerful than the Morning Star."

Fury didn't look convinced, but she didn't argue. "The Morning Star has a solid grip on Azrael. Iliana was able to break it a couple of times, but each time, he quickly regained control."

"That honestly makes me feel a little better."

"Why?"

"Because there's no way Azrael can be responsible for the things Claymore did. But we have a problem. The Morning Star planted some kind of bomb inside Az. If we try anything, Azrael will die."

Fury swore.

When we reached our door, I waved my hand in front of the lock, but it didn't click open.

"You're powerless, aren't you?" Fury asked as she stuck her key into the lock.

"Completely, I'm afraid."

She pushed open the door. "Me too."

The soldier followed us inside, and we immediately began shoving the things we'd bought the day before into our new travel bags. "Is he taking us to the base on Palawan?" I asked the guard.

"That's classified."

Of course it was.

When we finished, the guard followed us back to the top of the hill. Nathan and Sloan were walking out of the dining room. Sloan's eyes were red from crying.

Two other soldiers approached. I tensed, ready to fight. I was certain they were coming to take my sword. I couldn't let that happen.

Surprisingly, they didn't.

One of them grabbed me. The other grabbed Fury. They were separating us. I jerked my arm free and quickly grabbed the back of her head, pulling her in for a hard and fast kiss. "I won't let anything happen to you."

She nodded, but doubt filled her eyes.

Michael got into the back of the SUV. Azrael was in the leading Humvee. Anya and Reuel (he had his sword too) were loaded into the first van. Nathan and Sloan were in the second, and the rest of our group was behind me. The guard pulled me toward the SUV.

Great.

Once more, I expected him to take my sword. He didn't.

I got in the back and sat on the black leather bench opposite the Morning Star. The sword pressed uncomfortably against my back, but there was no way in Nulterra I would take if off.

Neither of us spoke for what felt like an eternity. I watched as the rest of my group was herded toward the convoy. Iliana was escorted by Orin and two guards, one on each side. They put her and Fury into the van directly behind me.

"This has gone better than expected," Michael said, breaking the silence.

"How did you expect it to go?"

"Oh, you know." He held up his hands and mimicked the way we could blast our power from them. *"Pew pew pew."*

"You can thank my daughter for that."

"I plan to." His words made everything inside me tense. "How's your mom?"

I wanted to dive across the car and pound his face in. Before he'd been reborn, he'd possessed my mother's body, holding her for ransom to ensure my father's compliance. She'd died because of him. I grasped the door handle and forced myself to look outside.

"Did I hit a nerve?" he asked.

My face whipped toward him. "Cut the shit, Michael. What do you want?"

"I want you, of course."

I rolled my eyes and shook my head.

"Eden is gone, Warren. The sooner you accept that fact, the happier and more peaceful your existence will be."

"No existence with you in charge will mean happiness and peace for anyone."

"You judge me so harshly. You don't even know me."

"I know enough."

"At one time, I was the shining light of Eden. The crystal water that flows through Zion was created from that light. It breathes life into everything it touches. With that being true, how could I be all bad?"

"That's a good question. How could something created so pure become so poisoned?" I couldn't even look at him. "I'm not interested. So if that's the only reason I'm here, perhaps you should send me back with the others."

"Hear me out." He turned toward me on the bench. "Together we can build a new Eden. An Eden *here* that's accessible to everyone, not just those whom some relic deity deems worthy."

"No. Just the ones *you* deem worthy. Just the ones who survive whatever destruction you throw at them. Tell me, how many humans died in the virus?"

He frowned. "I let nature take its course. That's all."

The soldier who'd escorted me and Fury to our villa got in the driver's seat. Another man got in the passenger's seat. The driver looked over his shoulder at Michael. "That's everyone. We're ready to roll if you are, sir."

"Let's go."

The convoy started rolling.

With a wave of his hand, the space between us and the front seats rippled. He'd put up a wall between us and them. "Warren, think about it. I can give you safety, power, rank. You and your family will never want for anything."

"And what would you have me do?"

"I have been with the angels since the beginning of time. They are my brothers, my sisters. The Angels of Death could be a great asset in this new world we're building. You are the Archangel. They will follow your lead. If you join me, so will they."

"And if I don't join you?"

His brow tightened. "Then I will destroy you all."

*Well.*

"Soon will come a time when all those who do not follow me will be put to death. I wish to shed no angel blood. Please assist me in saving your choir."

"Aren't you the benevolent leader," I said with a smirk.

His face darkened. "You can either accept my generosity, or you can perish with your angels."

I leaned toward him. "I'll fall on my own sword."

He stared straight ahead for a moment. At least I knew I could frustrate him. I sat back in my seat and reclined against the headrest.

"If this is how it is to be, then there's something you should know."

I didn't bother to look at him.

"As you've probably deduced by now, your father is being kept alive at my pleasure. So is Adrianne. So are your younger brother and sister. If anything were to happen to me, should you or your daughter try to kill me...if I die, so will they."

My stomach flip-flopped.

"And if somehow you succeed in turning your father against me, I will kill every member of the Claymore organization."

I thought of the sickness I sensed inside the soldier who'd cuffed me. My fists tightened as our car rolled down the bumpy road.

"I want your father's blood stone, Warren."

"I don't know what you're talking—"

"Lies," he hissed.

His hand stretched toward me, and the chain rattled under my shirt. The vibrations heated the metal until it singed my skin. My shirt started to smoke. "All right! All right!" I reached beneath my collar and pulled it out and over my head. I threw it at him. "Happy now?"

"You can't even imagine."

The Morning Star held the stone in front of my face and closed his fingers around it. Light beamed from between his fingers until, finally, there was a loud *crack!*

He opened his palm and the blood stone was broken. It withered and cracked until nothing remained but dust.

Laughing, he rolled down his window and let the island breeze carry it away.

I sat back hard in my seat, glaring at the road ahead. We were nearing the harbor. A military transport ship was docked in the marina.

"Where are you taking us?" I finally asked as we parked near it.

He looked across the car and smiled. "To the prison your father once built for me. Where else?"

# CHAPTER NINE

It was two more days before we landed in New Hope, if that was what you could still call the military city that had replaced the old Claymore headquarters.

We'd been held overnight in the brig on Palawan, then flown in on a Claymore jet that was twice the size of the old one. We hadn't been allowed to speak to each other, but from what I could tell, everyone looked whole.

Once, as we were being led to the brig in Palawan, Iliana had caught my eye and smiled. I wondered what she was up to.

*"Trust me,"* she'd said.

I did, but being locked in a four-by-five cell, completely cut off from humans and angels alike, made it hard.

I didn't speak to the Morning Star or my father again, but I saw them plenty between the tiny military base and the sixteen-hour nonstop plane ride. Azrael's expression was pained every time our eyes met, but he did nothing to help me or any of the rest of us.

They'd taken our bags when we boarded the plane, but even as we were led across the grounds at Claymore, I had my sword on my back and the duplicate of Azrael's blood stone in my pocket. Somehow, I'd find a way to get it back to him. And somehow, I'd get him to see the truth inside it.

My hands were shackled behind my back, still cuffed in high-Z, as I was led across the Claymore tarmac. Where it had once been a tiny airstrip with an aluminum hangar, it was now a full-blown aviation center with a small airport and business center.

A Claymore bus waited across the tarmac. The Morning Star and my father were waiting for us, as they'd been driven in a HOK, a high-occupancy ATV.

Michael crossed his arms as we approached. "Have you had a change of heart, Warren?"

"You know, I believe I have." I watched Michael straighten with surprise. "I've decided I prefer the old plane to the new one. You weren't on that one."

His surprise melted to anger.

I laughed. "For supposedly being so smart, you really are a dumbass." The guard shoved me up the steps of the bus.

A sheet of aluminum blocked the view of the driver and the windshield, and the windows were blacked out all the way down the bus. It was obvious we weren't the first prisoners to be carted around base in this thing.

My hands were reshackled to a chain around my waist before I was pushed down into the first barely padded seat.

"Don't take your eyes off her," I heard Michael say outside as Orin followed Iliana onto the bus. "And keep her away from Warren!"

Iliana smiled again—and winked—as they passed me.

Jett was loaded after Iliana, and he was placed midway between us on the bus.

Somewhere outside, a car door slammed. "Azrael, what's going on?" a woman shouted.

Adrianne.

I'd know her angry bark anywhere.

"Sloan?" she asked, her voice horrified. "Michael, seriously, what the hell? In chains was *not* what I had in mind when I asked you to bring them back!"

"It's just a precaution, my love." Azrael's voice was soothing and *unnatural*. "Some of them are dangerous."

"Dangerous? Some of them are *family*," she argued.

At least Adrianne hadn't been completely brainwashed.

"Mom, please stay out of it."

It made my blood boil to hear the Morning Star call Adrianne *"Mom."*

"Stay out of it?" she shrieked.

There was commotion. A scuffle of shoes against concrete and gravel. Adrianne was fighting someone.

"Adrianne!" Sloan cried out.

"Calm down!" Michael snapped. "Get her in there."

Sloan was fighting and craning her neck to see what was happening. She stumbled up the bus steps as a guard shoved her. "Adrianne!" she screamed again, tears streaking her cheeks.

"Sloan, look at me," I said calmly.

Her face whipped around. "Warren, I can't do this."

I tried to reach for her, but the shackles jerked my arms to a painful stop. "You can, and you will. We'll get through this, I promise—"

"Shut up!" The Claymore guard elbowed me in the side of the head as they passed.

I jerked on the chains again with all my strength and with all my power, but nothing happened.

"Appa!" Iliana shouted from the back of the bus.

Seething and murderous, I settled back in my seat as the guard moved Sloan somewhere behind me.

Nathan came next. His face was worried and afraid. "Where are they taking us?" he asked quietly as they passed.

I lifted my shoulders because I had no idea. I'd only heard speculation that Azrael might be building a prison for the Morning Star. He had never volunteered the information, and I had failed to ask. I'd mistakenly thought I had all the time in the world to get the details when Fury and I got back.

Damn me for being so naïve.

Reuel was behind Nathan, and for the first time in all the years I'd known him, he looked helpless…in addition to looking hungry.

Cassiel didn't look at me as she was escorted past. Perhaps she was still sore from our conversation the other morning.

Everyone else was loaded onto the bus. The last was Sandalphon, who shuffled slower than the rest of us.

He was seated across the aisle from me with Samael, and I wanted to talk to them, but the guard stood between us with a rifle ready to fire.

The bus ride was short, less than five minutes. I closed my eyes and tried to envision the base. The nose of the bus had been pointing east when we boarded, and I hadn't felt any hard U-turns. We'd turned left, sped up for a while, then turned left again.

Unless I'd grossly miscalculated, we were being taken to the armory.

The bus's brakes squealed to a stop.

I half expected them to put hoods over our heads before leading us off the bus. They didn't. Again, I was taken first, and when I stepped outside, Azrael and the Morning Star were nowhere to be seen.

It was the armory.

Or, at least, it used to be the armory. The building had received a facelift in the time I'd been gone. When we walked inside, the interior had been completely redone as well. The room had been divided, split by a wall with windows and a metal door. And where there once had been cages, weapons, and ammo, there were now waiting-room chairs and a welcome desk.

The only guns around were the ones strapped to the guards.

We were corralled into the lobby, and Nathan shuffled toward me. "I know this routine." He looked around at the guards. "This is a jail."

"I know. And beneath this room is a vault. Seventeen years ago it was one of the most sophisticated ones I'd ever seen. I can't imagine what they've done with it since. I guarantee you that's where we're being taken."

He swore.

The door behind us opened, and Azrael propped it open with his boot. Two more guards walked in. "These two," he ordered, pointing at Sloan and Nathan.

One of the men grabbed Sloan.

"Mom!" Iliana cried.

I started toward them, but Nathan stepped in front of me, shaking his head. Starting a fight would get us nowhere.

"Warren, keep her safe!" Sloan screamed as she was dragged out the door.

"I promise," I said to Nathan as two heavy hands closed around my arms. I was pulled backward with so much force I stumbled. Impressive strength, as I was six two and over two hundred pounds. The guard jerked me around to face forward as he hauled me toward the metal door.

His eyes were mismatched, brown and green. He could see angels. On the shoulder of his Claymore uniform was a rectangular patch of a skull with wings.

This was the Morning Star's new version of SF-12.

There was a loud buzz, and the door slowly opened on its own. When we were inside, he shoved me against the wall and held my face against the cool cinderblock.

"What the hell are you doing?" I shouted as he began to pat me down.

"Keep your mouth shut." He grabbed the strap of the sword's scabbard and jerked it over my head. I twisted to the side, out of his grasp, then charged him like a bull and slammed him into the desk behind him. The scabbard was caught under my armpit.

I headbutted the man as hard as I could.

Two more guards jabbed me in the ribs with electric prods. My knees collapsed under the volts of blinding electricity. I slumped forward onto the tiles.

Someone jerked the scabbard off my arm with a violent yank. Probably the guy I'd attacked. The steel toe of a boot connected with my ribs.

"Take him down!" a deep voice ordered as lights twinkled around the corners of my eyes.

I was heaving on the floor when I was grabbed under both arms and jerked upright. Two guards dragged me to an over-sized elevator, a definite addition since the last time I'd been underground.

There were three levels. There had only been two before. Or, at least, I'd only *seen* two before. The armory and the vault below. We rode all the way to the bottom, of course.

I was on my feet by the time the elevator stopped, and I walked out with both guards holding my arms. There were six cell doors down a single hallway. Cameras, each with a bright green light, pointed in every direction.

"We don't have space for all of them," one guard said to the other. He was young, probably fresh out of the military with his GI Bill for college—if that was still a thing.

"We'll double them up for now," the other guard said, who was obviously in charge. He was older, sturdier, probably former Special Forces, knowing the types of guys Azrael usually gave authority.

He touched his ear. "Open sub cell six."

I noticed the patch on his shoulder. A skull with wings. Same as the guy upstairs.

The first door on our right opened. They threw me into it. "Unshackle him, but leave the wide silver cuffs in place. He's one of *those*."

The younger guard's eyes widened. "He's a fairy?"

"Yes. Let's make sure not to put more than one of them in a cell together."

I brushed my black hair out of my eyes as I waited to be released. "A fairy? That's what you're calling us now?"

The young guy didn't answer, but he crept forward with a key. His hands were shaking as he released my shackles.

I growled, and he jumped backward.

I laughed.

He scurried out of the cell and slammed the door. The older guard touched his ear again. "Sub cell six, secure."

The heavy lock tumbled closed.

Interesting. With all their advanced technology, they still relied on an operator to open and close the cells.

One by one, everyone was led downstairs. Reuel had also been relieved of his sword. Kane, Cruz, and Nash were missing their weapons.

Fury was bleeding.

"Are you OK?" I asked as a different guard dragged her past my cell.

She didn't answer. She glared. It was a look I hadn't seen in a while. Blood drizzled over her lip and dripped off her swollen chin.

"Open sub cell two," the guard said to whoever was listening in his ear. His voice sounded familiar.

With my face pressed against the small bar-covered window, I watched as he threw Fury into the cell diagonal from me. With an angry scream, I pounded the silver cuffs against the bars.

They didn't budge, but the guard charged toward me. That was when I saw his bloody face and his mismatched eyes. It was the same guard I'd fought upstairs. Blood was now smeared around his nose.

He struck the metal door with his baton. "Keep that up, and I'll chain all four limbs to the wall!"

I was seething through clenched teeth.

"Are we going to have another problem?" he asked, visually daring me to lose my temper again.

Despite taking my sword and nearly splintering my ribs, he'd been an afterthought upstairs. A detail. Part of the process. But now, I memorized every inch of his square face. Severe underbite. Freshly broken nose. Mismatched set beneath unruly brown eyebrows.

Bruising and swelling crept across his forehead, and his knuckles were red, likely from where they'd punched my girlfriend in the mouth.

A name patch sewn on his uniform said *Thacker*.

"They won't keep me here for long," I said, resting my cheek against the cold door. "And when I get out, I'll find you."

Fear flashed in his eyes, but he blinked it away. "I can't wait." Then he turned and walked back to the elevator, out of view.

When I heard the doors close behind him, I grabbed the bars. "Fury? Can you hear me?"

I knew she could. Even without my supernatural hearing, I could hear Cruz and Nash breathing in the cell beside me.

"Allison, please answer me."

"I…fine." The swelling, and probably the pain, distorted her speech.

"Did he hit you?"

"I *hia hia fus.*"

*She hit him first.* That made me smile, but she clearly couldn't move her mouth. Her voice was weak and raspy.

We needed to get out of here.

"Kane, what are these cuffs made from, and how do we get them off?" I asked him in the cell directly across from mine.

He looked through the small window in his door. "They're made of high-Z and neodymium. They work together to create a crippling magnetic field for angels. The only way to get them off without Iliana is with a keystone. We have one, but it's with Rogan in Manila."

"Where did you get it?"

"Huffman smuggled a set out to us."

"So they were developed by the Morning Star?"

"Az actually started the project, but yeah, the Morning Star finished it. They tested them on Rogan when they had him. It's how we knew about it."

The elevator *whooshed* through the floors again. This time it was Anya. They put her in the cell with me. Her long hair was disheveled and worry filled her eyes.

She gripped the bars in the window when the guards were gone. "Fury!"

No answer.

Anya turned to me. "Is she OK? Is she hurt?"

"She's OK, but I think it probably hurts her to talk. The guard busted her lip open. Did you see what happened?"

"I didn't see it, but I heard it. It sounded like he got handsy with her. I think she broke his nose. Did you see the blood when he brought her down?"

"I did."

"Warren, I heard him hit her through the walls. It was hard."

I felt sick.

"You gonna kill him when we get out of here?"

I looked at her. "Is that even a question?"

"What a mess." She raked her fingers through her long hair, taming it back into the elastic band. "What was Iliana thinking?" When she finished retying her hair, she knocked her knuckles against the wall. "We aren't getting out of here."

I didn't want to confess that I doubted my daughter. But I doubted my daughter.

The walls were at least a foot thick. They wouldn't be easy to break through even if they weren't made from high-Z.

Cassiel came down next. When they led her past our cell, she finally made eye contact with me. She looked like she might cry, but I doubted she would give the guards the satisfaction.

The sight of her saddened me. Still in her white dress, two days after I'd first seen her in it. Her exposed skin was dirty and tears had stained her face.

As angry as she had made me, I wished I could comfort her. Cassiel had once admitted to me she wasn't cut out for life on Earth. Now she was stuck beneath it in an angelproof cell.

With Fury.

The guards pushed her inside and slammed the door.

"Oh god," I heard her say a second later.

I crossed the cell in one long stride. "What's wrong?" I asked when the guards left again.

"Fury's unconscious."

Anya pushed in front of me. "Unconscious?"

"She's breathing, and her pulse is OK, but she's out." A second later, Cassiel groaned. "She has a mandibular fracture."

"English, Cassiel," Kane said.

"That *was* English. Her lower jawbone is broken. Her gums are split, and a few teeth are displaced."

My fists clenched.

"Is she going to be OK?" Anya asked, gripping the bars.

"She's lost some blood, but I think so. She probably passed out from the pain."

Anya's legs wobbled, and I caught her around the middle before she dropped to her knees. "Iliana can heal her," I said, shaking her just enough to get her attention.

Her fingers curled into my shirt. "Where is she?"

"They haven't brought her down yet."

Anya's fingers went slack. "They brought her down before me. She's not here?"

My chest tightened. "No."

"They're separating us. Samael and Sandalphon were taken elsewhere also. They took them back out the front door," Nash said from the next cell.

Anya walked to the corner and slid down the wall. "What do you think that means?" She pulled her knees up and draped her arms across them.

I paced the cell. "I'd imagine Azrael built something more long term for the Morning Star." I looked at the ceiling. "She's on the floor with the vault."

"She's probably *in* the vault," I heard Nash say. "Azrael converted it into a high-security cell."

"More secure than these?" Kane asked.

"Yep, but also more livable for long-term prisoners. It has a separate bathroom."

"What about Sandalphon and Samael?" Cassiel asked.

"The Morning Star wants to convert the Angels of Death. He didn't have any luck with me, so he's probably starting on Samael. Sandalphon, too, I would assume, since all the angels of Eden respect him."

"Think they'll cave?" Anya asked.

I shook my head. "Not a chance."

Anya leaned her head back against the wall. "What about Sloan and Nate?"

"I'm hoping Az took them to see Adrianne. From the sound of it, she's very much in control here."

"She is," Nash agreed.

"I don't know Adrianne," Anya said.

"She's Azrael's wife now. Before all this, she and Sloan were inseparable best friends."

"She's the one who gave birth to the Morning Star?"

I nodded.

"When we were back at the airfield, she wasn't quite as zombie-like as Azrael," Anya said. She'd been outside the bus to witness it all.

"What happened?"

"This really tall woman pulled up in some fancy black SUV and jumped out like she might kill someone."

I smiled, but it was sad. "Sounds like Adrianne."

"She started to go to Sloan, and the Morning Star got in her way. She fought against him, but he had guards take her back to her car. I think she punched one of them in the ear."

My brows drew together. "So she's not under the Morning Star's control at all. Interesting."

"She wouldn't be," Cassiel said.

I walked to the cell door so I could hear her better. "Why not? She's a human."

"But she shares DNA with the Morning Star. He can't control her like he can control other humans. Angel-offspring relationships are different."

"Kasyade could summon Sloan," I said.

"Was she able to control Sloan?" Cassiel asked.

"No. It would've probably made the demon's job of getting us together a whole lot easier if she could."

"Exactly. The Morning Star can influence his earthly mother to a degree, but he can't outright control her."

"So we might have an ally on the inside?" Kane asked.

"I don't know if we can call her an ally. Sloan said they hadn't seen or talked to each other in years," I said.

"But she was definitely worried about Sloan," Anya said. "She was very upset by all of it."

"I agree," Nash said. "Adrianne's been skeptical about her son for a while."

"You know her?" I asked.

"I worked for them for years before I was deemed a traitor. Adrianne's probably the only reason I wasn't killed."

The elevator doors opened, and the guards—one of them was Thacker—led Jett past my cell.

"Hey, we need a doctor down here," I said as they waited for the door operator to open the cell at the end of the hall.

"I don't give a shit what you need." Thacker didn't even turn to look at me. "Keep your mouth shut."

"She needs a doctor. I fear she's in danger of bleeding to death," Cassiel argued.

I hoped Cassiel was being dramatic in order to get Fury some help.

"That's your problem, bitch."

A buzzer sounded, and the cell door opened. They put Jett inside. When it closed, they walked past me again.

"You broke her jaw!" I shouted.

Thacker stopped in front of my door. "She's lucky it wasn't her neck. Stupid cunt."

Rage short-circuited my brain. I slammed my fist into the bars. As stars exploded in my vision, I remembered the cell was impenetrable. With an audible *crunch,* my fingers and knuckles shattered, sending splintered bones slicing through my skin.

My whole body slumped against the door as Thacker turned toward me. He was laughing.

Blood splashed onto my boots and the concrete, and I quietly screamed in pain as I cradled the mangled limb against my chest. Anya jumped up to help me.

"Geez, Warren. What were you thinking?" She stripped down to her sports bra and used her teeth to rip her T-shirt down the middle.

I slid to the floor as the guards laughed all the way back to the elevator.

"Let me see it," Anya said when she'd finished tearing the shirt into several large strips.

I hid the hand behind my elbow as I held the arm. "I don't think you want to."

"I promise I've seen worse. Give it here."

When I showed her my hand, she gagged. "Oh my god."

"I told you it was bad."

"It looks like it went through a meat grinder. Holy hell." She gagged again, turning away like she might actually vomit.

"Just wrap it as tight as you can. It will heal."

"An injury like this will take a while, even for you."

Holy shit, it hurt. I was an idiot. A bullheaded idiot.

"Try to hold still." Anya draped the first strip of fabric over my knuckles, which were the worst. Bone and cartilage poked through the skin. She wrapped the fabric around once more before tying it tight against my palm.

I swore, gritting my teeth as the pain ripped through my entire arm.

Our friends were talking through the other cells, but I had no idea what they were saying, nor could I care at that moment.

When Anya finally finished, I exhaled for the first time in what felt like minutes. My fingers were going numb from the loss of blood, which I was honestly thankful for.

"Better?" she asked with a grimace.

"It will be. Shit, that was stupid."

"You've gotten too dependent on your powers. You've forgotten that even you have limits."

"Warren, are you okay?" Cassiel's voice echoed down the hallway.

"Yeah. I'll be fine." Blood seeped through the strips of fabric.

"What did you do?" Cassiel asked.

"He thought he could punch through the bars," Anya answered for me.

"I don't recommend trying it," I said.

"*Es en ket?*" Reuel asked.

"Remember when that train crushed your arm in Chicago?" I asked, leaning against the door.

"*Tek.*"

"It's not quite that bad, but there's a lot of bone showing." I turned back toward the window, bracing my shoulder against it. "Cassiel, how's Fury?"

"Still unconscious, and for her sake, I hope she stays that way."

"We need Iliana," Kane said.

I don't think I'd ever heard him say he needed anyone or anything in all the time I'd known him.

"She's here somewhere. I watched them bring her down," Jett said.

I looked out the window. A piece of my flesh had splattered onto the metal. "She didn't come to this floor."

"Wherever she is, we need to get her out," Jett said. "The Morning Star has no need for her now that he's destroyed the spirit line. I fear he means to kill her."

I thought of Orin guarding Iliana with his sword. "Got any bright ideas on how to do that?"

No one answered.

"Huffman," Kane finally said, looking at me from across the hall. "Maybe he'll find out we're here and break us out."

"That's a tall order for a human," Cruz said.

We were all quiet for a long time. Anya and I both sat down on the floor again. My hand had begun to heal, and the blistering pain made my eyes water. With gritted teeth and toes curled in my boots, I tried to think of an escape.

There wasn't one.

Quiet moaning broke the silence.

Fury.

I jumped up.

"She's waking up," Cassiel said with a sickened tone. "This is going to be bad."

Before long, the groaning became a stifled wail. I thumped my head against the cell bars.

Cassiel quietly consoled her. "Fury, I know it hurts, but we're going to get you some help. Try to be as still as possible."

I leaned my forehead against the door as her cries seared my spirit. Even more than my hand, everything inside me ached for her.

"*Wah-en,*" she said.

"He's close by," Cassiel told her.

"*Wah-en,*" she said again, more forceful but just as distorted.

"What?" Cassiel asked.

I straightened. "What is it?"

"She's pointing up," Cassiel answered.

Kane popped up in his window. "Cassiel, is Fury wearing cuffs?"

"No."

I looked at the ceiling again.

Anya stood beside me. "Fury can see power."

"Even through these walls?" Kane asked.

Mentally, I crossed my fingers. "Maybe so."

"Shh, listen," Cassiel said.

There was a faint *whirr* above us, like a saw cutting through metal…

Like a saw cutting through steel, lead, and high-Z.

It was right above us.

I pushed Anya back against the wall as pebbles and dust began to fall from our ceiling. A crack of light broke through, shining like a spotlight and illuminating our cell. Concrete crashed in big chunks onto the floor as a bright hole opened wider and wider.

Finally, the light dimmed.

My sword clattered to the ground. Reuel's fell on top of it. Then a third fell onto both of them.

Iliana stuck her head through the hole. "I told you I'd get us off that island, didn't I?"

___

## CHAPTER TEN

___

"*O*rin came to kill me," Iliana said as she curled her hands around the cuffs binding my wrists. They turned ice-cold and frosted over. Then they shattered in fragments of ice—not metal any longer. "He failed."

"He's dead?" Anya asked.

"No, when I took his sword, he grabbed a human shield. But I pushed them both into the tiny bathroom and sealed the door. They won't be going anywhere for a while, and that's five swords accounted for."

"Damn," I said, my voice full of awe.

Iliana smiled.

Dad-mode switched back on. "We could have found another way off the island. You could've gotten hurt, or worse."

Her brow crumpled. "You knew I could break through high-Z."

*I did?*

"The panic-room door," Anya said.

My eyes widened, remembering the story Nathan had told us at dinner our first night back.

"And I did that in middle school. You think this place is going to stop me?" She smirked.

"How did you get the other swords back?" Anya asked.

"Orin carried them into my cell in a case marked *Armory*. I assume he was going to take all three of them there after he killed me. Idiot." She turned my arm over, examining the bloody makeshift bandages. "What did you do?"

"Lost his temper and punched the door," Anya answered.

With a sigh, my daughter shook her head and started to unwrap the bandages.

"Wait." I grabbed her hand. "We don't have much time, and Fury needs your help."

"What's wrong with Fury?"

"One of the guards shattered her jaw," Anya said.

Iliana started on Anya's cuffs, but she looked at me. "Guess he's a dead man."

"Why does everyone just assume I'm a lethal maniac? Anya asked the same thing," I said.

"You love her," Iliana replied with a shrug.

I picked up my sword and eased my injured arm through the scabbard's strap. "I do love her, but I'm not just going to kill every human who—"

"Are you going to kill him?" Iliana asked.

"Well, yeah, but—"

"Men." Iliana rolled her eyes and shared a smile with Anya.

"Oh, shut up and get us out of here," I said, turning toward the door.

She laughed.

Once Anya's cuffs were gone, Iliana blasted through the cell door like it was made of glass rather than impenetrable metal. Anya nudged me with her elbow. "Your kid is a badass."

I smiled. "Don't I know it."

Iliana went straight to Cassiel and Fury's cell without

having to ask which one they were in. She opened the cell door with me and Anya right behind her.

Cassiel was on the floor, holding Fury's head in her lap. Fury's face was so swollen now, she was almost unrecognizable. Blood was crusted all around her mouth and in dried rivers across her cheeks.

I hung back as Iliana went inside for fear that as an Angel of Death, I might inadvertently make Fury's pain worse.

Iliana dropped to her knees and conjured bright white light into her hands. Cassiel shielded Fury's eyes from the light as Iliana lowered it toward Fury's chin.

She cried out when my sensitive ears heard the jawbone snap back into place. My stomach lurched for her. As often is the case, the only thing more painful than the injury was its healing.

It was over a moment later, and Iliana moved out of the way so I could pull Fury off Cassiel's lap and cradle her in my arms instead. As I kissed Fury's damp forehead, I saw Cassiel's dress.

The white was stained red with Fury's blood.

"Thank you," I said, pointedly looking into Cassiel's icy blue eyes.

She nodded.

"We must hurry," Kane reminded us from his cell. "They have cameras all over this place."

"I disabled the cameras," Iliana said.

Of course she did.

"And I locked all the doors, shut down the elevator, and jammed their computer system."

"Nicely done," I said.

Several others clapped or cheered.

Fury stretched her mouth wide and closed it a few times before sitting up.

"You OK?" I asked, carefully studying her face.

"I'm fine." She looked at Iliana. "Thanks to you."

Iliana smiled as she stood.

Fury grabbed Cassiel's arm. "And you. Thanks, Cassiel."

"You would've done the same for me," Cassiel said.

Fury gave a slight nod.

Before our journey to Nulterra, I might have doubted that. As the daughter of Abaddon, the Destroyer, Fury had never had much sympathy for angels—demons or otherwise. I believed the new Fury. She was infinitely kinder and gentler and was—for the first time since we were in Iraq—a true team player.

And for better or worse, she and Cassiel were on the same side of this war.

I stood, pulling Fury up with me, and we all followed Iliana out of the cell. One by one, she opened the rest. When she reached Jett, she ran in and hugged him.

Fury and I looked at each other.

"Nobody greeted me like that," Kane said behind us.

We turned to look at him as Reuel opened his arms wide. Laughing, Kane pushed him away.

"Here." Iliana handed Reuel his sword.

He beamed. *"Bon velai."*

"Thank you," she said, picking up the third. "Who gets this one?"

We all cast glances around the group.

"Anya should have it," Cassiel finally said.

Anya's head snapped back. "Me?"

"You're the Archangel of Protection now. It makes sense," Cassiel said.

Rogan nodded. "Agreed."

"Seconded," Jett said.

Reuel put his hand on her shoulder. *"Munra."*

"I don't even know how to use one of these," she admitted.

"Neither does Warren." Fury jerked her thumb toward me. "Doesn't stop him."

I couldn't argue, so I just shrugged.

With a laugh, Anya took the sword. "How the hell do I carry it?" Hers was the only one without a scabbard.

Reuel grunted and held out his hand. She gave it to him, and he wedged it in with his.

"He can carry it for now, and we have a couple of scabbards in the Echo-5 armory," Kane said.

I looked at him, surprised.

"Right after you left, your dad took up sword collecting," he explained.

Sounded about right.

Iliana returned to me and pulled on my arm. "Let me see what you've done. If we have to fight our way out of here, we're all going to need you to have both your hands."

I gently started removing the bandages. "Probably a good idea. As Fury said, I can barely handle my sword as it is. There's no way I could fight off demons left-handed."

"Geez, Warren." Fury's face soured as she looked at my mangled hand. "What did you do?"

"He tried to go all *Reuel* on the cell door," Anya said. "He failed."

Reuel came over to look as well. He scoffed and rolled his eyes.

"OK, so maybe it's nothing like your arm when we were in Chicago."

He looked at me with an expression that said, *"You think?"*

Iliana's healing light made me wince.

Reuel laughed. *"Kulan."*

"I'm not a baby," I said and winced again.

"Hold still," Iliana ordered.

Reuel walked down the hall, shaking his head.

Sirens blared through the hall and red lights flashed.

"I think they're on to us," Nash said, looking around at the cameras on the ceiling. They were lit with green lights again.

Iliana's light fizzled out. My hand was better. It no longer looked like raw meat, but it was definitely going to scar.

"I'll work on it more later," she said.

I rubbed my knuckles. "It will be fine. What now?"

"We fly up the elevator shaft." Iliana gestured to it. "Reuel?"

With the swords strapped to his side, Reuel balled a massive fist, then slammed it into the right sliding door. The metal caved, creating a gap wide enough between the doors for his hands to wedge between them.

With hardly a strain, he wrenched them apart.

Iliana leaned into the elevator shaft and looked up and down. Loud voices echoed from above as the elevator engine started turning. "They're coming," she said.

"Hello again, Warren," a woman's voice carried over a speaker.

I looked up. "Chimera."

Chimera, part-Angel of Knowledge and world-class tech genius, had, no doubt, repaired the disabled security features of the building.

"How was Hell?" she asked.

"Quite interesting. Met your dad."

There was a pause.

"Where is he?"

"Safe. For now."

Chimera didn't care about Torman's safety. She cared about her own. If—*when*—we killed him, part of her would die as well. Unless I could find her now. Then *all* of her would.

"Nash, do you know where the control room is for this building?" I asked.

Iliana spun toward me. "I know what you're thinking. There's no time to find Chimera now. We have to get out of here and regroup. And we need to find my parents."

She was right. I *hated* that she was right. So many of our enemies were so close. So vulnerable.

And everything inside me wanted to destroy them all.

"Humans, if you're not bulletproof, get in a cell," Iliana ordered.

Beside me, Fury hesitated.

I cupped her jaw. "You're unarmed, and you've lost a lot of blood. Please, get in the cell."

She nodded, which must've been hard for her. Nothing in her nature would ever want to sit out a fight.

Kane hooked his arm through hers and dragged her into the first cell where I'd been held.

Surprisingly, Cassiel stood with us. She hated physical confrontation almost as much as she hated gunfire. Both were surely coming on the plunging elevator.

Iliana stepped in front of us all, and I stood beside her. She raised her hands toward the shaft.

The elevator's brakes squealed as it reached the bottom. When it stilled, the inner doors slid open, and bullets— hundreds of them—exploded toward us.

And slammed against Iliana's invisible force field.

The gunfire slowed, the guards too stunned to even reload. The last few bullets bounced off the force field, clinking against the metal and concrete as they tumbled into the shaft.

"What the hell is she?" one of the guards asked, his voice quivering with fear.

Iliana's eyes narrowed. "Not a fucking fairy."

Had I been any prouder, my heart might have exploded in my chest.

"Seize them!" someone shouted.

Thacker.

He was on the right side of the front row of guards. "You," I said before anyone moved. He flinched when I raised my hand, but there was nowhere for him to run.

With my power, I ripped him forward until my hand closed around his throat. "I told you I'd find you." I pulled his face close to mine. "Thanks for making it easy."

I threw him against the wall beside the elevator so hard his skull *clacked* against the concrete.

The other guards were frantically pushing buttons to try to escape. "Lock them up," Iliana said to Jett.

"You don't want to kill them?" he asked.

"No. They're only following orders."

Thacker crumpled onto himself in a heap. I stood over him, grabbing a fistful of his brown hair. I jerked his fearful eyes up to meet mine. "How does it feel to be overpowered by someone stronger than you?"

Panic radiated off him.

And on his soul, it was clear: Thacker was a murderer, responsible for at least two human lives.

He might have been under the direction of the Morning Star, but in his case, it didn't really matter. Whether he was doing the devil's dirty work or not, Thacker was guilty. He'd taken pleasure in the suffering of others. And the fear in his eyes told me he knew that I knew it.

I turned his head toward Fury. "Now apologize."

Thacker was shaking. "I-I'm sorry."

Fury backed against the wall behind me.

"Let's show her just how sorry you can be." I grabbed his face, forcing his jaw open. Then I reached into his mouth, curled my fingers over his back teeth, and plunged my thumbs under his jaw on the outside.

Crying, he fought against me, but my hands twisted away

from each other until his mandible broke with a violent *snap*. I pulled until the lower gums split, his bottom front teeth separated, and blood poured down his throat.

Screaming and choking on the blood, his eyes rolled back, and his body went limp. Part of me wanted to wake him, forcing him to feel what Fury had felt for as long as possible.

But I refrained.

I shoved his head against the wall again before standing and wiping the blood and saliva onto my jeans.

When I turned, my friends were watching me, a clear mix of awe and horror on their faces. My eyes locked with Fury's. "Did he deserve it?" she asked.

She understood such a brutal retribution wasn't just because of what he'd done to her. He had killed and would likely kill again.

"Yes. He deserved it." I jerked my thumb toward him. "You want to get a swift kick in? He deserves that too."

"I know what he's going to go through when he wakes up. That's payback enough for me."

Down the hall, Iliana was sealing the cell doors, welding them shut with fire blasting from her hands.

Fire I had taught her to use.

When she was finished, she dusted off her palms. "They're not going anywhere for a while." She looked up at one of the cameras and shouted, "Chimera, go ahead and try to let them out!" Then she laughed and walked back to the elevator, shaking her head. "Let's get the hell outta here."

We blasted through the top of the elevator shaft and didn't stop flying until we were well outside Claymore's gates. It took longer than I would have anticipated, indicating just how much the base had expanded over the years.

In broad daylight, we flew inland to what looked like a wildlife preserve, or national park. We landed near a wide river, far away from civilization.

"Where are we?" Anya asked as she tamed her wind-whipped hair.

"Roanoke River," Jett answered. "John used to bring me out here camping when I was a kid."

Fury froze in front of me and turned toward him. "Really?"

"Yeah. A lot, actually. We're about thirty miles outside Claymore's new fence line."

It was clear Fury didn't care about the fence line. It was the only detail she'd been given about her son's childhood.

"That's great and all, but where are my parents?" Iliana opened her eyes. "I can't sense their spirits at all."

"I'm sure Azrael took them to his house on Kill Devil Hills Island," Jett said.

Iliana looked at me.

I shrugged. "It makes sense. Azrael, or even the Morning Star, would take them to see Adrianne. Even if for nothing else than to shut her up."

Jett touched her arm. "And it's probably even more secure than Echo-5."

"How are we going to get them out?" Anya asked.

"We're not," Cassiel said behind us.

We all turned and looked at her. Her golden hair was matted from the flight, and her shoulders were slumped in defeat. "There's no way we get that close to where the Morning Star sleeps. He's too smart for that."

My head fell to the side. "He's not smart enough to realize how powerful Iliana is. The design of that prison shows just how much he's underestimated her."

"I agree, but we could easily get Sloan and Nathan killed," Cassiel said.

Iliana looked up at me. "She's probably right."

Cassiel was usually right about things. It was equally one of the most annoying parts and helpful parts of who she was.

"I doubt he'll do anything to hurt them. He doesn't have anything to gain by their deaths," Cassiel said.

I sighed. "But he sure as hell can use them as leverage."

"We need to lure the Morning Star away," Kane said. "Get him alone and minimize the casualties."

Shaking my head, I crossed my arms. "It's not that simple. Somehow he's rigged all the humans close to him. If anything happens to him, they will die."

"What do you mean?" Fury asked.

I turned to my daughter. "When they showed up on the Island of Fire, you saw it in Azrael, didn't you?"

"I don't know what I saw, but yes. There was something inside him."

"What are you talking about?" Cassiel asked.

"I'm not sure if it's a bomb of sickness, or what. But there's something concealed inside Azrael's body that I'm afraid might kill him."

"*Utam katave*," Cassiel said, almost to herself.

"What?" Iliana asked, likely echoing everyone's thoughts.

"*Utam katave*," Cassiel repeated. "Lethal sickness encapsulated. It's something we discovered the Morning Star was trying to perfect when he was working with Kasyade, Phenex, and Ysha to spread the disease that makes humans sterile."

"He tried to sterilize humans?" Anya asked.

Fury nodded. "Yes. While you were gone. Warren stopped them."

"Sloan stopped them," I corrected her. "Her biological mother, Kasyade, was working with the Morning Star to infect child prostitutes with an antibiotic-resistant strain of gonor-rhea. They were going to use this *utam katave*?" I asked Cassiel.

"Yes. It was a failsafe in case they were caught. Should the demons be killed, the girls would die too."

"But what is it?" Fury asked.

Cassiel made a fist with her right hand and covered the fist with her left. "Warren was right. It's like a bomb of sickness, covered by a layer of life." She released the fist. "Remove the life, and the sickness consumes the host."

"Can I heal them from it?" Iliana asked.

"I don't see why not. You've already proven you can heal the virus," Cassiel answered.

Iliana looked at me. "So I heal them from it, and then we kill the Morning Star."

I shook my head. "You might be able to save those closest to us, but you wouldn't be able to save the entire Claymore Army. The Morning Star said they're all infected, which means a few hundred thousand will die."

"And that's a bad thing?" Jett asked. "They chose their side, and casualties go hand in hand with war."

Leave it to an angel to oversimplify the choices of humans. I thought of Huffman, my friend and longtime Clay-more operative. He'd been with the company even before I'd joined, and he'd likely stay as long as Azrael was in charge. He hadn't chosen the wrong side; the wrong side had trapped him.

Nash was apparently thinking of himself because he beat me to the argument. "Do I deserve to die too?"

We all looked at him.

"Most of Claymore's manpower has never even seen the Morning Star, much less chosen to follow a psychopath. We're talking about innocent lives. And the innocent lives of their families and communities."

"He's right," Cruz said. "You unleash that sickness again, and you're helping him wipe out the rest of the planet."

"We need more time to figure out how to eradicate the disease in the soldiers before Iliana kills the Morning Star," Kane said.

"Got any idea how to do that?" I asked Cassiel.

"I'm not sure. We first need to figure out how he got it in there," she answered.

"They were given vaccines for the virus. I'm almost sure of it," Nash said. "One of my buddies said I got out just in time. That whatever new shots they were required to have hurt worse than the anthrax vaccine."

"Papa Jordan suggested we might be able to use my blood to create a vaccine or a cure," Iliana said.

We looked at Cassiel.

"It's worth some research," she said with a shrug. "Perhaps I could talk to Dr. Jordan."

"We need to get back to Asheville anyway. I'm sure word has gotten out that we've escaped, and the Morning Star is probably looking for us," I said.

"They'll have Wolf Gap surrounded by now," Nash said. "They've had units in place there for a while. And, if I'm being really honest, I wouldn't put it past the Morning Star to drop a shit ton of bombs on the compound."

Kane shook his head. "Bombs won't matter if everyone's underground. They could drop a nuclear warhead on the bunker, and it wouldn't even rattle the pictures on the walls."

"Are they underground though?" Cruz asked. "That wasn't the order when we left."

"I'll send some angels to make sure everyone is safe." I touched my ear and started to walk away.

"Already done," Iliana said. "I called out to Lachlan on our way here. He promised to stay close to Asheville when we left, so he may already be at the house."

Lachlan was an Angel of Death. An angel in *my* command—and also in Iliana's, I remembered.

She looked at Kane. "I told him to put Wolf Gap on Threat Level Five. He'll report back soon."

"Threat Level Five?" I asked.

"Everyone goes into the bunker, and everything above-ground is completely shut down," Kane explained. "We'll be safe there once we get inside."

"So we have a plan," I announced. "We return to Asheville."

Cassiel stepped forward. "What about Sandalphon and Samael?"

"I'm not sure there's anything we can do," I said.

"They're both fully capable of taking care of themselves," Jett added.

"Are they? Even stripped of their powers? Samael will be fine, but what about Sandalphon?" Cassiel's voice had jumped up an octave. "Those cuffs have reduced him to little more than a mortal. His body is old. He's suffering."

Her concern was moving, but I didn't know how we could help him.

"If we can get in touch with Huffman, our friend on the inside, maybe he can find out what conditions Sandalphon's being held in," Kane told her.

"And Iliana ruined all the high-security cells they have that I'm aware of, so he won't be any place too heavily locked down," Nash added.

Nodding and hugging her arms, she walked toward the water, perhaps to get her emotions under control.

It was clear, life on Earth was beginning to take its toll on Cassiel. Emotionally, this realm was heavy for angels and humans alike, but angels who kept residence in Eden struggled particularly hard with coping.

Stress, anxiety, and negative emotions didn't exist on our side of the spirit line, allowing us to disconnect completely from the temporal chaos of Earth.

But here there was no escape.

It was one of the main reasons she'd never wanted to live here. And it was the primary reason I felt guilty for my part in her being trapped here.

I touched Fury's elbow. "I need to talk to her."

She nodded and stepped back out of my way.

I jogged down to the water's edge to catch up with Cassiel. When I reached her, she was wiping away tears.

"Don't look at me," she said, looking upriver as she pressed her wrist against her nose.

I curled my hand around her arm, hoping my touch alone might bring her some comfort. We all carried a piece of Eden inside us, and that dose of energy could sustain us when we were away.

It was why some angels, like Rogan and Malak, always traveled together. And it was why others avoided their kind altogether on Earth. The only thing worse than the high was the withdrawal when we were forced apart.

It was likely the reason she and Sandalphon had been inseparable since even before my return.

"Cassiel."

She wiped her cheeks again before turning to face me. Her eyes were wet and tinged with red. She sniffed and blinked hard to keep more tears from falling. "I'll be fine."

"I know you will be. This is hard for all of us. It's okay to accept a little support."

"Support from you?" Her words stung. "You called me a traitor forty-eight hours ago."

"I said you had an agenda, but I never called you a traitor. I believe your intentions are pure. I just don't trust how far you might go to carry them out."

She looked across the water, but I closed the space between us and took hold of both her arms. "I still care about you. You're in pain, and I want to help."

"I think I can help," Iliana said, walking up behind Cassiel. She reached behind her neck and unclasped the sanctonite-stone necklace. "Here."

Cassiel shook her head. "I couldn't possibly—"

"Of course you can." Iliana lifted the necklace over Cassiel's head. "Hang onto it until we can find Sandalphon."

When the stone rested on Cassiel's skin, peace washed over her face, and she exhaled like she hadn't breathed in a week. She gathered her hair over one shoulder and let Iliana fasten the chain around her neck.

Cassiel grabbed Iliana's hand before she pulled away. "Thank you, Iliana."

Iliana smiled. "Don't mention it."

When Iliana had returned to the group, Cassiel's eyes followed after her. "She really is remarkable, Warren."

"She is." I looked at Cassiel again. "Now you see why I had to come back."

She nodded. "And I understand how hard it must be that you missed so much."

My eyes fell for a quick second, but I forced them back up. "This isn't over, Cassiel. We haven't lost everything. Not yet."

Cassiel took a deep breath and looked back at the group. "If anyone can restore the spirit line and help us get home, it's Iliana. No matter what you believe about my intentions, I'm going to do all I can to help her do that."

"I know you will." I offered her my hand, the most vulnerable I could make myself to an Angel of Knowledge. "Truce?"

"No." She took my hand. "A truce is between enemies. You will never be that for me."

"For me either." I pulled her into a hug.

"Come on," she said, starting up the bank. "Let's rejoin the group. We're acting like a couple of humans."

Fury was watching us.

Cassiel noticed. "She loves you."

"I know. I love her too."

"It's as it should be," she said.

I'd once said those words when Sloan married Nathan. It was strange to hear them now being said about me. "Are you going to be all right?" I asked Cassiel because I meant what I'd said. I *did* care about her.

"Yes. Just as soon as I get home."

"Then let's hurry up and make that happen," I said with a smile.

We rejoined the group, and I walked over to stand beside Fury. "What's the plan?"

Fury sighed. "We have one, but you're not going to like it."

"Try me."

"We need to get to Asheville, but the only way to do that from here is to drive," Iliana said.

"Well, fly first. Then drive," Jett said.

"Drive what?" I asked. "And fly where?"

"That's the part you're not going to like," Fury muttered.

"To see Uncle John," Iliana said.

"Uncle John." I pointed at Jett. "*That* Uncle John?"

Iliana nodded. "He's only a half hour from here by air, and he can help us get across the state."

My internal "oh shit" meter blew a fuse.

The last interaction I'd had with John McNamara, Fury's ex, hadn't been friendly. It hadn't even been civil. It was days before Fury and I had left for Nulterra, and he'd just found out that Jett wasn't his biological son.

He'd given us two weeks to save Anya and come back, threatening to drop Jett at the Claymore gate. We'd never returned. And for him, that had been seventeen years ago.

This reunion wouldn't be pretty.

"Does he know we're back?" I asked.

Jett shook his head. "We thought it best not to tell him until we had to."

I raked my hand through my hair.

Iliana grinned. "You OK?"

Shaking my head, I blew out a sigh. "I think I'd rather deal with the Morning Star."

# CHAPTER ELEVEN

We stayed by the river until sundown, then flew farther inland toward Raleigh. When I'd known him, John had lived on the outskirts of Durham. He ran a hole-in-the-wall bar and grill called Johnny Bones.

Those days were gone.

Jett said he closed the restaurant when the economy took a nosedive during the virus. He'd sold his house and moved into a camper on some hunting property he owned well outside the city limits. Over the past couple of years, he'd built a one-bedroom cabin, completely off the grid.

No internet.

No cell phone.

No electricity.

We landed just outside a locked gate in the middle of the woods. The land was densely covered with pine trees.

"This is it?" I asked, stretching my arms. My muscles were spent from carrying Fury. The other angels were doing the same. Especially Reuel, who'd carried both Cruz and Anya.

"This is it." Jett waved to a small camera perched on the gatepost.

I inspected it. "I didn't think there was electricity."

"He has his own solar setup. It's enough to power the lights and a few small electronics." Jett waved his hand in front of the lock, and it fell open. The gate gave a shrill shriek when he pushed it wide.

"What about running water?" Anya asked as we started up the dirt road.

"There's plenty of fresh water out here. He has a well and septic tank."

"Man," Nash said, turning all the way around. "This is my dream. Think he'd mind a squatter?"

Jett chuckled. "Yeah, he'd mind. John doesn't do humans anymore. Not since…"

"Not since I left him?" Fury asked, saying aloud what we were all probably thinking.

Jett didn't answer.

"He's not all bitter and angry though," Iliana said, glancing over her shoulder at Fury and me. "I happen to like Uncle John very much."

"When's the last time you saw him?" I asked.

She thought for a moment. "It's been a couple of years, I guess." She looked at Jett. "I don't guess I've seen him since we moved you to Wolf Gap."

Iliana had finally answered my question that she'd been dodging for a while.

"Yeah, and I've only been back once since then," Jett said.

"So you live at Wolf Gap?" I asked him.

Iliana looked back at me, clearly ready to roll her eyes. "He and Rogan have apartments in the bunker. He doesn't live in the house."

That didn't make me feel any better.

"Uncle John taught me how to fish out here," she said, wisely changing the subject. "And how to build a fire and find drinking water."

It wasn't hard to imagine John being a friendly lumberjack of an uncle. Before he'd been screwed over by Fury, I had actually liked the guy. Or at least I *would* have liked him had he not been sleeping with the woman I loved.

I certainly respected the hell out of him, even if he'd never believe it. John was a former Navy Seal with a good heart and a strict moral code.

Right up until he put his hands on Fury. That was the line for me. I threatened to kill him then, and friendly relationships don't exactly come back from that. No matter how much time has passed.

Thick trees flanked both sides of the dirt road. At the end of it was a small cabin with a wide front porch. A gentle breeze rustled the pine trees, and a strange smell floated with it. Something akin to sweet, stinky feet.

"He's mellowed out a lot," Iliana said. "You two would get along if you could actually get past the—"

The unmistakable ratchet of a shotgun echoed through the trees. As if purposely blowing Iliana's point all to hell, John stepped out of the tree line with the barrel aimed straight for us.

Correction.

The barrel was aimed directly at me. I moved protectively in front of Fury.

"You've got a lot of nerve showing up here," he said.

John's head was shaved, and he had a thick white beard. He was smaller than last I'd seen him, but taut muscles pulled against his shirtsleeves.

Creases had settled in his face like canyons, mostly concentrated across his brow and between his eyes. John had done a lot of scowling in his day—exactly like he was scowling now.

Fury stepped to my side. "John?"

His eyes, but not his gun, shifted to her face and back to mine. Then he did a quick double take, his eyes widening with shock. He lowered the weapon and looked at her, his mouth gaping.

"Allison?"

She held her hands up and slowly walked toward him. "Yeah. It's me."

He blinked a few times, probably wondering if his sight was deceitful. "Is that really you?"

"It's really me."

I took a step forward, and the barrel jerked right back up toward my face. I froze.

"John, put down the gun," Fury said gently.

He didn't take his eyes off me. "I'll put down the gun when he gets off my property."

Jett stepped between me and the shotgun. "Dad, we need to talk to you. Please put it down."

Fury's head whipped toward her son. The intimate title snagged in all our ears. Everyone's eyes were on Fury, except Jett didn't seem to notice. Why would he? He'd never had a mother before.

I touched the small of her back and felt her tense, as if she knew I'd peeked behind the curtain, exposing some great secret. Her eyes darted off toward the woods.

"Talk about what?" John demanded. "I have nothing to say to them."

By *them,* I assumed John meant me and Fury.

"You're not even a little curious where they've been all these years?" Iliana asked.

"Or why they look exactly the same," Jett added. "I know you're curious."

And he was. It was obvious from the way John's eyes kept flicking toward Fury. He shifted nervously on his feet, like he was debating whether to relax or start shooting.

I hoped for the former, but the whites of his knuckles around the shotgun's barrel warned the latter was a real possibility.

"Don't make me disarm you," Jett said. "You can't kill him anyway, remember?"

That got John's attention. With a frustrated huff, he lowered the gun and swore under his breath. Then he turned on his boot and started toward the cabin.

We all looked around at each other, then Jett started after his *dad.* Everyone else fell in step behind him, but Fury's feet were reluctant to move.

"You all right?" I asked quietly.

Her back straightened. "I'm fine. Come on. Let's get this over with."

Reuel, Kane, Nash, and Cruz waited outside. Mainly because there wasn't room for everyone in the living room.

"Uncle John, can we have some water?" Iliana asked as he put the shotgun on a rack above the fireplace mantle.

"There are cans in the storage pantry."

"Cans?" Anya asked. "Of water?"

"Humans stopped using plastic bottles about a decade ago," Cassiel explained.

"Who the hell are you?" John asked her.

Cassiel bowed her head. "My name is Cassiel. It's nice to meet you, John McNamara."

"You're one of *them*?" There was that word again. Spat like a curse from his lips.

"I am an Archangel of Eden," she said.

His blue eyes turned toward Anya. "And you're the sister? The rescue mission?"

"Yes. Thank you for your sacrifice. They saved my life."

John's face softened. Missions. Rescues. Sacrifice. Those were all things he understood. John may have had his moments of being a complete asshole, but he was a hero—no doubt about that.

He finally looked at Fury. "Wanna explain to me why the hell you look like you just left here?"

"Because I did," she said.

He stared, waiting for an explanation.

"We were in Nulterra for less than two days."

"Bullshit."

"It's true," Jett said.

John pointed at him. "A little heads-up would have been nice."

Jett shrugged and sat down on the sofa. "You would've left had you known we were coming."

John didn't argue.

Iliana returned to the living room with an armful of canned waters. She passed them out, and when she reached Cassiel, Cassiel held out both hands. "I'll take the rest outside to the others."

"I'll help you," Anya said, rushing to her side to help.

Couldn't blame them. The tension in the house was toxic.

When they were gone, Iliana cracked open her own water and sat next to Jett. I watched her touch her ear, then static crackled in mine. *"It's not going well, is it?"*

I shook my head.

*"Should we give them some privacy?"*

I shook my head again.

The last time Fury and John had been in a room together,

he'd almost hit her. There was no way I was leaving her alone unless she explicitly asked me to.

John walked over and sat down in an old recliner. "Two days?"

Fury took that as her cue to move closer. She sat across from him on the edge of the coffee table. "I swear, John. For us, less than a week has passed since we saw you at Claymore."

"It's been seventeen years, Allison."

"I know. I still haven't really come to grips with it." There was a hitch in her throat. "John, I missed everything."

"Yeah, you did." There was a bite to his statement.

I waited for him to launch into a tirade about how he had to raise a boy who wasn't even his son. How she'd dumped her responsibility on him and took off.

He didn't.

Instead, he visibly swallowed, choking back emotion. "We thought you were dead."

"I nearly was." She leaned forward and reached for his hand. "I didn't disappear on purpose. I never meant to not come back."

He pulled his hand from hers. "But you didn't come back. And now, here you are. What do you want?"

"We need to get to Asheville," Jett said.

"So flap your arms. I assume you flew here."

"It's too far. We need the RV." Jett sat back. "And some cash."

John sat back with a *humph*. He stared at Fury. "Shoulda known you needed something."

"It wasn't my idea to come here," she said.

"Of course it wasn't." He got up. "I'm sure this would be the last place you'd show up of your own free will. It's not like you'd come here to apologize or anything."

She started after him. "I did want to apologize. I never meant for any of this to happen."

"I have no doubt. Can't imagine you'd willingly spend a couple of decades in Hell." He stopped and faced her. "*If that's really where you've been.*"

"You know it is."

He started walking again. "I don't know shit."

"I promise we were stuck there. I had no idea how much time had passed."

"She's telling the truth," Jett said.

"Maybe. Maybe not."

Fury huffed.

John opened a door on the far side of the room. Behind it, on a shelf, was a small safe. He punched in a digital code, and the box clicked open. "Still, it doesn't change anything. You walked out on me, and you walked out on him." John pointed something at Jett. It took a second for me realize it was a stack of money.

He pressed the money against her chest. "So here's the money."

"John, I—"

Ignoring her, he lifted a key ring off the hook on the inside of the door. "And here are the keys to my RV. Take them and don't ever come back here again."

"John, I'm here now. Can we please talk about this?"

"What's there to talk about?"

"Uncle John." Iliana stood, and all eyes in the room turned toward her. She walked slowly toward him, holding her hands up in surrender. "We all understand why you're angry, and no one faults you for it, but for years, you wanted to know what happened to Fury. *Prayed* to know, even. I remember."

John looked caught.

"Now, here she is. Are you really just going to turn her away without getting any answers? Without finally getting some closure on whatever this is?" Iliana gestured between John and Fury.

John's whole body visibly relaxed. For a moment, I wondered if Iliana might be using her powers on him. Whatever was happening, John had clearly been disarmed.

The anger in his eyes faded to bewilderment...and something that looked a whole lot like sorrow. His Adam's apple bobbed with a hard swallow.

Fury took a step closer to him, taking advantage of the crack in his resolve. "Thank you," she said, looking him dead in the eye.

He blinked and fell back a step. It was clear that of all the things that needed to be said, he hadn't expected her gratitude.

"I never deserved your help or your support, or even your kindness. I deserved for you to walk out on me and Jett and never look back, but you didn't. You were the parent Jett deserved to have." Her eyes turned upward. "Apparently, someone somewhere knew that. So thank you."

John shifted uncomfortably on his feet. "It wasn't his fault you and I screwed things up. I couldn't leave him alone."

She closed the space between them, took his hand, and lowered her head. "I was wrong for the way I treated you. I should have told you the truth, and I'm truly sorry I didn't."

My eyes widened so much they ached. It was the most brazen act of humility I had ever seen Fury demonstrate.

John looked baffled too. He recoiled. "It's done now. No need to dredge up the past."

He turned and walked to the kitchen out of our view, but my sensitive ears heard him let out a sigh of relief? frustration? hatred? Whatever it was, the old frogman was shaken.

I joined Iliana and Fury in the center of the living room, and I squeezed the back of Fury's neck. "You okay?" I asked quietly.

She gave a silent nod.

John returned with the distinct *pop* and *phshh* of an opening can top accompanying the sound of his footsteps. He tilted the beer up to his lips, sucking down a few gulps before lowering it.

He didn't offer anyone else a drink. Not that I could blame him. Jett and Iliana were technically underage. Fury rarely drank, and I was still *me*.

John plopped into his recliner. An improvement since he'd done so without yelling. Iliana returned to her seat, and Fury and I stood by the wood-burning fireplace.

"So you closed the bar?" Fury asked, lightening the conversation while there was still a break in the tension.

"Yep." John balanced his beer can on the armrest. "When all hell broke loose with that virus, folks either died or got the heck out of Dodge. Nobody was hanging out in bars anymore, so I closed up shop and moved out here."

John finally looked at me. "Jett says your old man, Azrael, is behind that virus. Is it true?"

I was surprised. Partly because John was finally acknowledging me and partly because of how much he knew—and accepted as truth—about our situation. The last time I'd seen John, he still believed Azrael was my brother, Damon. "I doubt he knows about it, and if he does, he's not doing it willingly."

"If he spreads that compound any farther east, he's going to swallow up this property," he said, almost to himself.

"Will you sell to him?" Iliana asked.

He sipped his beer. "Doesn't sound to me like he does as much *asking* as he does *forcing*."

"Are you aware that Azrael's other son is the one running the show at Claymore?" Fury asked.

John took another long drink. "Yeah. I hear he's an angel who can control people, like Iliana." He slid a sideways glance at her. "Don't think I don't know you hoodoo'd this whole situation just now."

Iliana tucked her hands beneath her thighs and stifled a grin. "I don't know what you're talking about, Uncle John."

"*Mmm-hmm.*" John rolled his eyes back toward me and Fury. "Jett's told me a lot."

"Obviously," I said.

"John, you may not be safe here in Claymore's backyard when this comes to war," Fury said. "The Morning Star will probably come after everyone he might be able to use against us."

"Jett told me that too, and I'll tell you the same thing I told him. I can take care of myself."

"They might even track us here," I admitted.

"He's right. You should come with us to Asheville," Jett said, leaning forward and balancing his elbows on his knees.

John chuckled and lifted his beer again. "Sure. One big fucked-up family. That'll be the day." John wiggled his fingers in Iliana's direction. "And don't try using your superpowers to change my mind."

She rolled her eyes. "If I thought it was that easy, I would've done it years ago."

"I'll take my chances." John stood and put his beer down on the coffee table. "But on that note, you'll forgive me if I don't want y'all hanging around here, drawing attention."

"Of course," Iliana said as she and Jett stood.

"You should blend in fairly well in the RV. They're commonly lived in now." He looked at me. "As long as all the *fairies* stay hidden inside."

I groaned, but I couldn't help but smile. It was the most normal conversation the two of us had ever had.

Fury was clutching the stack of fresh bills and the key ring. "We really appreciate you helping us get back."

John's head tipped slightly forward, but he didn't comment. After a second, he let out a deep breath. "Ah, damn it. Come here." He pulled Fury into his arms. "I'm glad you're OK."

Iliana took the money and the keys so Fury could hug him back. Fury locked her arms around his neck and buried her face in his shoulder. "Thank you, John."

He sniffed and kissed the side of her head. "It wasn't all bad." He flashed a grin at Jett. "For being an angel, he makes a pretty good hunting buddy."

She laughed as he pulled away.

"Hold on. I've got something else for you." John walked past us down a narrow hallway, then disappeared through a side door. He returned a moment later with seemingly empty hands. "Here." He turned his hand over and uncurled his fingers. In his palm was a small USB flash drive. "I'm not sure if you can find any computer able to read it, but I'm old school, and this is high tech for me."

Fury picked it up. "What is it?"

"Pictures. Memories." John tilted his silver head toward Jett. "He was a cute kid."

A quiet sob erupted from Fury's throat as she clutched it. "Thank you, John." She hugged him again. "For everything."

He gave her back a patronizing pat. "I know. I know."

"We will pay you back," I said, touching the small of Fury's back as she stepped away from him.

Iliana came over beside me and handed me the cash with a grin. "For this, or the seventeen years of back child support?"

John pointed at her. "Kid's got a point."

We all laughed.

"Are you sure you won't change your mind and come with us?" Jett asked, offering his hand to his father.

"I'm sure." John pulled him into a one-armed hug. "Try to keep that battle away from here."

"I'll do my best."

John kept a hand on his shoulder. "Call me if you need me, son."

"Thank you," Jett said.

I looked down at Fury. She was smiling. I touched her waist. "You ready to go?"

She was holding the flash drive. "Yeah, I'm ready."

Iliana inhaled deep, her eyes wild with excitement. "Let's go home."

# CHAPTER TWELVE

It should have been a four-and-a-half-hour drive back to Asheville, but John's motorhome was a throwback to the days when Fury and I had first left Earth.

It burned through gasoline like there was an infinite supply of it on the planet, which there was *not*, and gas was almost ten dollars per gallon. It sputtered down the interstate, nearly dying about every hundred miles, as electric cars whizzed by.

Electric cars had already begun to rule the West Coast by the time we left, but the cars we saw on the drive home were another level entirely. They looked like something out of a sci-fi movie. Sleek lines, massive windows, and reflective paint jobs. Cassiel explained that nanoparticles in the paint actually charged the car. A detail my pea brain couldn't even comprehend.

I drove the last leg of the trip, well into the early hours of the morning. All the humans and Reuel were asleep when we took the Highway 280 exit toward the Asheville airport. Cassiel sat up front with me while Jett sat far in the back, keeping watch out the rear and side windows.

Static crackled in my ears. "Warren?"

It was Lachlan. "Yeah?"

"Welcome back."

"Thanks."

"Where are you guys?"

"Almost back to the Wolf Gap property. You?"

"I'm here now, circling. Just a heads-up, there's a Claymore unit sitting on the drive up to the building."

"Damn it."

"What do you want me to do?"

I thought for a second. "Stay close, but don't engage. We'll handle it when we get there."

"What's the matter?" Cassiel asked.

"Soldiers are waiting for us."

"Not surprising. Claymore set up an installation not far from the property, between Wolf Gap and the airport. It wouldn't have taken long for them to find out we escaped."

"What do you think we should do?" I asked her.

"Try not to kill them if they're human."

"Getting through them won't be a problem, but we both know reinforcements will be sent. What then?"

"Underground, we'll be protected, but they could trap us. Starve us out, or cut off the oxygen supply."

I'd already thought about that.

"We sealed our fate by breaking out of that prison," Jett said from the back of the motorhome. "The Morning Star *will* retaliate, even if only to save face. Peacetime is over."

I looked in the rearview mirror and noticed Iliana's head on his lap.

"Warren!" Cassiel's voice ripped my eyes back to the road. I jerked the wheel to pull us back into our lane.

"Do you need me to drive?"

"No." I gripped the wheel with both hands.

She turned to look at what I'd been gawking at. Then, shaking her head, she sat back in her seat. "Humans."

"I don't like it," I whispered quietly enough so that Jett couldn't hear me.

"My experience with teenage girls is limited, but if you push her about him, she's not going to respond in the way you hope."

I turned my palms up on the steering wheel. "So I just keep my mouth shut? She's a child, and he's a few billion years older than she is."

Cassiel's head tilted to the side. "I don't remember you having much of a problem with me being billions of years older than you."

"That was different."

"Is it? Would you rather her fall in love with a human boy who will be dead in sixty years?"

"Yes. Dead boyfriends are the best boyfriends."

"You're being ridiculous."

"No, I'm not."

"Malak has been protecting mankind since before even you were born. He might be the best thing to happen to Iliana. Have you thought about it that way?"

"No," I grumbled.

"I don't think Malak has ever cared for anyone besides Rogan. Angels falling in love is very rare."

I didn't miss the wistful tone of her statement. I let it linger between us for a mile or two. "Cassiel, I'm sorry for how you and I left things. I meant what I said, but I don't want tension between us."

She stared ahead. "It never would've worked with us anyway. We are too different. If nothing else, you finding it unforgivable that I would seek out the truth proves that much."

"I want the truth as well, but I'm not willing to sacrifice my integrity to get it."

"You call it *integrity*. I call it *necessity*. You didn't even know what to look for in the blood stone."

"Perhaps not, but you should have asked me."

"Maybe, but let's not fight about it anymore."

"I like the sound of that."

She tapped her window. "You missed your turn."

"Damn it."

She chuckled.

I turned onto the next road.

"Are we there yet?" Anya asked, half-asleep on the pull-out sofa behind me.

"Almost," I answered in the middle of a seventy-three-point turn on the narrow road. I raised my voice. "We need everyone awake."

Fury's head appeared in my mirror. "Where are we?"

"Not where we're supposed to be," Cassiel said, biting back a laugh.

"You wanna walk?" I asked.

She laughed again.

Three full minutes later, we were back on the highway, and Cassiel had filled everyone in on the situation awaiting us. I took the next left turn onto what used to be an unmarked road. "It has a road sign now. That's why I passed it."

"OK," Cassiel said with a smirk.

I turned onto Dead End Lane and slowed as we passed the sign. "Dad named it," Iliana volunteered before I could ask. "He thought it would deter visitors."

I grinned. "Sounds like Nate."

"Did it work?" Cassiel asked.

"No. A lot of teenagers get busted smoking pot and making out just past the Echo-5 turnoff now."

I switched on my high beams as I drove up the mountain. The road and the scenery were mostly unchanged, except for the old and crumbling pavement shifting beneath the tires of the motorhome. The road had been dirt the last time I'd been here. After a while, I took a left turn toward Echo-5 and rolled past the guard shack, which had fallen into disrepair.

It had been empty for quite some time.

I looked at Kane in the rearview mirror. "No more guard?"

He shrugged. "Not enough manpower."

"Or cash flow," Cruz added.

"The cameras are functional, however." Iliana waved through the side window as we passed it.

Cassiel looked over at me. "With a direct feed back to Claymore, I would assume."

Dread swelled inside me as we crested the hill toward the building. Two armored Humvees flanked the road, and weapons were raised in our direction.

"Great. More guns," Cassiel said, dropping her hands into her lap with a frustrated sigh.

Kane leaned forward. "That's definitely not our guys."

High-powered flashlights blinded us.

I shielded my eyes with my hands. "I'm not sensing any angels out there. Cassiel?"

Her hands were in front of her face too. "Only humans."

"Step out of the vehicle with your hands where we can see them!" a man called over a loudspeaker.

I turned to look in the back of the RV. Everyone was squinting from the lights. "No lethal force. We are *not* killing humans."

"We have secure holding cells in the bunker," Kane said.

Of course they did. That would've been one of Azrael's top priorities.

"Angels, stay in front of the humans in case they open fire." I looked at Fury. "Don't be a hero. You're unarmed."

Behind her hand, she rolled her eyes. It made me smile.

My smile quickly faded as I put the RV in park and killed the engine. Then I pushed open my door and raised my hands over my head. Cassiel did the same, and Kane opened the back door.

"We don't want any trouble!" I called out to whoever was beyond the high beams.

"Turn around and place your hands behind your back!"

"I'm not going to do that." I walked slowly forward, carefully placing one boot in front of the other. "We can talk about this peacefully, or I can end this standoff right here."

I heard whispers among the humans.

"You know what I am, and you know what I'm capable of." I let my energy sizzle to life in my hands, inciting a few quiet gasps from the other side. "Don't make me do this."

There was painfully long silence as I inched forward until…

"Fire."

A single bullet ruptured from a chamber before I blasted my power forward, extinguishing the lights and shattering the bulletproof glass on the Humvees. Bullets sprayed wildly through the air as the humans, now visible in the moonlight, were knocked off their feet.

The soldier quite obviously in charge had been shot by one of his men in the back. It had blown open a hole in his chest. He was bleeding profusely and writhing next to the Humvee on the left. I grabbed his rifle, unloaded it, and tossed it to Kane. "Disarm them."

Another soldier rolled and began firing at us again. Reuel knocked him sideways, but not before Cassiel cried out in pain.

*Shit.*

Before he could shoot again, Kane took the man's rifle and handed it to Cruz. The two of them swept the area of guns while Reuel and Jett used their power to restrain everyone.

I went to Cassiel.

She was hunched over and holding her stomach. I looked down and saw the blood seeping through her fingers.

"Every damn time I'm with you, I wind up downrange from a machine gun."

"Technically, those are rifles. Not machine guns."

"Oh, shut up!" She twisted in pain as I tried not to laugh.

I looked around for Iliana. "We need your help."

Cassiel grabbed my arm. "No, no. I'm fine. But that guy needs help." She pointed a bloody finger at the soldier who'd been shot.

With a nod, Iliana started toward him, and Jett followed her. "You're going to heal him? They tried to kill us," he said.

"He's a soldier following orders." My hand on Jett's chest held him back. "And yes, she's going to heal him." I looked around at the whole group from Claymore. "She's going to heal all of them." I was certain, even though I couldn't see through their armor, that each of them carried the virus.

Iliana started with their leader, dropping to her knees at his injured side. I spread my wings of light behind me, illuminating the scene. The man on the ground was easily in his late thirties. Average height with a warrior's build. He was black with a clean-shaven jaw and two dark-brown eyes.

Eyes that were currently fighting back tears.

"What's your name?" Iliana asked gently as she covered his wound with her bright healing light.

Sweat had beaded across his forehead. "Kelvin. Kelvin Holmes."

"Hi, Kelvin. I'm Iliana."

After a moment, his shaking began to calm, and surprise replaced the agony on his face. "Why are you doing this?"

"Because not all fairies are evil," she answered with a wink. "But the one you work for certainly is."

"Warren…" Cassiel's voice behind me was weak.

As I turned toward her, she fell to her knees. Anya was closest, and she closed her arms around Cassiel's shoulders to keep her from face-planting in the grass.

I closed the distance between us with my wings. "Cassiel, what's the matter?"

She was bent over on Anya's arm. "I… I don't know. Pain." She groaned and spewed blood from her mouth.

"It's ruptured her stomach or esophagus." Fury knelt beside us.

"That shouldn't matter. She should be getting better, not worse. Help me lay her down."

The three of us eased Cassiel onto the grass. Reuel stood nearby with his wings outstretched to cast light over the area.

"I'm sorry, Cassiel." With both hands, I grabbed hold of the low-cut collar of her dress. I ripped it down the middle. Black streaks spiderwebbed through the skin surrounding the hole in her stomach. It wasn't healing. It was getting worse.

Thick black ooze bubbled up from the wound.

"Warren, what is that?" Anya asked, her voice horrified.

I had no idea.

Fury stripped off the zip-up jacket she was wearing and covered Cassiel's exposed breasts. Bras weren't a thing in Eden, and Cassiel considered them a curse for women everywhere.

Cassiel's midsection violently arched off the ground as her bloodcurdling screams echoed through the mountains. Her whole body convulsed.

Iliana ran toward us, collapsing on top of Cassiel with all

her healing power. She literally curled Cassiel's body, letting her light consume them both.

I scrambled backward in horror. Fury's hands were clamped over her own mouth, her eyes wide with terror. Everyone around us, even the soldiers, were frozen.

Iliana strained. "It isn't enough."

Finally, her light went out, and she rolled off Cassiel, panting. Cassiel gasped loudly for air.

I crawled back toward Cassiel as Iliana pushed up onto her knees. "I can't heal it completely," Iliana said, trying to catch her breath. "I've never seen this before. It's like something exploded inside her."

"The bullet." I grasped my chin and nervously pulled my mouth down. "They planted some kind of bomb or poison inside her."

She was breathing, but only just.

"Can it kill her spirit? Or just her body?" Fury asked me.

"I can't imagine anything of this world could kill her spirit, but I wouldn't bet any of our lives on it. Either way, this is bad news."

Jett came closer, his mismatched eyes clouded with worry. "Only Angels of Death have ever been able to destroy the bodies of other angels. If whatever this is has the ability to cripple us, then this war just got a whole lot more dangerous."

Iliana checked Cassiel's pupils. "Let's get her inside so I can continue treating her."

I looked behind me. "Reuel, can you carry Cassiel to Echo-5?"

"*Amam.*" Reuel knelt down and scooped her up into his massive arms. He started toward the building, but Iliana stayed, staring wide-eyed at his back.

"You OK?" I put my hand on her shoulder.

She blinked a few times. "I've never failed to heal anyone before. Human or angel."

"I think you healed her more than you know." Anya visibly swallowed hard. "You may have just saved her life."

Fury stood and offered Iliana her hand. "Come on. You'll need to get us in the building."

The three women set off after Reuel, but Jett raised a hand to stop me. "What the hell was that, Warren?"

I shook my head, afraid to voice my fears aloud.

Behind him, Kane, Nash, and Cruz were guarding the soldiers. My eyes fell to the leader Iliana had healed. He was inspecting the bloody hole in his uniform. I walked over to him and knelt down, keeping my wings just bright enough so we could see the area. "What's in those magazines?"

He hesitated, and Kane raised the barrel of the man's own rifle toward his chest. "Maybe we shoot him with another round. This time in the stomach."

Fear flashed across the soldier's face. "I'll tell you." His voice broke with emotion. "Please don't shoot me."

Interesting. Zero loyalty to Claymore.

Kane lowered the rifle.

"It's called a 5.56 Yahweh."

"Yahweh?" Jett asked. "That's the name for God in Hebrew."

The man was shaking. "I don't know about all that. I just know they're fairy killers."

"*Angel* killers," I corrected him. "Kane, hand me one." I heard a *click* followed by metal sliding against metal as he removed the magazine.

"It's a hollow-point." He handed it over my shoulder.

Hollow-point bullets expand as they tear through a target. The expansion slows the bullet down. In a human, there would still likely be an exit wound—a violent one, like the soldier's mangled shoulder. But in an angel? The bullet would be trapped inside.

I rolled it around across my palm. 5.56-YWH was imprinted on the bottom, encircling the primer.

"Inside the bullet is a poison pellet. When the membrane ruptures inside the body, it's lethal to your kind," he said.

"Lethal how?" Jett asked.

The man was trembling. "I don't know."

"He's telling the truth. He just shoots what they give him." I held the round between my thumb and index finger. "Is this the same bullet that hit you?"

"Yeah," the man answered.

"So humans can be healed but angels can't," I said, almost to myself. "Is all of Claymore packing these now?"

He shook his head so hard I was sure his brain rattled against his skull. "Only those of us in Legion Nine carry them."

"Legion Nine, is that your angel-fighting army now?" Kane asked.

"Yes, sir." He tapped a patch on his shoulder. A skull with wings. It was the same patch the guards had worn at Claymore's armory prison.

"How many soldiers are in Legion Nine?" I asked.

"Around nine hundred."

I gulped, suddenly remembering the current scope of Claymore Worldwide Security.

"All of them armed with bullets lethal to both humans and angels." Kane slipped the magazine back into the rifle. He jammed it into place harder than the rifle required.

"How do we find out what that poison is?" Jett asked.

I stood, the cartilage grinding between my joints. "These guys won't be able to help us."

Kane sighed. "Too bad Cassiel's out of commission. She's the one good at figuring out answers."

A single light was now shining inside Echo-5. I started toward it. "Come on. Let's lock these guys up in the bunker. We need to focus on Cassiel."

Jett double-stepped to catch up with me. "Warren, what if that poison has the power to destroy her spirit?"

I'd been worried about the same thing.

"Then this whole war just changed."

# CHAPTER THIRTEEN

*E*cho-5 was dark and stuffy.

"Threat Level Five puts everyone underground and kills the internet and power to the building," Kane explained as we crossed the first floor, which was lit only with security lights. Two of the detained soldiers were with us. "I hope you don't mind stairs. The bunker is a hundred feet underground."

He opened a door that once led to a closet, if my memory served me correctly. Inside was an elevator and a door to a stairwell. "Start walking," he told the two men in front of us.

"I don't remember a prison on the original blueprints," I said as we followed them down.

"Early in the construction process, Azrael converted the business center into a high-security prison block. It was meant to house up to four humans and one angel, so these guys will be a little cramped, but they won't be dead."

One of the men smirked. The same man who'd shot Cassiel. I wanted to punch him.

"What was supposed to be a theater is now an office, and

there's an armory, a gym, a huge commercial kitchen, and an infirmary."

On the fourth or fifth landing, I looked over the railing. We still had a long way to go. "Everyone is down below?"

"They're supposed to be. All the staff bedrooms are Lower Level One, and the private apartments are on Lower Level Two."

"Did you move into Enzo's house that connects to the bunker?" I asked.

"No, sir. A garage went up over the escape hatch instead. The plans for the house were scrapped when—" Kane froze and looked at me.

"When Fury and I never came back?"

"That was the beginning of all the changes, sir. Things really fell apart when Azrael began losing his memories. We all made necessary adjustments to adapt. Me and the guys live in the staff quarters of the bunker."

"I'm sorry, Kane. I'm sure that sucks after all those years living in barracks."

"Not to worry. My life has been perfectly fulfilling. I lived at the command center in your old house for quite some time, so I was quite comfortable."

Kane and several of the others had given their entire lives to Azrael and Claymore. Kane had been with my father since before I even knew Azrael existed. He and Enzo had trained me when I first joined the company, and he'd been part of every mission we'd been on since.

I couldn't imagine how the current state of things must've affected him. How it had affected *all* of SF-12. And now that we were back, Enzo's absence was glaring. He'd been more dedicated than any of them.

"When did Enzo jump ship?" I asked.

"A *long* time ago. Even before Iliana came of age."

"He just left?"

"He wasn't happy about it, but he said it was an offer he couldn't refuse."

"Sounds very Godfather-ish."

Kane lifted a shoulder. "It kind of was. It always felt like he was forced into it."

"You think the Morning Star had something to do with it?"

"Jett was with us around the time Enzo left. He was just a kid then, but he could see power the way Fury can. He said Enzo wasn't being controlled."

"Huh. Maybe the government pays really well these days."

He cut his eyes toward me. "More than Claymore?"

"Good point."

"And you never hear from him?"

"Not a single word."

"Damn."

When we finally reached the bottom, a long, dark concrete hallway glowed green from security lights, and the sound of our footsteps echoed off the walls.

At the end of the hall, Kane waved to a tiny red light above a large steel door.

A buzzer sounded, and a lock tumbled.

"There's power down here?" I asked as he opened the door.

"Yes. I'll explain later." Kane's head tipped toward our prisoners.

He led us past a couple of decontamination showers and through two more massive double doors. On the other side was an open lobby where my old friend Lex was half-asleep behind a security desk.

"Warren." He jumped up and came around the table to greet me with a firm handshake. "Welcome back from the dead."

I pulled him into a one-armed hug. "Thank you. You're still here?"

"Of course I am." He looked at Kane. "Where else would we go?"

I smiled. "I appreciate you taking care of my family." I split a glance between Lex and Kane.

Kane shook his head. "We're protecting a whole lot more than just your family."

He was right. As personal as the war felt, it was much bigger than any one of us or even our whole group collectively.

"Is Iliana in the infirmary?" Kane asked him.

"They just came in. What happened to Cassiel?"

"We're not sure," I said with a sorrowful sigh.

Lex looked at the two soldiers with us. "Is this part of the band of misfits who's been sitting on our driveway all night?"

"Claymore's finest," Kane replied with an eye roll. "Cruz and Nash are coming down with a few more. Six total."

Lex started toward an interior wooden door with a narrow vertical window above the handle. "Well, let's show them to their accommodations."

We walked down a long, narrow hallway, passing a large living area on the right, the kitchen and dining room on the left, then a long glass wall marked with a medical cross.

Beyond the glass, Reuel covered Cassiel with a blanket, and Iliana held her hands over Cassiel's midsection. Bright light pulsed between them.

Fury caught my eye and excused herself.

Kane and Lex continued on with the soldiers, but I waited as Fury walked toward the door.

"We'll be through the last door on the left," Kane said over his shoulder.

"I'll be right behind you." I reached for Fury when she walked through the electric sliding double doors. "How is she?"

"She's still unconscious. Iliana is doing all she can, but I'm worried. Cassiel's skin is gray and ice-cold."

"She's losing blood."

"A lot of it, I'm afraid."

"Will you stay with her? I want to help them secure these prisoners, and then I need to search for answers."

Fury nodded. "I won't leave her side."

I touched her cheek, then kissed her.

Jett entered the hallway, holding two more of the soldiers by their elbows.

"Go," she said. "I'll let you know if there's any change."

"Thank you."

Fury returned to the infirmary, and I waited and fell in step with Jett. "We need to get in touch with someone on the inside at Claymore. We need to find out what's inside those bullets."

"I'm hoping your friend who's on the inside can help us. If he works at the armory, he should know something about this."

Jett was talking about Huffman, and I was thankful he didn't say his name out loud in front of the prisoners.

"Why would the Morning Star keep our friend around, given our history with him?" I asked.

Jett shrugged. "I've heard he was never on payroll as part of SF-12. It's likely the Morning Star simply doesn't know."

It was hard to imagine the Morning Star *not knowing* something, but Cassiel had once told me, as smart as he was, he wasn't omniscient. And Huffman would keep his mouth shut about the connection, so maybe—hopefully—Jett was right.

"We'll see what info Kane can find out," Jett said.

"Info about what?" Kane asked when we entered the doorway. Inside were four narrow metal cages, two on each side. Each cell had a cot and a metal toilet.

Across the room was another metal door with a small window at my eye level.

Kane had put Kelvin into the first cell and had locked the door. He put the second soldier in the cell beside him.

"Have you been able to make contact with Huffman?" Jett asked, loud and clear for all to hear.

My eyes doubled, and I turned toward him.

"What?" he asked with an oblivious shrug.

"You know Huffman?" Kelvin grasped the bars of his cell.

"Great." I held a hand toward the soldier, glaring at Jett. "Now we're going to have to kill this guy."

Kelvin stepped back. "Kill me?"

"Kill all of you, actually," Kane said, locking the last cell door.

We couldn't risk a Claymore soldier getting away knowing that we had connections on the inside. It was a matter of life or death for our friend—something Jett wouldn't understand as an immortal angel.

But for now, the cat was way out of the bag. Might as well use our mutual connection to get as much information as possible. "You know Huffman too?" I asked the guy.

"For a very long time."

Not surprising. Huffman was a friendly and funny guy. Everyone liked him, and he'd been with the company for longer than I even knew.

"Is he still working at the armory?" I asked.

"Yes. I talked to him yesterday."

I blinked. "Yesterday?"

He nodded.

I looked back at Kane as he put the other two soldiers in the cells behind me. "You haven't had time to contact him, have you?"

"Not yet, sir. And once I do, it will probably be a while before we hear back. The only way to make contact outside Claymore's network is through an old online forum that's basically defunct now. A few of us have fake accounts, but we don't check them often."

"I could get a message to him for you." Kelvin gripped the bars again. "Tell him to check that forum."

Kane and I exchanged a worried glance. "Why would you do that?" Kane asked.

Kelvin lowered his voice. "Because maybe you'll let me live if I help you."

My eyes narrowed. "I'm not buying it." I remembered how quickly he'd cracked on the battlefield. "You want out, don't you?"

His eyes darted around the room. The other soldiers were silent, but I knew what Kelvin was thinking. These were his men, and what he was talking about doing could get them all killed by Claymore.

"Kane, is there someplace private where Kelvin and I can talk?" I asked.

Kane thought about it. "The bedrooms are soundproof. If you go back to the living room, there's a door inside it that leads to three rooms. All of them are empty."

"Thanks." I passed my hand in front of the lock on the cage. Nothing happened.

"Here." Kane tossed me a set of keys.

Old school. I liked it, but it would take some getting used to.

"Everything's gotten so high tech that low tech is hard to beat these days," he said.

The second key I tried opened the cell door.

"I'll come with you," Jett said.

"No. I'll handle this one alone."

Jett looked surprised. Clearly, he wasn't used to being denied.

Kelvin held out his hands for me to cuff them.

I glanced down at his hands. "Is that necessary, or will you behave?"

He dropped his hands. "I'll behave."

He and I walked past Jett and out of the jail door. Cruz and Nash were coming down the hall with the last two soldiers. Both of them carried an armload of assault rifles, and they each had magazines shoved into every pocket on their cargo pants.

Kelvin and I flattened our backs against the wall to allow them room to pass. "Everything okay?" Cruz asked, eyeing Kelvin.

"We're all good. I'll see you in a few," I answered.

Cruz tipped up his chin, and they continued on down the hall.

At the end other end of the hall, we entered the living room. It was empty. Across the room, more doors opened to a shorter hallway with three rooms off the right side.

I opened the first one to a small room that could have been plucked from a college dorm. There were two twin beds, a nightstand between them, and a desk on each side of the room. Just inside was the door to a tiny bathroom.

I gestured to one of the beds. "Have a seat."

Kelvin sat down, and I sat on the other bed facing him. I leaned forward, resting my elbows on my knees, and clasped my hands. "One of the first things I learned when I joined Claymore back in 2010 was that we never give up company secrets. It was beaten into us, almost literally."

His eyes widened. "You worked at Claymore?"

"For a short time, I *owned* Claymore."

Kelvin's head pulled back with surprise. "Who are you?"

"My name is Warren. Damon Claymore is my father."

His jaw dropped, and he ran his hands down his cheeks.

"Damn." He studied my face for a moment. "You do kind of look like him."

I straightened. "You know what Damon looks like?"

Kelvin lifted a shoulder. "Of course. He's the CEO and the owner."

Azrael had always been the CEO and owner of Claymore. He hadn't always let himself be known. I had worked there for years and had never seen his face.

Damon Claymore was a ghost. A legend.

Now, something about him being so recognizable reminded me of his finite mortality.

"So you're Michael's brother?" With the mention of the name, concern flashed across Kelvin's face.

"Michael and I are *not* related."

Kelvin visibly relaxed.

"Why do you ask?"

He shifted on the mattress.

"You can speak freely. Nothing you say in this room will ever get back to your men. I promise you that."

After a moment of silent deliberation, Kelvin finally spoke. "I was among the first group of Claymore recruits who were given the new vaccine four years ago. We were about six weeks into training when they pulled us out of the chow hall one morning and sent us to the infirmary.

"It was surprising because we'd all gotten our shots on day two of orientation. It was even *more* surprising to see Michael Claymore—a kid, and the heir to the whole damn dynasty—there to watch us be injected."

"That had to have been strange. I don't guess he shows up often," I said.

"Never. It definitely stuck with me, you know?"

I nodded.

"Well, when I was in line to get my shot, I overheard one

of the veteran soldiers saying the vaccine should protect us from a new disease. All the way across the room, Michael perked up and looked over at the guy, like he'd heard him talking. Then two guards removed the dude, and we never saw him again."

"What do you think happened to him?"

"Honestly?" He looked around the room and lowered his voice. "I think they killed him. I tried looking him up a few times. His name was Carmichael, and I couldn't find him anywhere."

"What happened with your injection?"

"That shit hurt like hell. It was huge."

"And Michael was there the whole time?"

"The whole time and a few times after that. Like he was coming to check on us. Now, I think we were a bunch of guinea pigs."

I nodded. "I think that's a reasonable assumption."

"Fast forward a year, and people on the outside started getting sick. All those people died in Blackmouth, right down the interstate from our headquarters. Back then, I wondered if this was the reason for the new vaccine. And something in my gut told me Michael Claymore at least knew about it...or that he was behind it. It was just too damn coincidental."

*Coincidence.*

The word rattled around in my brain. It had always been a buzzword for me and Sloan before we knew what we were. So many strange events we couldn't find any better way to explain. Everything that had happened since she and I had met began with some kind of unexplainable *coincidence.*

"By the end of that year, almost everyone in my family was dead." His voice cracked. "They had moved to New Bern to be closer to me, and every single one of them got sick." He started counting on his fingers. "My mom, my dad, my two sisters,

LaShae and Katrina. Even my grandmother. LaShae was the only one who survived."

Leaning on my knees again, I steepled my fingers and rested my forehead on my fingertips. "Kelvin, I'm sorry."

"LaShae still needs around-the-clock care. The doctor's say her lungs and heart will never fully recover. We were lucky to find help when I was transferred to Asheville. Almost nobody got sick here."

"I know."

"It's because you're here, isn't it?"

I shook my head. "It's because my daughter is. She's the one who healed you."

A crease formed between his eyebrows. "Your daughter? You can't be old enough to be her dad. Your *sister*, maybe."

"It's a long story."

"I've got a feeling you could tell a lot of long stories."

"You have no idea."

"What I do know is Michael Claymore is responsible for the virus that killed my family. I have absolutely no doubt about that."

"Yet you still work for him."

"My sister depends on me. I'm all she has left. I have to provide for her, and it's not like I can accuse anybody of anything. You know they'd kill me just like they killed that guy, Carmichael."

Kelvin was probably right.

"When your daughter told me my boss was evil, I knew you guys were on the right side of this battle. And Michael's so afraid of you; I think you're the only person who can take him down."

"He's not afraid of me." I smiled with the satisfaction of knowing how dangerous Iliana was. "He's afraid of *her*."

"Iliana," he said.

I nodded.

"Is what she said true?" He visibly swallowed. "You're angels?"

"Yes, and Iliana is the most powerful one who's ever existed."

"And Damon and Michael Claymore?"

I thought for a second. "Damon is…a long story as well, but Michael is definitely an angel. A fallen one." I took a deep breath. "And you're right, he did kill all those people and your family."

Kelvin broke, slumping over onto his knees and burying his face in his hands. I didn't move. I didn't speak. I just let him cry.

After a minute or two, his sobs subsided. He sniffed and wiped his nose on his uniform's sleeve. "Are you really going to kill me?"

I chuckled. "Not unless I have to. Will you help us?"

Kelvin sobered. "I'll do anything I can."

"Those bullets, the angel killers, I need to know what's in them."

"My girlfriend works in the lab. She can probably find out."

I lifted an eyebrow. "Claymore has a lab?"

He nodded. "I actually met her because I was snooping around to see if it was true that they had developed a biological weapon. Turns out, her division is just one of many. She works in biological security."

"What is biological security?"

"The team that works on restraints for fairies"—he stopped himself—"for *angels*, I mean. They developed the cuffs that can take away your powers."

"Would she know about the bullets?"

"If she doesn't, she can put us in touch with someone who does."

"Think she'll be on board?"

"Oh yeah. A lot of employees would be. Most of us are just too scared to leave."

"You're right for being scared. And helping us will be dangerous. For you and for her."

He thought for a moment. "No more dangerous than working for a man who murdered a quarter of the world."

"Don't underestimate him. Your boss is not a man. His name isn't Michael Claymore; it's the Morning Star." I leveled a serious look at Kelvin. "And the Morning Star is Satan himself."

# CHAPTER FOURTEEN

*"Pssssst."*

I rubbed my face and rolled toward Fury. In the darkness and under the warmth of the covers, I curled my arm around her and nuzzled her bare back.

*"Pssssssssssssssttt..."*

Something grabbed my foot.

I bolted upright in bed with a loud gasp.

A woman screamed.

Then Fury screamed and reached for the pistol on the nightstand Kane had given her before bed. She and I were both panting.

The woman in our bedroom cowered back against the wall with her hands raised over her head. A picture frame crashed to the floor and shattered. She screamed again.

"What the hell is that? Another ghost?" Fury was aiming at the figure across the room.

"Not a ghost." The woman's soul was very familiar to me.

"Ahab, turn on the lights," Fury said to the computer system that controlled Echo-5.

Nothing happened. "I don't think that works down here." I brightened my wings.

The light reflected in a pair of bright blue eyes as wide as saucers.

Taiya.

Her hands were still raised in the air, and the tips of all her fingers bent in a silent wave of greeting.

My whole upper body slumped with relief. I pushed Fury's gun back down. "Taiya, what are you doing in here?"

With a groan, Fury put the gun back on the nightstand. She pulled the comforter up over her head as she flopped back down onto the mattress.

"I-I say hello?" Taiya stammered in English.

My head pulled back with surprise. She'd only ever really spoken Katavukai before. I smiled. "Hello. You can relax."

Slowly, Taiya lowered her arms.

Had I not known who she was, I never would've recognized her. Her red hair was still red, but rather than being long and stringy, it was thick and healthy and cut short at an angle toward her chin. Her face was lined with age, but her cheeks were plump and rosy.

She looked so much healthier than the last time I saw her. No longer malnourished. No longer pale and fragile.

She was the same age as Sloan, but thanks to constant exposure to her now-deceased demon father, Ysha, her mental development had stopped somewhere around age six. Consequences such as this were the main reason I was unable to raise my daughter.

That, and my unintentional seventeen-year absence.

I rubbed my eyes. "Did you need something?"

She ran across the room and threw her arms around my neck. With a startled laugh, I hugged her back. "I've missed you too."

Suddenly realizing I was naked under the covers, I eased her back and tugged the sheet up a little higher around my waist.

Taiya clasped her hands beneath her chin. "Miss Kathy says breakfast."

"Okay. We'll be upstairs soon."

My stomach growled at the thought of a home-cooked breakfast by Nathan's mother. Then my stomach dropped with the thought of having to tell her that her son was missing.

With a smile and another wave, Taiya skipped from the room, leaving the door open behind her. Light poured in from the hallway, and I dimmed my wings.

I picked up my boxer briefs off the floor and pulled them on before standing up.

"What time is it?" Fury asked, her voice muffled by the covers.

I closed the door and flipped on the bathroom light. Then I searched the room for a clock without finding one. "No idea."

"It feels like it's the middle of the night." She rolled onto her back.

"That it does." I gathered my clothes off the floor. "Nathan's mom is a wizard in the kitchen. I promise whatever she's made is worth getting up for."

"I know."

Of course she did. She and John had lived down the road from the McNamaras for a while.

Fury draped her arm across her forehead. "I am starving."

I stepped into my pants. "I want to check on Cassiel before I eat, but you can go on up without me."

"You still really care for her, don't you?"

"I do. Does it bother you?"

Fury shook her head. "I'd probably think something was wrong with you if you didn't. And we need her."

"Yes, we do. We have to find out what's in those bullets."

Fury rolled onto her side toward me. "I felt much better when you were truly bulletproof."

I smiled. "Worried about me?"

"Yes. If Iliana hadn't been there last night, Cassiel wouldn't have made it out of the yard."

"I hope we'll have some answers today."

"From that Claymore soldier?"

I nodded and stuck my arms through the sleeves of my T-shirt.

"Can we trust him?"

"We don't really have a choice. The only person who could tell us if he's lying is the one who needs his help most." I sat down to put on my socks and boots. "We're just going to have to revert to giving people the benefit of the doubt."

"People who work for the Morning Star."

Worry tumbled through my spirit. "We don't have another choice," I said again, as much for my own benefit as for hers.

"That sucks." She laid on her back again.

There was a knock at our door. "You guys OK in there?" Anya called. We'd shared one of the two-bedroom apartments with her.

"Come on in," I said.

She opened the door with a yawn. "I heard screaming." Anya's sweatshirt was on backward, and her hair was matted on the right side.

"We had an unexpected visitor." I tied my right boot. "Everything's fine. Taiya came to tell us breakfast is ready."

"Ugh. I'm going back to bed." She backed out of the room without another word.

I smiled back at Fury. "You two look alike, but that's about where the similarities end."

"Because she doesn't wake up in a panic?"

"That's one thing." I chuckled as I stood. "I was afraid bullets were going to fly."

"Anya isn't as easy to kill as I am," she said with a sigh.

"You are *far* from easy to kill." I walked around to her side of the bed. "Do you want to walk upstairs with me?"

"I'm going to see if there's hot water. If there is, I'd like to take a shower before I rejoin the world."

"All right. If you don't mind, I won't wait for you then."

"I don't mind. Go check on Cassiel. If I don't see you in the dining room, I'll save you a plate."

I leaned over her, bracing my arms against the mattress. "How are you doing? Seeing John yesterday must have been tough, and we haven't had any time alone to talk about it."

Her shoulders rose. "It was better than I expected. I thought for sure he'd shoot us both."

She was making light of it, a clear Fury-signal that she didn't want to rehash the situation. At least not before coffee.

I kissed her. "I'll see you in a little while?"

"Yeah."

I walked out of our apartment, a little disoriented. I'd been pretty tired the night before, and all the doors looked the same. Both doors at the ends of the hallway had exit signs.

With a mental coin toss, I turned right. That door was locked. I used my power to try to open it, but nothing happened.

"Wrong door," a voice said over an intercom. "That goes to the escape hatch."

Feeling like an idiot, I walked all the way to the other end of the hallway. That door was unlocked. I took the stairs up to the lobby, and the smell of sausage flooded my senses.

My knees wobbled, and my stomach growled.

Kane was cleaning a rifle at the lobby table.

"Man, do you ever rest?" I let the stairwell door close behind me with a heavy thud.

"About as much as you." He put the weapon down. "Sorry, we should've labeled the doors."

"It's OK. Seriously, did you get any sleep?" I asked.

"A couple of hours. I'll sneak a nap when Cruz is awake. You?"

"Yeah, but I don't even know what time it is."

He looked at his watch. "Eight thirty."

Fury and I had fallen into bed just before four.

I pointed up at the light bulb. "Explain to me why the power is on down here and not upstairs in Echo-5?"

"The bunker is on a completely separate power grid from the building. Az didn't want them linked if Echo-5 was compromised."

"Ironic," I said.

"You're telling me. There's Wi-Fi down here too. It's maddeningly slow, but it's so archaic it's almost unhackable. When I logged into the forum last night, I had a message waiting from Huffman."

I jerked upright. "And you didn't tell me?"

"You were finally going to bed, and he didn't have real info for us yet. I knew it could wait till morning."

"What'd he say?"

"He's been trying to reach us. Sent a warning while we were gone about a new weapon. Guess we know which one."

"What'd he say about it?"

"Nothing more than we were already told, but I asked for details. I'll let you know if I get a response."

I nodded. "Have you seen Cassiel yet?"

"Everyone was asleep when I went by there this morning to check on our prisoners. I didn't want to disturb them."

"Have you thought anymore about the risks of letting that guy Kelvin contact people on the inside at Claymore?"

"Thought about it? Sure. But I haven't come to any other conclusions besides *it's risky.* The alternative though is Cassiel will probably die."

"And lots of other angels might get killed as well."

"Weighing it out, I think it's worth letting him try. What's the worst that could happen? Claymore finds out where we're hiding, and the Morning Star tries to kill us?"

I smiled. "You're right."

"Rumor is, for the past few years, they've been flagging all calls into Claymore from this area, but if we use the computer upstairs, I can hook him up with a secure line that doesn't originate from this area. Again, risky, but worth it."

"I agree. We don't want to put our contacts on the inside in danger either if we can help it. Do we have any way to contact the Father? I feel like he and the other angels should be aware of this."

"The last we heard, he was traveling with Gabriel. I'll have Ionis contact him."

"Where is Ionis? I haven't seen him yet."

"He's probably asleep. He says he needs all the beauty rest he can get."

"That doesn't surprise me." I started toward the door.

"If you're hungry, breakfast is ready. You should probably get in there fast. Reuel just came up," he said.

"I want to see Cassiel first."

"Give her my best."

I gave him a thumbs-up as I walked into the hallway. Voices carried through the partially open door of the dining room, but I didn't pause for fear of being stopped before I could see Cassiel.

When I reached the infirmary, I saw Iliana asleep in a chair beside the bed. Because she had slept in the RV, she insisted that Fury and I get some sleep. She had stayed with Cassiel the rest of the night.

Across the bed, a human spirit hovered.

Dr. Robert Jordan.

It was a jarring sight. Outside Eden, I'd never seen the human soul of someone I knew so well. Dr. Jordan had almost been my father-in-law. I'd grown to love him like one, and he'd always treated me like a son.

Now his soul appeared old and weary. A consequence of being stuck in this realm.

When he saw me, he came out into the hallway, passing through the door without opening it. "Warren, my son." He embraced me. "Oh, how we've missed you."

I pulled back and held him at arm's length. "It's good to be home."

"How are you?"

"I'm well. Thankful to be back."

"Is what I've heard true?"

"That I thought I was only gone two days?"

He nodded.

"Yeah. It was a shock."

"I'm sure."

"And it's a shock seeing you like this."

His smile was sad. "I must count my blessings where I can find them. I'm no longer sick or in pain, and for that, I am thankful." He looked down at his ethereal body. "And this won't be forever, right?"

"Right. We are going to get you home to Eden."

"I'm sure you will." He glanced back into the infirmary. "But perhaps it's for the best that I'm here now. Your friend is very sick."

"Do you know what's wrong with her?"

"Without being able to do any tests, hemolytic anemia would be my guess. It seems something is destroying her red blood cells faster than her bone marrow is able to create more."

"Any idea how we stop it?"

"Not without knowing the cause. You should call in a medical professional to test for toxins."

"Toxins shouldn't affect angels," I said.

His head tilted forward. "Neither should swords."

Good point.

"We're waiting on news about what exactly was in that bullet."

He nodded. "You should hook up Cassiel to some monitors. We should be able to tell a lot from her vitals."

"Is it the same with angels as with humans?"

"Warren, a human would long be dead."

"You think the poison is deadly for everyone?"

"A human wouldn't have survived the bullet, never mind whatever's inside it."

He was right. Kelvin only survived because Iliana had been right there.

Dr. Jordan looked back through the glass. "You need a proper doctor and nurse. Someone who can at least start an IV and run some blood tests."

"I can start an IV."

"You can?"

I nodded. "I had basic field-medicine training when I was with the Marines. I started an IV on Fury when we were in Nulterra."

"OK. She needs fluids, at the very least, and probably something for the pain. There's morphine in the locked cabinet at the nurse's station."

"Our bodies metabolize it too quickly."

"Her cellular function is clearly inhibited. I think the morphine is worth a try."

"OK. Is there anything else we can give her that might slow the poison?"

He hesitated.

"What is it?"

"I wonder what might happen if she's transfused with some of Iliana's blood. Rh-null blood is called 'golden blood' for a reason. It can be given to anyone, regardless of blood type. And with Iliana's powers…"

"It might save Cassiel?"

He shrugged. "I really don't know."

"Any suggestions for a doctor we might call? Someone who isn't easily shocked, with the ability to keep their mouth shut?"

He thought for a moment. "I'll see if I can come up with some names."

"Thank you."

"I wish I could do more to help, but I seem to be cut off from everything material in this world." His eyes fell. "I can't even hug my own daughter."

I put my hand on his shoulder again. "It won't be forever," I repeated.

"I know. Where are Sloan and Nathan? I asked Iliana, but she was very vague with her answer."

I crossed my arms. "They're with Adrianne."

"You mean they're with the Morning Star."

"Yes, but we have no reason to believe he will harm them."

Dr. Jordan lifted an eyebrow. "He *will* use them as leverage. They aren't safe there."

There was no point in arguing. He was right.

"What can I do to help?" he asked.

"I don't know yet."

"But if you think of anything, you'll tell me?"

"Of course."

"I'll look in later on Cassiel."

I watched him walk down the hall toward the door. "Dr. Jordan?"

He looked back.

"Can you walk through doors and walls?" I asked.

The ghost smiled. "Only windows, my son."

Interesting. "How will you get out of the bunker?"

"Kane will let me out. We have a system."

The thought of their *system* intrigued me, but right now, Cassiel needed my attention. "We'll chat more later."

"Of course we will." Then he turned and disappeared through the door at the end of the hall. It had a window into the lobby.

"Damn," I whispered to myself.

When I walked inside, I realized Jett was asleep, sitting on the floor beside Iliana's legs. I blew out a sigh and walked past them to the nurse's station. Using my power, I opened all the locked cabinets until I found a morphine stash, a couple of bags of saline, and an IV start kit.

I carried them back to Cassiel's bedside, and the overwhelming stench of rotting meat burned my nose. Restraining my gag reflex, I hooked the saline bag onto the IV pole by her bed. The squeak of its rolling wheels echoed around the room.

Jett's eyes popped open with a startled jerk. "Warren."

I ripped open the IV supplies with my teeth. "Morning," I said and spat a piece of plastic onto the floor.

Jett pinched the bridge of his nose. "What time is it?"

"Eight thirty." I straightened Cassiel's arm. Her skin was hot to the touch, and her cheeks were red and splotchy. I tied a tourniquet around her upper arm.

"What are you doing?" Jett asked, standing.

"Her body needs fluids." I swabbed the inside of Cassiel's

elbow with alcohol, then slid the needle into an unnaturally black vein.

The needle prick exploded the vein, and a black starburst spread under her skin. I pulled out the needle and swore. "Jett, wake up Iliana."

He turned toward her. "Iliana."

She groaned, sounding just like her mother.

"There's a problem," he said.

In the corner of my eye, I saw her bolt upright. "What happened?" she asked.

"Blew a vein." I moved out of Iliana's way. "They're really weak."

She spread her healing light over Cassiel's arm. After a few seconds, Cassiel drew in a raspy breath.

Iliana looked over at Jett. "The smell is getting worse."

"What is it?" Jett asked.

"Death," I answered, and I wasn't joking. It was the same smell that emanated from freshly rotting corpses.

"I think the bleeding under her skin stopped." Iliana pulled her hands away and moved back. "Want to try the needle again?"

"Yeah." I found a different vein. One that appeared normal compared to the last. My hands trembled as I slid the needle in through the skin again.

That time, it worked.

I let out a slow exhale and finished hooking her up to the bag.

"I didn't know you could do that," Iliana said.

"I didn't either," I replied with a smile. "It's a skill I learned a few lifetimes ago, and I have had to do it twice in the last week." I moved to the head of the bed and felt Cassiel's forehead. "She's burning up."

"She's fighting hard. I'm not surprised she has a fever." Iliana sat on the bed. She gave a violent yawn.

I palmed the back of Iliana's head. "Why don't you go get some sleep? I'll sit with her a while."

"Did you sleep at all?"

"I did. Thank you. Now it's your turn."

She flexed her fingers a few times. "I'll give her another treatment, then we'll go."

*We?* My eyes flashed across the room to Jett, but by some miracle, I kept my mouth shut.

Iliana's healing light burned in her palms, weaker and dimmer than it had been the night before.

"How many times did you treat her during the night?" I asked.

"About once an hour until I was too exhausted to continue." She pressed the light into Cassiel's chest, and immediately, Cassiel's breathing steadied.

I studied Iliana's tired face. "It takes a lot out of you, doesn't it?"

"I'll be okay." She forced a weak smile.

"Your grandfather said we should get a doctor in here to test for toxins," I said.

"Papa was here?"

"When I came in."

She looked surprised. "I saw him last night, but I didn't hear him come in this morning."

I cracked a grin. "Would you?"

"Yeah, I guess you're right," she said with a smile.

"I told him about your mom and Nathan."

Iliana grimaced. "I didn't want him to worry until we knew more."

"Wondering makes parents worry even more," I said.

She nodded, but I could see her own concern bubbling in her tired eyes.

I stood and hooked a finger under her chin to lift her face. "Iliana, we will get them back. If I have to burn down the whole state of North Carolina, I will get your mom and dad out of there."

"I know you will." She stretched on her toes to hug me.

I held her head against my chest and pressed a kiss into her hair.

"Where is he?" A shrill shriek behind me sent a shiver up my spine. I turned and saw a blonde with inch-thick makeup and a messy morning updo.

"Shannon Green," I said.

"Shannon Green-Reese," she snapped, without looking at me. She was glaring at Jett with her hands on her hips. She wore a maroon velvet jumpsuit and pink slippers with white pompoms on top of the toes.

Clearly on a mission, she stalked across the room and pounded her finger against Jett's breastbone. "I know you know where he is. Where's Nico?"

Jett held up his hands and backed a few steps away. "As far as I know, Rogan is trying to get back here, but I haven't talked to him today."

For the first time since we'd met, I actually felt bad for the guy.

"You get him on the phone right now!"

"He doesn't have a phone," Iliana said.

Shannon's hands flailed wildly beside her ears. "Then use your angel walkie-talkies, and tell me where my son is!"

"It isn't safe," Jett said.

Jett most certainly had been communicating with Rogan, but there was no way on earth he'd tell Shannon of her son's whereabouts. Shannon's personality had always screamed *liability*, but now she seemed downright hysterical.

I wondered if the Botox had seeped into her bloodstream.

"Shannon? Hello?" I said, waving my hand toward her face.

This time, she did a double take when she registered who I was. "My god. Warren?"

"In the flesh."

Her eyes doubled, and she crossed the room, moving Iliana out of her way. Shannon grabbed my face and studied it. "Goodness, what's your secret?"

"My secret?"

"You haven't aged a day!"

Shannon couldn't say as much about herself. The skin of her face seemed to have been pulled back with the strength of gravity, and concealer, a shade too light, was caked under her eyes.

Iliana had stumbled into Jett, and he was holding her arm. "He's been stuck in Hell, Shannon," she said.

Shannon dropped her hands. "Haven't we all, honey?"

"Are you living here now?" I asked.

"Oh no, but one of the thugs who works here came and picked us up a couple of days ago. He forced us to come."

"Forced you?" Jett said, his voice laced with doubt.

"He was *very* insistent," she snapped. "Said there was trouble again. Is Nico part of it? He'd better not be…"

Behind her, Jett rolled his eyes. "Rogan isn't even here."

Iliana took a step toward her. "Nico is fine. You being here is just a precaution until things settle down."

"What things? Where's Sloan?" Shannon whirled around like Sloan might be hiding in a corner.

"She's with Adrianne," I said.

Shannon's head snapped back with so much force she could

have fractured a vertebra. "Adrianne *Marx?*" She twisted Adrianne's last name like it tasted bad in her mouth.

I chuckled. Some things were as constant as the rising and setting of the sun.

"Yes. She and Nathan are at Adrianne's beach house," Jett said.

"Beach house? Sloan's at a beach house while I'm stuck in this dump. We don't even have any power upstairs!" Midrant, Shannon's eyes drifted past me and settled on Cassiel. They widened with shock, like she hadn't even noticed her before. "What's going on with Angel Barbie?"

Oh, I bet Cassiel loved that nickname.

"She's sick," Iliana said.

Shannon wagged her finger at all of us. "But Nico told me you guys can't get sick."

I shook my head. "We can't, yet here we are. Obviously, we don't know exactly what we're up against right now. So we need you to stay close so we can keep you safe."

"Keep me safe?" She pointed at the bed. "Looks like you can't even keep yourselves safe."

Iliana sandwiched Shannon's hand between her own. "Nico would want you to wait here until he returns."

I wasn't so sure about that.

But it seemed to be the magic words Shannon needed. "He'll worry if we're at home?"

*No.*

"Yes." Iliana pulled Shannon's hand closer to her heart. "You don't want to make Nico worry."

Shannon's eyes were glazed over. Iliana had her under some kind of spell. Angels of Life were a tricky bunch.

"OK." Shannon gave a singsong sigh. "We'll wait. Is there anything I can do to help her?" She glanced toward Cassiel.

"Know any good doctors who could treat an angel without

asking too many questions?" I asked without too much thought.

"Yes."

My eyes darted toward her. "What?"

"Dr. Swain has been treating Nico since his *incident*. She's become a close friend of the family."

The "incident" would have been Rogan's kidnapping.

Iliana looked up at me. "He was really sick when we got him back."

"I guess this is why," I said, nodding toward Cassiel. "Was the doctor able to make Nico better?" I asked Shannon.

"Honestly, I think Iliana helped him most, but Dr. Swain is a fine physician."

"Can you call her?" Iliana asked.

Shannon held up her hands. "Not from inside this fortress."

"Jett, take Shannon to the lobby. Tell Kane she needs to use a phone A-sap," I said.

With a nod, Jett walked to the door.

"Hold on! What do I tell her? Doctors don't just make house calls anymore," Shannon said.

"Tell her to bring supplies for a blood transfusion," I said.

"A transfusion?" She looked at Cassiel again. "Is it that bad?"

"Yes," I said. "We also need her to test Cassiel's blood for toxins. We think she's been poisoned."

"Poisoned…oh my."

Iliana stood in front of Shannon. "Can you do this for us? For Nico?"

Shannon's head twitched. "Yeah. I'll do it."

"Thank you," Iliana said.

Shannon left with Jett, and I looked at my daughter. "You just used your power on her."

"No. That was straight manipulation." Iliana returned to Cassiel. She put her hand on her forehead. "Her temperature is coming down, I think, but it might go back up once my power wears off."

"Hopefully, it won't before you've had a chance to get some rest," I said.

The statement triggered a yawn from her. "On that note, I'm going to lie down."

"Where will I find you if there's an emergency?"

"In the big apartment downstairs. Kane and Jett have keys."

"Jett won't be with you, then?"

"No, Appa," she said, shaking her head. She kissed my cheek. "Send for me if she gets worse."

"I will."

When Iliana was gone, I sat on the edge of the mattress and took Cassiel's cold hand. Someone had dressed her in a thin hospital gown, and she was covered in two thick blankets. There were no machines. No heart monitors or respirators. Just her, lying helpless on the bed.

I stroked her hand. The skin was so pale it was almost clear. I could see the tendons and tiny bones, and her veins had all but disappeared. When I felt for a pulse in her wrist, it was so faint I almost missed it.

Her hand twitched, and I looked up to see her eyes cracked open. I stood and pushed her golden hair off her forehead. "Cassiel, can you hear me?"

The slightest flutter of her eyelashes confirmed she could.

"We're getting you some help. I need you to hang on a little longer."

Tears leaked from the corners of her eyes as a faint sound escaped her cracked lips. I leaned my ear close to her mouth, and the sound came again. It was barely a whisper.

"Hurts."

My throat clenched. "I'm sorry. I'll get the morphine."

I stepped away, but she let out a dry grunt in protest.

Her fingers stretched toward me.

I took her hand again and eased back down beside her.

She closed her eyes again. Just when I thought she'd fallen from consciousness, she sucked in a shaky breath. "I'm going to die."

The words were barely audible.

"Don't talk like that. You're not going to die because I won't let that happen."

The corners of her mouth twitched like she was trying to smile. "Always in control."

"Me or you?" I asked, making a pathetic attempt at being lighthearted.

When she didn't answer, I leaned closer. "Cassiel, I need your help. You're the smartest person I know."

Her eyes opened to slits again.

"Is there *anything* that might have done this to you? Any kind of poison or weapon that could harm an angel like this?"

She shook her head just enough for me to know the answer.

I looked down at her hand in mine "Are you worse with me being here?"

If Cassiel were human, she'd already be dead with me so close.

"Stay," she whispered.

"I'm not going anywhere."

She was quiet for a little longer. Her breaths were ragged and shallow. I feared she might be right. She sounded like she was dying.

"San…" She wheezed in. "Sandalphon."

"I haven't heard anything yet, but we're trying to contact someone on the inside. As soon as we get word, I'll tell you." I gently squeezed her fingers. "So I need you to hold on until we get word."

"You…need…to find…swords."

"Swords can wait until you're better."

The sliding door opened behind me. I turned and saw Fury as she walked past the nurse's desk holding a bag and two coffee mugs.

"Hey," I said as she came in. "That was fast."

"I worried Reuel might get to the food before we did, so I came on up. I ran into Iliana in the dining room. She said you were staying in here. Figured I'd bring you some breakfast." She lifted the bag.

"Thanks." I tilted my head toward the rolling bed table. "You can put it there. I'll get to it in a few."

Fury put down the bag and one of the mugs. "How is she?"

"She's awake right now." I looked back at Cassiel. Her eyes were closed again. "She's in a lot of pain."

"Can we give her something? If this is like the triage rooms in Azrael's other bunkers, there's probably pain meds in one of these cabinets."

"I don't think she wants any. I am going to stay with her a while," I said.

Fury carried her mug over to me. "OK. I'm going to eat and go back to the apartment."

I nodded.

"Can she hear me?"

"Yeah."

Taking care not to spill her coffee, Fury leaned toward her face. She spoke softly in Katavukai. *"Ciyet ai kayam. Ala rattanai ain alis."*

"Thank you," Cassiel breathed. "But Fury…"

Fury paused.

Cassiel's blue eyes opened. "There's no one to hear your prayers."

# CHAPTER FIFTEEN

"Oh. My. God. It's true?"

I'd recognize that high-pitched voice anywhere. I dropped my feet off Cassiel's bedside and sat up as Ionis came into the room. "Hey, you."

Ionis tore his worried eyes from Cassiel and blinked a few times when he looked at me. Then his face softened, like he'd suddenly realized who was standing in front of him. "Oh, Warren." He threw his arms around me, pinning mine against my sides.

I laughed. "I missed you too." I wiggled one arm free and hugged the small messenger.

"We thought you were—"

"Dead?" I pulled back. "I've heard that a *lot*."

For the first time I'd ever seen, Ionis's hair was long and straight. With his pale skin and chiseled cheekbones, he was only lacking pointy ears to be an elf from *The Lord of the Rings*.

"You were in Nulterra the whole time?"

"The whole time. Which was only a couple of days for me and Fury. We figured out how the Morning Star sidestepped his fate in the Thousand Year Prophecy. Time all but stood still down there."

"Is it true you destroyed Nulterra completely?"

I nodded.

"What happened to the fallen?"

"I assume they're gone. None of them followed us out of that hole."

An unmistakable flash of sadness crossed his eyes.

"You all right?" I asked.

"Yeah, but it's big news. The angels…" He swallowed. Then he jerked his head upright. "But don't think I'm sorry. I'm not—"

I put a hand on his shoulder. "Calm down. They got what they deserved, but that doesn't mean you have to be happy about it. The angels have been together since the beginning of time. If their demise didn't affect you, I'd worry you were a psychopath."

"It's a little hard to stomach." His eyes shifted back to Cassiel. "We're supposed to be immortal."

"I know."

"Do you think she's dying?"

"I think her body is dying, at least. Not sure about her spirit." I walked over and checked Cassiel's forehead temperature again.

"But her body." Ionis looked down at his own figure and whimpered. "I really like mine."

"Yes, we all know you do."

Fury and Anya walked in. Fury's hair was damp from the shower. "Ionis?" she asked.

He spun around so fast his white hair whipped over his face. "Fury. Whoa…and Fury's twin, I presume?" Ionis did a small bow in front of Anya. "No need to ask which one's the evil twin." He pointed at Fury.

Anya laughed and nudged Fury with her elbow. "I think my sister had some quick anger management down in that pit."

Ionis looked up at me. "You have something to do with that?"

I grinned.

"Oh yeah?" He thrust his hips forward a few times.

I shoved him sideways. "Ionis!"

He laughed. "You should be proud. No telling how many lives you"—his eyes sank to below my belt—"might have saved."

Fury crossed her arms. "I say we test out one of those bullets on Ionis."

"Eek!" He hid behind my arm.

Something beeped overhead. We all looked up.

"Warren, it's Kane. Can you meet me on the main floor of Echo-5?" Kane said over a loudspeaker I wasn't aware existed.

I looked at Fury.

"Go," she said. "We'll sit with Cassiel a while."

I kissed her. "Thank you. Iliana is in the large apartment downstairs if there's a problem."

"OK."

I looked back at the messenger. "Ionis, are you coming with me? I need to talk to you."

"You bet. Angel business is *my* business." His chest puffed out proudly.

I kissed Fury's cheek once more before Ionis followed me to the hallway. "Have you talked to Kane yet this morning?" I asked.

"Was I supposed to?"

"He was going to find you. We need you to get in touch with Gabriel and tell him what's happening with Cassiel. All the angels need to know about this threat."

"To do that, I'll have to go outside." His nose scrunched at the idea. "I don't wanna get shot."

"I'll take you myself."

"So brave." He smiled and batted his eyelashes up at me. I was pretty sure he was wearing mascara.

The door to the kitchen and dining room was open when we passed by. "Warren?" a woman asked.

Ionis and I stopped, and I looked inside.

"Bless my soul." At the sink, Kathy McNamara covered her mouth with her rubber-gloved hands. "Warren?" She peeled off the gloves and dropped them beside the sink as I stepped inside.

Nathan's mother was the cookie-baking grandma nursery rhymes were written about. She was round with wavy white hair and glasses with bright red frames.

"Is it really you?" she asked, grabbing my biceps.

"It's really me. Hi, Kathy."

She hugged me. "Lord, have mercy. I can't believe you're alive."

Over her shoulder, I saw her husband, whose name escaped me, getting up from one of the tables. Sitting with him was a young man with shaggy black hair and olive skin. His eyes were mismatched, brown and dark blue.

Kathy pulled away from me and turned toward her husband. "Warren, you remember James."

James came closer with his hand extended. "Good to see you again, son."

The title somehow comforted me. These grandparents to my daughter could have easily believed that I'd abandoned her all those years.

I smiled as I pumped his fist. "Good to see you again too, sir. Thank you both for helping take care of my little girl."

James tilted his gray head. "I do believe she's the one taking care of us."

"I'm learning that about her."

"Any word from Nathan and Sloan?" he asked.

I shook my head. "We're working on that, but I'm sure they're OK."

*For now.*

James's unconvinced eyes told me he was thinking the same.

Kathy seemed to be holding her breath, and when I didn't elaborate with any news, her eyes searched the room like she was searching for something good to hold onto. She found the boy at the table, and she immediately perked up.

"Oh! I don't guess you've met our other grandchild." Kathy snapped her fingers toward him. "Come here and say hello."

The young man peeled himself from his chair with all the speed and enthusiasm of an arthritic ninety-year-old. He tossed his head to the side, swooshing his dark bangs out of his eyes.

"You must be Luca." I offered him my hand, and he shook it. "I'm Warren."

"You're Iliana's dad?"

I nodded.

"Did you really go to Hell?"

"Luca!" Kathy snapped. "Language."

"It's a place, Nana," he argued.

"He's right, but only humans call it Hell. It was called Nulterra."

Luca smiled, his hair falling back into his eyes. "That's *stupe.*"

"Stupe?" I asked, confused.

"Badass," he translated.

"Luca!" Kathy said again. "Go finish the dishes. And wash your mouth out with soap while you're at it."

Luca waved. "Nice to meet you, Warren."

"You too."

James smiled. "I swear, kids these days have their own language."

"I'm afraid it's going to take me a long time to catch up." I smiled at Kathy. "Thanks for breakfast. As always, it was delicious."

"Oh, thank you. I'm glad you got to eat. This kitchen is not quite as nice as the one aboveground, but it will do."

James glanced up. "Any idea when we might be released to go back upstairs?"

"Yeah. The connection speed down here is killing me," Luca added.

"Kane and I need to address some security concerns with the building, but I hope we'll get that resolved today."

James patted my arm. "You're busy. We won't keep you."

"Hopefully, we'll have plenty of time to chat soon. I don't plan on getting stuck anywhere else for the next seventeen years."

He smiled. "We all certainly hope not."

I waved as Ionis and I walked back out and continued down the hall.

Lex was at the desk in the lobby. "Morning," he said, looking up at me from his coffee. "Kane's looking for you."

"I heard. I'm on my way up now. Any idea why?"

"Didn't say. He took one of the Claymore soldiers up to the control room upstairs. Ground level. The door across from the living room."

"Is the power back on up there?" Ionis asked.

"Must be. The cameras in the building are working."

"Hallelujah!" Ionis sang.

I frowned as we started toward the door. "Don't get excited. It's probably not staying on."

"I am excited. We can take the elevator." He linked his arm through mine as we crossed the decontamination room. "Do you *know* how many steps it is up to the top?"

"We came down them last night."

"But you haven't had to go up them." He patted my forearm. "Trust me, you should be thankful for the elevator too."

When we entered the long concrete corridor, Reuel's back was toward us, far up ahead. He turned around when he heard the door.

"Hey!" I called. "Where are you headed?"

Reuel pointed up.

"I think he was looking for a more specific answer," Ionis said, shaking his head.

"*Kupa aral,*" Reuel clarified.

"Us too. Did Kane call you?" I asked.

Reuel nodded. "*Akai enta ai utal vliye.*"

Ionis stopped walking. "Kane needs your help *outside*?"

Reaching back, I grabbed the front of his shirt. "Come on. Stop being such a baby."

We caught up with Reuel. "Did Kane say why?" I asked.

He shook his head.

Reuel let out a happy, quiet squeal when he saw the lights on above the elevator.

Ionis pointed at him. "See? Reuel gets it."

I grimaced. "Maybe this isn't a good—"

"You're being ridiculous." Ionis pressed the up button, and the elevator roared to life. "You just survived Nulterra. You can't be whining about an elevator. I get so dizzy trying to fly up that staircase." He whirled his finger up in a spiral.

I cocked an eyebrow. "You don't even walk?"

"Of course not."

It was a long wait until the elevator doors opened. Unsurprising since we were a long way beneath the ground.

The three of us stepped inside, and I pressed the button for the ground level.

*"Iru ai Cassiel?"* Reuel asked.

I lifted both shoulders. "She's about the same. It doesn't look good."

"But Iliana can keep her alive, right?" Ionis asked.

"For now. We're working as hard as we can to find—"

The elevator lurched to a stop, and the lights cut out.

Ionis squeaked. "Oh no."

"Damn it, Ionis. Why do I listen to you?" I brightened my wings. "Kane must have cut the power to the building again."

Ionis was biting down on the insides of his lips. "My bad." He started pushing buttons on the panel. "Maybe Kane is rebooting something."

We waited for a few moments, but the power never came back on.

Ionis was fanning his face with his hand. "Anybody else feel like this space is getting smaller?"

I let out a frustrated sigh and put my hands on my hips. "So how do we get out of here without destroying anything?"

Above us was a covered escape hatch. It was too high for me to reach, and the elevator was too small for me to use my wings. "Can you give me a boost?" I asked Reuel.

With a nod, he bent his knees and laced his fingers together. I put my boot in his hands, and he hoisted me up with so much force I smacked my head against the ceiling. "Ow!"

He grimaced. "Sorry."

When the stars dancing around my vision stopped, I used my power to open the lock on the outside of the hatch—a trick I'd watched my daughter perform during our escape from

Claymore. This elevator was much smaller than the one in the prison, but luckily, it was a similar design. The lock opened, and I pushed the hatch door up and out of the way.

Reuel helped me up through the hole, and I climbed out and stood on top of the elevator. The dark tunnel disappeared high above me into blackness. We were very far below the surface, and it was a thousand degrees inside the tall shaft.

I stretched my wings. There was just enough room for them to miss the walls and cables. Still, flying up the tight space would be precarious. We'd done it when we escaped from Claymore, but that had been like bull-in-a-china-shop flying. Here, we couldn't afford to demolish the elevator shaft.

"Warren, a hand?" Ionis called from down below.

Kneeling down, I reached through the hole and grasped Ionis's small hand. I pulled him up with little effort.

Ionis moved over as Reuel reached up and easily grabbed the rim of the hole. He jumped, and the entire metal ceiling bowed under his weight. I stumbled forward but planted a foot across the concave surface before I fell.

Ionis latched onto me.

"Oops." Reuel reached through the deformed square and pulled himself up. His shoulders wedged through one at a time, but somewhere around nipple-level, he got stuck. His eyes widened with worry.

"Oh shit," I said.

The metal creaked under his weight. He threw his large shoulders side to side, but his body didn't budge.

"Can you drop back down?" I knelt again. "I can fly up and get Kane to turn on the power."

Reuel wiggled. I pushed against his shoulders, and Ionis jumped up and down. But nothing happened.

Ionis tapped Reuel's forehead. "This is what happens when you eat four breakfasts."

Reuel frowned.

The elevator lurched again. I grabbed hold of the cables attached to the top of it, and Ionis, who was crouching, grabbed onto Reuel. Gears turned overhead, and we started to rise.

Fast.

"What do we do?" Ionis asked, panicked.

The bloody elevator scene from *The Shining* flashed through my mind. I imagined the outer doors being coated with our blood as our bodies were crushed against the ceiling.

Looking up, light was shining near the top. We needed to stop. Now.

*Brakes. We need brakes.* The walls were concrete and too far apart for me to reach, so manually stopping it—if I even could —was out.

The elevator ran between steel guides in the corners of the shaft. I held my hands toward two of them and blasted them with laser-sharp energy. Sparks showered down on us, and the metal peeled up as we rose, rolling and bending over on itself, like two large balls of crumpled aluminum foil.

When we neared the top, I dropped my hands and knelt down over Ionis and Reuel, shielding them from whatever our fate was above. With an ear-piercing *shrieeeeeeeek* of metal grinding against metal, the elevator slowed.

And stopped.

I let out the breath I'd been holding and sat back on my heels. Sweat drizzled down my forehead. We were close enough to the ground-floor doors that I could stand and touch them.

"Oh my god! You saved us!" Ionis threw his arms around my neck, toppling me over onto my ass.

When he released me, I bent my knees and rested my arms

over them, sucking in deep breath after deep breath to steady my panting. "That was close."

Reuel grabbed my foot and squeezed.

The gears were still humming, and I caught a whiff of smoke. But the elevator, thankfully, wasn't going anywhere.

I stood when I finally caught my breath.

With a loud hiss, the gears stopped, and the elevator shaft went dark again. A moment later, there were footsteps on the other side of the doors.

"Warren!" Kane yelled.

"We're in here!" I called back.

"Hang on. I'll get you out." I heard the clinking of keys. "I called Lex on the radio to see where you were, and he said you were on your way up. I yelled through the stairwell and didn't hear you, so I assumed you were stuck on the elevator after I shut it down."

The double doors to the lobby finally slid open. Kane stuck his head through and looked down. "What the hell happened?"

"Warren saved us!" Ionis replied.

"Save you from what?"

"From being crushed to death," Ionis said.

Kane's brow crumpled with confusion. "What?"

"We had gotten on top of the elevator to fly out of here, and Reuel got stuck. When the elevator started to rise, we were trapped," I explained.

Ionis slapped my chest. "This guy stopped the elevator before it smashed us against the ceiling."

Kane grinned and pointed up. "You know there's like eight feet between the elevator and the ceiling, right?"

My mouth fell open.

Kane started laughing. "How did you stop it?"

My jaw shifted to the side. "Uh…"

"He jammed up the tracks with metal," Ionis answered for me.

Kane pinched the bridge of his nose. "Well, that won't be easily fixed."

I cringed. "My bad," I said, quoting Ionis from earlier.

Still chuckling, Kane reached down into the shaft. "Come on, I have something to show you."

# CHAPTER SIXTEEN

"I'm really sorry about the elevator," I said as we followed Kane to Echo-5's control room.

"Don't worry about it. It won't kill anyone to take the stairs for a while." He pushed open the door.

The control room had one whole wall of flat-screen televisions with security-camera footage. In front of it, Kelvin Holmes was handcuffed and duct-taped to an office chair.

I looked at Kane.

He shrugged. "I told him I don't trust him as much as you do, and that I can't kill him without making a mess."

Kelvin's eyes widened, and everyone else snickered.

Kane rolled him to the side and sat down in another chair at the desk. "I think I've figured out a way to bring the power back on but keep the system completely offline."

"How?" I asked.

He pointed to one of the video feeds outside. It was the "tree" Nathan had installed, a powerful cell-phone tower that connected the building with Claymore headquarters.

He looked back at me. "We need to take the whole thing down."

"You want to chop down the ugly fake tree?" Ionis asked.

"Well, it's made of titanium, so chopping isn't an option." Kane looked at Reuel. "Ripping it out of the ground, however, should be an easy task for you."

Ionis scowled. "An easy task? This guy couldn't free himself from the elevator hatch."

Reuel argued in Katavukai that if he could've wedged his hands between himself and the hole's edge, it wouldn't have been a problem.

Ionis cut him off. "Sure, sure. Good to know the strongest angel of the auranos can be defeated by a hula hoop made of steel."

Kane chuckled, but he held up a hand to silence them. "We don't have a lot of time here."

"Reuel, can you take down the tower?" I asked.

He gave a single confident nod.

"Okay. I'll go out with him and Ionis when we're done here. Ionis is going to contact the Father," I said.

"Good," Kane said.

Ionis clasped his hands beneath his chin. "If the power is coming back on, does that mean we can all move back upstairs?"

Kane grimaced. "We just need the power to run the cameras and the electric fences around the property. I don't recommend anyone staying aboveground until we have a lot more information."

"I agree. It's too risky right now," I said firmly.

Ionis sighed.

I ignored him. "Are we ready to make a phone call to Claymore?"

"Ready if you are," Kane said.

I looked at Kelvin. "You ready?"

"Y-yes, sir." Kelvin certainly didn't *sound* ready, but he used his feet to scoot closer to Kane. "Wait a second."

We looked at him.

"Claymore's cyber-security team will know if you call from this building. I don't want them to suspect my girlfriend of anything." He lowered his voice. "I don't want her to get hurt."

"We don't want that either," I said.

Kane tapped a few buttons on the computer's keyboard. "We can mask the location by sending the call through a VPN. Even if Claymore sees a call come through, they won't know it's from us."

Kelvin nodded nervously.

I really wished Cassiel was with us. She would know for sure if he was trustworthy. By doing this, I wasn't just entrusting him with her life, but potentially all of ours.

I turned his chair for him to face me, and I leaned down so we were almost nose to nose. "Kelvin, if you betray us, I will see to it that you and everyone you love dies a slow and painful death."

It was a good thing Kelvin couldn't tell I was bluffing. I wasn't above taking human lives in war, but I would never go after his innocent loved ones.

He didn't have to know that.

I let him shake with fear on his office chair. "I promise. I only want to help." Poor guy looked like he might have to change his pants.

I turned him back toward the desk and gave Kane a nod.

"Okay, what's your girlfriend's number?" Kane asked, his fingers ready above the keyboard.

As Kevin spouted off the digits, Kane tapped them into the computer. He hit send, and a moment later the room was filled with the sound of the line ringing.

On the third ring someone picked up. "This is Chimera."

All the oxygen was sucked out of the room.

Kane's hand slammed onto the keyboard, ending the call before Kelvin could speak—or before anyone else could gasp with horror. I covered my eyes with my hand and groaned.

"What? Why did you hang up?" Kelvin asked.

I peeked at him through my fingers. He was either genuinely confused or the absolute best liar I'd ever met. And I'd met the Morning Star, so that was saying something.

"Reuel!" Kane spun around in his chair. "Open that metal panel by the door and flip the big red breaker."

Reuel opened the panel door, flipped a switch, and the whole room went dark.

I dropped my hand. "Your girlfriend is Chimera?"

"Yeah?" Confused, he didn't sound so sure.

I brightened my wings, and Kelvin scooted back in his chair. "Whoa."

Kane looked at me. "Can we kill him now?"

"What's the matter?" Kelvin asked, casting desperate looks around the group.

Ionis walked over and thumped Kelvin on the forehead. "You're sleeping with the enemy, soldier!"

"Huh?" Kelvin struggled against his handcuffs. "Chimera's really high up in the company. She could get you whatever information you want!"

I crossed my arms. "How long have you two been dating?"

Before Kelvin could answer, Kane raised his hand. "About as long as you've been working here in Asheville?"

Kelvin's mouth parted. "Well…"

Kane sighed and sat back in his chair.

"What's happening? I don't understand!" Kelvin's voice was higher than ever.

"Hate to break it to you, Kelvin, but she's using you to spy on what's happening here." I walked over beside Kane and leaned my arms on the desk. "Now what?"

"Now we wait to hear back from Huffman."

"Hold on just a damn minute," Kelvin said. "Are you serious? Chimera is using me?"

Ionis shook his head in disbelief. "What women say is right. Human men really are stupid."

I straightened. "Chimera is part-angel, part-human. She's been working for the Morning Star since before he was even born."

"Before he was born? How is that possible?"

"It's a *lot* to explain. You'll have to trust me," I said.

"But long story short, we won't be getting any help from Chimera," Kane said.

Kelvin blew out a shaky breath. "I swear I didn't know. Please don't kill me."

I shook my head. "No one's going to kill you."

"Really?" Kane asked.

I ignored him. "Have you checked to see if anything's come through from Huffman?"

"A few times. Nothing yet."

"Why not call him?" Kelvin asked. "I have his number in my phone."

Kane and I looked at each other. He lifted a shoulder. "It's your call, man."

Calling Huffman—our friend—directly was dangerous, but Cassiel was running out of time and we were out of options. "You're sure the line is untraceable?" I asked.

"It's *supposed* to be," Kane answered.

My head felt like it might explode. I rubbed my temples and pressed my eyes closed, playing out all the scenarios that might happen if we were to act…

And all the scenarios that might happen if we didn't.

"Do it." My eyes popped open. "Call Huffman."

Kelvin swiveled toward me. "I need my phone back."

"We have his number," Kane said, his worried voice barely audible. "Reuel, the power."

Reuel flipped the power breaker again, and my heart raced as the computer booted back up. Kane finally tapped the number into the keyboard, and the line began to ring.

I leaned my arms against the desk again for support.

"This is Huffman."

The room was dead silent.

"Hello?" he asked.

"Huffman, it's Shadow," I said, referencing an old nickname, a throwback to my days as a Marine.

More silence.

I felt sick. "Do you copy?"

"Holy shit. Is it really you?" Huffman asked.

"It's really me."

"Where did we first meet?"

This was a test. "About a hundred and sixty klicks north of Sadr City in a shithole concrete building." I grinned. "You promised to be my worst nightmare."

He chuckled on the other end of the line. "I still am, you bastard. Where the hell have you been?"

"Stuck between worlds."

"Seriously?"

"Unfortunately, yeah. I'm afraid we don't have much time."

"Your whole group is being watched," he said quietly.

"I'm not surprised. Listen, what do you know about this new round Claymore has developed? It's called the…" I looked at Kelvin.

"The 5.56 Yahweh," Huffman answered before Kelvin could.

"Yeah, that's it."

"I got Kane's message. I've been trying to figure out a way

to get this information to you guys. The round was just officially released a few weeks ago."

"What can you tell us?"

"Inside the bullet is a pellet containing an engineered chemical agent called *hydrogen necroxide.* Once the pellet membrane dissolves and the chemical is released into the bloodstream, it binds to Rh-null blood cells. Have you seen elephant's toothpaste?"

"Yes," Kane said.

My brow crumpled. "Is that a real thing?"

"Search online for a video when we get off here," Huffman said. "In this case, it's sort of like pouring peroxide onto a cut. You know how it fizzles?"

"Yeah," I said.

"Instead of fizzling, the toxin combines with the Rh-null blood cells to form a foam. A highly toxic foam that destroys everything it touches. It basically melts angels from the inside out."

I thought of how hot Cassiel's forehead was. "It only binds with Rh-null?"

"Correct."

Kane looked up at me and lowered his voice to barely above a whisper. "Explains why Iliana could heal Kelvin and not Cassiel."

I closed my eyes, swallowing hard all the emotion that threatened to bubble up from my chest. "Does it have the ability to destroy the spirit as well as the body?"

"It might. It's rumored they melted down a sword like yours for the compound, but I have no proof. That's way above my pay grade."

I swore.

"What about a treatment?" Kane asked.

I wasn't the only one holding my breath.

"They say there isn't one."

I hung my head.

Ionis whimpered.

"So I'd stay clear of it, if I were you," Huffman said.

I sighed. "Too late."

"Shit. Really? Anybody I know?"

"Not important." The less Huffman knew, the better. "We need to find out all we can about hydrogen necroxide."

"Oh." Kane looked up at me. "We got in touch with that doctor. She's coming later today."

"Good."

"A doctor isn't going to be able to help you," Huffman said. "This stuff is so highly classified that even I wasn't told 5.56-Yahweh ammunition existed until we started distributing it to Legion Nine operators. The only reason I found out what's inside it is because I pulled some serious strings to get the information. Hydrogen necroxide doesn't exist outside Claymore labs."

Kane drummed his fingers on the tabletop. "Huffman, how many rounds of 5.56-Yahweh have been distributed?"

"Each member of Legion Nine was issued seven thirty-round mags," Huffman said.

Kane looked at Kelvin. "And how many members are there in Legion Nine?"

"Nine hundred," Kelvin answered.

Reuel let out a low whistle.

Ionis was mumbling numbers to himself. "Two hundred and ten angel-killing bullets each," he finally said out loud. "Times nine hundred. That's math I can't even do in my head!" He held up his hands. "That's it. I'm not going outside."

"Thank you, Huffman. This has been really helpful," I said.

"Warren, man, I'm afraid that's not all that bastard in the top office has created," Huffman said.

"I know about the virus."

"It came from us. I'm sure of it, but I couldn't leave." Huffman sounded sick. "There are so few of us left who know the truth."

"You did the right thing. We're going to win this war because good men like you stayed."

"I'm trying, man. I wish I could do more to help."

"You can, I hope. Sloan and Nathan are possibly being held at Azrael's house. Do you have access there?" I asked.

"None. That place is locked up tighter than Fort Knox."

I'd figured as much. "What about the old armory? I think they might be holding a couple of angels prisoner there."

"Yeah. That I can do. What do you want to know?"

"Just how they're doing, and where exactly they're being held. Their names are Samael and Sandalphon."

"Black guy with crazy golden eyes?" Huffman asked.

"Samael isn't a *guy*, but yeah," I said.

"They're holding him at the old Echo-10 building. Saw him last night when they were moving him. He was chained and cuffed, but he was fine."

That made me feel a little better.

"What about an old, wrinkly dude?" Kane asked. "Looks a bit like Saruman with a shorter beard."

"Haven't seen anyone like that. Sorry."

"Are they holding high-risk prisoners in Echo-10?" I asked.

"Not supposed to be. Only the old armory is equipped for that, but I guess there was an *incident* there yesterday. I don't suppose you had anything to do with it." I could almost see Huffman's grin through the phone.

"I don't know what you're talking about."

He laughed softly. "Sure you—"

Commotion in the background cut him off.

Men shouting.

Static cutting in and out.

Furniture being slammed around.

Horrified, I scrambled away from the computer, like somehow putting distance between myself and the speaker might save my old friend.

There was a loud crackle of electricity, followed by the sound of Huffman screaming.

Then the line died.

And the only sound left was the pounding of my heart in my ears.

# CHAPTER SEVENTEEN

I eased onto the bed beside Iliana. She was on her left side, curled around a pillow. It was the same position her mother always slept in. I placed a hand on her shoulder. "Iliana."

She didn't respond. Or move.

"Iliana."

With a moan, she slid her arm under her pillow.

"I'm sorry, kiddo. We've let you sleep as long as we can. The doctor has come to help Cassiel, so we need you downstairs."

"I'm awake." Her breathy muffled voice said otherwise. She rolled onto her back and beyond, resting both forearms across her face, to shield her eyes. "How long have I been asleep?"

"Not long enough. Three hours, maybe."

"How is Cassiel?"

"No better. Getting worse again."

She dropped her arms onto the mattress and blinked her eyes a few times. She squinted up at me. "What's wrong?"

"I have good news and bad news."

She pushed herself up and leaned back against her pillows and headboard.

"We found another sword."

She perked up. "Really?"

"Yes, it's part of the poison that's killing Cassiel."

"What?"

"Yes, and I'm afraid the information might have cost our friend Huffman his life."

"What happened?"

"We called him on a secure line, but someone must've been listening in. We heard him being captured before the line went dead."

"I'm so sorry. You guys were friends for a long time."

I nodded, my eyes on the floor. "But before they took him, he told us the bullets are filled with a poison called hydrogen necroxide. Apparently, it attacks Rh-null blood cells, which all angels born into human bodies have."

"What does it do?"

"It binds with the blood cells to create a necrotizing foam. It destroys everything it touches inside the body."

"And it contains helkrymite?"

"Afraid so."

"So it will kill her spirit too."

My eyes fell.

"How do we fix it?"

I lifted my shoulders. "I don't know if we can."

"This is bad," she said, staring at her ruffled gray comforter.

"Very bad. The Father and Gabriel are on their way here."

Iliana straightened, and her wide eyes met mine. "What happens if the Father gets struck by one of these bullets?"

"I don't even want to guess. Anyway, Rogan's doctor just arrived. Kane watched her pull in on the security cameras upstairs."

"Upstairs?" she asked.

"Yes. Reuel and I took down the communication tower outside, so we could turn the power back on to the building and the cameras without risking a connection to the Claymore servers."

"You took down the tree that wasn't a tree?"

"Yeah."

"Dad's gonna be pissed. He loved that thing."

"Really? It looked ridiculous."

"He would agree with you, but he was really proud of it. Even decorated it with a crane a few times for Christmas when I was little."

I laughed softly, imagining Nathan decorating the tower. Iliana's smile had wilted. I touched her cheek. "You worried about your mom and dad?"

With a nod against my hand, she closed her eyes.

"Come here," I said softly, pulling her into my arms. I rested my head against hers. "We're going to get them back. I promise."

She sniffed. "Can't we just fly out there and go all Big Bad Wolf on the house?"

I laughed softly. "I like the way you think." I stroked her hair. "We'll figure out a plan."

When I pulled away, she held me close. "I'm so glad you're home."

"Me too, Iliana." I kissed the top of her head and lingered, inhaling deep the scent of green apples and Sloan. "Me too."

After a moment that could have never lasted long enough, she sat up. "I'll change and meet you in the infirmary?"

"I'll see you there."

Out in the hall, I walked to the last door on the left, the apartment I was sharing with Fury and Anya. When I walked in, Anya was asleep on the sofa. I crept past her to the master bedroom.

Fury was sitting on our bed, with a laptop open on her lap. She looked up like she'd been caught. "Hey."

I eased the door closed behind me. "Hey. What are you doing?"

Guilt washed over her face, and she turned the laptop around for me to see. On the screen was a paused video of John holding the bike seat for a little boy wearing a helmet.

I walked over and grinned as I sat beside her. "You look like I busted you committing fraud and espionage."

She wiped her wet cheeks. "I just feel stupid. I don't get sentimental."

"It's okay to have a heart." I leaned toward her and winked. "I promise I won't tell anyone."

She laughed and closed the laptop. "I wasn't expecting to see you down here."

"Ionis is with Cassiel. The doctor is here to treat her."

"Any word about Huffman?"

I shook my head sadly.

She put her hand on my cheek. "Huffman knew what he was doing when he chose to talk to you. The same as he knew what he was doing when he stuck with the company all these years. He stayed because he wanted to do good. And if he dies for that, then he already deemed it a worthy cause."

She was right, but it didn't make me feel any better.

"We're running out of time," I said, resting my forehead against her shoulder.

She threaded her fingers up the back of my hair. "Look at us. Me feeling sentimental. You feeling hopeless. Don't tell me this isn't a day when the unexpected can happen."

If she was trying to make me smile, it wasn't working.

A speaker on the nightstand beeped. "Warren?" Cruz asked.

"Yeah, I'm here."

"The doctor is in with Cassiel now."

"On my way." The speaker beeped again and went silent. I looked at Fury. "You coming?"

"Of course. I'll be right behind you."

I stood and started toward the door.

"Warren?"

I looked back.

"Don't give up."

"I won't."

I hoped that was true.

---

Rogan's doctor was a woman, wearing a suit instead of a lab coat, with neatly parted black-and-gray hair and glasses. She was listening to Cassiel's heart through a stethoscope when I walked inside.

Shannon and her husband were standing by the nurse's desk. "Thanks for helping us, Shannon," I said.

She nodded. "Warren, you remember my husband, Tyrell. Everyone calls him Reese."

The man reached for my hand, and I shook it. "Of course. Good to see you again, Reese."

"Do you know where our son is?" he asked.

"I hope he's on his way back here."

"So that's a *no*," Shannon said, crossing her arms.

"We have no reason to believe Rogan is in any danger, but as soon as I know anything, I will tell you."

"Thank you," Reese said.

Ionis walked out to join us. "Warren, you should go in. The doctor has some questions."

"Can you go find Dr. Jordan?" I asked Ionis, as none of the

other humans in the room would be able to see Iliana's grandfather.

"Already here," a man's voice said behind me.

I turned as Dr. Jordan floated into the room. I hadn't heard or felt him come through the glass doors. It was a little creepy.

"Can you help make sure I don't forget to tell the doctor anything?" I asked him.

"Of course."

Shannon and her husband exchanged a confused glance, and Shannon searched the room for who I might be talking to.

Dr. Jordan followed me to Cassiel's bedside, opposite from the doctor. He elbowed my arm. "Oh, she's good," he whispered, like the woman might be able to hear him.

I ignored him. "Hi, Dr. Swain. Thank you for coming."

She took the stethoscope out of her ears. "This woman isn't a human?"

I shook my head, a little surprised by her blunt delivery and curt tone.

She turned back toward Cassiel. "She was shot?"

"Yes. In the abdomen."

"With?"

"A hollow-point 5.56 round. It did not exit the body and did a lot of damage inside."

"Isn't she self-healing?"

"Yes. Normally, she would heal quickly, but the bullet contained an engineered toxin that is causing her body to—"

Dr. Swain stuck her hand in my face. "Decompose." She peered over the top of her glasses at me. "I can smell it."

The doctor peeled Cassiel's blanket from the foot of the bed. Her legs were swollen, and her feet were covered with lesions. "Her kidneys are shutting down."

She pulled up Cassiel's gown, exposing her belly. The black

hole had spread, so that we could peer down inside the crater. Her insides were mostly liquified.

Even Dr. Jordan gasped with horror.

Dr. Swain covered her back up. "I'm sorry. There's nothing I can do for this woman."

"Tell her to do a direct blood transfusion from Iliana to Cassiel," Dr. Jordan said, gripping my arm.

"She needs a direct blood transfusion from my—"

Dr. Swain cut me off. "We can't do a direct blood transfusion. That's ridiculous to even suggest." She started spouting off all the reasons why it was unsafe and insane, but my mind was spinning on another idea.

My eyes fell to Cassiel's midsection. To all the blood that had turned a putrid black...

"No. Iliana's blood won't work." I turned to look at Dr. Jordan. "The toxin joins to Rh-null blood cells. Iliana's blood would only feed the poison." I grabbed his shoulders—which I was sure looked to Dr. Swain like I was grabbing onto air.

"We need crystal water," I said.

Ionis was hovering near the doorway. "Crystal water? Of course! Let's just hop back to Eden and get some. Except, oh wait...*we can't.* Or have you forgotten that already?"

"The Morning Star told me he created the crystal water of Eden. Iliana is a more powerful Angel of Life than he is, so she should be able to do the same."

"Genius." Ionis crossed his arms. "How are you going to do it?"

"I have no idea." My excitement over the revelation deflated like a punctured balloon.

"The patient needs to be in a hospital. She needs tests, medicine, round-the-clock care."

"That isn't an option. We really need you to help her here."

Frustration was laced in the creases across the doctor's forehead.

"I'm sorry. It just isn't possible," I insisted.

She huffed. "The patient—"

"The patient's name is Cassiel," I said a little louder than I intended. "Trust me, Doctor, you should let this case get personal, and you should treat this woman as if she were your own sister. Because if she dies, we all die. Including you and everyone you love."

Dr. Swain jerked back. "Are you threatening me?"

"Absolutely not. But this poison is killing the only things"— I gestured around at all the angels—"standing between what's left of the human race and total annihilation. Blackmouth Fever was only the beginning of the plans our enemies have for mankind, and the only way we can save you is if you first save us."

"He's telling you the truth," Reese said from the nurse's station.

The doctor looked at Shannon.

With an eyeroll, Shannon nodded.

Before the stunned doctor could gather her wits and reply, a flash of movement caught my eye in the hallway. Iliana and Jett ran into the room.

"What did I miss?" Iliana asked.

"Your dad wants you to create crystal water," Ionis said.

Iliana's eyes widened. "I don't know how to do that. I'm not even sure exactly what it is."

"No one is sure," Jett said. "And we don't have access to it here."

"What is crystal water?" Shannon asked.

"It's the life water of Eden," Jett told her.

Dr. Swain's eyes pinched with skepticism. "The *what* of *where?*"

"Crystal water is the main fuel source where we live. It has incredible healing powers," Ionis explained. "We don't know how it was created."

I looked at Cassiel. "I'll bet she does." Returning to Cassiel's bedside, I took her hand. "Cassiel, can you hear me?"

Nothing.

I leaned closer. "I really need you to find the strength to be my favorite know-it-all again."

Nothing.

Dr. Swain pried open one of Cassiel's eyes and flinched. I looked over her arm. The corners of Cassiel's eyes were webbed with black.

With a heavy sigh, the doctor let the eyelid close. Then she backed slowly toward the nurse's station where Shannon and Reese were waiting.

I pressed my eyes closed and swore. "Ionis, we need another Angel of Knowledge. Who's here on Earth?"

"Besides Cassiel, I think the only other Angel of Knowledge here and on our side is Sandalphon. From what I've heard, you guys lost him."

I thought of our conversation with Huffman. "But I know where to find him." I squeezed Cassiel's hand. "Hold on a little longer. I'm going to get help."

Iliana grabbed my arm. "You can't go back to Claymore. Do you want to end up like Cassiel?"

"Illy, I can't just stand by and let her die. We still don't know if this stuff has the ability to destroy her spirit or not. And even if it doesn't, you don't understand how difficult it is to be trapped here on this planet without a body. I can't do that to her."

"Then I'm going with you," she said.

"You can't. You're the only thing keeping Cassiel alive now.

If you go, she'll die before we even find out if we can save her or not."

"No," Jett said.

We both looked at him.

"Rogan has Torman. He's an Angel of Knowledge, and he's been close to the Morning Star all these years. If anyone knows, he will."

"But we don't know where Rogan and Torman are," I reminded him.

His eyes flashed toward Shannon and Reese at the nurse's station. They were talking quietly with Dr. Swain. "Rogan is back in the States. He borrowed a car in New Jersey. They're going to drive all night until they get here."

"Borrowed?" I asked.

Jett grimaced. "Apparently, he ran out of cash trying to get back."

Behind us, alarm bells sounded on Cassiel's heart monitor.

"Iliana!" Dr. Jordan called.

She pushed past me with her healing light ready. She pressed it straight down into Cassiel's chest. Almost instantly, Cassiel's heart rate returned to normal.

Dr. Swain returned to the bedside, her eyes wide behind her glasses. "What are you?" she asked Iliana.

"She's the most powerful angel in this room," Ionis answered.

"She's the most powerful angel in *any* room," Jett corrected him.

I turned toward him. "Rogan has until morning to get back here, or I'm going to Claymore."

He nodded. "I'll tell him."

Cassiel moaned in pain, a downside of being brought back from the brink of death.

"Give her the morphine," Dr. Jordan ordered.

"I tried earlier, but she didn't want it," I said.

"Give it to her anyway. She's in too much pain to argue."

"Yes, sir."

"Sir?" Confused, Dr. Swain looked around the room. "Who do you keep talking to?"

I walked around to the bedside table. "Do you remember Dr. Robert Jordan?"

"Geriatrics practitioner? Sure. He was a good man. I was sorry to hear of his passing," she said.

I carried the bottle of morphine over to her. Then I pointed to Dr. Jordan's spirit by the bed. "Dr. Jordan is right over there."

"What?" Her voice was horrified.

"Ghosts are real, and a lot of them are stuck here right now. I know this is a lot to ask you to believe, but some things must be making sense to you now."

"It's true then?" Dr. Swain took a slow and steady breath. "Blackmouth Fever was an act of terrorism?"

"Cosmic terrorism." Ionis wiggled his fingers in the air.

"Yes, and worse is coming." I held out the bottle. "So do you want to administer this, or shall I?"

Dr. Swain looked like she might faint. She swallowed hard but took the bottle from my fingers. "I'll do it."

"Thank you. Please do anything else you think might make her comfortable," I said.

When Iliana's light extinguished, she slumped over Cassiel's thighs onto the bed.

"Illy?" I asked, reaching for her arm.

She pushed herself up. "I'm...I'm OK." Her head drooped. "It's getting harder and harder to recover."

"You're putting so much of yourself into her," Dr. Jordan said.

I pulled her against me, out of the Dr. Swain's way. "You sure you're all right?"

She wobbled a bit, but she nodded.

Dr. Swain injected Cassiel's IV with the morphine. Then she uncovered Cassiel's abdomen again and began to clean it. "I'll take some blood samples to the lab. Maybe something will show up on a tox screen or culture plate."

"Thank you," I said.

Iliana sat in the chair, leaning heavily on the armrest. "What are we going to do about my parents?"

"I'll talk to our prisoner and see if he knows anything about the security setup around Azrael's house. This is probably a dumb question, but have you tried summoning them?"

Her face wilted. "I can't even feel their spirits anymore. That house must be spiritually impenetrable."

"If they're even in that house," Jett said.

"True." I sighed. "I wish we could at least get them a message. Tell them we're out and holed up here because of Claymore's new ammo."

Iliana weakly raised a finger. "And see if they can get somewhere I can reach them."

"But how? Claymore has eyes on everything," Jett said.

I thought of Huffman and felt sick again. "No. And there's no way we could get past the guards without putting ourselves and them in a lot of danger."

"We might not be able to"—Iliana straightened in the chair—"but Papa can."

Dr. Jordan turned around. "Papa can what?"

"Get a message to my parents." She looked up at me. "There's probably a bunch of human soldiers guarding the house. They won't be able to see him."

"Yeah, but neither will Sloan and Nathan," I said.

"No, but he can communicate with Mom."

"How?"

Dr. Jordan walked over. "I can speak into her dreams."

"Really?" I asked.

He nodded. "And it only seems to work on her."

"This might work, but I'll need to check with our prisoner to find out how many angels are hanging around that house. Can anyone else see any holes in this plan?" I asked.

Dr. Jordan raised his hand. "How will I get there?"

"I can drive him," Jett offered.

"An angel would be too risky. We need a human," I said.

"One of the SF-12 guys?" Iliana asked.

I shook my head. "They're too recognizable. If there's a wanted poster anywhere at Claymore, you can expect their faces are on it, along with all of ours. We need someone that would be off Claymore's radar."

Iliana and I locked eyes as the same idea occurred to both of us. We both slowly turned toward Shannon and Reese, who were talking quietly.

Shannon noticed us staring first. Her face shifted quickly from acknowledgment to concern. She held up a finger. "Oh no. Whatever you're plotting, I don't want any part of it."

"We really need your help." I walked toward them, and Iliana jumped up, right on my heels.

"Please." Iliana clasped her hands beneath her chin. "We have to warn my mom and dad."

"Absolutely not," Shannon said.

Reese pulled her behind him. "What do you need us to do?"

"I need you to drive to the Outer Banks," I said.

"Sure."

"Excuse me?" Shannon barked, clawing at his arm.

He spoke over his shoulder to her. "Nate and Sloan are in trouble, and I'm going to help them. If you want to stay here, then be my guest."

I was sensing Reese might be hoping for a quiet car drive.

He looked at me. "I'm in."

"Thank you."

"What do I do when I get there?"

"Nothing. We need you to take Sloan's dad to Kill Devil Hills."

"Sloan's dad…the *ghost*?" Reese's eyes darted around the room.

I grimaced. "Yeah. He'll be able to get inside the house and get a message to them."

"He's the best chance we have," Iliana said.

"Then I'll do it." He lowered his voice. "But how will I know when he's in the car? What if we stop somewhere and he gets out or something?"

"He won't. It's not like he'll need to use the bathroom," I said with a smile.

"But once we're there. He goes in and does his thing…how will I get him back?"

I hadn't thought that far ahead.

"He won't." Dr. Jordan came up between me and Iliana. He looked at me. "Tell him to drop me off, and I'll figure out my own way back."

"Papa, we can't just let him leave you in the middle of some island, off the coast," Iliana argued.

"You can, and you will. Sending an angel will put your mother in danger. I won't have that." His translucent hand cupped Iliana's chin. "Sweetheart, this is the only way."

She held onto his wrist. "How will you get home?"

"I'll find a way. Most humans in my situation are stuck here without the assistance of those who can see us. They've adapted. So will I." He released her and turned to me. "I'm ready. I want to do this."

"I'll get my keys," Reese said.

Shannon grabbed his arm. "Hold on. It's going to be dark soon."

"Our van has headlights." Reese looked at his watch. "If we leave now, we'll get there around two in the morning. Is that too late?"

"No. It will probably be better. Security will slack off with the night shift. It always does," I said.

"One question," Dr. Jordan said. "How will Sloan know I'm really there and that she's not just dreaming? Before, Iliana has told her."

I thought back to the island. To the night Fury and I had been awoken by a ghost. I smiled. "Well, that depends. How good are you with electricity?"

# CHAPTER EIGHTEEN

"Hey, Warren?" Cruz stuck his head into Kelvin's cell later that night.

I looked up from my notes. "Yeah?"

"Fury's looking for you."

"Great." I closed my notebook and held it up. "Thanks for this, Kelvin."

"Hope I was helpful."

"I hope so too." Hopeful, yes. Doubtful, a little. After all, Kelvin hadn't known he was dating the Morning Star's right-hand demon.

"I have some bad news," I said as I stood. "We need you to share a cell with one of your buddies. We have another prisoner on his way here that needs the extra precautions of this cell."

"Sure. I understand. Think we can get some food? My guys and I haven't eaten since dinner yesterday."

"I'll talk to your guard."

"Thanks, Warren."

I walked out of the cell and gestured for Cruz to follow me

into the hallway. "Move Kelvin out of the secure cell and put him with one of the other guys. We'll need the cell for Torman."

"When will they be here?"

"Maybe the middle of the night. Where's Fury?"

"Infirmary, I think."

"Thanks." I started out the door but paused. "And get these guys something to eat. This isn't Camp X-ray."

He smiled. "Yes, sir."

"Warren!"

I turned and saw Fury standing outside the infirmary door. "We need you. Now." She disappeared back inside.

When I reached the doors, I saw Jett embracing Iliana. Her head was tucked beneath his chin, on his chest, and they were both facing away from me.

It took a second for me to tear my eyes away from the romantic scene and realize they were listening to something Dr. Swain was saying on the other side of Cassiel's bed.

Fury and Anya were waiting by the nurse's station.

Iliana looked over when I entered the room. Her eyes were at half-mast eyes, her arms were limp, and Jett seemed to be holding her *up* rather than just holding her.

"What happened?" I asked, alarmed.

"She's exhausted," Jett said, rubbing her back.

Dr. Swain scribbled something on a clipboard. "The patient —I mean, *Cassiel*—flatlined again."

"I can't fix this." Iliana's voice was barely above a whisper as she stumbled back a step. I grabbed her arm to steady her. "I'm barely keeping her alive, and it's taking all I've got. If the Morning Star has this kind of weapon, there's no way we can—"

I pulled her to me. "Don't give up on us now. Rogan and Torman will be here soon. We'll get some answers out of him."

She nodded. Barely.

Dr. Swain shined a penlight into Cassiel's eye. The black webbing had crept closer to her irises. "Perhaps we should treat Iliana's power like any other medicine."

"OK," I said, hopeful that the doctor was taking us seriously.

"Let's try setting a schedule for Iliana to give her regular, *smaller* doses, rather than having her expend all her energy when Cassiel nears death."

"That's a great idea," I said.

Iliana rubbed her bloodshot eyes. "I'll try anything."

"It should be better for both of them." Dr. Swain looked at Iliana. "You don't look like you have much left to give."

She really didn't.

Her hand clutched my shirt like it was barely grasping a lifeline, and I wished for a way to transfer my strength to her. Because in that moment, I realized now that Iliana was here, the world no longer needed me—but she did. And there wasn't anything more I could do to help her.

Dr. Swain looked at the clock behind the nurse's station. "The healing power seems to be wearing off after about three hours." She thought for a moment. "Iliana, go rest for about an hour. Then come back and give Cassiel a small booster."

Iliana blinked and tired tears streamed her cheeks. "OK."

I rubbed her back. "We'll come get you if we have to. Now go. We need you strong."

She nodded and shuffled toward the door.

"Jett, go with her. See that she makes it to her room." I couldn't believe I was saying it. "Then come back and stay with Cassiel until it's time for her next treatment."

"Yes, sir." He jogged after Iliana.

"Thank you, Dr. Swain," I said when he was gone. "I trust Shannon told you, we will compensate you well."

I wasn't sure with what money we'd compensate her with, but I'd sell my bodily fluids if I had to.

"I'll send you a bill," she said with a tired smile. "I started her on a broad-spectrum antibiotic. However, it doesn't seem to be helping. And I've given her a second dose of morphine. Tomorrow, I'll bring something stronger."

"You're coming back?" I asked, surprised.

Fury and Anya walked into the room.

"Yes," Dr. Swain said. "I'll take her bloodwork to the lab tonight and pick up the results after my class tomorrow afternoon."

"You're in school?" Fury asked.

"No, I'm giving a lecture tomorrow to the medical students at the university."

Fury's head pulled back. "To all the students?"

"It's open to all of them. Usually a hundred and fifty or so show up."

"What do you teach?" I asked.

"The ethics of experimental medicine."

"I didn't realize testing out new treatments was cause for an ethics conundrum," I said.

"In most countries, medical professionals try to avoid it now, but some horrific things have been done in the name of science. The Tuskegee syphilis study, Dr. Mengele's experiments on prisoners at Auschwitz, Unit 731 and Japan's biological warfare experiments..."

"Bet you don't have many students falling asleep in that talk," Anya said.

Dr. Swain smiled for, I think, the first time since we'd met. "No, I don't. Tomorrow we're doing an overview of some of the most extreme cases in history."

"Sounds brutal."

"It is." Dr. Swain picked up her bag. "Her catheter bag will need to be changed every few hours, and hang a new bag of saline when that one is finished."

I nodded.

"Call me if there's anything I can do."

"Thank you," I said again. "Anya, would you mind sitting with Cassiel while we walk out with the doctor?"

"Of course not." She sat in the chair. "I had a nap earlier, so I'll take first watch tonight. You guys haven't slept much, and I know you'll want to question Torman when he gets here. Go on to bed while you have the chance."

"Thank you," Fury told her sister.

We followed the doctor out into the hall. "I'm sorry you were dragged into this," I said to her as the three of us walked toward the lobby.

"Is my family in danger?" she asked.

I didn't want to answer, but she deserved the truth. "Yes, but the rest of the world is too."

We walked a few steps in silence.

"Is your family local?" Fury asked.

Dr. Swain shook her head. "I have a sister in Cashiers, but the rest of our surviving family is in Arkansas. We lost about half of them in the fever."

"I'm sorry," Fury said.

"It's part of the reason I'm glad to help." The doctor's face fell. "Though I don't feel very useful."

"I think you were exactly right about having Iliana give Cassiel smaller doses of power more regularly. You might have saved both of them," I said.

"Please keep me updated on how it goes."

"We will," Fury said.

Laughter from the living room stopped us as we passed by. Inside, Taiya was playing a card game with Luca on the coffee table. They were both throwing cards down onto a pile until Luca slapped the deck and threw his head back, laughing.

"Cheat!" Taiya shouted, pointing at him.

He pulled all the cards toward his chest. "Nope. You lost fair and square."

"*Nooo,* I won fair and *circle*!" Taiya dove across the table toward the cards.

Luca laughed and let her have them.

She glanced over and saw me. "Hey!" She pointed to the cards. "Play *flapjacks*?"

"*Slap* jacks," Luca corrected her.

I laughed. "Maybe tomorrow. I'm going to bed." I pointed at her. "No sneaking in our room tonight."

Taiya's cheeks flushed. "OK." She pushed her hair out of her face. "Fury play flapjacks?"

Luca groaned.

"Not tonight." Fury pointed back down the hallway. "But Anya might play with you. She's in the infirmary."

"Nana says to stay out of the sick lady's room," Taiya said.

I smiled. "You can tell Nana I said it's OK as long as you're quiet."

Taiya held a finger over her lips. "Shh."

"Shh," I echoed. "We'll see you in the morning."

"Night night!" she called.

"Who is that?" Dr. Swain asked when we started down the hall again.

I opened the door to the lobby for her and Fury. "Taiya has become like a little sister."

"Little?" the doctor asked, confused.

Shit.

Taiya had once been younger than me, but now she was obviously much older.

"Figuratively speaking," Fury chimed in.

Kane, Cruz, and Nash were all behind the lobby desk when we walked in. Kane stood. "All finished for the night?"

"All done," I said. "Would one of you mind walking Dr. Swain to her car?"

Nash stood from where he'd been sitting on the desk. "I'll do it. I didn't go to the gym today."

Dr. Swain groaned. "Oh. I'd forgotten about the stairs."

"Yeah, sorry about that," I said with a grimace.

She waved her hand. "Good for the heart, right?"

"That's right." I shook her hand. "Thanks again for coming."

"You're welcome. I'll see you tomorrow. My lecture is at one, so I'll probably be here closer to dinnertime."

"Well, I hope you join us to eat," I replied. "See you tomorrow."

Nash picked up a rifle to escort her out.

"Going to bed?" Kane asked.

"Yes. Please wake me when Rogan and Torman arrive."

"Will do."

"Any word on Huffman?" Fury asked.

Kane shook his head.

"He'll be fine," Cruz said. "It's not the first time that knucklehead has slept in a cell."

I certainly hoped so. "What about Reese and Dr. Jordan?"

"Reese sent an email when they reached Raleigh. They have a few hours to go," Kane said.

"Come get me if there's news," I said.

Kane held up his thumb.

Fury and I took the stairs to the lower level. When we reached our hallway, I offered her my hand. She stared at it—for less time than usual—before sliding her fingers between mine. "I think this is getting easier," I said, swinging our hands between us.

She laughed softly. "You're so weird." When we reached our

door, she opened it. "You know, I think even after all this time, Taiya's still in love with you."

I tipped up my chin. "You jealous?"

"Maybe a little," she said with a wink.

I closed the door and pulled her to me. "Need me to prove my loyalty?"

She looped her arms around my neck. "It sure as hell wouldn't hurt."

I bent and wrapped my hands around the backs of her thighs. Then I lifted her and settled her legs around my waist. She raked her fingers through my hair as I carried her to our bedroom, and I kicked our door closed behind us.

## CHAPTER NINETEEN

"Warren?"

Someone was knocking on our bedroom door when I opened my eyes. Fury groaned and rolled over toward me. "What time is it?"

I looked at the alarm clock I'd swiped from one of the staff bedrooms. "Five a.m." Six hours of solid shut-eye. That had to be some kind of record here lately. I checked to be sure Fury was decent before I called out, "Come in!"

The door opened, and light spilled into the dark room. Lex stuck his head in. "Sorry to wake you."

I shielded my eyes from the light. "What is it?"

"Rogan and Torman just pulled in, and Reese sent a message to say he and Shannon are going to stop and rest a few hours before driving back home."

"OK. Thanks," I replied as I sat up.

"We're in the lobby when you're ready."

"I'm going to jump in the shower, so I'll be up in a minute. Where's Kane?"

"Asleep, sir."

"Good." I dropped my legs off the side of the mattress as Lex walked out.

Fury sat up behind me and laid her head against the back of my bare shoulder. "I feel like I'm never going to be caught up on sleep. Just one night it would be nice to sleep until I woke up on my own."

"Stay here and rest for a little while longer. I'll come get you if there's big news."

"You sure?"

"Absolutely."

I took a quick shower and dressed quietly in the bathroom. When I crept back through our bedroom, Fury didn't even stir. I took the stairs two at a time until I reached the lobby. Lex was at the desk, and Cruz was standing in the doorway to the main hallway.

"Morning," Cruz said.

"Morning," I replied.

"There's coffee." Lex nodded toward a pot in the corner.

I walked over and picked up a paper cup. "Where are our *friends*?" I poured a paper cup full.

"On their way down now," Lex answered, turning one of the security-camera monitors toward me. On the screen was a fuzzy shot of the two angels coming down the staircase.

"OK." I held up the pot. "Anybody need a refill?"

"No thanks," Lex answered.

"Nah, I'm heading to bed as soon as Kane is up," Cruz said.

I slurped the steaming coffee. "What did Reese have to say?"

"He said they arrived in Kill Devil Hills around two a.m. They slept for a few hours at a rest area, then headed back," Lex said.

"Where did they drop off Dr. Jordan?" I asked.

Lex grinned. "Well…Reese *thinks* he dropped him off at the

end of the road that leads to the house. He said he got out, opened the back door, and hoped for the best."

I laughed, and hot coffee shot up my nose. My eyes watered as I coughed. "Shit, that's funny."

"Man, did you ever imagine we'd see the day that we were using ghosts as a messenger service?" Cruz asked, almost to himself.

Lex laced his fingers together behind his head and leaned back in his office chair. "Freaks my shit out, if I'm being honest."

The door opened, and Rogan and Torman trudged in. They were the visual definition of *bedraggled.* Rogan's blond hair so desperately needed a wash that it was almost brown. His clothes were wrinkled like they'd been washed in a sink and wrung dry.

Torman's clothes were straight-up filthy, and his shirt was buttoned wrong. His hair in the back was standing almost completely vertical. He was also missing a shoe.

My head tilted to the side. "What the hell happened to you two?"

"Don't get me started," Rogan said, shaking his head.

Torman's hands were cuffed behind his back. "This is cruel and unusual, even for a bunch of angels."

To be honest, I was a little surprised Torman had survived the trip. Though I was sure that was only because Rogan didn't have means of killing him permanently.

"Come on. Let's take him back to the secure cell." I said.

"It had better have a shower," Torman snarled.

It didn't.

"We'll figure something out." I could smell them both from five feet away.

Rogan grabbed my arm. "Is Shannon here yet?"

"Not yet. You have a few hours' reprieve."

He sighed with relief. "Thank the Father."

"Whoa," Cruz said, pinching his nose as the three of us walked through the door he was holding. "What's that stench?"

Rogan held up his middle finger without saying a word.

The four of us walked down the hallway. "How did you get back?" I asked.

"It took a couple of days, but we finally found someone to forge travel documents. Unfortunately, they were pretty shoddy, so I didn't want to risk flying through one of the major airports if we could help it.

"A guy in Manila told us about an airline in Vietnam that has pretty lax security. But it added another day to our trip. We flew from Manila to Ho Chi Minh City, then all the way across the Pacific, where we landed at LAX. We have a friend on the inside there who works at the airport in customs."

"That's convenient," I said.

"It's by design. Cassiel and Samael have been working the past couple of years to get angels stationed in all the major airports to help us with issues such as this."

"Smart." Not that I was surprised.

"Still, we were detained for another day before we made it to Chicago. By the time we got there, we were broke."

"I heard you stole the car," I said.

He smiled. "Yeah. One of the company cars outside a Claymore recruiting office."

I burst out laughing. "Jett didn't tell me that."

"Nice car. Had enough battery life to get us all the way here," Rogan said.

Torman smirked. "Yes, and with a detour halfway to Knoxville."

"Shut up, Torman," Rogan snapped.

"Why would you take direction from an Angel of Knowledge anyway? It's not like we know anything—"

Rogan squeezed Torman's arm, buckling Torman's knees. "I said, shut up."

"Shh," I said, pulling them apart. "The rest of this place is asleep."

"He's making me crazy," Rogan grumbled.

"I can tell."

I paused at the infirmary window and looked inside. Iliana was asleep on the second hospital bed. Jett was asleep in the chair. Taiya was, surprisingly, laying right next to Cassiel.

*Weird.*

Rogan took a step toward the glass. "How is she?"

"It's bad. She's going to die if we don't figure out how to help her," I said.

"Die?" Torman whirled toward me. "Angels can't die."

"Apparently the Morning Star has found a way. Do you know anything about an engineered toxin known as hydrogen necroxide?" I asked him.

Torman shook his head. "I've been in the same hole with you, remember? What is it?"

"Our friend Huffman…"

*Huffman.*

My throat thickened. I cleared it, then told him everything we learned from Huffman as we escorted Torman past the sleeping Claymore prisoners.

Inside the eight-by-ten cell, Rogan gave Torman a shove toward the mattress. He stumbled across the room and sat down. "Is that necessary?" Torman asked.

"Yes." Rogan walked over and turned on the metal sink. He splashed his face with water, then dried it on his dirty shirt.

"Anyway, the poison is killing Cassiel." I leaned against the concrete-and-high-Z wall. "And if we can't reverse the effects, it might kill a whole lot more of us. Legion Nine, Claymore's special-ops trained to deal with angels, have been issued about two hundred thousand rounds of ammunition containing the poison."

Torman looked around at his accommodations. "Never thought I'd be thankful to be locked up."

Cruz brought in a chair, and I sat down. "I might find you a more comfortable bed if you help Cassiel."

"Me? What can I do?" he asked.

I leaned forward, balancing my elbows on my knees. "Tell me how to make crystal water."

Torman laughed. Then his head pulled back. "You're serious?"

"Do I look like I make a lot of jokes?"

"You can't. The only Angel of Life powerful enough to create it is the Morning Star."

"Iliana is stronger than he is."

Torman clearly hadn't thought of that. "Technically, she should be able to do it, but it would be nearly impossible to pull it off outside Eden."

"*But* it is possible," I said.

"Do you know how crystal water is made?" he asked.

In the doorway, Rogan crossed his arms. "Would we have been in such a hurry to get you back here if we did?"

Torman scowled at him. "If you want my help, I suggest you lay off the insults."

I turned toward Rogan. "You should leave us. I'm sure you'd like to shower and get some rest."

Rogan appeared offended at having been asked to leave, but he didn't argue. When he was gone, I closed the secure cell door and removed Torman's cuffs.

He rubbed his wrists. "Thank you. I haven't felt my fingers in days."

"You're welcome."

His eyes were on my coffee cup. Reluctantly, I handed it to him.

He sipped it slowly. "What do you want from me, Warren?"

"We need your help. And if you get caught in the crossfire, you'll need a cure for that poison too."

"That's what I'm afraid of."

"Would the Morning Star ever take the time to save you even if you were completely on his side?"

Torman just stared at me. He didn't need to answer. "Like I said, it will be nearly impossible to make crystal water outside Eden. But yes, it can be done."

"How?"

"You need human tears. A *lot* of human tears."

"Tears? But there are no human tears in Eden," I said.

"You forget that Eden isn't some distant realm. Eden is here." He spread his arms and turned his palms up, slowly gesturing around the room. "Eden is everywhere, just across the spirit line."

"I understand that."

"Tears shed here on Earth evaporate. They are drawn in and pressurized by the power of the auranos. The light from the Eden sun burns away all the impurities. Then the vapors are forced into condensation coils that empty into the life water fountain in Zion."

"You mean *suns*," I corrected him. "There are two."

Torman blinked with surprise. "Oh. Of course there are. A new sun would have appeared when your daughter was conceived."

My jaw dropped. "Iliana is the reason there are two suns in Eden? I've been there all this time and no one has bothered to tell me that?" My brain triggered memories of conversations in Eden.

Several angels had referred to her as the "Light of Eden."

Even Cassiel had once said, "At least you always have a piece of her nearby." She had gestured toward the sky.

Then there was the prophecy that had foretold her birth. It had called her the *Daughter of Zion, light of the world.*

And when Sloan became pregnant, Samael had told us, "All the angels can see her now."

I'd thought they were all being figurative. As angels often are.

"Is Iliana's sun the big one or the smaller one?" I asked.

"I'd imagine she's the biggest star."

Of course she was. "And the smaller one represents the Morning Star?"

"Not represents. It's part of him. The Morning Star isn't just a name; he is, even now, the light of Eden's sun. His sun will remain as long as he lives."

"Which is why using crystal water outside Eden reopened the spirit line to him," I said as all the bits of information clicked together like Tetris pieces in my brain.

"Yes. The moment your girlfriend consumed the crystal water, it became a living entity. Its power opened a direct connection with the light of Eden, shattering the veils around Nulterra and the spirit line. Almost like knocking down a lead wall between two magnets."

I sat back in my chair and stared at the ceiling. "I can't believe Iliana is the second sun."

"They really didn't tell you?" Torman asked.

I shook my head. "Once again, I think everyone has highly overestimated me."

He smirked. "The Morning Star certainly hasn't."

I realized this was probably as close to a compliment as I would ever get from Torman or any of the demons.

"But back to your original question." Torman cleared his

throat. "All of that is to say that creating crystal water is an incredibly complicated process. And without the auranos, you would never be able to collect enough tears to create even a drop."

"But a drop is all we really need to save Cassiel, right?" I thought of the tiny vial Fury drank in Nulterra that saved her life *and* destroyed the veils hiding the spirit line and the underworld.

"A few drops, probably, if the damage is as bad as you say. And you would need a few thousand tears to create them."

I stood. "But there *is* hope."

Torman rolled his eyes. "Humans and their optimism."

"Say we somehow get enough tears, how do we duplicate the process here on Earth?"

He folded his arms over his chest. "I'm not saying another word until I, at the very least, get some water and something to eat."

I frowned.

"I've been cooped up in a sedan since New Jersey, and if it's OK with you, I need to use the facilities." He nodded toward the toilet.

I could have gotten my sword from the safe, but a meal and a bit of privacy was a small price to pay to keep our association from turning hostile. Torman helping us willingly was what we all needed.

With a frustrated sigh, I stood and walked to the door.

"How's it going in there?" Cruz asked when I closed the door behind me.

"It's *slow.* Where's Rogan?"

"Bathing in disinfectant, with any luck."

Fury was coming down the hallway with Kathy and James when I walked out. The three of them were about to enter the kitchen, but I gestured them forward.

"Good morning, Warren," Kathy said with a bright smile as they approached.

"You're both up early," I said.

They met me in front of the infirmary. "I know shift change is at six for the boys on duty, so I wanted to make sure Cruz and Lex got something to eat before they went to bed," Kathy said.

I smiled. "That's very thoughtful."

"Well, I can't assist much with angel business, but I can keep everyone fed."

"You do a fine job of it," James said, kissing her temple.

"Agreed." I looked at Fury. "Couldn't go back to sleep?"

She leaned into me. "Bed was cold."

I squeezed her hip and nodded toward the glass. "Anybody know why Taiya is down here having a sleepover?"

James crossed his arms. "I woke up just after midnight and came up here to check on Iliana. I found them like this then. Jett said Cassiel seemed a little better with Taiya around, so he asked her to stay."

Interesting.

"Why would Cassiel get better around Taiya?" Kathy asked.

"I'm not sure, but Taiya used to be part-Angel of Life. Perhaps some of her healing powers lingered," I said.

"Sloan got some of her powers back," Fury said. "So I think it's possible."

Unlike Iliana, Taiya had never had much control over her healing powers. It had been more like a healing *aura* that followed her wherever she went.

An aura that was now keeping Cassiel's heart beating while everyone slept. My tuned ears could hear the heart monitor through the glass. "Wonder when Iliana treated Cassiel last," I said.

"Iliana doesn't look like she's moved. Maybe she's been asleep since I was down here," James said.

"God, I hope so," I said.

We all walked to the kitchen. Inside, Rogan was at a table with a huge bowl of Lucky Charms.

"Rogan, if you can wait, I was about to make breakfast," Kathy said, turning on the oven.

"Can't," he said around a mouthful of cereal. He swallowed. "But thank you anyway."

"Suit yourself." Kathy walked to the commercial-sized refrigerator and took out a pallet of eggs. She pulled a bag of something from the freezer before walking to the counter.

My stomach growled.

Rogan pointed his spoon at me. "Did you find out anything useful?"

I pulled out a barstool and sat down. "Torman knows how crystal water is created, but he refuses to answer any more questions until he has something to eat."

"I can whip up some eggs and bacon in about eight minutes," Kathy said.

"Thank you, Kathy."

"What'd Torman say?" Fury asked from the coffee pot. She was pouring two mugs full.

She brought one to me as I parroted back Torman's play-by-play of making crystal water. At the counter, Kathy chuckled.

We all looked over at her.

"Sorry." Kathy was arranging what looked like white hockey pucks onto a baking sheet. "It just sounds like you're making moonshine."

James laughed as he carried a package of bacon to the stove. "You're right. All except the human tears part. Heat, pressure, condensation coils…"

At the table, Rogan had stopped chewing. He was staring at me. "Have you ever drunk crystal water?"

*Holy shit.* I'd always joked that crystal water was the white lighting of the afterlife.

I swiveled toward James and Kathy. "Please, tell me everything you know about making moonshine."

"You oughta talk to John," Kathy said, opening the large box of eggs.

James placed a frying pan on a burner. "Yeah, my brother's taken up illegal distilling since he moved out into the middle of nowhere."

I really had no desire to consult with John about anything. "Can you give me an overview?"

James carefully laid strips of bacon across the frying pan. "I've seen his setup a couple of times. He basically cooks up the mash, lets it ferment for a few weeks, then heats the liquid till it evaporates into the coils. The liquor drains out into glass jars."

Kathy cracked an egg into a glass bowl. "He's going to go jail if he's not careful."

Jett walked and yawned loudly. "Morning." He did a double take when he saw Rogan. "You're back." He crossed the room but quickly stopped short of Rogan. Jett's face soured. "Whoa. You stink."

Rogan shoveled another heaping spoonful of cereal into his mouth. "I know. Don't care."

"Jett, how's Iliana?" I asked.

"She's asleep." He looked relieved. So was I.

"What happened?" Fury asked.

Jett walked to the coffee pot. "I'm not really sure, except Taiya came into the infirmary last night to play some game with Anya. When Iliana and I showed up an hour later, Taiya left for bed. As soon as she walked out, Cassiel's vitals deteriorated. So Iliana brought Taiya back in. Cassiel didn't get better, but she stopped getting worse so quickly. It was the weirdest thing."

The pans under the counter clanged together as Kathy retrieved a second frying pan. "You know..." Her voice was muffled by the cabinets until she stood upright. "Sloan told me Taiya's mother almost survived the fever. They traveled for several days to try to get here before she died. That's unheard of for the virus."

"I'd forgotten about that," James said as the bacon started to sizzle. He looked back over his shoulder. "Whatever the reason, I'm glad Iliana was able to get some rest."

"Hear, hear." I sipped my coffee.

"Warren, you should ask Jett about John's setup. He'd know better than me," James said.

"Setup for what?" Jett asked, pulling out the chair across from Rogan.

"They were just telling me John is distilling moonshine now," I said.

The corners of Jett's mouth tipped up. "Yeah. I told him he's turning into a redneck in his old age. Didn't you smell it when we got there?"

I thought back to our visit. "All I remember about our arrival was a gun in my face."

"That was because we probably interrupted him doing a run."

"I figured it was just because he wanted to kill me."

"Maybe a bit of that too," Jett said. "You taking up bootlegging?"

"I'm wondering if we can use the same process to create crystal water."

"Crystal water? I can't help you there." Jett leaned his elbows on the table. "Can it be created here on Earth?"

"Torman thinks so. Will you bring him in here?" I jerked my head toward the hallway. "He's in the cell."

"Sure." Jett got up and left the room.

The oven beeped. Kathy handed James her spatula and then carried the baking sheet and hockey pucks to the oven.

"Kathy, what is that?" I asked.

"Biscuits. I made them yesterday and froze them so I wouldn't have to make them again today."

My stomach growled again. This time so loud that Fury looked over. She laughed and shook her head.

Jett returned with Torman. His hands were no longer chained together, but he was wearing the cuffs that would inhibit his powers and drinking the coffee I'd given him.

He frowned as Jett led him past me. "I thought you'd forgotten about me."

"Food is almost ready," I replied, annoyed.

Jett put him in the chair beside Rogan.

Rogan scowled. "Why by me?"

"I'm trying to contain the stench to that side of the room," Jett said, joining me and Fury at the counter.

"Warren, can you get some plates?" Kathy asked, turning the eggs in the pan. "Upper cabinet by the fridge."

I put my coffee down and crossed the room. In the cabinet was a stack of white plates. I placed them carefully on the counter.

"Thank you, son," Kathy said, turning off the burner on the stove.

"Torman, is it possible that, even though Taiya no longer has an angelic spirit, she still carries healing qualities?" I asked, retaking my seat.

"Of course. All bodies, angel or otherwise, retain some qualities of the spirit, even long after it's removed. You're an Angel of Death. Do you not sense bodies buried in the earth?"

My eyes widened. "Yeah, I do."

"You're not detecting flesh and bone."

Interesting.

"The Father has the same kind of healing qualities, even when he's in human form. The spirit is not easily removed," Torman said.

"He's on his way here," I said.

Gloom flooded Torman's face. I wondered if this might be the first time since the First Angel War that the two had seen each other.

"Can the Father make Cassiel better?" Kathy asked.

Torman took a sip of coffee. "His presence might help, but even he won't be able to heal her completely. Not with the limitations he puts on himself here. I'm afraid crystal water is her only chance."

Kathy wiped her hands on a dishtowel. "What exactly is crystal water?"

James chuckled as he turned the bacon. "Sounds like angel hooch to me."

"I've had it, and it kind of is," Fury said.

Disgust washed over Kathy's soft face. "Liquor made from human tears? Sounds evil, if you ask me."

"It's quite the opposite." Torman put down his coffee. "While crystal water can be used recreationally, it's vital to all human spirits in Eden. It's the reason there's no pain or sadness there. The humans' tears on Earth are payment for never having to suffer again."

The room fell silent.

"*For he has stored my tears in a bottle and counted each and every one,*" Kathy mumbled almost to herself. Her hand was over her heart.

"What was that?" I asked.

"A song my grandmother used to sing when I was a little

girl. Saintly woman. She always said God counted our tears and kept them forever."

Torman nodded. "In a way, that's true. Crystal water nourishes the ground and filters into all the water sources. Even the plants release it into the air like oxygen."

Kathy looked like she might cry as she filled one of the plates with food. "That's the most beautiful thing I've ever heard."

My eyes narrowed. "It is, but it sure as hell doesn't sound like something the Morning Star would create."

Kathy carried the plate to Torman, and he didn't say thank you.

"The Morning Star didn't do it by choice," Jett said.

"You knew about this?" I asked.

"I didn't know the details, but the Father commanded the Morning Star to create the crystal water."

Rogan nodded and picked up his fork again. "It fueled the rebellion that led to the First Angel War."

"That sounds more like him." I drummed my fingers on the countertop. "Torman, can we use something like a distilling setup to create enough crystal water to save Cassiel?"

He swallowed the bite in his mouth. "Theoretically, it's not out of the question, but you won't get enough tears to do it."

"What about artificial tears?" James asked.

"Must be human," Torman answered.

Our whole group was quiet. Kathy and James stopped washing the dishes. Even Rogan stopped eating. Torman, apparently, didn't care. Collecting tears to save Cassiel wasn't a more worthy cause than filling his belly.

"How many humans do we have here?" Jett asked.

I started counting on my fingers. "Fury, James, Kathy, Luca, Kane, Cruz, Lex, and Nash. Taiya is part-human. So nine?"

"John, if he comes," James said.

Fury pointed at Rogan. "Shannon and Reese, when they get back."

I held up ten fingers.

Torman shook his head. "No way that's enough."

"Dr. Swain," I added. "She's coming by later today."

Fury's lower jaw fell an inch. "Oh shit. I have an idea." She looked at me. "How many students did she say would be at her lecture today?"

"A hundred and fifty, I think."

Her eyes widened. "She said it's brutal. Lots of tears, I bet."

My brow stitched together with doubt. "I don't see a bunch of college kids getting weepy in class."

Fury smiled. "They would if a bunch of angels made them." She looked over at Torman. "Angels of Ministry can manipulate emotion, right? If they can make humans happy, surely they can make them sad."

"My god, Fury, you're brilliant." I sat forward on the edge of my stool and grabbed her thigh.

"Damn," Jett said, nodding his head with a raised brow and a smile.

Fury beamed as she awaited Torman's answer. Even he looked impressed. "Sure, they could do it."

She turned to Jett. "How many Angels of Ministry do we have in the area?"

Jett thought for a moment. "Most are outside Asheville, comforting those who are still losing relatives to Blackmouth Fever, but there are a few here. Ionis could call them in."

Rogan raised his spoon. "Hold on. Let's say you can get a room full of humans to cry. How would you collect their tears? Have us all stand by with paper cups to catch them as they drip off their cheeks?"

Good question.

"Give them tissues," Torman said. "Then soak the tissues in

water to release the tears from the fibers. Just like making moonshine mash."

"Yeah." James pointed at Torman. "The water is siphoned off the mash, and that's what makes the alcohol."

"Exactly," Torman said.

I split a glance between Jett and James. "Do either of you have a way to contact John?"

"He has a prepaid cell that's only for emergencies," Jett said.

"Can you get him to come and bring his equipment?"

He grimaced. "I doubt it, but I'll try."

"So will I," James added.

Fury looked at me. "Even I will beg if I have to."

I pulled her to me and kissed her.

When I let go, Jett was watching us. No. He was staring past us toward the door. I looked over as Iliana walked in.

"Morning," she said through a yawn. When her mouth closed, her eyes drifted curiously around the room. "What are you guys doing?"

I squeezed the back of Fury's neck. "Just another day of trying to save the world."

"And my mother"—Jett flashed an approving gaze toward Fury—"has figured out how to save us all."

## CHAPTER TWENTY

"Are you all right?"

I looked across the bench seat of the passenger van at Fury. "Yeah, why?"

She glanced at my knee, which was bouncing up and down. "It feels like an earthquake in here."

"Sorry." I pressed my palms against my thighs. "Just worried about leaving Iliana behind. She's going to try to summon Sloan and Nathan, so they'll have to open the protective shutters around Echo-5."

"She'll be fine. She's with Kane and Jett, and if anything good has come out of all this shit, we now have a few of the enemy's weapons designed to kill angels, right?"

"True."

I searched the sky. Iliana wasn't all that worried me. It had been *too* peaceful since we'd been home. No reinforcement troops had been sent after Kelvin and his crew went MIA. We'd had no trouble getting humans or angels on and off the property. And there'd been zero activity when all of us had left Echo-5 that morning.

It wasn't a good sign.

An old drill sergeant once told me, "There's only silence on the battlefield for one of two reasons. Either the enemy's dead, or he's just reloading. You'd better know which before you stick your head out."

The Morning Star certainly wasn't dead. And if he'd pulled his troops back, that could only mean he was mounting an even bigger attack.

All of us were vigilant as we rode through the city. Cruz was driving. Reuel was in the passenger's seat, and Anya and Rogan were sitting behind us. Taiya had tried to come, and she'd cried when I told her she had to stay home.

On our drive to downtown Asheville, I believed what my friends had told me about the growth of the city since we'd been gone. The interstate now stretched eight lanes across, and all eight lanes were bumper-to-bumper. Corporate buildings dotted what was once undisturbed mountainsides, and skyscrapers had replaced the office buildings along Biltmore Avenue.

We passed a cluster of brick shops that sparked some memories. One of the stores should have had a black-and-white striped awning, but now it was gone. The sign above the door said "The Holistic Apothecary."

It wasn't until Reuel turned all the way around in the passenger's seat with his eyes fixed on the building that I remembered what it used to be.

A bakery.

"That's where Brienne's shop was," I said.

Without a response, Reuel looked forward again. His stony silence reminded me that Fury and I weren't the only ones who'd missed out on a lot here on Earth. Apparently, Reuel had been entertaining a hush-hush romance with a local sweets peddler. For a quick second, I wondered if she'd gone out of business due to lack of his patronage.

They truly would have been a match made in sugary heaven.

The heart of downtown was still recognizable. Pack Square was still dominated by a massive stone pillar. The courthouse and Sloan's old office building still stood. And Tupelo Honey, Sloan's all-time favorite restaurant, still had a line out the front door.

The people were also just as diverse, just as eclectic, as they'd always been.

Only now, there were many more of them.

Business people sipping coffees. Teenagers on skateboards. Young mothers pushing strollers. Street musicians playing for spare change. There were crew cuts and dreadlocks, power suits and broomstick skirts.

People had always spoken of the mystical draw of Asheville, but that had never been more true than now that Iliana was here. She was the beacon drawing wandering souls to the mountains.

We passed a billboard advertising the seventh-annual Asheville Brews-N-Tunes Fest happening this weekend.

"Asheville Brews-N-Tunes Fest?" I searched my memory. "I think that's the festival where I first saw Sloan."

"Sort of," Cruz said from the driver's seat. "The festival changed names and owners several years ago. Sloan was pretty upset about the change when it was announced. We used to go every year. We'd all raise beers to you."

I smiled as we turned onto Merrimon Avenue. From there, I recognized nothing until we passed the turnoff to Sloan's old townhouse. A chill rippled my spine.

The Asheville University School of Medicine was a shining

new campus on the west side of the city. "Damn," I said, awed as we drove in. "How long has this been here?"

"It opened this year," Rogan answered behind us.

Cruz looked at me in the rearview mirror. "Asheville drew a lot of attention from the medical community when people didn't get sick here."

"Does the doctor know we're coming?" Fury asked.

I shook my head.

Fury pointed past me. "They're here."

I followed the direction of her finger. Ionis and seven Angels of Ministry waited in front of a large white-granite building. The ministry angels were all in spirit form, a typical choice for their choir.

We parked and walked up the path to meet them.

Ionis stretched out his arms with a bright smile. "Did I do good, or what?"

"You did very well," I said as we approached. "Thank you all for coming."

A few of the ministers gave slight nods. Angels without bodies, particularly ministry angels, rarely spoke. Audibly, anyway. These would be no exception.

But we didn't need them to speak; we needed them to act.

Ionis stepped over beside me. "I explained why they're here, but I wasn't sure exactly what you needed them to do."

One angel floated a few inches in front of the others. He had yellow eyes that set him apart from the rest of the group. Ionis gestured toward him. "Warren, this is Shem. He leads the others."

"Hello, Shem."

He gave absolutely no sign of greeting.

I moved over in front of them and kept my voice low. "We're going to be in a classroom with about a hundred and fifty students. They'll be listening to a lecture dealing with difficult subject matter for humans. Some students will become emotional. Rather than helping them feel better, we need you to make them feel worse. We must collect as many tears as possible."

"You got that?" Ionis asked Shem.

Shem didn't respond. At all.

"I think he's got it," Ionis said.

I lifted a skeptical eyebrow. "Shall we?" I motioned toward the steps of Norton Hall.

The ministry angels went ahead of us and floated through the doors like they weren't closed at all. I tried the handle, but it was locked. As I moved to pass my powers over it, a young guy with a ponytail tapped a card onto a silver card reader. The lock clicked, and he yanked the door open.

I caught it before it shut. Fury stood beside me as our friends filed inside. She and Kane carried bags full of tissue boxes. I took hers and looked in it. "How many did we get?"

"Ten boxes. Should be enough, right?"

"I hope so."

Reuel carried in a couple of small metal trashcans.

"Think this will work?" I asked Fury quietly.

"Nope."

At least she was honest.

I walked in behind her, letting the door close behind us. Up ahead, Anya led the way, searching the door placards for room 203. We drew curious stares from the college students passing through the halls.

"This is it," Anya said over her shoulder. She pulled open a door and went inside. We followed her into a short hallway that turned right, then left and finally led into a large open auditorium. It had stadium seating for the hundred-plus students.

Dr. Swain spotted me from the front row. Her eyes widened with alarm and she stood.

"Wait here," I said to my friends before walking to her.

"What's wrong?" she asked.

"Nothing. We were hoping to sit in on your lecture."

"Why?"

"It sounds interesting?" My response didn't sound much like an answer.

Her eyes narrowed. "What are you really doing here?"

"Do you trust me, Dr. Swain?" I asked.

"Not really, no."

I smiled. "I appreciate the honesty. I promise, no humans will be harmed while we are here."

It was a tricky statement. She would immediately wonder if we were protecting them all from some greater danger. In a way, we were, but it was manipulative nonetheless.

She pointed beyond me. "You and your friends can sit on the back row at the top. Hopefully, there, you will be less conspicuous."

"You won't even know we are here."

"I'd better not." She slid her glasses down the bridge of her nose and looked at the bag I was holding. "What's that?"

"Tissues." I took out a box, ripped off the tab, and pulled out a single white tissue. "Given your subject matter, we thought they might come in handy."

"We're academics. Medical professionals not ruled by emotions."

I smiled. "OK."

Neither she, nor any of the students, would be able to see the ministry angels.

She rolled her eyes and shook her head. "Someday, I hope to understand all this."

"Dr. Swain, I sincerely hope you never do."

She looked at her watch. "It's almost time to start. You and your friends had better behave yourselves."

"We'll be perfect angels," I said with a wink.

Before going to our seats, Reuel and I placed trashcans at the bottom of each staircase. Fury and Anya put tissue boxes at the ends of alternating aisles. When we all finished, we found seats together near the center of the top row.

The Angels of Ministry divided into groups and positioned themselves along the stairs. Students passed around and through them, none the wiser.

Ionis leaned across Fury toward me. "Shem is waiting for you to nod. When you do, he'll signal the others to begin."

Across the room, the yellow-eyed angel was watching me so intently I worried my hair might start smoking. It was creepy.

"Do you understand?" Ionis asked.

I nodded.

Suddenly, one of the students let out a loud whimper. I realized it was the kid with the ponytail who'd let us into the building. He was a few feet in front of Shem, and the angel's yellow eyes were set on him.

I cleared my throat loudly until Shem, finally, looked at me. I swiped my fingers across my throat, which was hopefully a cosmically universal sign for "Cut it out!"

The angel blinked, and Mr. Ponytail quieted down immediately. Luckily, the girl at the end of the aisle passed him a tissue.

I closed my eyes. "This is going to be a catastrophe."

Beside me, Fury was muffling a giggle behind her fist. "At least it will be entertaining."

"Ionis," I whispered. "Can you ask them to be more subtle? We just need tears, not therapy sessions afterward."

"You got it, boss," he replied, then touched his ear.

The bell rang at exactly nine o'clock.

Almost every seat in the auditorium was filled. With a quick count of the seats, I guessed there were closer to two hundred students present.

I leaned toward Fury. "If we can get ten tears out of each of them, that's a couple of thousand."

"Will that be enough?"

"Torman said it would take a *few,* so fingers crossed."

A man in a suit with Albert Einstein hair walked up to the front podium. "Hello and welcome. I am Dr. Wyatt Murray, director of the Department of Health Management. Welcome to the first presentation of the three-part lecture series, 'Medical Ethics and Human Subject Experimentation.'

"We are honored to have Dr. Leona Swain, a physician and former professor of bioethics at the University of Maryland. Dr. Swain is the author of *First, Do No Harm: A Dark History of Human Experimentation*, which won the 2017 McCauley-Wilson Award for Book of the Year in Medical History. Please welcome, Dr. Swain."

The classroom erupted in applause as Dr. Swain walked to the podium. Shem caught my eye. I shook my head and mouthed the words, "Not yet."

"Hello, students, and thank you, Dr. Murray, for that warm welcome." She folded her hands on top of the podium and looked thoughtfully around the room. "*Primum non nocere.* Can anyone tell me what that means?" The words flashed onto the screen behind her.

Hands shot up around the room. Ionis's hand was one of them.

"First, do no harm," a woman answered loudly a few rows in front of us.

"Yes. First, do no harm. It's a phrase that's hopefully been drilled into your minds since your first day of medical school.

Hippocrates wanted you to remember it. Your professors want you to remember it. Your patients will certainly want you to remember it."

There were a few laughs around the room.

"But what does this mean? Surgery causes harm. Chemotherapy causes harm. Doctors don't always know when the benefits outweigh the risks, am I correct?"

Without thinking, I nodded right along with most of the students.

Ponytail guy cried first.

It took a second for my brain to connect the dots. By the time it did, tidal waves of emotion, from both sides of the room, crashed down onto the audience. Shem was so fixated on the students, there was no getting his attention. No pulling back the hysteria unleashed on the room.

The entire row in front of us wailed almost in unison. Grinning wildly, Ionis passed forward a box of tissues.

"Students, students, please!" Dr. Swain could hardly be heard over the sobs. Her eyes were wide with alarm, frantically searching the crowd for something to explain the commotion...

She spotted me.

I sank down low in my seat. Between the heads of the two kids in front of me, I saw the doctor's face darken. She put a fist on her hip and shook her head.

I sank lower.

Dr. Swain hadn't even shown the first slide.

"You've done it now," Fury said, chuckling beside me. I looked over and saw she was laughing through the tears streaming down her cheeks. She was trying to catch them in her palms.

Rogan reached over the shoulder of the girl in front of him

and plucked a few tissues from the box she was holding. He passed them across me to Fury.

Still laughing, she dabbed her cheeks and eyes. "How the hell are you going to explain this?"

I leaned my elbow on the armrest and covered my eyes. "Beats the shit out of me."

After a few seconds, I sat up and surveyed the chaotic scene. The bright side was the plan was working. Flashes of white tissues were everywhere. Even at the front, the doctors were now crying.

My supersonic ears couldn't hear what the two doctors were saying, but they were clearly trying to figure out what was going on. A couple more faculty members entered the room, and before long, they too were dabbing at their eyes with tissues.

The commotion lasted several minutes before a confused Dr. Murray stepped up to the podium. He gripped both sides of it and leaned toward the microphone. "Let's take a ten-minute break while we figure out what is going on." He looked at the clock and had to wipe his eyes before he could read it. "Class will resume at exactly nine twenty-five."

I jumped up. "Come on. We need to collect those tissues."

The wastebaskets were half-full by the time I reached the first one. I handed it to Reuel, then sidestepped my way through the bodies to grab the other on the opposite staircase. I held it out toward every student that passed.

Rogan, Anya, and Fury handed out tissues to students who needed more. Before the room had emptied, our wastebaskets were full, and I was crushing the tissues down to make room for more.

I needed to wash my hands.

"What did you do?" Dr. Swain marched over to me and threw her tissue on top of the pile.

"I didn't do anything," I said, semi-truthfully.

Another sob rippled through her.

Hesitantly, with my fingertips, I picked up the same tissue she'd discarded and offered it back to her.

She swatted my hand down. "I know this was you and your friends. What is it? Some kind of bioweapon? Is it harmful?"

"No, no. Nothing like that."

She cried out again.

I whirled around to look for the angel that was causing it. "Shem, that's enough!"

The angel jerked upright, and the crying around the room faded as quickly as it had begun.

Shock replaced the sadness on Dr. William's face with a flash. "Who's Shem?"

I looked over her shoulder as Dr. Murray approached. "Leona, I wonder if we shouldn't have the police or the city come in and test for toxins—"

"I don't think that will be necessary," she said, still glaring at me. "Whatever it was seems to have passed. Maybe the kitchen was cooking onions and peppers."

He looked even more confused. "The cafeteria isn't in this building."

"I think we'll be fine to resume class in a few minutes." She cast a questioning glance at me.

I looked around the room before nodding. The Angels of Ministry were leaving. Some through the walls. Others via the hallway.

"We'll chat later, Dr. Swain," I said with a smile as I backed toward the exit. "Great lecture." I grabbed a few more tissues off the floor as I left.

Rogan met me in the hallway when I walked outside. "Warren, we have to go. Kane needs you back at Wolf Gap."

"John's here," Rogan announced when we pulled onto the Wolf Gap property. A blue pickup, vintage now by any standard, was parked in the lot outside Echo-5.

Beside me, Fury sighed. "I can't believe you asked him to come."

"I can't believe he agreed," I said.

Cruz parked beside the truck, and we all got out. It was hot out, hotter than I remembered Asheville ever being. But it was the middle of August, and I hadn't exactly spent a lot of summers there.

I looked up at the building as we crossed the lot toward it. All the high-Z shutters were closed over the windows except for one.

"What is it?" Fury asked.

I pointed to the window. "I think that's the control room. Maybe Iliana was able to make contact with Sloan and Nathan." I breathed in fresh mountain air and looked down at her. "We're finally making some progress."

She smiled, squinting against the sunlight.

Beyond the building, near the tree line, was a four-car garage. "Hey, Cruz. Is my car in there?"

"It was the last time I saw it," he replied.

"Thinking of going for a spin?" Fury asked.

"Wouldn't that be nice?" I said with a sigh.

When we reached the door, I waved to the camera that was connected to the bunker. A buzzer sounded, and the lock clicked open.

Kane stepped out of the control room when we walked inside the lobby. His face was pale. His expression grave. "H-how'd it go?" he stammered.

My good mood crashed.

Reuel held up the three economy-sized trash bags filled with tissues. Before leaving campus, we'd scavenged the trash cans around Norton Hall.

Kane smiled, but his eyes were dead. "Nice work."

"You all right, man?" I asked.

His head jerked toward the door. "I need to see you in the office."

"OK."

"John is down in the bunker setting up."

"He brought his equipment?" I asked.

Kane's head gave a noncommittal tilt. "Well…he brought some equipment."

I didn't like the sound of that. I looked at Rogan and Torman. "Take the tissue to John. Bring Torman in and flash one of the swords around. That should make him more willing to help. Where's Iliana?" I asked Kane.

"With Cassiel."

"Did she make contact with Sloan?"

He shook his head and swallowed.

Something was wrong. Terribly wrong.

I turned to the rest of the group. "Don't wait on us to start making the crystal water. We'll be down soon."

Rogan nodded and led the group toward the door that would lead to the steps below. Fury stayed with me, and when the others were gone, we followed Kane into the control room.

"You're freaking me out, man," I admitted.

Kane pulled out the desk chair and sat down. "Close and lock the door behind you."

That didn't help my rising blood pressure.

When the lock clicked into place, he turned toward the computer and pressed a key on the keyboard. The picture flickered to life on the screen.

Fury gasped and covered her mouth.

I took a step back.

Two people wearing black hoods were chained to a wall in front of the camera.

One had a soul.

The other did not.

Between them, taped to the wall, was a sheet of white paper with "2 PM" written on it in red.

"What the hell is this?" I asked, though I knew exactly what it was. As a Marine, I'd seen too many similar videos during the Middle Eastern wars.

"I received a message from Huffman in the forum about an hour ago. It was a link to a video, but the connection was too slow in the bunker to play it, so I came up here, opened the window, and used my cell to connect. This feed is what came up. As far as I can tell, it's live." Kane looked at his watch. "It's one fifty-four."

We were four hundred miles as the angel flies from New Hope. Without the spirit line, there was no way for any of us to intervene in six minutes.

Fury gripped the back of Kane's chair and leaned over his shoulder. "Is this being recorded?"

"What?" I was a little horrified.

Kane clicked a few keys. "Everything is disabled. I can't make any changes."

"Can you use your phone?" Fury asked.

Panic pulsed through my veins. "Why?"

Fury straightened and faced me. "Because if they do what I think they're about to do, the world needs to see it. Our government needs to see it."

Nausea swept over me.

Kane picked up his phone off the desk. "She's right."

I paced the room, pulling my fingers back through my hair

as my mind went through the roster of everyone the Morning Star was holding prisoner.

Sloan.

Nathan.

Huffman.

Samael.

Sandalphon.

1:57.

1:58.

1:59.

I rocked on my heels behind Kane. Fury held onto my waist. Kane lifted up the phone in front of the screen and tapped *record* on its camera.

Another hooded figure walked into view. They wore nondescript black cargos and a long-sleeve shirt with black boots. They carried an assault rifle over to the prisoners, and first removed the hood of the angel.

Samael.

They pulled off the human's hood next.

Huffman.

Both of my friends' jaws were set. Expressions and hearts steeled, they stared straight ahead, visibly emotionless.

The guard used a serrated knife to cut open Samael's shirt, exposing his smooth, ripped chest.

Without warning, without last words, the guard stepped back and shot Samael. Three rounds straight to the chest. His back slammed against the wall, and he writhed against his restraints.

This wasn't just an execution. It was a demonstration.

The bullet holes didn't close. Steam rose out of them first, followed by thick black sludge that oozed down his torso. He gagged and sputtered as he tried to breathe through shredded lungs. Black blood trickled from his mouth before his whole body began to convulse.

Everything in me wanted to look away, but I didn't.

I couldn't.

I don't know how long it took—it felt like hours, but it couldn't have been more than a minute—until we got the answer we'd feared since Cassiel had first been shot.

In a shower of black sparks, the once-eternal spirit of the angel who guarded the spirit line exploded with a screeching, final hiss. The full weight of his body sagged against the chains, and his eyes—open and black—stared into nothingness.

Samael was gone.

My friend, who wouldn't even have been on this planet had it not been for the mess I helped create.

The executioner stepped over in front of Huffman.

His death wouldn't be so dramatic. A 5.56 of *any* kind at such close range would be fatal instantly for a human.

The gunman aimed straight at Huffman's forehead.

"Warren," Huffman said, staring straight into the camera. His eyes narrowed. "Kill them all."

Then blood splattered the camera lens.

# CHAPTER TWENTY-ONE

Dazed, Kane and I followed Fury to the bunker. Of the three of us, she was the most adept at keeping her shit together under all circumstances. But even her hands trembled as she reached for the door to the lobby.

Nash was behind the desk, thank the Father. Had it been Cruz or Lex, I might not have been able to keep the anguish off my face. Like Kane and Fury, those two had worked with Huffman for many years.

"Whoa, what's wrong with you guys?" Nash asked, sitting up straight.

Kane ignored him. "Where is everyone?"

"Most everybody's in the kitchen, I think. John's here."

"Can you find Iliana and bring her up here?" I asked him.

Nash stood and walked quickly to the door. When he was gone, Kane put his hands on his hips. "We don't need to tell anyone about this. At least not right now."

"I agree. It will cause nothing but panic, but Iliana must know. We need to make contact with Sloan and Nathan now more than ever," I said.

Kane nodded. "I'll take her upstairs if you want."

I put my hand on his shoulder. "No, I'll do it. Take a break, brother. I'm sure as hell going to find a dark corner and stew for a while as soon as I can."

He held up his phone. "I'm going to send this video to Enzo. He's on the inside at the Pentagon. Maybe he can help shut Claymore down and keep Azrael's name out of it."

"That's good." If I trusted anyone in Washington, it was Enzo.

"I'll come find you later," he said.

In an unprecedented move, Fury hugged him. They'd served with Huffman for years before I was in the picture. "I can't believe he's gone."

"Me either," Kane said, emotion thick in his throat.

The door opened. Fury released Kane and wiped under her eyes, sniffing back tears.

"What's going on?" Iliana stepped cautiously into the lobby.

"I need you to come with me," I said.

"Why? What's the matter?"

Nash walked in behind her.

I looked at Fury. "Go to our room. I'll have Anya come find you."

Fury lowered her voice to a whisper. "I don't keep secrets from my sister."

I nodded and pushed her hair behind her ear. "Tell her. I'll be back as soon as I can." I kissed her cheek. "I love you."

"I love you too." She and Kane walked out the door to the stairwell below.

"Nash, have you seen any movement on the cameras outside?" I asked.

"No, sir. Not since you all got back from the university."

"Thank you. Can you go find Anya and ask her to see Fury in our room?"

"Sure."

Iliana followed me out into the decontamination room. "Appa, what's happening?"

"We have to find your mother. Even if we have to fly out there and blow the house down."

She took a step closer. "You're scaring me. What's wrong?"

"I need you to keep a secret. I don't want to cause a panic in the group."

She nodded.

"They've killed our friend Huffman." Emotion choked me. "And Samael."

Iliana's throat closed with a squeak. Her eyes widened with horror. "Samael is dead?"

"Yes."

"Like *dead* dead?"

"Yes. They shot him with the same bullet that got Cassiel. I watched it destroy his spirit."

Her hand covered her mouth. "We have to save Cassiel."

"We will, but right now we have to find Sloan and Nathan. I need you to try summoning them again."

"OK."

We took off in a jog down the long hallway to the stairs. It was an excruciating walk up the stairs to Echo-5. My thighs were burning when Iliana and I finally reached the lobby. We were both panting.

"We've got to fix that elevator," I said, bending over to grab my knees and catch my breath. "I understand now why Ionis flies."

She recovered faster than I did. My body had been made *better* when I became an angel, but I was far from perfect. And I certainly wasn't an Angel of Life. I could feel the death searing through my muscles.

"Come on," Iliana said, tugging on my shirt.

I slowly jogged after her to the front door of the building. "Wait here."

She started for the door handle. "It's fine. Those bullets can kill you too."

I clotheslined her with my arm. "You're far more valuable than I am. Stay put while I check to make sure it's clear."

She sighed. "All right."

I walked outside. The sun was sinking low in the sky. I spread my wings and soared to the top of the building. My spirit detected no human life, or angelic, as far as the Wolf Gap property stretched through the mountains.

I returned to the ground and opened the door. "Come on out."

Iliana stepped outside and let the door close behind her.

"That's far enough," I said.

She closed her eyes, and a ripple of energy knocked me back a step.

*Whoa.*

I'd forgotten just how powerful she really was. Suddenly, her eyes popped open. "She's there."

"Your mom? Where?"

"I don't know, but she's out." Iliana's voice jumped up a few decibels. "I can feel her. I can feel them both."

"They're alive." I grabbed Iliana and hugged her. "Oh, thank the Father."

Iliana pulled back to arm's length. "We should go tell the others."

"You're right. I certainly need to focus on some good news."

She held back when I started to pull her forward.

"What is it?"

"If I go inside, my connection with Mom and Nathan will be broken." Her eyes were on the building—the angelically secure building.

I was confused. "So? When your mom was an Angel of Life, summoning someone was enough."

Iliana looked at me like I had three heads. It may have been the most "normal" moment of our father-daughter relationship thus far. "No offense, but Mom's power was nothing like mine."

Of that, I had no doubt.

I crossed my arms. "Please explain."

"As I understand it, Mom's power almost seemed coincidental. Mine isn't. As long as I maintain my connection with them, I can not only bring them here, but I can keep them safe."

"What?"

"I control life *and* death." She said it as matter-of-factly as she might have told me she ate bacon and eggs for breakfast.

"You can control it from hundreds of miles away?"

"If I'm focused enough...which I won't be if we go back inside."

I looked at the building and then back at her. "It isn't safe right now. You need to go back inside. I know your mom and dad would agree."

"You went to West Asheville and back today and nothing happened," she argued.

"Illy, those bullets aren't meant for me. I am not a target like you are. By comparison, I'm a nobody. But you..." I gripped her shoulders and turned her to face me. "You're the hope of this whole planet."

Her teenaged, quarrelsome face softened, and she took hold of my wrist. "You're not a nobody."

"Thanks," I said with a half smile. I cupped her face in my hands. "I promised your mother I would protect you. Please let me."

Still, she hesitated.

I released her. "I certainly can't force you. God knows you're stronger than me." I pulled open the door and waited.

She took a deep breath and blew it out slowly. "OK." She closed her eyes one more time, and the energy around her rippled again. "They're closer than before." She looked up at me. "Maybe they're on their way here."

"If they're free, I'm sure they are." I gestured to the doorway. "After you?"

With a cute smirk, she walked inside.

Our descent back to the bunker was, thankfully, less hurried than our ascent out of it. We took the steps one at a time, and side by side.

"I'm really sorry about your friends," she said when we were halfway down.

"I am too," I said, my heart heavy.

"I never met Huffman, but Dad spoke highly of him."

"He was a great guy. So funny. Took me out for my first beer after I'd joined Claymore."

"When you got out of the Marines?"

I nodded.

"So you knew him a really long time."

"Yeah. I wonder who will tell his family," I said almost to myself.

Huffman had a wife and three-year-old daughter when Fury and I left for Nulterra. He could have easily had more children during our time away. It was gut-wrenching that I didn't even know.

"When will the Father be here?" she asked, perhaps trying to change the subject.

"He was in Canada when Ionis made contact with him, so I doubt he'll be here today." Acid burned up the back of my throat. "He'll be devastated to learn about Samael. Everyone will be."

"I really liked Samael. He taught me a lot about using my powers."

"Really?"

"Yeah. He visited often after you left."

"He was a good friend. Saved my ass a few times."

"Mom said he was one of the first angels you guys ever met."

"That's true. The day your grandmother died." I looked over at her. "He'd come because he was excited at the possibility of *you*."

"Me?"

"All the angels were in an uproar when they heard your mom and I were together."

"Because of the prophecy?"

I lifted an eyebrow. "You know about the prophecy?"

*"I have heard the cries of a woman in labor breach the auranos, as the Daughter of Zion, light of the world, commander of Life and wielder of Death, is born unto man, the savior of us all."*

"I'm impressed. Even I hadn't heard of the prophecy until I got to Eden. Cassiel told me."

Iliana grinned. "Yeah. She told me too. And she said they didn't tell you while you were human because they thought it might freak you and Mom out."

"They were probably right." I laughed. "How is Cassiel? Jett told me about Taiya."

"Taiya's really helping her. Helping us both, really. She's keeping Cassiel stable for longer periods of time so I can rest. I slept for almost four straight hours last night."

"That's good. We were all really worried about you."

"I was worried about myself. And about Cassiel. I couldn't have kept it up. She would probably already be dead if it weren't for Taiya."

When we reached the lobby, Nash was chuckling behind the desk, watching the security cameras.

"What's so funny?" I asked.

"Just watching an Angel of Knowledge get told off by a human. It's pretty entertaining."

I opened the door to the main hallway. "Torman and John?"

"Oh yeah. It's a battle of wits, and the angel is losing."

"Bet that's going over well," Iliana said as we started down the hall.

We heard raised voices before we reached the kitchen.

"But the boiling point of water is two hundred twelve degrees Fahrenheit," Torman was arguing.

"And I'm saying a hundred and sixty-five degrees should be plenty high enough," John countered. "You don't want it to release too much steam. The steam is where the alcohol's at."

"There is no alcohol, you hillbilly moron."

"Hey, they called in an expert for a reason!"

Iliana followed me inside. "What the hell is going on in here?" I asked.

John and Torman were engaged in their shouting match across the kitchen island. On it was a camping stove, a kerosene bottle, a large pressure cooker, an orange five-gallon paint bucket, and some copper tubes. John was holding what I guessed was a thermometer in one of the many pots on the actual kitchen stove.

All our friends were watching the show from a safe distance at the tables. Luca was filming with his cell phone. Ionis was eating popcorn.

John actually looked relieved to see me, which was a statement in itself of how heated this conversation had gotten. "Warren, do you want me to do this, or what?"

I put my hands up in defense and approached the scene slowly. "What are you two arguing about?"

"Everything," Ionis said, popping a kernel into his mouth.

John waved a hand toward the large pots on the stove. "He says we need to cook down all these tissues until they start to disintegrate, but he wants me to turn it up so high that all the good stuff will float away." He wiggled his fingers through the air.

"He's being overly cautious." Torman rolled his eyes. "This would go a lot faster if he would turn. Up. The. Damn. Stove."

"Torman, stop talking. We've got one shot at this, and if John thinks we need to be overly cautious, we're going to be overly cautious."

John flung his hand toward me. "Thank you!"

"Never thought you two would be allies," James said with a grin, at the table.

I nodded. "You and me both."

Torman huffed and shook his head.

Iliana and I walked closer to inspect the pots. Five of them were filled to the brim with cloudy water and floating tissue paper. John was alternating between checking the temperature of the water and stirring the pots with a long wooden spoon.

He scooped up a spoonful of the dripping tissues. "See? The paper is already starting to dissolve."

I slapped the back of his shoulder. "Nice work."

"You wanna tell me exactly what the hell it is we're doing here? This guy"—he cut his eyes at Torman—"says it's none of my damn business."

"Didn't Jett tell you?" Iliana asked, looking around for Jett.

Rogan caught her eye. "He's in with Cassiel and Taiya."

"Oh, OK." She turned back toward her uncle.

"All Jett told me was something about a poison deadly to angels. He said whatever has made that blonde sick could kill him. Could kill all of you. Said the cure could only be made with my still, and he asked me to bring it."

I jerked my head toward all the other seemingly random equipment. "Is that what all this stuff is?"

"Well, no. It's taken me a long time to perfect my setup. Didn't want to dismantle it when this is capable of doing a small run."

I frowned. "Looks like a meth lab."

"You want to jump in with the insults too?"

"No. I'm sorry. Thank you for coming. What's the next step?" I asked, splitting a glance between him and Torman.

"I'm keeping my mouth shut," Torman said, swiveling away from us.

He wouldn't for long.

"John?" I asked.

"Well, if we were doing this the normal way with normal ingredients…" John scooped up another spoonful of tissues. "I'm not even sure what the hell we're doing with Kleenex."

"We are extracting human tears," I said.

His head pulled back. "That's creepy as shit."

"Yes. Now as you were saying," I said expectantly.

"As I was saying, if we were doing this the normal way with normal ingredients, we'd let our mash"—he nodded toward the pots—"sit and ferment for a few days, holding the temperature at ninety-five degrees. But I don't know how to ferment tears and snot so…" He gave a dramatic shrug.

Torman turned back around, just like I knew he would. "You don't need to ferment it at all. You just need to extract it." He got up, walked over to a large hard-sided cooler on the ground, and picked it up. He slammed it down with more force than necessary onto the countertop.

"Empty all the pots into here, stir them around, then use this spout here on the side to drain the water into the pressure cooker. That's it."

Because John was a little out of his field of expertise at this point in the process, he just smirked. "Then I guess we do that."

"Then what?" I asked both of them.

Torman lifted the long copper coil.

"Hey, don't mess with that." John shooed Torman away from the coil, waving his spoon. "The caulking probably hasn't set yet."

I inspected the setup closely. The thin coiled copper tube was connected on one end to the lid of the pressure cooker, and the other end was fed down through a hole at the bottom of the orange bucket. A messy caulking job sealed the hole around the pipe.

John tapped the pressure cooker's lid. "We'll lock this onto the pressure cooker, put the whole thing on the camping stove, and—"

"You don't need the stove for the next part," Torman interrupted.

"We need a heat source, and I can control the temperature better with the—"

"Iliana is the heat source!" Torman almost shouted.

John's face snapped toward her. "What?"

"She's the only way this works. We don't need kerosene heat. We need *supernatural* heat." Torman seemed ready to start pulling out his hair. "Iliana will heat the mixture of tears, the steam will condense in the coils, and the crystal water will drip out of the pipe in the bucket, into the Mason jar."

"You forgot you have to fill the bucket with cold water to cool the liquid so it doesn't evaporate," John said.

Torman shrugged, so annoyed. "Sure. Whatever."

"Those are the basics of the process," John told me.

"That's actually pretty genius. I never thought I'd be impressed by a moonshine still."

"I told him he should have become a science teacher instead of a bootlegger," Kathy said.

"How much longer do you think on the tissues?" I asked.

Surprisingly, John turned to Torman. "You wanna give your blessed opinion here?"

Torman got out of his chair like his body weighed a thousand pounds. He trudged to the stove. "They're translucent and starting to shred. I think that's enough."

"I think it needs a few more minutes," John said, stirring.

Everyone at the table snickered.

With a huff, the angel threw his hands in the air. "I give up. Do what you want." Torman started toward the door, but I sent up an invisible wall of power to stop him. He bounced off it and back a few steps, swearing.

"You're not going anywhere," Rogan said.

"Please, Torman," I said calmly. "We need your help."

His eyes narrowed to angry slits. "I still don't know what I'm getting out of all this."

Rogan suddenly stood. "Cassiel is crashing."

I dropped my wall, and Iliana took off running from the kitchen. I started after her, but stopped. "John, Torman, you should both come with us."

John grimaced. "I don't know."

"I'm *asking*. Please," I said.

"All right." He put the wooden spoon on the counter.

"Torman?" I asked with a little more don't-make-me-say-it-again in my tone.

He begrudgingly trudged after us.

Iliana was already treating Cassiel when we reached the infirmary. Taiya ran out of the triage room and into my arms when I stopped at the nurse's station. She was crying. And trembling. "Shh," I said, rubbing her back.

Torman walked closer to the door. "My word. Is that stench

coming from Cassiel?"

"She's rotting from the inside out," I said. "Iliana and Taiya are barely keeping her alive."

"I-I not," Taiya cried into my chest.

I ran my hand down her hair. "You're doing fine, sweet girl."

Cassiel's eyes were partially open, but the irises were mostly indistinguishable from the whites—now, *blacks*—of her eyes. The black webbing had spread to her face and neck.

She was worse, if that was possible.

Much worse.

John was staring, slack-jawed. "That could happen to my son?"

Torman beat me to an answer. "That could happen to all of us. What has the Morning Star done?"

Even for a demon like Torman, a line had been crossed. Stormed through, judging by the horror in his voice.

"Your daughter helped create this," I reminded him. "They are no longer discriminating between humans and angels."

"I see that."

"You understand now?" I asked.

He turned slowly to face me. "Yes. I understand. He's truly turned on his own."

"You'll help us then? *Really* help us?"

He nodded, something akin to *repentance* in his eyes. "Yes. I will help you."

"So will I," John said. "And I'll shut up and get along with the angel."

If he was waiting for Torman to agree to something similar, he'd be waiting forever.

Torman turned toward me. "As soon as Iliana is finished, we'll get to work. But be warned, it's going to take everything she's got."

## CHAPTER TWENTY-TWO

"*W*arren, you have a visitor." I could hear a smile in Nash's voice over the intercom.

Several of the guys and I were watching *Die Hard* in the living room. The bunker had a limited collection of "Emergency Apocalypse Films"—the box was labeled—and most of them were on DVD. The television was a beast compared to the slim-line mounted screen I'd spotted upstairs in Echo-5.

"Wonder who he's talking about," I said to whoever was listening.

"Fury?" Reuel asked.

I shook my head. "Fury and Anya are in the gym."

The *click-clack* of angry heels down the hallway prickled the back of my neck.

Dr. Swain stepped into the doorway, a crease already between her eyebrows. She pointed at me. "You have some explaining to do."

Ionis paused the movie.

I took my boots off the coffee table and dropped them to the floor. "I can explain."

She put her hands on her hips. "I certainly hope so. What did you do in my classroom today?"

"Would you like to sit down?"

"No."

"We needed human tears to create a cure for Cassiel."

She turned her head, her eyes narrowed to slits. Her expression was caught somewhere between amusement and *are-you-serious?* "Come again?"

I got up and crossed the living room. "You heard me correctly. My daughter can create a cure from human tears that no disease can stand against."

"You think that teenage girl of yours can create a broad-spectrum antidote for all diseases?"

"Yes."

"From human tears?"

"Yes."

With a smirk, she shook her head. "You're all crazy."

"It's true," I argued. "And we needed enough humans in one place to get it done. I'm sorry the only place I could think of on short notice was your classroom."

She put up a hand to silence me. "Let's say I believe you. How did you do it? An odorless gas of some sort?"

"No, no. It was completely harmless."

"How is it harmless? You took two hundred of the brightest minds in this city and reduced them to blubbering crybabies."

"We had the help of some other angels. Angels who can manipulate emotion. I promise, there will be zero lasting effects from today."

She looked skeptical.

"Have you had any lasting symptoms today?"

"No."

"Completely harmless." I started toward the door. "Come. I'll show you what we're working on."

With an exasperated sigh, she followed me across the hall to the kitchen and dining room. Kathy McNamara was working around the moonshining equipment to make dinner.

Dr. Swain stopped halfway through the room. "It looks like a meth lab in here."

I sniffed the air. It smelled a lot like the *osteria* where Cassiel and I had eaten in Rome. My stomach growled in response. "Kathy, what are you making?"

"Lasagna. I hope you're hungry."

"I'm always hungry now."

As if on cue, Reuel walked into the room and headed straight for the refrigerator.

"What is all this?" Dr. Swain asked.

"Well, it's a moonshine still," I answered.

"You know moonshining is illegal in this state, right?"

My head pulled back. "Really? After all these years?"

She didn't speak, but her eyes were asking, "Where have you been?"

She wouldn't believe me if I told her.

"Why are you making moonshine?"

"We're not. But we are using a modified process to distill the tears we collected today from your classroom. We do something similar to create a healing liquid called crystal water where we come from."

She lowered her voice. "Where *do* you come from?"

I smiled. "That's a conversation for another day. I apologize again about the disruption in your lecture. I hope things improved after we left."

We'd left the Angels of Ministry behind to calm the emotions of the students. Help them focus and be a model classroom after the disruption we'd caused.

She lifted an eyebrow. "They may have been the best students I have ever taught. *After* you and your friends left."

"Glad to hear it."

She looked over all the equipment. "You really think you can cook up a cure with all this?"

"We hope so. It's the best chance we have. We're going to try here in a moment. Perhaps you'll be here to see the results."

I had hoped we'd have this finished by now, but Iliana needed to rest after treating Cassiel again. Her grandmother had ordered her to bed. Poor kid was worn thin.

Dr. Swain reached into the bag she was carrying. "I got the results of Cassiel's bloodwork." She handed a sheet of paper to me.

On it was a list of acronyms and corresponding numbers. None of which meant anything to me. Most of the numbers had asterisks beside them, indicating the numbers were out of normal range. There were a lot of them.

"We also found an incredibly high amount of a foreign toxin. It might be a heavy metal or an element we don't have on our periodic table. I took it to some of my coworkers in the lab, and they said it has similar characteristics to arsenic. Her symptoms show the same."

"So how do you treat arsenic poisoning?"

"At this stage? You don't." Her face was grim.

I held up the paper. "So this is worthless?"

"Afraid so."

I crumpled it. "Anything else?"

"Her blood-cell count is almost nonexistent. There's no way a human would survive with her levels. She needs a blood transfusion, but her blood type is the rarest on the planet. She can donate blood to anyone, but there are only a handful of other people around the globe who could donate blood for her."

"Rh-null blood."

Her head jerked. "You know?"

"The golden blood type. All angels have it. She's in a bunker full of donors right now, but I'm afraid it might only fuel the poison. Whatever is killing her was designed to seek out and latch onto those blood cells. The blood cells survive long enough to kill everything in their path before they too are destroyed."

She looked at all the equipment again. "Then, for your friend's sake, I hope this works."

"For all our sakes, I hope so too. Want to check in on Cassiel?"

"Yes."

We started toward the door, but I stooped and looked back. "Reuel, you coming?"

Standing in front of the refrigerator, Reuel still hadn't chosen anything to eat. He closed the door, glanced quickly at me, and shook his head.

He hadn't spoken much since we'd left that morning. Not exactly out of character for him, but now he wasn't eating. Come to think of it, he hadn't joined us for lunch, and I couldn't remember seeing him snacking *at all* that day.

Something was definitely off.

I looked at the doctor. "Go on to the infirmary. I'll catch up."

"OK."

When she was gone, I walked over to him. "You're not hungry?"

He sighed.

"What's going on?" I asked.

"I think she's dead," he answered in Katavukai, the language he was most comfortable speaking.

"Who?"

"Brienne."

"Oh."

"I asked Nathan about her when we were on the island. He said she closed the bakery and moved away from Asheville before the virus hit." His eyes fell. "Luca helped me look for her online today when we returned from the university. We found nothing."

"Maybe no news is good news. She could be fine."

Or she could easily be dead.

He lifted his giant head, but I could see in his eyes, he didn't believe me. I put a hand on his shoulder. "We'll find out. I promise."

A small window of time existed between allowing Iliana to rest and Cassiel needing another treatment. Jett brought her to the kitchen at dinnertime, as Nana insisted Illy eat first.

The second we'd all finished the amazing meal, it was time to get to work.

"Place your hands on either side of the pot, and channel all your healing energy into it," Torman instructed, standing beside her.

"Will the metal of the pot reduce its effectiveness?" Rogan asked.

"Yeah, there are no pressure cookers in Eden," Jett added.

Torman tapped his creepily long fingernails on the metal side. "Do you really think this is any match for an angel's power? Iliana, go ahead. *Only* your healing power of life. Please don't turn this thing into a projectile."

"Please," I echoed.

Iliana's hands brightened, and the pot to began to vibrate against the granite countertop.

"More," Torman instructed.

She gave it everything she had until I could no longer see the pot or her hands around it for the light.

"Good. Keep going. As the liquid inside heats up and forms steam, the pot will pressurize. The steam will travel through the copper tubing, through the bucket, and will hopefully empty out into the jar," Torman explained.

"How long will it take?" I asked.

Torman lifted both shoulders. "As far as I know, this has never been done before. The only other angel capable is the Morning Star, and he wouldn't have much use for it."

"The Morning Star?" Dr. Swain asked from her place at the table.

"Yep," Ionis said. "Satan himself. He's not really in the business of healing people anymore."

The doctor visibly shuddered.

Everyone watched in bated silence. James stood behind Kathy, near the refrigerator, with his arms around her shoulders. Kathy's hands were clasped in the prayer position, beneath her chin. Her eyes were closed, and her lips were moving. I didn't have the heart to tell her that prayers were worthless without the spirit line.

My heart thumped nervously, and my hand was sweating around Fury's. She finally pulled away and wiped her hand on her pants.

Soon, sweat glistened across Iliana's forehead. "Is anything happening?" she asked through gritted teeth.

John was leaning against the counter behind her, by the stove. "Doing this the human way can take ten to fifteen minutes or more for the pot to pressurize. It will take even longer for the steam to begin collecting in the tube."

She groaned loudly.

Jett curled his arm around her waist for support. For the

first time, it didn't bother me. She needed all the help she could get.

The minutes ticked by slower and slower. It didn't help that my eyes were set on the clock.

Finally, John wrapped his hand around the copper tube. "It isn't working."

I walked over. "What do you mean?"

"Feel it."

I touched the metal. And shrugged my shoulders.

"It should be hot by now. Whatever she's doing isn't enough to build up the steam."

With a frustrated guttural scream, Iliana let go and grabbed onto the countertop for support.

I grabbed her waist to hold her upright when her knees wobbled. "Breathe," I said calmly in her ear.

"I can't do it. I don't have anything else to give."

"What do we do?" I asked Torman.

He was sitting at the far end of the counter, leaning his elbow on the countertop. "I was afraid this might be a problem."

"So how do we fix it?" Jett asked.

"She needs rest and food." He cradled his head in his hand. "I'm not sure she's going to be able to produce enough power to do it, even if she had a vacation to the Caribbean to recover. Her human body hasn't been purified by Eden. She'll never access all she is until that happens."

"So what do we do?" Rogan asked.

"What if we bring Taiya in here?" I asked Torman. "Iliana can use the power of other angels, and you said it yourself, Taiya still has healing properties buried in her body's cells."

"Taiya's the only thing keeping Cassiel alive right now. You pull her in here, and we might as well not even do this," Iliana said.

I hung my head. "Dammit."

"Warren, we have company outside," Kane said over the intercom.

"Who is it?" I replied, raising my voice toward the speaker in the tiles overhead.

"I have no idea. It's an old guy and another dude who kinda looks like Thor with black hair."

Every angel in the room except Torman, me, and Iliana jumped up and bolted toward the door. My whole body relaxed, and I exhaled for what felt like the first time in hours.

Dr. Swain looked around confused. "What? Who's here?"

I kissed Iliana's temple. "The Father."

# CHAPTER TWENTY-THREE

*R*eality had threatened to break my brain many times since Fury and I had leapt seventeen years into the future. But not even Iliana being all grown-up was as jarring as the sight of the Father, God Almighty himself, hobbling with a cane down the hallway.

I had finally given up waiting and went to investigate what was taking so long. Upon seeing him, the delay made immediate sense. I was a little surprised it hadn't taken him a year to get down all the steps.

As long as I'd known him, Father John—as he went by on Earth—had been an old man. Now? He was *elderly*.

Hunched.

Shriveled.

Feeble.

Even though they told me he'd been in Eden most of the time I was gone, the Father seemed to have aged more than the rest. Had it not been for the birthmark shaped like South America stamped on his forehead, I might never have believed it was him.

His wrinkled old face brightened when he saw me. "Warren," he said, breathing heavily from the journey to the bunker.

Gabriel and the other angels were behind him, but greetings for Gabriel could wait.

I closed the space between us in a couple of strides and embraced the Father gently, so as not to break his certainly brittle bones. "Father." I'd only ever seen him in the form of an old man, but now he felt small and frail in my arms. I pulled back to search his tired eyes. "Forgive me, but you're so…"

"Old?" he asked with a smile.

"Yes."

"This body ages here on Earth as any other would. Except, I fear the complete absence of Eden's power is fueling the process." He glanced back and chuckled. "And those stairs didn't help any either."

After almost wrecking reality in a negotiation gone sour with the Morning Star, the Father had imposed limits on himself for his visits to Earth. Never again would he be able to travel here with access to his full power, for his own fear of unintentionally undoing everything he created.

"Sorry about the stairs. I'm afraid that's my fault."

"So I heard," he said with a smile.

"I'm really glad you're here. Thank you for coming all this way."

"I told you, Warren, I'll always come when you ask me. Even if I am falling apart." His bony fingers reached up to touch my cheek. "You, on the other hand, haven't aged a day. How are you?" His eyes were deep pools of emotion, filled with questions well beyond how my day had been. They were pained. Sad. Maybe even a little regretful.

My gaze fell an inch. "Did you know?"

"About the time difference in Nulterra?"

I nodded.

"Prophecies cannot be avoided. They aren't guesses; they are glimpses of the actual future. So I suspected the Morning Star had tampered with time." He took my hand. "I'm sorry I didn't tell you."

"I've thought a lot in the last few days about why you didn't."

"And?"

"I would have gone to save Anya, even had I known." The shock of the moment I saw Iliana grown fluttered once again in my chest.

The Father must have noticed because his head fell slightly to the side, and a small smile played at his thin lips.

"I'm pretty sure anyway," I added quickly.

"Of course you would have. It is because of my certainty in this that I didn't tell you. I'd hoped to save you from even a few days of this pain. Now, I wonder if I made the right choice."

I would probably spend the rest of my life, however long it was, wondering the same. But he was right, as always. There's no way I could have lived with myself, knowing that an innocent woman was trapped in Nulterra when I had the power to free her.

Not to mention, Fury would have gone with or without me, and I would have died had anything happened to her.

But there was no use in pondering the what-ifs. Life only makes sense when looking back from tomorrow, and if we didn't hurry, tomorrows would be in short supply. I certainly didn't summon the creator of the universe to Asheville for an explanation.

"You've heard about Cassiel?"

"I have. How is she?"

"Not well. Not well at all. Would you like to see her?"

"Yes."

When I turned to offer him my elbow, I saw that everyone

had gathered in the hallway. Iliana, Fury, Anya, Kathy, James, John, and even Luca, who never seemed impressed by anything, were crowded behind me.

Kathy's hands were clutched over her heart. "Is it really…" She gulped, apparently unable to make any guesses.

"You haven't met?" I asked, a little surprised.

Everyone except Iliana and Luca shook their heads.

Even Fury.

The Father shuffled toward her first and reached for both of her hands. "Allison."

In all the years I'd known her, I'd never seen Fury dumb-struck. Her eyes were wide as he clutched her hands. "H-Hello," she managed.

"You've done well," he said in a loud whisper, leaning closer to her.

She blinked and swallowed hard.

Before she could recover, he looked at Anya. He reached for her. "You made it home, my child. I'm sorry for your ordeal."

Her mouth opened, but no sound came out.

"Sometime, I'd love to hear all about it," he said.

Her head bobbed up and down, but it was more like a nervous twitch than a nod.

James and Kathy were next.

The Father stepped toward them. "James, Kathy. Hello."

Kathy's knees sunk a few inches. "Oh my."

James shook his hand. "It's very nice to meet you, sir."

"The pleasure is mine," he said, and I absolutely believed him.

He patted Luca on the shoulder. "I daresay you've grown six inches since the last time I was here. How's baseball?"

I swear Luca blushed. "It's good, but this is the offseason. It doesn't start back until January."

"Maybe I can come to a game," he said quietly with an excited smile.

"I'd like that."

John was next. He looked far more confused than everyone else. I wondered how much Jett had told him about the hierarchy in Eden.

"John McNamara," the Father said.

John reached to shake his hand, but the Father stretched his skeletal arms around John's neck instead. John stood frozen for a moment before slowly closing his arms around the old man's back. "Uh, nice to meet you."

"It's so wonderful to meet you. Thank you," I heard the Father whisper.

John flinched as he pulled away. Then he gave a small nod and glanced behind us toward Jett. The guardian was beaming.

When the Father released him, he turned toward Iliana, who was leaning against the doorway. "Illy," he said, opening his arms.

She walked into them, and when she rested her chin on his shoulder, I watched her face fill with color. Perhaps her loss of strength had been so gradual over the past couple of days, I hadn't even noticed how pale she was.

She gave a heavy sigh of relief. "I'm so glad you're here."

He patted her back. "It's going to be okay."

I hoped he was right.

As he hugged her, he peeked into the kitchen. "Quite a setup you have in there, John," he said, pulling away from Iliana with a teasing grin.

John stammered again. "Um…uh…"

The Father grabbed John's wrist and shook it. "I'm only joking. Apple-pie moonshine happens to be my favorite." We all laughed, and he gave a John a wink before taking a closer look into the kitchen.

Torman had slinked out of immediate view from the door, probably in hopes of going unseen.

"I see you, Torman," the Father said. "Don't make my old knees chase you down."

Torman stepped out from behind the pantry door.

"Come here."

Torman slogged across the kitchen like the floor was made of molasses.

A hand touched my shoulder. "Gabriel." I greeted him with a firm hug. "Thank you for coming."

"Where else would we be when the weight of the world hangs right here?"

I groaned. "Do you have to put it like that?"

He lifted his shoulders.

"It's good to see you."

"You too." His eyes flashed behind me. "This should be interesting."

I turned back around as Torman stopped a few feet shy of arm's reach of the Father. He didn't utter a word, but the wilt of his shoulders betrayed his shame.

The Father closed the space between them, and after a long break of loaded silence, he hugged the demon. Torman stood rigid with his arms at his side, like a runaway kid who'd been forced back home.

"It's been too long," the Father said, taking a step back. "I've missed you."

Torman didn't speak, but his Adam's apple bobbed with a strained swallow.

The Father gave Torman's arms a final squeeze, then came back to me. "Shall we see Cassiel now?"

He hooked his arm through mine, and we started down the hall. "How much have you been told?" I asked.

"Ionis told Gabriel about the poison. He also said you're attempting to brew crystal water."

"That's true. Do you think it will work?"

He lifted his free hand. "I honestly don't know. I do know that it will be very difficult to create."

"We've already tried. Iliana is tired and weak from keeping Cassiel alive. I was hoping you might be able to help them both while you're here."

"You know I'm without my powers in this form."

"I do, but I also know people still get better around you. That's why you've been traveling far and wide, seeing people with Blackmouth Fever."

"Yes, that is correct."

"So will you help her?"

"Of course I will."

We continued down the hallway, but he stopped suddenly before we reached the glass sliding doors. He put his hand on the window, and his tiny shoulders sank. "Oh, my beloved Cassiel."

Taiya was with her. She had made balloons out of the latex gloves at the nurse's station. She was swatting them all over the room and chasing after them around Cassiel's bed.

Cassiel looked about the same. Still threatening to charge down death's door.

The Father was visibly shaking. I curled my arm around his shoulders. He shuffled toward the door beside me, and we walked in arm in arm.

Dr. Swain, who'd gone to check on Cassiel when everyone else took off outside, was at the nurse's station. She was bobbing and weaving around Taiya's balloons as she worked on some paperwork.

Suddenly realizing we'd entered the infirmary, Taiya spun around and let all her balloon gloves fall to the floor. "Oh!" She pushed her hair out of her wide blue eyes. She knew exactly who was with us.

When the Father reached for her, she grabbed his hand and hugged him until he winced. "I've missed you too, sweet Taiya."

She started babbling in Katavukai.

He put his hand on her face. "Thank you. You're doing a fine job taking care of her. I'm so proud of you."

She kissed his cheek.

He laughed cheerfully. "Thank you for that."

"Taiya?" Kathy called from the door, beckoning her forward.

Taiya skipped across the room to join the others waiting behind us. The Father's gaze followed her. "Such sweet innocence in that one," he said to himself.

He turned to Cassiel's bed and touched the peak of one of her toes under the blanket.

Part of me expected Cassiel's eyes to open and for her to leap off the bed at his magical touch. That part of me was disappointed.

"This is not supposed to happen. Angels are not supposed to get sick and die." He looked at me. "Of all the things he's done, how could he do this to his own kind?"

I didn't need to ask who he was talking about.

I shook my head sadly. "When I was in the military, I saw the worst of humankind. Bombs driven into school buildings. Women and children starved in prison cells. My buddies getting their legs blown off by roadside IEDs. I often asked myself the same question."

"This is because of me," he said solemnly. "So many atrocities are committed in my name, but this…" He tipped his head toward Cassiel. "This was done directly to cause me pain. A weapon that can kill all my creations alike."

He walked around to the head of the bed and picked up

Cassiel's dead and gray hand laying on the mattress. Her dangerously low heart rate picked up a few beats.

Dr. Swain walked up beside me. "That's 'the Father'?"

She actually used air quotes, and I might have laughed had the whole scene not been so grave. "Yes. That's Father John."

"And he's an angel too?"

"Oh no. He's something else entirely."

We watched him put her hand down carefully and move closer to her head. "Cassiel?" He leaned down and lowered his voice. He spoke softly in Katavukai, and I intentionally tuned out his words. They weren't for me.

"I doubt she can hear whatever he's saying," Dr. Swain said.

I crossed my arms. "I'm sure she can. Her spirit and her ears are two very different things. We can all hear his voice."

The doctor was watching Cassiel's vital-signs monitor. "Whatever he's doing, it's helping her. Her stats have only been that high after the first time I saw Iliana treat her."

"He has that effect on people."

When the Father straightened, I saw tears on his face. He wiped them on the back of his hand. "Let's go. Let's make a cure."

"The steam is rising," John said, his hand wrapped around the tube. Gasps and whispers floated around the room. "It's slow. I'm afraid the power isn't enough."

At the end of the kitchen island, the Father's hands now covered Iliana's on the pressure cooker. Her face was red and sweaty. She'd stripped down to a tank top and had pulled her hair back.

I looked at the clock. It had been half an hour since the Father had seen Cassiel. "Reuel, bring Taiya in here."

"Is that a good idea?" Fury asked.

"We don't have a choice. Cassiel is dead either way." I looked at Reuel. "Hurry."

He rushed out of the room.

Kathy dabbed Iliana's forehead with a towel. "You're doing great. Just a little longer."

"Nana, could you get me some water?" Iliana asked.

Luca beat everyone to the cabinet. He pulled down a glass and filled it at the refrigerator for his sister. He carried it to Kathy.

"Thank you," Iliana said.

Kathy held it to Iliana's lips as she sipped.

A moment later, Reuel returned with Taiya. She was running behind him, and she skidded to a stop when she saw all of us gathered around the kitchen counter. Her head fell to the side. "We eat again?"

"No. We need your help. Come here, please," I said.

The Father released Iliana's hands, and she immediately slumped forward like all the strength had been sucked out of her. "Taiya, put your hands on Iliana's," he directed.

Obediently, Taiya placed her hands on top of Iliana's. "Good. Stay just like that." He covered Taiya's hands with his own.

Energy surged back into Iliana so fast her head swirled around. "Whoa."

Jett grabbed her waist to steady her. "You OK?"

She nodded and refocused on sending her energy into the pot.

We all waited nervously. James paced the room. I chewed my thumbnail until it bled. Ionis quietly hummed the old theme song from *Jeopardy!*

"Will you shut up?" Rogan snapped at him across the table.

Ionis held his hands up. "Excuse me."

When he was silent, I could almost hear the seconds ticking by on the clock. It was more maddening than the angel ever could have been.

*Tick.*

*Tick.*

*Tick.*

John's hand moved farther along the coil. "It's moving."

Judging from where his hand was, six inches above the top of the bucket, the steam wasn't moving fast enough.

We needed more power.

We needed another Angel of Life.

Out in the hallway, the heavy door to the lobby opened and shut. Shannon's voice echoed off the concrete. Rogan sank down in his chair and shielded his eyes with his hand.

Reese walked into the kitchen first. His head snapped back when he saw us. "What is this? A party?"

Shannon walked in right behind him. She was saying something over her shoulder.

Two more people followed her inside.

Sloan and Nathan.

"Oh my god," I said.

"Yes?" the Father answered.

My mouth fell open. I rushed to them. "You're here," I said, grabbing Sloan by the arms and pulling her to me.

Kathy and James were right behind me. Kathy cried as she hugged Nathan.

Adrianne entered next. Her hair was long, straight and bleached blonde, and she seemed shorter than I remembered. I looked down and saw she was wearing sneakers instead of her usual high heels.

"Adrianne?"

"Hi, Warren."

She held a young girl by the hand. A boy, almost as tall as

his mother, trailed behind them, playing something on his phone.

All of them, I realized, were wearing high-Z cuffs.

And they each had the same black *spot* inside them that I'd seen in Azrael. They were rigged to die.

Sloan and Nathan too.

I searched Sloan's chocolate eyes, my thoughts tumbling like boulders down a mountainside. "But…what? Why? I mean, how are you here?"

"Hey!" John called. "Never mind all that. We are running out of time over here!"

"John?" Nathan couldn't have sounded more shocked if Santa Claus was in the kitchen.

John was right. Questions could wait. I grabbed Sloan's hand. "We need you."

She stumbled as I pulled her to the counter. "What on Earth is going on here?" She did a double take of the Father's face. "You're here too?"

"My dear, we will explain everything. But right now, I need you to place your hands under mine."

Sloan was obviously confused, but people who know him rarely question the Father. She nodded. "Whatever you need."

"On the count of three, I will remove my hands. I need you to place your hands on top of Taiya's and give it all the power you can."

"OK."

The Father and Taiya shifted apart to make room for Sloan at the counter. She stepped between them and opened her hands.

"Ready?" the Father asked her.

"Ready."

"One… Two… Three!" The Father let go.

Jett held Iliana to keep her from falling.

Sloan closed her hands around Taiya's.

The Father covered Sloan's with his. "Now! Everything you've got!"

From the other side of the island, I could see Sloan's power surge through Taiya's hands into Iliana's. Fury put her arms around my waist, and I held her. Her other hand clasped Anya's. Everyone in the room gathered near.

Watching.

Waiting.

Soon, Iliana's light was so bright everyone was squinting against it.

John slipped on his sunglasses. He was still holding the coil. "It's moving!" His hand inched farther along the tube until it reached the bucket. "James, get the water jugs out of the refrigerator."

James and Luca brought over four gallon-sized milk jugs. He poured them into the bucket. "What's that for?" Anya asked.

"The cold water will condense the steam back into liquid." He poured in one of the jugs of water. "Which, hopefully, is liquor…or whatever the hell it is we're making."

"Crystal water," several of us—including the Father—said at the same time.

"Crystal what?" Shannon asked.

When all the jugs were empty, John placed a Mason jar with a plastic funnel on a stool. He slid it beneath the end of the copper tube jutting out from the bucket's base.

He reached into the cold water to touch the coil again. "It's working!"

We all held our breath…

Finally, the first drops drizzled into the jar.

whiff of the jar made my eyes water. "I'd say it worked." I handed the crystal water to the Father for inspection.

"Well done, everyone," he said, nodding with approval.

Taiya cheered. Everyone else clapped. Well, most everyone. Torman was very ho-hum at the counter. "That's less than two shot glasses full. Definitely not enough to protect all of us."

The Father passed it back to me.

I screwed on a lid. "No, but it might be enough to save Cassiel." Half the amount is what had saved Fury in Nulterra. "And now we know it can be done. Hope is half the battle of the war."

Torman smirked. "Okay. I'll remind you of that when you're in front of a firing squad with Uzis filled with that stuff."

Rogan grabbed him by the arm. "I think we promised you a more comfortable room. Anybody mind if I lock this asshole up in one of the staff bedrooms?"

"Be my guest," I said

Rogan looked at Reuel. "Want to help me?"

With a grunt, Reuel followed Rogan and Torman out of the room.

Shannon started to go after them, but Reese held her back.

Iliana went to her mom and dad, tears sparkling in her tired dark eyes. "I'm so glad you're back."

The three of them embraced. Nathan kissed Iliana's forehead. Sloan pulled back to look at her. She pushed Iliana's hair behind her ears. "You found us today."

"You felt it?"

"I did, just when I was about to give up hope." Sloan hugged her again. "I'm so proud of you, Iliana."

When she released her again, Sloan reached for my hand and squeezed it with a grateful smile.

I sighed with relief. The black spot inside Sloan was gone, erased by Iliana's power. The spot inside Nathan, Adrianne, and the kids remained.

Iliana saw it at the same time I did. She reached for Nathan. I grabbed her wrist to stop her. "Try the crystal water."

She looked at the jar. "But there's so little."

"We need to make sure it works on whatever is inside them. You have a whole army to cure, remember?"

She nodded. "Nana, can you hand me a spoon?"

Kathy went to the cutlery draw and returned with a teaspoon.

"It should only take a drop," the Father said.

"What's happening?" Nathan asked, wide-eyed.

"You're gonna be our guinea pig," Iliana said, dipping the spoon into the jar. She let almost all the liquid drain off it before holding it up to his lips.

Nathan recoiled. "What is it?"

"You don't want to know." Grinning, I crossed my arms. "But if you don't drink it, you might die."

"He booby-trapped us, didn't he?" Nathan asked.

"Yes. Drink," Iliana ordered.

Nathan obeyed and coughed when he'd swallowed the liquid. "Shit, that stuff's awful."

Iliana and I stood back, watching the spot in his chest. Slowly, it fizzled away. She squealed and hugged me.

"It worked?" he asked.

"It worked," the Father said.

"Hey, Nate, you just drank a bunch of strangers' tears and snot," John called across the kitchen.

Nathan gagged. "Seriously?"

Iliana laughed. "We need to get this stuff to Cassiel."

I offered it to her. "I think you should be the one to take it. After all, it's your creation."

"Agreed!" James cheered.

When she reached up to take it, I held onto the jar. "I'm proud of you too."

She smiled. "Thank you."

"Me too," added Taiya loudly.

We all laughed.

Together we walked to the infirmary. The whole group trailed behind us. They gathered around the window as Iliana took the crystal water to Dr. Swain.

The doctor lifted an eyebrow. "This is it?"

Iliana held it up against the light from the overhead bulbs. "This is it."

The Father came in behind us. "It may not look like much, but I think you will be quite impressed with its results."

Dr. Swain took the jar and unscrewed the lid. "What's the dosage? How do we administer it?" The smell made her head snap up. "Whoa."

"Start small, that's all we have," I told her. She took a

syringe and vial out of her bag. "Five milliliters to start?" she asked.

When she held up a syringe, I nodded. "Looks good to me."

She poured the liquid into the vial, stuck the needle inside it, and drew the liquid into the barrel. She took a deep breath and picked up Cassiel's IV line. "Everyone say a prayer."

I glanced down at the Father. "You heard that?"

He chuckled.

Dr. Swain pressed the plunger, sending the crystal water in through the IV. She dropped the syringe into the sharps container and stepped back beside the three of us. Iliana took my hand. She was trembling.

When Fury drank the crystal water in Nulterra, it was an immediate and explosive reaction. Shattering the veils around reality and tearing down walls between worlds.

Here, nothing happened.

I worried that was a bad sign.

The doctor's eyes were on the monitor. The rest of us watched Cassiel's face for any change. Any sign of life returning.

*Beep...beep...beep...*

Cassiel's heart rate increased first.

"My god," the doctor said, checking Cassiel's pulse in her wrist. The blood pressure cuff inflated and released. "Her blood pressure is rising."

Iliana's hand tightened around mine.

Cassiel's temperature dropped.

104.6

103.9

102.4

Dr. Swain pulled the blanket down to Cassiel's waist and opened the front of her gown. With a gasp, the doctor dropped the fabric and stepped back with shock.

Cassiel's entire abdomen oozed puss and bloody black sludge from the gaping hole in the center, but the webbed veins of necrosis wrapping all the way around her sides were beginning to shrink. Slowly, but visibly, even for the stunned human.

The Father walked over and stood beside Dr. Swain. "It's working."

As the infection shrank, the black diffused to a dark purple. Then it turned from green to light brown to yellow before finally fading into the creamy peach tone of her skin. Scar tissue crept across the open wound until it closed.

A sniff made me look up. Dr. Swain was crying.

So was Iliana.

The color returned to Cassiel's face last. Her breaths had deepened, but she didn't open her eyes.

"One more dose of your power wouldn't hurt if you have it in you, Iliana," the Father said.

She nodded and flexed her fingers a few times as she walked to the bedside. She recovered Cassiel with the gown before letting the white light surge in her hands once more. She carefully lowered it to the center of Cassiel's abdomen.

With a powerful gasp, Cassiel shot up in bed so fast she nearly knocked heads with Iliana.

Our friends in the hallway erupted into cheering. Ionis squealed, jumping up and down. Everyone was hugging.

The doctor covered her mouth with her hands.

I was so relieved I feared the weight of the whole situation might go out through my knees. I grabbed the nearest body to me for support.

Jett.

With a laugh, I put my arm across his shoulders. Fury joined us, and I pulled her against my side.

Iliana took Cassiel's hands to calm her. "Cassiel?"

Cassiel's bright blue eyes were now clear. No longer painted with black. They darted frantically around the room but stopped when they passed over the Father. "What...what are you doing here?"

"Welcome back." He hugged her, but she was too stunned to even move her arms.

"Back? Back from where? What happened?"

"You've been unconscious for days," Iliana said, sitting down on the edge of the bed beside Cassiel's legs. "We almost lost you. A few times."

Cassiel's hands went to her stomach. "I remember being shot." She looked at me, as I was always the cause for gunfire around her. "Then I woke up here."

I walked toward her bed. "Congratulations. You were our first test subject to create a cure for a poison devised by the Morning Star to kill us all."

"What?" she asked, horrified.

"The Morning Star created a new poison called hydrogen necroxide. He melted down one of the swords to add helkrymite to the compound. We almost lost you for good," I said.

"Iliana kept you alive until she could create crystal water," the Father added.

Cassiel was amazed. "Crystal water?" She looked at Iliana. "That isn't possible. No angel is powerful enough to create it without the auranos."

The Father put his hand on Iliana's head. "Yet this one *did*."

The doctor lifted the vial. "Yeah...we need to get more of this stuff."

"How are you?" I asked Cassiel.

She looked bewildered. "I feel great. *Confused*, but great." She lifted the neckline of her gown to her nose. "I smell really bad."

"Hydrogen necroxide binds to our red blood cells and causes our bodies to rot from the inside out," Iliana said.

Cassiel gagged. "I've been rotting?"

"For three days." The doctor shook her head, amazed. "I can't believe you're alive."

"Who are you?" Cassiel asked.

The doctor extended her hand. "Dr. Leona Swain. I can honestly say, it's been a privilege to treat you and experience all this." She looked over at me. "Thank you for convincing me to stay."

I bowed my head slightly. "You're welcome."

"Now about that crystal water…" Her eyes cut toward the jar again. "How can we get more of it?"

Iliana laughed weakly. "I'm gonna need one hell of a nap first."

"You've earned that, little girl." The doctor picked up the jar. "Can this stuff cure Blackmouth Fever?"

"Crystal water can cure anything," Cassiel said.

"Wow." Dr. Swain raised the jar toward me. "I think I just changed my fee."

Slowly, our friends began to trickle in behind me. Sloan grabbed the side of my shirt, and I pulled her against me. I kissed the top of her head. "Your timing couldn't have been any better."

"We have Reese and Shannon to thank for that," she said.

"I was going to message you guys, but Adrianne advised against it," Reese said.

"Communication is too dangerous with Michael and Chimera," Adrianne explained, coming into the room. Her kids were sitting in the hallway. Luca and Taiya sat with them. "They've always watched this place, but I'm sure it's even worse since the shit hit the fan last night."

"What exactly happened?" I asked.

"Dad came to me in a dream last night," Sloan said. "He told me what had happened here with Cassiel and warned us about the new weapons of Legion Nine."

Nathan smiled. "We woke up when the bedside lamp exploded. Not sure what he did to it."

"He was afraid you would think you were only dreaming. We tried to teach him how to mess with electricity so you would know he was really there," Iliana said.

Nathan chuckled. "Oh, we had no doubt. He almost burned down the house."

"How did you escape?" I asked. "I can't imagine they just let you walk out of the house."

"Michael was the most irrational I'd ever seen him this morning," Adrianne said. "I'm not sure what he and Azrael were arguing about, but Michael stormed out. During lunch, Azrael got a phone call and left in a hurry. Something was going on at the base."

"Samael and Huffman." I hadn't realized I'd said it out loud until the whole room fell silent.

"What about Samael and Huffman?" Nathan asked.

I tensed and exchanged an uncomfortable glance with Fury. "Samael and Huffman were executed today."

A wave of shock and horror pulsed through the room.

"No," the Father said with a gasp.

Tears welled in Sloan's eyes. "They're dead?"

I nodded.

"Are you sure?" Nathan asked.

"We watched it happen," Fury said.

"What do you mean *dead*?" the Father asked.

I swallowed hard. "The poison contains helkrymite. Samael is gone."

The Father's knees faltered. Iliana grabbed him and eased

him down next to Cassiel. Nathan swore and raked his fingers through his hair.

I returned my watery eyes to Adrianne. "That's why Az left in such a hurry. It happened at two o'clock."

We were all silent for a while. Nathan held Sloan as she cried. Adrianne hung her head and turned to look at her kids out in the hall.

The Father held Cassiel. "What about Sandalphon?" she asked quietly.

"We have no news on Sandalphon. But that also means we have no news that anything has happened to him. He must be safe, or they would have told us," I said.

"We were able to escape because of them," Nathan said. "They gave us a window to get out of that house."

"You're right. Their last acts on this Earth saved the lives of others." I put my arm around Fury. "They would have wanted that."

"True," she said.

"That doesn't explain how you all wound up together," Anya said.

Adrianne hugged her arms. "Michael disabled my car as soon as he realized we were gone, I'm sure. It died in the middle of I-40, and we barely got it to the side of the interstate. Thankfully, we were near an exit, so we walked to a gas station. Low and behold, guess who we found?"

Shannon waved her hand.

"I can't believe I'm going to say this…" Adrianne looked mildly guilty as her eyes slid toward Shannon. "Thank you for rescuing us."

Shannon leaned toward her. "Come again?"

"Thank you for rescuing us," Adrianne said again, sounding slightly less grateful.

Shannon smiled. "You're welcome."

We'd never hear the end of it.

"We were really lucky you were there today," Nathan said to Reese.

Gabriel shook his head. "That was too fortunate for it to have been luck. Someone was watching over you all." He looked over at the Father. "Any idea who that might be?"

"I really don't, but I'd like to find out," the Father said.

"What time was it?" I asked Nathan.

He thought for a moment. "We'd been driving about three hours, so probably around three."

"It was Iliana," I said.

Her brow rose. "What was me?"

"You're right." Sloan took Iliana's hand. "We were on the side of the road when I felt your spirit."

"Somehow, you made Reese and Shannon stop at that exit." I looked at the Father. "Did you know she could do that?"

"It's well within the power of an Angel of Life to move the energy of the universe to protect others. Doing it without intention…that is remarkable," he said.

Iliana blushed, and Sloan hugged her.

Nathan put his hands on his hips. "So what now?"

"Now, I'm afraid we prepare for the fallout. The Morning Star will come after us. He's probably already on his way," I said. "Adrianne, do you have any insider information?"

"Michael doesn't tell me much, but I know they've been working around the clock this week. They're preparing for something."

"War," Gabriel said.

I nodded. "You're exactly right. We need you to summon all the angels you can."

"Of course."

"We need a plan," Cassiel said.

Kane came forward. "She's right."

The Father looked at Anya. "Send the guardians to the city. Their instinct will be to protect the people."

She nodded. "I'm on it."

"I'll position the messengers outside the area, maybe even between here and Claymore, so they can keep us informed of the Morning Star's movement," Gabriel added.

"Tell the Angels of Death I want them here. They battled the fallen here the last time and won," I said.

"Where do you want me?" Iliana asked.

I pointed to the floor. "Right here."

She scowled.

"You're the prize. If we keep you here, we might keep this battle out of the city," I told her.

"We'll have the advantage if they attack from the main road. We can crank up the voltage on the electric fences along the perimeter," Kane said.

"The demons can disable it," Cassiel said.

Nathan nodded. "Maybe, but the fences are rigged with tear gas if anyone, angel or otherwise, tampers with the power."

"Nice," I said.

"Whatever happens," the Father said solemnly, "spare as many human lives as you can. Remember, those in the employment of the Morning Star know not who they serve."

"Nonlethal force against mortals," I repeated. "Gabriel, go. Call everyone you can."

He bowed his head. "Ionis, come with me," he ordered.

Ionis saluted, then did some sort of ballerina twirl toward the door. When they were gone, Cassiel scooted toward the edge of her bed. "I'm not doing anything until I've had a shower." Her legs wobbled when she stood, and I reached out and grabbed her arm.

"I'll take you," Fury offered, rushing to help.

Cassiel looked surprised. "Thank you."

"We'll both help," Anya said, stepping to Cassiel's other side.

The two sisters supported Cassiel across the room. "We'll be downstairs if you need us," Fury said to me.

I smiled as they walked out.

Shannon looked at her husband. "I want to find Rogan."

"OK." Reese touched the small of her back as she started toward the door. "I'm really glad everything worked out here."

I walked over to shake his hand. "Thank you, Reese."

"You're welcome."

"I need to be going too," Dr. Swain announced. "I certainly wish I could take this stuff with me." She carried the jar of crystal water to the nurse's desk. "I'm gonna lock it up in the drawer for safekeeping. If word gets out that you've got something like this, demons won't be the only attackers you'll have to worry about."

"That's a good idea," I said. "Once this is all over, we might put your research team to work figuring out a way to mass distribute this stuff."

"Like a vaccine…" Iliana said quietly. She looked around. "Where's Papa?"

No one had told Iliana that her grandfather was MIA. He hadn't returned with Sloan and the others.

"Yeah, where is he?" Sloan asked.

I grimaced. "We really don't know."

Her eyes doubled. "You lost my dad?"

"Not *lost*, exactly. He'll find his way back here."

"Warren!"

"We'll find him, I promise," I said, putting my hands on her shoulders. I needed to change the subject. Fast. "Kane, can you take Dr. Swain to her car?"

"Of course."

We all thanked her again before she left, then followed them out of the infirmary. Jett and Iliana helped the Father.

Kathy and James were waiting in the hall with the kids and Taiya.

"Tell me about Azrael. What's going on with him?" I asked as we started down the hallway.

"We didn't see much of him," Nathan said. "But he's definitely not himself."

"He's a puppet," Adrienne said.

"You know Michael is controlling him then?" I asked her.

"I've known for a while. I should have listened to you all. He's not my son."

"No, he's not," the Father said. "He's mine."

We all stopped walking. It wasn't exactly a revelation, but hearing the Father take ownership of the Morning Star was still jarring.

He shuffled toward Adrianne. "I'm sorry you've been caught in the middle of all this. It's not fair what he's done to you and your family."

It was clear, she was unsure of what to say.

He touched the top of the little girl's head walking beside her. "But I'm sure these little ones have brought a lot of joy."

I wasn't sure Adrianne's son qualified as *little*. He was easily pushing six feet, not shocking since both his parents were tall. It was odd how much he looked like me when I was thirteen. His hair was lighter, and he had a slim frame like his mother, but the face was all Azrael, just like mine.

In the center of his chest, glowing deep inside him, was the black spot. The capsule of death implanted by the Morning Star.

"What's your name?" I asked him.

His attention was buried in his phone. Adrianne nudged him with her elbow. "Hey, Warren's talking to you."

He looked up.

I smiled. "What's your name?"

"Phillip." He turned back to his phone.

Adrianne rolled her eyes. "He's named after my dad. He's very happy to meet you."

"And what about you, princess?" the Father asked the little girl.

The kid looked up at her mom, as if for permission to talk to a stranger.

Adrianne nodded.

"Sloan," the girl answered.

"Hey! That's her name too," Taiya said, pointing at grown-up Sloan.

We all looked at Sloan. "Did you know?" I asked her.

"Not until today," she said, her eyes sparkling. She leaned down in front of the child. "Sloan, that's my daughter, Iliana."

Iliana stuck out her hand. It was glowing with a small amount of healing power. "Hi. It's nice to meet you."

The instant little Sloan touched Iliana's hand, the black spot disappeared. "Hi," she said quietly.

When Iliana pulled her hand away, she touched Philip's arm. That was all it took.

Adrianne, none the wiser to what Iliana had just saved them from, was fighting back tears. "Iliana, I can't believe how grown-up you are."

Iliana walked over and hugged her—and healed her, too. "We've all missed you, Adrianne."

Tears flowed then. "I wanted to reach out so many times. I just felt so trapped."

Sloan walked over and hugged her. "It's done now. We'll get through this." She pulled away and looked at Luca. "Why don't you and Taiya take Phillip and Sloan to our apartment downstairs? Find a movie or something."

Luca obviously wanted to object. Babysitting wasn't cool for a senior in high school. To his credit, he nodded. "Sure.

Come on guys. We have a lot of old, really crappy"—he flashed a *look* at Nathan—"movies downstairs."

Nathan pointed at him. "You watch your mouth, sinner."

Luca laughed.

"We'll go with them. Give you all a chance to catch up," James said to Nathan.

"Thanks, Dad."

"Who wants a snack?" Kathy asked. "Maybe Nana will whip up some cookies."

The little girl hesitated, looking up at Adrianne. "It's OK," Adrianne said. "These are our friends."

Taiya knelt down in front of her. "Do you play?" she asked, hopefully.

Little Sloan nodded.

"Me too!" Taiya offered her hand, and the little girl took it and immediately smiled. Taiya had that effect on *everyone*.

Adrianne was wiping the mascara under her eyes as we watched the kids go toward the lobby. "It's been so hard on them."

"I'm sure it's been hard on all of you," Sloan said, rubbing Adrianne's back as she steered her into the living room. "Nathan, can you open a bottle of wine?"

"Of course." He went into the kitchen as the rest of us followed Sloan and Adrianne.

"We have to get Azrael back," Adrianne said, crumpling onto the sofa.

"We will," I said firmly. "Does he know he's being controlled?"

Adrianne shook her head. "I've tried to tell him. He thinks I'm being paranoid."

I sat down in one of the recliners. "Where'd you get the cuffs?"

"I've been stealing them for the past year. One pair at a time whenever I've come across them." Sloan handed Adrianne a tissue, and Adrianne dabbed her eyes. "I knew we'd have to get away at some point, and I didn't want Michael to be able to follow us."

"Do they work on humans?" Iliana asked. She and Jett sat on the floor near her mom.

"We made it here, didn't we?" Sloan answered. "Claymore helicopters were circling the interstate the whole way across the state. They were definitely looking for us."

"They limit the control Michael can have on us," Adrianne said. "I overheard him say to one of the guards once to never put human prisoners in the cuffs. I knew there had to be a reason."

"We need to get Azrael into them," I said.

"I've tried. Wrestled him to the ground one night with them, but then Michael found out and took the cuffs away. He didn't know I had other sets."

Nathan returned with a bottle of wine and as many glasses as he could carry. He handed one to Sloan and one to Adrianne. When he offered one to me, I shook my head.

"I'll take one," the Father said with a smile from the other armchair.

Nathan handed it to him, then poured his glass half-full.

"Thank you, Nate," the Father said.

"Anything for you, sir." He returned to fill Sloan's and Adrianne's glasses. "Warren, thought you'd want to know that John is in the kitchen packing up his stuff. He's about to head out."

John.

In all the excitement, I hadn't even realized he wasn't in the infirmary. I got up. "I'll go talk to him."

"It's too dangerous out there tonight. Convince him to stay. Only you can," Nathan said.

I doubted that, but I walked toward the door, determined

to try. Jett started to get up, but Nathan held out a hand to stop him.

John was at the sink washing out the cooler when I walked in. "You need some disinfectant for that thing?" I asked.

He grinned. "I'm going to bleach the shit out of it when I get home."

I picked up a towel and started drying the pressure-cooker lid. "Why don't you stay? We've got plenty of room."

"Sit tight while you all bring the apocalypse down on our heads? No thanks." He dumped the water out of the cooler, into the sink.

"We'll be safe underground. I can't say the same for the roads between here and Claymore."

He put the cooler on the counter and wiped another drying towel over it. "I appreciate what you're trying to do, Warren, but I'm ready to go home. I did what I came to do, and now I'd like to get back behind my gate."

I admired his resolve. "All right." I put the lid back onto the pot and placed the whole thing into the cooler. He coiled the copper tubing around it and closed the cooler's lid. "Any of this other stuff yours?" I asked, looking around at the pots on the stove.

"Nope. This is all." He carried the cooler to the door, and I followed him.

Out in the hall, I offered him my hand. He stared at me for a second before putting the cooler on the floor and accepting. He gave me a firm handshake. "Thank you, John. We couldn't have done this without you."

"Well, you almost had to. I still can't believe I came."

"Why did you?" I asked, for the first time wondering if somehow Iliana had manipulated him into it.

He looked into the living room. "I came for him." He was

looking at Jett. Iliana was nearly asleep, leaned against his chest.

"You're a good dad."

He slapped my shoulder. "Well, I'm pretty sure that boy is *your* problem now," he said with a chuckle. "Good luck with that."

I laughed. "Thanks."

"Can you ask him to see me out?"

"Sure. Fury will want to say goodbye."

His face suggested that wasn't a good idea. "I'd rather not. I've had enough goodbyes with that girl to last a lifetime."

I nodded.

"Take care, Warren."

"You too, John."

He picked up the cooler and started toward the lobby.

I returned to the living room. "Jett, your dad is heading out."

Nathan was on the couch beside Sloan. "What?"

"Sorry. Couldn't argue with him."

Jett got up.

The Father reached out. "Take me with you. I'd like to say goodbye."

Jett helped him out of the chair.

"I'm coming too," Iliana said, dragging her weary self off the floor.

When they were gone, only the four of us remained.

Me, Sloan, Nathan, and Adrianne.

Adrianne patted the seat beside her. Obediently, I walked over and sat down, still, after all these years, unwilling to put up a fight against her. She leaned on my arm. "You started all this shit, you know?"

"Me?" I asked.

"We were doing just fine until you showed up in Asheville missing a soul."

Sloan laughed. "If we're pointing fingers, I'm pretty sure Detective McNamara is to blame."

Nathan turned toward her in his seat. "What the hell did I do?"

"You're the one who plastered my face all over the news to begin with. Warren wouldn't have ever seen me and come to Asheville had it not been for you trying to force me to become some kind of superhero."

"Yeah, Nathan. How dare you bribe her with cheese grits?" Adrianne added.

We all laughed.

And it felt good. *So* good.

"Maybe," Nathan conceded. "But think of all we've built."

Sloan looked at me. "And all we've made."

*Iliana.*

"As much hell as it's been, I wouldn't have chosen anything different." Adrianne rolled her head along the back of the sofa to look at Sloan. "Except for maybe walking away all those years ago. I'm sorry."

Sloan took her hand, threading their fingers together. "I love you."

Adrianne rested her head on Sloan's shoulder. "I love you too."

Fury peeked into the room.

"Hey, you," I said.

She hesitantly walked inside. "Am I interrupting?"

"Absolutely not," Sloan said with a genuine smile. "Come join us."

"Want some wine?" Nathan asked, reaching for the last empty glass on the coffee table.

"Sure." She sat down next to me as Nathan poured the wine. He handed it to her. "Thank you."

Adrianne leaned forward to look at her. "Hello, Allison."

We all had the same reaction. Pure shock.

Fury lifted an eyebrow. "You've hated me since the day we met, and now you want to use my Christian name?"

"It's been almost two decades. If we all live through this, I guess we'll be seeing a lot more of each other since Sloan told me the two of you are together now. It's time we start over." Adrianne raised her glass to her lips. "And I can't take you seriously calling you Fury."

Fury smiled. "OK."

"OK?" I asked, surprised. "It took years for you to allow me to call you Allison."

She gestured toward Adrianne. "It's been *years* for her too, Warren."

We all laughed again.

"How's Cassiel?" Sloan asked Fury.

"I think she's going to be fine. The crystal water seems to be working its magic," she said. "Anya is with her."

"It worked a lot more slowly for her than it did for you," I said.

Fury sipped her wine. "I figure angels are a lot harder to kill, so they're probably a lot harder to heal too."

"Good point." I leaned my head back and stared at the ceiling. "When those guns show up, we're going to need a hell of a lot more of that stuff."

Sloan straightened, shaking her head. "I don't want to be sad or afraid tonight."

"Sorry," I said.

She raised her wineglass. "So let's toast to the next seventeen years. Of all of us *together*."

Everyone but me raised a glass. Nathan reached forward and grabbed the wine bottle. "Here."

I smiled as I raised it with the others. "To the next seventeen years, and to Huffman and Samael."

"To Huffman and Samael," they echoed.

"Cheers," Sloan said as they clinked their glasses—and I, the bottleneck—together.

I drank straight from the bottle.

Adrianne kept her glass in the air. "And if we're all going to die tonight, I'm glad it's with you jokers."

## CHAPTER TWENTY-FIVE

We didn't die that night.

Quite the opposite, actually. It was the first full night of sleep I'd had since we returned to Asheville. No one woke me up in the morning, and Fury was still asleep beside me. The clock on the nightstand said 7:07 a.m.

Crazy.

Of course, the world could have gone to hell above the surface, and I might've slept right through it.

Rolling toward Fury, I curled my arm around her. She gave a soft moan in the darkness, and I pressed my lips against the back of her bare shoulder.

"We're alive," she said sleepily.

"I guess miracles are still a thing even, without Eden."

We'd all gone to bed early the night before to catch as much sleep as possible before the Morning Star's inevitable attack. Fury and I had made love until we were both too spent to continue. We'd slipped on our underwear in case people or sirens woke us during the night.

"Have you heard anything since I fell asleep?" she asked.

"Only you snoring."

"I don't snore."

"Oh yes, you do. When you're good and exhausted."

She arched her spine so that her ass pressed against me. "Then if I did, it's all your fault."

I slid my hand up her arm to where it disappeared beneath her pillow. I meshed our fingers together and smiled against her skin. "I'll gladly take the blame."

"You haven't heard from anyone?"

"No, but I'm sure things are hopping upstairs." I could hear the shuffle of feet overhead.

Before we'd gone to bed, seventeen other angels had already arrived. The Father had taken it upon himself to play host up in Echo-5 once all the beds were filled in the bunker.

"Do you think more angels will come?" she asked.

"I hope so. We need all the help we can get. The Morning Star will attack, but who knows when?"

"I thought for sure he'd sweep in during the night."

We'd all thought that. My fear now was that he would know we would rally everyone here. Then he'd fly in and start shooting us like fish in a barrel.

But I couldn't think about that yet. Not during what could be our last peaceful minutes together. I released her hand and hooked the strap of her tank top, sliding it slowly down her arm.

"What are you doing?" I could hear the playful smile in her voice.

"The world might end today. And one more time with you would be my dying wish."

She laughed softly. "That's exactly what you said last night."

"We've been given a second chance. We shouldn't waste it." I pushed my hips against her, and she reached back and threaded her fingers through my hair.

My hand skimmed her breast as it dove beneath the sheets to slide her panties down her thighs. It was my turn to moan as I entered her from behind.

Someone knocked on our door.

I swore and flattened my palm against her stomach to hold her against me. "If the building's not being bombed, go away!"

Whoever was outside the door hesitated, but they didn't leave. I could feel them standing there.

"What?" I shouted.

"No bombs yet, sir." I heard Nash clear his throat. "But the Morning Star is on his way."

A lightning-fast cold shower had done little to defuse the situation below my belt, so I took the stairs to the lobby two at a time to get my blood pumping to *other* areas. It was an uncomfortable hike.

Lex was behind the lobby desk. He motioned me over and slid his chair back.

"What's happening?" I asked, walking over beside him.

"Sorry to wake you, man, but Kane needs you upstairs." He pointed to the ceiling. "All the way upstairs."

Over his shoulder, I looked at the monitors. Vehicles were parked all over the grounds outside, all civilian as far as I could tell. "All these angels have been cleared to be here?" It wouldn't be too hard for members of the fallen to infiltrate this swarm.

"Cleared by the Father himself. Most of them are yours."

The Angels of Death.

"Cassiel has been checking loyalties at the door since sunrise, just to be safe."

She would know if any of them were lying to get inside. I was thankful she survived all over again.

"Where's the Morning Star?" I asked.

"Inbound. You should hurry."

"And Iliana?"

"With her parents downstairs."

"Good. Use physical force to keep them down here if necessary."

He gaped. "Physical force against *Iliana?*"

"Try," I said and started toward the exit. "And tell Fury where I've gone. She's supposed to get my sword from the safe and bring it to me."

"Warren, wait up!" she called behind me.

I turned.

No. Not Fury. It was Anya, now carrying her own sword strapped across her back. She caught up with me as I entered the concrete hallway. "Is it true?"

I didn't slow my pace, and she had to double-step to keep up. "Is what true?"

"That the whole damn army is headed this way?"

I stopped. "What?"

"That's what Nash just told me. He said they're watching it on the news upstairs."

"Shit." I broke into a run, and Anya stayed right behind me. She and I were both half-dead by the time we reached the ground floor.

Upstairs, Angels of Death and messengers had taken over Echo-5. Most were in human form; others were not. A few greeted me, but there were so many that I passed by most without being noticed.

I spotted Cassiel and the Father near the front door, but they would have to wait. I ducked into the control room and found Kane and Cruz at the computer watching several news stations on the big screens.

My jaw dropped. "What the...?"

"I was able to patch into a few local channels," Kane said as we walked up behind them.

I pulled both hands back through my hair. "Holy shit."

On each screen was aerial footage from different news cameras. Military convoys filled the interstates, some taking up all lanes of traffic in both directions.

"The media is just now putting it together that all those troops are inbound to Asheville. All the interstates and major highways from *all* sides," Kane said, pointing to the different screens. "I-40, I-26, 74, 25, 191, 280…It looks like the 2003 invasion of Iraq, sir."

"What the hell are they doing?" Anya asked.

"There are too many of them to all be coming here," Cruz said.

A boulder landed in my gut. "They're going to seal off the city. The Morning Star's not attacking us. He's going to attack the city."

"That's what it looks like," Kane agreed.

"How close are they?" I asked him.

"By road? Forty miles, max, via I-40."

"There's more *not* by road?"

"Helicopters have been circling the sky for the past twenty minutes."

"What kind?" I asked.

"Three light-assault birds, two chinooks, and the fancy transport helo. It's passed over a few times. My guess is the Morning Star is about to make a grand entrance any minute now. The Father confirmed he was aboard."

"What about Azrael?"

Kane shook his head. "No way of knowing."

"Were the assault birds armed?"

"Four gunners each. That's why the Father started bringing everyone inside. He was afraid the Morning Star's plan was to pick everyone off from above, knowing you wouldn't want to harm the human soldiers."

"I was worried about the same thing," I admitted.

"There's more," Cruz said, his tone grim.

"A couple of fighter planes flew over a few minutes ago," Kane said.

"He's going to bomb the city." I couldn't believe the words even as they left my mouth.

"Why?" Cruz asked.

"His only other option would be to starve us out. That would take years, and he knows it," I said.

"And you don't show up to a party with that many people just to wait outside," Anya added. "If he attacks civilians, he knows we'll try to stop him."

I started toward the door.

"What are you going to do?" Kane called after me.

"I'm going to bring down that helicopter."

Anya followed me back out to the entry hall. I stopped and faced her. "Maybe you should go find your sister."

She lifted an eyebrow. "Why? Because us womenfolk belong in the bunker?"

I grinned and shook my head. "Never mind. Forgot who I was talking to."

"Warren!" Cassiel waved me over. She looked a million percent better. Clean hair. Fresh clothes. She was dressed in khaki cargos and a white T-shirt. She had a radio and a pair of high-Z cuffs strapped to her belt.

I sidestepped through the angels coming in. "Who all is here?" I asked.

"You told Gabriel to call them all." Her clear bright blue eyes were wild with excitement. "Almost a thousand have already been accounted for."

"Leave the Angels of Death here, but send everyone else to

the city," I said.

She pointed out the door, toward the sky. "But the helicopters—"

"He's going to attack Asheville. He knows it's the only way to draw us out of the bunker."

The Father looked sick. "He knows it's the only way to get to her."

By *her*, he meant Iliana.

"Exactly."

"He's right," the Father said. "Send everyone you can to the city."

"The guardians are already there," Cassiel said.

Anya looked up at me. "I should be with them."

It was hard for me to agree.

Perhaps the Father noticed. "She is their Archangel now," he said.

I stared at her for a moment. "Find Rogan. Have him take you in the car he stole from Claymore. At least, maybe then, you'll blend in."

She nodded.

"Anya," the Father said as she started away. She turned back toward us. "You have the power of the Archangel now. Use it to repel the people out of the city without causing a panic."

"I don't know how," she admitted.

He reached for her hand, and she took it. "Yes, you do." A wave of energy pulsed between them, and Anya rocked slightly on her feet.

When he released her, she shook her head to clear it. "I'll do it," she said, backing toward the stairs.

Watching him as he watched her, I lifted an eyebrow. "Powerless, huh?"

He smiled. "It's like nuclear energy, Warren. You can shut down the reactor, but the radiation lingers."

"Cassiel, how are you feeling?" I asked.

"Like I could kick somebody's ass today," she said, lifting her radio to her mouth.

"That's good. Looks like we might need you to."

She clicked the button on the radio. "Ionis, tell Gabriel to send everyone else to the city." She stopped an Angel of Death named Egris at the door.

"I can take care of mine." I touched my ear and silently called out to the Death Choir. Almost a complete hush fell over the building as the angels listened in.

"Change of plans. The Morning Star is preparing to attack the city. On my order, go and defend it. Take care to not use lethal force against human soldiers, but do whatever is necessary to prevent mass casualty. Watch for bombs overhead."

The Father was staring at me when I looked up.

"Sorry, Father, but they have bombers. If we have to sacrifice a pilot and crew to save thousands, so be it. They shouldn't have chosen to follow orders against civilians."

"I know, but I don't have to like it," he said.

I squeezed his shoulder.

Static crackled in my ear. "Warren, it's Lachlan. Shall we go now?"

I heard the faint *chk chk chk* of helicopter rotors outside. I touched my ear to answer. "I want everyone to meet me outside first."

"Outside?" Cassiel's voice dialed up a few decibels. "You saw what that bullet did to me."

I put my hands on her shoulders. "You're right. And I would rather be standing in front of those guns than anyone else. He's not going to go away, so the sooner he's dealt with, the safer everyone will be."

The Angels of Death were lining up at the door. Lachlan led them. I shook his hand. "Good to see you, old friend."

"You too, sir. Welcome back."

I stepped into the doorway and searched the sky. "Has anyone seen the Morning Star's helicopter pass over again?"

The Father shuffled forward to stand beside me. "Not in the last couple of minutes, but it's flying by regularly. I'm sure he'll be back."

"And you don't know if Azrael is in it?"

He shook his head sadly.

I started outside.

Cassiel grabbed my sleeve. "You can't be serious!"

"The Morning Star is circling because he's waiting on something. Probably me."

"Do you at least have crystal water?" she asked.

"It's locked in the desk in the infirmary." I turned to the Father. "But no matter what happens, promise me you won't let them use it on me."

I knew the Father would be the only one able to make that call. They wouldn't listen to anyone else.

Cassiel touched her temples, ready to launch into an argument. "Warren, that's the most—"

The Father held up a hand to stop her. "I will tell them," he said to me.

"Thank you."

Before Cassiel could argue further, I walked out. The Angels of Death were right behind me. At least fifty more angels were wandering the grounds. Most of them were Angels of Ministry, and only a few of them were in human form.

I recognized a spirit with yellow eyes. "Shem!"

He looked over, then glided toward me, inches off the ground. "Take your angels to the city. If you can't encourage the humans to get out of town, try to make them go inside."

He gave a slight nod, then signaled to the other angels to follow him. They all flew straight up into the air. I watched them until they disappeared. "That's still so weird," I said, forgetting other angels were gathering in behind me.

Lachlan was the closest. "What would you have us do?"

"Think we can crash-land some helicopters without killing anyone on board?" I asked.

Lachlan grinned. "Kinda picked the wrong bunch for keeping humans alive, sir."

"Let's give it our best shot, OK?" I asked.

He nodded and took a few steps toward me. "Can I ask you a question?"

I lifted my brow.

"Is Samael really dead?"

"Yes."

Lachlan flinched. I hadn't really thought about it before, but the Angels of Death had never lost *anyone*. Azrael had come close, and he was no longer an angel, but he still wasn't *dead*.

A worrying thought flashed through me. *What if Samael's death was only the beginning?*

My eyes searched the sky as the sound of helicopters echoed off the mountains in every direction. "Come on, you son of a bitch. Where are you?"

A helicopter flew by, but it wasn't one of Claymore's fancy transporters. It was a small attack helicopter, and Claymore guards were posted on outboards outside its doors. Their weapons rested in front of them, thankfully.

But I'd been part of this organization before. They were waiting for an order.

An order to open fire.

"That one, sir?" Lachlan asked.

"Not yet. We're waiting on the big one."

A few more minutes passed by.

"Warren! What the hell do you think you're doing?" Fury yelled from the building.

When I turned, I saw she'd been to the armory. A rifle was strapped across her chest and a handgun was holstered on her thigh. She wore an armored vest, but at close range, with such a large caliber as these soldiers were carrying, it wouldn't be enough.

My sword was on her back, and I needed it, but it would have to wait.

Reuel was standing right behind her in the doorway. I locked eyes with him. "Keep her there."

Fury wouldn't have been able to hear me, but Reuel's supersonic hearing hadn't missed the message. When she started outside, his massive arms closed around her.

If I lived, I'd have hell to pay for that later.

A deeper *whomp whomp whomp* of another helicopter drew my attention back toward the sky. After a moment, the aircraft crested the peak behind Wolf Gap. It was solid black, with Claymore written in gold down the tail.

Angelic energy surged inside it.

I touched my ear. "Let's bring that thing down without killing anyone."

Raising my hands toward it, I blasted my power at the tail, but it ricocheted off without touching it. Some kind of force field protected it.

The helicopter turned and lowered toward the field in front of us. My hair whipped wildly back and forth from the force of the helicopter's blades as it landed. Its engine died. This wasn't going to be a drop-and-run flight.

As the rotors slowed, the side doors opened. Four armed human Claymore guards got out, with what looked like M4s on steroids raised in our direction.

The scene was oddly familiar. Our island arrest was a fresh memory. I realized now that if he'd wanted us dead, the Morning Star could have killed us then.

*Why didn't he?*

The thought passed as quickly as it came because a woman, instead of the Morning Star, stepped out onto the grass.

Chimera.

Two angels were behind her. One of them was a guardian named Tabris. I'd heard stories from Azrael of when they'd battled during the First Angel War.

Half of Tabris's face was scarred from the fire Azrael had conjured.

The other, a female I didn't recognize. She was tall and thin with long, straight black hair.

As they approached, the noise waned from the helicopter. My spirit searched inside it. There were no other angels. Or humans.

Azrael wasn't here.

I folded my arms. "Chimera."

The Seramorta, part-human and part-Angel of Knowledge, hadn't aged quite as much as the rest of the people Fury and I had left behind. Probably thanks to her proximity to the Morning Star.

But she'd matured from the cyberpunk I'd known before. Her hair was still short, but no longer spiked, and she was missing her piercings. Instead of fishnets and combat boots, she wore a black button-up with the sleeves rolled up her forearms and simple gray slacks.

Her hands were stuffed in her pockets as she approached. "So it's true. You're still alive." She stopped in front of me.

"And you are still a conniving thief. I guess some things never change."

She smirked.

"What do you want?" I asked.

"You know what we want. We want Iliana."

"Not going to happen."

"Would you really let the entire city burn? Would she?" She looked around, probably hoping to spot Iliana nearby.

My eyes narrowed.

"Here's the deal." She looked at her watch. "In eleven minutes, all the main roads in and out of Asheville will be blocked with tanks and armed soldiers. No one will be able to escape. And five minutes after that, we lay waste to your beautiful city."

"Or?"

"Or she comes peacefully with us, and we pull back all our troops."

"Where's my father?"

"If Iliana complies, you can have Azrael too. The Morning Star has even promised to remove the poison inside him."

"Because promises from the Morning Star mean so much to me," I said. "Why does he want her?"

"Truthfully?"

"Can you manage such a thing?"

"He wants her dead."

Because without Iliana, he would be the most powerful angel on Earth. Not even the Father could rival him.

"One life for a few hundred thousand." She looked at her watch again. "You have nine minutes. Think it over. I'll wait." She started back toward the helicopter.

There was no way I was giving up my daughter. The Morning Star might spare the city *today*, but his mission was to destroy mankind. Hell, he might get Iliana and blow up the city today anyway. That's the thing with demons—the only thing you can trust is that you can't trust them.

Ever.

The Father hobbled outside, and I went to meet him. "He wants Iliana?" he asked.

"Yeah."

He grabbed my arm. "She's the only hope we have."

"I know. We need to keep her below."

"What do you want us to do?" Lachlan asked.

I touched my ear so he would hear me, along with all the angels standing behind him. But before I could speak, Cassiel rushed out of the building, carrying her radio. "Warren, we have a problem." She was looking all around.

"What's wrong?"

"Iliana is…"

An engine revving snagged my attention somewhere in the distance. There were plenty of cars on the property, but none of them seemed to be occupied. My first thought was Anya, leaving with Rogan, but I hadn't seen them come out of the building yet.

Then I saw it.

Across the property, one of the garage-bay doors opened. A black car screeched its tires on the concrete and sent up a cloud of black smoked as it peeled out.

My black car.

The Challenger.

Nathan and Lex ran through the smoke it left behind.

As the car screamed by, I saw Jett clutching the "oh shit" handle in the passenger's seat. Iliana had both hands on the wheel, her eyes set straight ahead.

I was so stunned, I couldn't even move.

When I finally turned, Chimera stood by the helicopter door, her jaw dropped. She touched her ear to use her phone, as she couldn't communicate like the angels. "Iliana is on her way to the city—"

Suddenly, sparks sizzled all over the helicopter. Electricity ripped through it like it had been struck by lightning, but it was a cloudless day. The pilot in the cockpit was blasted backward, his head bouncing off his seatback.

"Hello? Hello?" Chimera was calling out. She swore. "Phone's dead. What the hell happened?"

The confused pilot pulled himself back to the controls. He pressed buttons, then lifted his hands. The aircraft was dead. So was Chimera's communication.

A shimmer beyond the cockpit glass caught my eyes. Inside, Dr. Jordan was waving.

I touched my ear. "Angels, seize them!"

The Angels of Death swarmed the helicopter. Tabris and the tall female angel fought back. The guards opened fire. Two of my angels were immediately hit.

"Warren!" Fury screamed from the doorway.

I turned to see her holding my sword. Spreading my wings, I sailed forward and grabbed it by its hilt before spinning backward to dive-bomb the helicopter.

I buried the blade in Tabris's skull.

Lachlan had wrestled a gun from a guard. He used it to shoot the tall female demon twice. Once in the chest. The other in the center of her forehead. Neither bullet would kill her instantly.

Chimera was hiding behind her when she fell.

I landed a few feet in front of them. Chimera was visibly shaking as I approached, dragging the tip of my sword through the grass. The angel was convulsing on the ground as I stepped over her. I grabbed Chimera by the throat.

Then I tossed my sword up to flip my hand over. When I caught it, I drove the blade straight down through the demon's neck. Her spirit screeched and hissed as it fizzled to nothing.

Chimera was choking.

Good.

She fought against my arm, her feet kicking wildly as I held her inches off the ground.

"You want my daughter, huh?" I squeezed until my fingers

turned white. "Maybe torture her a bit before you kill her. Like testing weapons on her to kill us?"

She couldn't respond. No air was going in or out of her lungs.

Everything in me wanted to kill her.

Instead, I threw her down onto the ground with so much force that her head bounced off the grass. With a painful gasp, she curled into the fetal position.

"Cassiel!" I shouted. "Cuff this bitch and have someone lock her up downstairs."

Cassiel came over, unhooking the high-Z cuffs from her belt. She dropped to her knees beside Chimera, grabbing her arm. "Now you can see what it feels like to be *average* for a while." She snapped the cuff around Chimera's wrist.

The irony of it was a beautiful thing since Chimera had developed the restraint.

"Oh no," a male voice said behind me.

Rogan stormed toward me with Anya, Kane, and Cruz carrying an arsenal behind him. His face burned with hatred.

Before I could react, he grabbed my sword, shoved Cassiel out of the way, and pulled the blade back with both hands.

Chimera couldn't even scream before the blade sliced through her neck. Blood sprayed everywhere, splattering my face as her body crumpled one way and her head tumbled the other.

It takes a lot to shock me.

That one did. I turned my wide eyes toward Rogan as he pulled up his shirttail to wipe the blood from his face. I wrenched my sword out of his hand. "Give me that thing."

He smiled. "Bitch had it coming."

I guess I couldn't blame him after what she'd done to him. But still… damn.

Cassiel stood, her face covered in blood. "So this is a take-no-prisoners war, then?"

"No. We're taking human prisoners," I ordered.

Speaking of humans…

Dr. Jordan ducked out of the helicopter's side door. He looked slightly guilty, like he may have enjoyed causing so much chaos.

I clapped as he walked toward us. So did Cassiel and Rogan. "Nicely done, Doc," I said with a grin.

"I had good teachers." He embraced me.

"Where were you hiding? I didn't even know you were on board," I said.

"I tucked myself into the gun case when the humans were loading up. The angels never look in there."

"Nice work."

"Thanks." He looked toward the building. "Is Sloan here?"

"Yes. Downstairs." I kept my hand on his shoulder. "You got them out."

His smile didn't last. "But Iliana's gone?"

I nodded. "I'm heading there now."

"To the city?"

"Yes."

He hugged me again. "Come back to us, son."

I smiled. "I'll bring your granddaughter back too."

"I have no doubt." When he released me, he started toward the front door of Echo-5.

Several of my angels were holding the guards. "Cassiel, can you figure out a place to put these guys? I think we're running out of room in the bunker cells."

"I'm on it. You're going to the city?"

"Yeah."

She squeezed my hand and looked me square in the eye. "Don't die, Warren."

"I don't plan on it." I held her gaze for a moment before

turning to my angels. I touched my ear so even those out of earshot could hear me. "Three of you, go with Cassiel. Stay here to guard the building. The rest of you, fly to the city to support Iliana and the guardians. I'll be right behind you. Stay clear of those bullets, and remember, spare human life if possible."

Some angels on the field nodded before they launched into the sky.

Another helicopter was approaching. I searched the horizon. "We need to bring that thing down before they alert the Morning Star to what happened here."

"We care if he knows?" Rogan asked.

"The call Chimera made might have bought us some time. She told the Morning Star Iliana was on her way, and he's just arrogant enough to believe he's won. It will be a full-on assault if he finds out Chimera's dead."

An attack helicopter flew over the ridge. "Got it!" Anya yelled, her hand aimed at the sky.

The helicopter pitched sideways.

Rogan started toward Anya to help, but I held him back. "Hang on."

I'd always heard what a badass Anya was. Now, I wanted to see it for myself.

The helicopter tilted forward, tail over cockpit, tossing the gunners and pilots forward. Two gunners lost their weapons before she steadied the machine. Planting her feet, one in front of the other, she brought it down gently to the ground.

"Rogan! Disarm them!" she shouted over the noise of the rotors.

He looked as surprised as me. Then he laughed. "Damn. OK." He and Cruz ran toward the helicopter.

"Kane, can you fly this thing?" Anya asked.

"Nash can!" He clicked the button on his radio.

Rogan and Cruz threw the stunned humans out of the helicopter. Two of my angels grabbed them and hauled them toward the building with the others. They passed Nash as he jogged out of the building and to the cockpit.

Fury fought against Reuel again. "Put me down!"

"Let her go!" I yelled.

Reuel released her, and she ran toward me.

I grabbed Anya's arm. "Take Fury with you. Give her the best rifle we've got and plenty of ammo."

She turned an amused grin toward me.

I put my hands up. "I'll shut up now."

Anya put her hand on my shoulder. "I'm glad you love her. Now stand back, Warren." She leaned toward me. "You're about to see what she and I were born to do."

Excitement rippled through me. "Who's staying here?" I asked.

"The humans in the bunker. Lex is with them."

"Good."

Fury ran into my arms. At first, I thought she might punch me. She kissed me instead. Covered in blood, I kissed her back. "I'll see you in the city," I said against her mouth.

When I pulled away, she fisted my shirt. "Don't do anything stupid."

"I won't if you won't."

She smiled and kissed me again. Then she took off toward the helicopter with Anya, Rogan, Kane, and Cruz.

Gabriel and Reuel were walking toward me. "I'm with you," Gabriel said. "The Father is staying here."

The Father had walked out the front door. He locked eyes with me. His mouth didn't move, but I heard his voice as clearly as if he was standing right next to me.

"Be safe, Archangel. Protect your daughter at all costs and end this war once and for all."

## CHAPTER TWENTY-SIX

The city was peaceful from the sky.

As promised, all the main roads to and from the city were jammed up with Humvees, tanks, and SUVs. But none of them were firing on civilians.

Yet.

In the heart of the city, downtown Asheville seemed almost business as usual, except for the humans gawking up at the sky. Between the helicopters and flying angels, it was no wonder their attentions were above.

Gabriel and Reuel hovered beside me.

"He's late," Gabriel said.

I searched the ground. "Chimera bought us some time."

"*Lon ai Iliana?*" Reuel asked.

"I'm not sure where she is. She's not answering me." I rose higher for a broader view. I'd be able to sense her power before seeing her.

So would the Morning Star.

Gabriel joined me. "Anything?"

"Nothing. I hope she didn't wreck somewhere."

"Can't she fly?"

"Yeah." I wondered why she hadn't.

Something rumbled the mountains. I turned all the way around, looking for the sound. *"Lo!"* Reuel shouted beneath us. When I looked down, he was pointing toward the morning sun.

Two black specks were getting closer. Fast.

Reuel flew up to join us.

"Bombers." I spun around again, this time looking for an empty space to put them down. Asheville had grown so much, there wasn't much green space left on the mountainous horizon.

My eyes followed the French Broad River. Its widest point was just beyond where two of Asheville's interstates merged together.

"What are you thinking?" Gabriel asked.

"You remember that pilot Sully?"

Reuel grunted with a nod.

"Excuse me?" Gabriel was looking at me like I was speaking a language he couldn't understand—and he understood *all* of them.

"A pilot landed a 747 on the Hudson River back in 2009," I explained.

"I vaguely remember."

"We need to put those planes down in the river. How good is your aim?"

He held up his hands. "I'm a messenger. Haven't dealt much with planes."

I looked at Reuel. "I'll take one. You take the other?"

He nodded and pushed up his sleeves.

As they neared, I realized the plane on the right was much closer than the plane on the left. When it reached the city limits, a rocket blasted from its bowels. Before any of us could react, the bomb exploded somewhere near Biltmore Park, billowing up a cloud of smoke and rubble.

Reuel shot up vertically and grabbed the plane with ease, nearly halting it completely midair. With a forceful twist, he sent the plane in a slanted dive toward the city. It passed beneath us, and he somersaulted in the air to put it down in the river. The silver jet skipped like a pebble down the wide French Broad, sending up massive walls of water that flooded the streets running parallel to the river.

It was impressive, but there was no time for cheering or applause. The second aircraft fired a second rocket at the city.

Like Reuel, I rose, squared off in front of the plane, and grabbed it with my power.

Unlike Reuel, its surging energy blew me backward like a feather flitting on a summer breeze.

Gabriel joined me to help. Between the two of us, we slowed the fighter, and I managed to send a pulse of energy through it to fry its guidance system. Sweat blistered on my forehead as we fought to turn the jet toward the river.

Even without its guns, it was too dangerous in the air. The Morning Star could cause the pilot to dive-bomb the city.

"*Cey alis enta ai utal?*" Reuel asked, chuckling twenty yards beneath us.

I worried my eyeballs might pop out of my skull from the pressure of holding back the energy. "No, smartass, we don't need your help!"

A thick wave of black smoke rolled behind the jet as it strained to push forward. "Gabriel, go right!" Together, we banked the plane to the right, and I pulled it toward us.

The jet lurched sideways, and Gabriel lost his grip, sending the bomber into a nosedive straight toward a high-rise. A bank building filled with human souls.

"Reuel, I changed my mind!" I yelled.

His power rippled the sky as it wrapped like a lasso around the plane's nose. He pulled it back, steadying it in the sky.

Before he could send it into the river, something whizzed past me, followed by the *tat! tat! tat!* of a machine gun. We both dove sideways out of the bullet spray, losing our grip on the plane. By the time we recovered, it was speeding off toward the horizon.

"What was that?" Gabriel asked, searching the ground.

"An anti-aircraft gun…or anti-*angel* gun, in our case, would be my guess," I answered.

Reuel was watching the jet speed away. His hands dropped to his sides in defeat.

"Come on. You'll get it when it returns!" I called to him.

The south side of the city had erupted in flames from the air strike. Even from the sky, I could hear humans screaming.

Suddenly, a swell of power emerged in the center of downtown. Gabriel was pointing at it. "She's there!"

The three of us dove toward her. When we were close enough, I saw the black top of my Challenger parked sideways in the middle of the intersection of Patton Avenue and Broadway. Behind it was the tall stone pillar in Pack Square. It crowned the top of the hill, looking down Patton Avenue, a one-way street.

Iliana was at the top of the street.

The Morning Star was at the bottom.

Military trucks and utility vehicles jammed the road behind the Morning Star's SUV. He stood beside it, no longer dressed for a golf course. He wore ridiculous desert fatigues, a wannabe general if I'd ever seen one.

About a thousand soldiers were behind him and coming up the side streets, their weapons all pointed in Iliana's direction.

I had no idea how everyone had congregated in that spot,

but my daughter had pulled off one very important thing: she'd given herself the high ground.

Battle Strategy 101.

She was out of the car and standing on a half wall made of concrete. Her hands were stretched toward the sky, and open high-Z cuffs lay on the sidewalk beneath her. Jett seemed to be holding up some kind of invisible shield in front of her.

Reuel, Gabriel, and I landed so hard in front of the car that the pavement cracked under our feet. The sides of the Challenger were banged up and dented. They hadn't been when she left the Wolf Gap compound.

Nathan was right. She drove like she was in a bumper car.

I touched my ear to summon the Angels of Death. "We're in the center of downtown. Look for the giant stone penis in the sky."

The army retrained their weapons on us as the soldiers on the side streets pushed farther toward the center. Half of them wore Legion Nine uniforms.

The soldiers outside Legion Nine looked terrified. Most, if not all, of them would have never seen flying men or young girls summoning storms before. The barrels of their weapons vibrated with fear. Bad news for the innocent bystanders lining the streets.

"Fire," I heard the Morning Star say, his voice calm and even.

Gunfire exploded from the bottom of the hill. Reuel sent up another invisible shield, and the bullets ricocheted off it, shattering windows in the buildings surrounding us.

The people on the streets ran screaming then.

I pushed his arm down. "Too dangerous. If they hit us, they hit us, but no one else needs to get shot by bullets meant for angels."

With a grunt and a nod, Reuel lowered the shield. Then he

reached toward the army, and all their weapons lurched forward like he'd pulled them with a magnet.

A few weapons tumbled to the ground, then skidded along the asphalt up the street toward us.

The Morning Star smirked. "Despite your tricks, you're still outnumbered and outgunned, and you'll have to kill my men to get to me. Give up, so we can end this peacefully."

"Outnumbered?" I smiled and pointed up.

Everyone looked toward the sky. The Angels of Death, hundreds of them now, descended through the storm clouds Iliana was creating.

It was clear from their terrified expressions, most of the soldiers wanted to cut and run. Regardless, they didn't budge.

"He's controlling them," Jett said, holding the shield in front of Iliana.

"Fire!" the Morning Star yelled again.

Shots rattled off the buildings. Reuel's hand shot forward and slowed the bullets sailing toward us. We ducked and swerved out of their paths.

Above us, Lachlan sent a wave of energy toward the ground, to something out of my view. Suddenly, a large blue dumpster rolled from a side alleyway into the street in front of us.

Reuel pushed it down the hill toward the troops, like a massive rectangular bowling ball. The shooting stopped and yelling began as the men scrambled out of the way.

The dumpster was ripped off the ground and flung sideways into the glass walls of an office building.

The Morning Star was seething. "Is this how it shall be then?" he screamed.

*Tat! tat! tat!*

The angels in the sky scattered until one of them sent a fiery bolt to the ground, causing a massive explosion about a mile away. The rapid fire stopped, and black smoke rolled into the sky in the distance.

There was no time to celebrate.

A sound all too familiar ricocheted off the buildings. I heard it in slow motion, but my reflexes worked in real time. Jett fell backward before I could protect him.

The sniper's bullet had torn a massive bloody hole through the center of his chest.

"Jett!" Iliana screamed, her arms faltering.

I grabbed Reuel's sleeve. "Protect her. Keep her attention on the sky."

Reuel sent up a blindingly bright shield in front of her.

Dropping to my knees beside Jett, I tore open his shirt. He was gasping for air. I pulled a sliver of brass from the splintered bone around his heart.

"The wound isn't closing," Gabriel said.

"It's a Yahweh round. Same thing that almost killed Cassiel."

"Appa, what's happening?" Iliana asked.

I caught Reuel's eye and shook my head. Jett was going to die, and there was nothing I could do to stop it.

"Check his pockets!" Iliana shouted.

Another shot blasted from somewhere. Reuel's wings spread to deflect it.

"Jett's pockets?" I asked.

"Yes!"

A putrid smell rose from the wound as Gabriel and I searched Jett's clothes. Inside his left jeans pocket was the vial of crystal water.

After unscrewing the vial's lid, I forced open Jett's blood-smeared mouth and drizzled a few drops into the back of his throat.

I pushed his lower jaw shut and got in his frightened face. "Swallow!"

He gurgled.

Good enough. The wound began to close, and he sucked in a deep breath. I slumped over, bracing my hand on the concrete sidewalk. Never thought I'd feel such relief over keeping a boyfriend around.

Thunder rumbled through the sky, and cold, heavy raindrops pounded the ground.

"He's OK!" I shouted over the rain.

Iliana jumped down from the wall and fell to her knees beside Jett. He was panting as he grasped her hand. "I'm...I'm all right." He looked at me. "Thank you."

"Yeah, yeah," I grumbled, rising to my feet.

Gunfire blasted all around me before I could even fully straighten my spine. Reuel flipped the Challenger on its side, shielding us behind it. The car shook as bullets tore through the metal.

One of my angels dropped from the sky. I peeked around the Challenger's bumper to see who had fallen.

Lachlan.

Iliana started past me, but I grabbed the back of her shirt to hold her back. "Whoa! Whoa! You trying to get yourself killed?"

"It's Lachlan! We can't leave him to die!"

"I'll go," Jett said, stepping in front of her.

Panic flashed across her face. "What? You were just shot."

"And I was just healed." He grabbed her arms. "I have crystal water running through my veins. They can't hurt me."

That was true for actual Eden crystal water. I wasn't so positive about the concoction we'd cooked up in the kitchen.

"Will you cover me?" Jett asked, looking up at me.

I had to choose to keep this kid alive *twice?* Was there a father on Earth with that kind of willpower?

"Of course." I reached for one of the rifles Reuel had commandeered from the soldiers down the street.

As Jett turned to step out from behind the car, Iliana grabbed him and planted a hard kiss right on his mouth.

"Hey! Hey!" I shouted. "Do you want me to protect him or not?"

Jett's cheeks flushed red. I shook my head and pushed him toward the car's bumper. "Go on. Get out there."

Iliana was still smiling and touching her bottom lip.

I rolled my eyes and positioned the rifle in the groove of the tire well. Reuel stepped to the side of the car and extended his hand. This time, instead of the gunmen being pulled forward, they all stumbled back, allowing Jett a second to get to Lachlan.

The Angel of Death easily outweighed Jett by a hundred pounds. My eyes were focused on the recovering firing squad beyond him, but I watched Jett in my peripheral vision low-crawl toward Lachlan.

He rolled Lachlan onto his back.

One of the soldiers aimed. I fired first, my bullet striking the man's shoulder, toppling him backward. Reuel blasted all the troops backward again.

Jett was lying back-to-chest on top of Lachlan. Reaching back, he hooked his arm under Lachlan's leg. Then he rolled to the opposite side and up onto his hip, balancing Lachlan across his shoulders, executing a nearly flawless fireman's carry.

With only a slight stumble, Jett started toward us, with Lachlan's body oozing black sludge down Jett's arm.

A sniper's bullet zinged by my head, grazing my ear. I flinched, and the army opened fire again. I recovered and shot an operator in the thigh, but not before a bullet struck the back of Jett's leg. He crashed down onto one knee.

A helicopter soared over the top of the monument behind

us. I looked out from behind the car in time to see Fury aiming her rifle from the helicopter's outboard. With a single shot toward the roof of a neighboring building, the sniper plummeted to the street below.

She dropped the rifle, and Cruz handed her a grenade launcher. She fired at the Morning Star's SUV. Cruz fired down the side street to our right.

*Fwoomp!*

*Fwoomp!*

*Fwoomp!*

Someone else was shooting from the other side of the helicopter. Jett was limping along, mostly dragging his injured leg behind him.

A second later…

*Pop!*

*Pop!*

*Pop!*

*Hissssssss!*

Tear gas fogged the army, sending the soldiers scrambling for gas masks they didn't all have. It allowed Fury, Kane, and Cruz time to fast-rope through the pouring rain, to the ground. Anya and Rogan stayed in the helicopter.

Fury ran to Jett. She wrapped her arm around his waist and helped him limp back to the top of the hill.

Gabriel and I grabbed Lachlan when Jett and Fury were close enough. We eased him down onto the ground behind the car.

I wrenched the vial of crystal water from my pocket and unscrewed the cap. When I reached to pour some into Lachlan's gaping mouth, Gabriel caught my arm. "It's too late."

Lachlan's gray face was spiderwebbed, and his eyes were solid black and staring into nothing. He was gone.

I sank back on my heels and hung my head.

"He's dead?" Jett asked in disbelief.

"Yeah," I answered through gritted teeth.

The others ran behind the car. "Everybody whole?" Kane asked.

Fury shook her head.

"I was too late." Jett stared at Lachlan. His pant leg was pulled up. The bullet had torn through his calf muscle but had mostly gone straight through. Iliana was helping close the wound.

Fury walked over to her son and examined his bloody shirt. "Are *you* all right?"

"I'm fine." He looked up at her. "You saved my ass out there."

She lifted a shoulder. "What are mothers for?"

He gave a sad, but genuinely grateful, smile.

Fury knelt down next to me. "You OK?"

I fisted her hair and kissed her. "Nice shot, babe. Where'd Anya and Rogan go?"

"An RPG team was setting up a few streets over. They'll be back," Fury said.

"Better?" Iliana asked Jett, pulling her hands away from his leg.

"Better. Thank you."

"Iliana, you went completely dark when you took off in my car," I said.

"What do you mean, *dark*?" Fury asked.

"She's the most powerful angel alive. She's pretty damn easy to find, except for today." I looked at my daughter. "What did you do?"

"High-Z cuffs. I figured if they could stop my power, they could hide me from the Morning Star."

I'd have applauded her if I hadn't still been pretty freaked out by it.

She grimaced. "Sorry about the car. Claymore had all the inbound roads blocked off. I had to drive it up a one-way street."

I ran my hand down my face.

Gunfire was the only thing that saved her from a safe-driving lecture. The ceasefire ended as the helicopter returned.

Fury stood and tossed me a smoke grenade. "Smoke 'em!"

I pulled the pin and hurled it over the car and down the street. Kane, Cruz, and Fury did the same as the helicopter lowered overhead. A wall of thick purple smoke ballooned up between us and the army.

When the firing mostly stopped, Rogan dove out of the helicopter, and Anya slid down a rope. Once she was on the ground, she started barking orders. "Guardians, *unat oruku urak!*"

The guardians flew in from every direction. They lined up in front of the car, linking arms to form a massive wall of bodies in front of us.

"What are they doing?" I asked Fury.

"It's called a unity lock."

"I understood that much. What is it?"

"When they're locked together, they're impenetrable. Nothing will get through that line."

I shook my head, impressed. "Never saw Abaddon do that."

"You never saw Abaddon really lead anybody."

"True. Where'd she learn it?"

"Azrael."

The fog was beginning to clear, and once again, the remaining soldiers raised their weapons. But before anyone could fire, Anya raised her hands toward them.

Her mouth opened, and a shock wave of energy exploded from it. The wave rippled the air all the way down the hill. When it hit the soldiers, every single one let go of their weapons to cover their ears. Some crumpled. Some scattered. All of them were in obvious pain.

Behind her, I heard nothing.

Whatever it was, the firing stopped. Even the Morning Star had ducked and covered his head with his camouflaged arms.

Fury crossed her arms. "Pretty cool, right?"

"What the…what?" I couldn't even form words.

"Sound waves. You can only hear them if you're in their path, but they're deafening."

Iliana came and stood beside me. "OK, that's badass."

Most of the soldiers had run away.

Anya stopped, finally out of breath after nearly a solid minute of…doing *whatever* it was she was doing.

The Morning Star straightened, his face red with anger. He extended his hand toward the SUV behind him. Its back door flew open with so much force the top hinges snapped.

Azrael fell out of the backseat sideways, landing hard on the pavement, on his side. His hands were cuffed behind his back, and the aura holding his mind captive was so thick it shimmered like diamond dust around him.

The Morning Star jerked Azrael off the ground so that he hovered in front of him.

"Let him go!" Iliana ordered, pushing through the wall of guardians.

"Your life for his! That's the only deal I'll make!" The Morning Star curled and tightened his power around Azrael until my father was struggling to breathe.

"Have it your way," Iliana hissed.

She raised her hands toward the thundering clouds again. Like lightning rods, her arms drew the power of the skies. Streaks of white light surged through her, then her hands flew forward toward the bottom of the hill.

Lightning shot straight for the Morning Star, slamming him and Azrael against the side of the armored SUV.

Electricity sizzled through both of them until the aura surrounding Az exploded in a violent spray of sparks. The energy suspended him off the ground as it pulsed through him.

His eyes were open.

His mouth was screaming.

Iliana finally dropped her hands, and the beam of energy receded like a wave that had crashed onto the beach. The rain stopped as quickly as it had started.

The Morning Star crumpled in a heap against the tire. Azrael lay motionless on his back. And almost all the remaining soldiers scattered, now free of the Morning Star's hold.

The rest of us were stunned.

"Is he dead?" Jett asked, breaking the silence.

I wasn't sure to which *he* Jett was referring, but neither Azrael nor the Morning Star were moving. My father wasn't dead; I would have sensed it.

"Jett, Rogan, cuff them!" Iliana ordered.

We all set off down the hill. The few Legion Nine members left standing were relieved of their weapons.

Rogan took the high-Z cuffs off the belt of a soldier and slapped one onto the arm of the still-sleeping demon. When he went for the other arm, the Morning Star shot up and grabbed Rogan by the neck.

There was a flash of movement beside me. The tip of a shiny blade was pointed at the Morning Star's throat before I could even turn to see that it was Anya beside me.

"Let him go," she said calmly.

The Morning Star smiled. "Do you really want to kill me?"

I carefully placed my hand on top of her wrist. "No, she

doesn't." I was staring at Anya's profile as I gently pushed her arm down.

If she killed him now, the whole army—and Azrael—would die with him.

Reluctantly, she lowered the sword, but she stopped just below his belt line. "How about castration instead? Think you'll be able to regrow a dick that's been severed with a helkrymite sword?"

*Oh.*

The Morning Star's eyes widened. Then his hand released Rogan's neck. Coughing and gasping, Rogan fell to his knees.

I cuffed the Morning Star's other arm, and I *felt* his powers leave him. It was like shutting off a generator. We all relaxed.

"Reuel, help me move Az," Iliana said.

Reuel touched my father's arm, and a spark singed his hand. He recoiled.

"What the hell was that?" I asked, walking over to join them when Jett took hold of the Morning Star.

Reuel lifted both shoulders.

My father's foot twitched. And *sparked.* I looked at my daughter.

She turned up her palms. "I have *no* idea."

"Az?" I asked, taking a knee beside him. I lowered my hand toward his chest and watched the air crackle in the space beneath my palm. It was like static electricity with jumper cables. His body hummed with energy when I touched him.

A violent blast knocked me forward, and a spray of glass shards sliced my skin. Shielding my eyes with my arm, I looked back to see the side of an office building smoking. "Mortars!"

Anya searched the sky. "Guardians!"

Another round came from the east, striking the courthouse over the hill.

Anya glanced at me. "You good?"

I gave her a thumbs-up.

Without another audible word, she touched her ear, and two angels I didn't know lifted her into the sky. Rogan, Jett, and Reuel stayed behind with us.

Iliana's hands were on Azrael's chest, and she was sending her healing power into him. The black spot had disappeared, but nothing else was happening. "I don't know what's wrong," she said.

Death certainly wasn't the problem. Azrael's life was solidly intact. "Maybe nothing is wrong. Can you get those handcuffs off him?"

"Yeah."

Close by, car horns sounded. The city streets hadn't exactly been silent since the angelic had staged a coup, but this was different. This was desperate honking. *Angry* honking.

Another mortar blew apart the spired tower on top of one of the oldest skyscrapers in the city. Rubble rained down from above, and Reuel cast a shield over us.

Everywhere, humans were screaming. Iliana started to get up.

I grabbed her arm. "Where are you going?"

"To help."

"We don't know who else is out there. Someone is still obeying orders. It's too risky."

"I can't let them—"

"Iliana!" a man's voice echoed down an alleyway.

Nathan.

"Dad?"

Nathan and Ionis darted out from between two buildings, past the debris from the first mortar strike.

Iliana ran to him. "What are you doing here?"

Out of breath, Nathan jerked his thumb over his shoulder. "Your mom sent me to make sure Tupelo Honey was OK." He pushed the rifle he was carrying behind him, then grabbed her and pulled her close. "What do you think I'm doing here? Geez." He kissed the top of her head.

He was wearing his olive-drab ball cap. On the front was the "Regular Guy" patch I'd given him years ago.

"It's too dangerous out here," she said against his chest.

"You're my daughter. If you drive headfirst onto the battlefield, you can bet your ass I'm going to follow."

"I'm sorry," she said quietly. "I couldn't stay home and let—"

"Shh. It's done now. Besides, Gabriel told us you subdued Michael."

"From the looks of it, he was right." Ionis looked over at the Morning Star and let out a slow whistle. "Hey, Mike! You look sexy in handcuffs!"

The Morning Star ignored him. He was glaring at Nathan. "Hello again, Mr. McNamara. We didn't get to say goodbye before your departure yesterday."

Nathan smirked. "Isn't that a shame?"

"You know what else is a shame?" Ionis asked out of the corner of his mouth. He pointed to the Morning Star. "That you didn't drown him at birth."

The Morning's Star's eyes narrowed.

Nathan chuckled and walked toward the demon. "How does it feel being abandoned by everyone who's supposed to love you, or at least follow you? We saw the Claymore vehicles hightailing it out of the city." He tapped his finger against the Morning Star's chest. "And your own mother drove us across the state to get away from your ass."

"I have no mother," he hissed.

Nathan smiled. "I think she'd agree." As he turned back toward Iliana, Nathan's gaze snagged on Azrael, who was still hidden behind Reuel. "Is Az…?" Nathan swallowed.

"Unconscious," I said.

As if he had heard his name, my father groaned in pain.

I grabbed his hand. "Azrael, can you hear me?"

With a gasp, he bolted upright, and his eyes popped open. The dark irises were swirling with energy, like a midnight sea after a storm. His hands rose slowly in front of his face, sparks popping at his fingertips.

"Holy shit," I said.

Iliana crouched down beside me. "Is that magic?"

"Magic," Azrael whispered, mesmerized by his hands.

I smiled at her. "You know, he hates it when people call it that."

She grinned.

"Too bad he doesn't remember how to use it," the Morning Star said with an eyeroll.

"What's happening to me?" Azrael asked her...or me, I wasn't sure.

"He needs the blood stone." Iliana grabbed my wrist.

The Morning Star laughed. "Warren, did you tell them about our car ride?"

Iliana looked at me. "What's he talking about?"

The corner of my mouth tipped up. "I have no idea."

"Now who's a liar?" the Morning Star asked. "Tell them about the blood stone. Tell them how you watched me destroy it."

I pulled the chain around my neck, hauling the duplicate stone from beneath my shirt. "You mean this blood stone?"

"Impossible." The Morning Star started forward, but the barrel of Cruz's rifle at the center of his chest stopped him. "I destroyed that stone myself."

I lifted the chain over my head. "You know what's really interesting about this stone?"

He didn't answer.

"*You* created it."

He scoffed.

"It's true," Fury said. "With one of your illusions in Nulterra."

"But illusions aren't reality," he argued.

"Maybe not." I fisted the stone. "But the penicillin, food, and water worked the same way down in that pit, and I'll bet this thing does too."

The shock on his face told me I was right.

I offered the stone to my father. "Put this on, and if you think about it hard enough, I'm pretty sure you'll remember why your hands are buzzing."

He reached for the stone, but hesitated.

"It's OK," Iliana said gently.

He looked up at her, then took the necklace and put it over his head. I was pretty sure she was *encouraging* him, but it clearly didn't matter. My father's eyes rolled back the instant he put it on.

"What's it doing to him?" Iliana asked.

Nathan crouched next to us and put his hand on her shoulder. "Oh, just a few hundred thousand years of data dump." He smiled at me, and we both laughed. I'd said the same thing to him the last time we'd been through this with Azrael.

The Morning Star moved so quickly no one could react fast enough. He swiped a handful of debris off the hood of the car and flung it in Cruz's face. Then he threw one arm over the barrel of the gun and drove his free arm down between Cruz's hands. The Morning Star twisted and used his body weight to drive them both to the ground.

He'd learned that move from Azrael.

Cruz collapsed on top of him, trying to wrestle the gun back out of Michael's hands. It went off. Cruz's head flew backward with a bloody spray of bone and brains.

The only thing between my family and that weapon was me.

Spinning toward them, my arms and wings spread wide, shielding them from the bullet spray that followed. I felt each round as it tore through my skin.

One…

Four…

Nine…

Twelve 5.56 Yahweh rounds disintegrated inside me.

Everything went black.

# CHAPTER TWENTY-SEVEN

*K*nock.

*Knock.*

*Knock-knock.*

*Knock...*

On the other side of the thin drywall I heard my little sister, Alice, giggle. After all these lifetimes, it was still one of the sweetest sounds on any planet.

When the giggles stopped, she answered.

*Knock! Knock!*

I blinked, and when I reopened my eyes, the scene had changed.

Fury was messing with a button on the front of my shirt. I felt dizzy. Maybe it was the internal blood loss. Maybe it was the Vicodin. Maybe it was the clean-shot view I had straight down her cleavage.

She stretched up on her toes and touched her lips to mine. I pulled back, certain I was high. Certain I might regret this when I was sober.

But my eyes fell to her mouth as she trapped the side of her lower lip between her teeth.

"Fuck it," I said, stepping into her before my better judgment could talk me out of it. I grabbed her waist and pulled her hips against mine, bending until tears sprang to my eyes and my mouth crashed down on hers.

Everything in me twisted in agony.

And in pleasure.

I slid my arm around her back to pull her up and tighter against me. And when I did, a broken rib shifted enough to make me cry out in pain.

I laughed as she cupped my face in her hands.

Then I blinked, and the scene changed again.

2:23 a.m.

I should have been in bed, but sleep—especially alone—was so overrated. I scrolled down the job postings for positions abroad. I flagged all the ones in active war zones, since that was the only place my life seemed to make sense.

A flash of red in the corner of the screen caught my eye.

*New message. User Fury_308.*

My chest tightened, and I hated myself for it. I clicked on the flashing message anyway.

*New post. 2:24 a.m.*

A single link to a news station.

Unable to help myself, I clicked on it.

A news spotlight filled my screen. "Breaking news in Buncombe County. A little girl is home safe with her family tonight after surviving a nightmare..."

The video cut to side-by-side photos of a man and a beautiful young woman—a beautiful young woman that *wasn't* Fury.

She had long dark hair.

Chocolate-brown eyes.

And absolutely no soul.

My lungs forgot to inhale.

She wore a black hoodie with the name N. McNamara printed on the front left side.

For the first time in my entire life, nothing and everything made sense…

I blinked.

"Warren, I'm pregnant."

Every drop of blood inside my body pooled in my feet. The starry courtyard started to spin.

"Warren?"

I worried I might faint. Or vomit. Or both. "You're pregnant?"

Sloan nodded.

"Pregnant?"

Sloan was fidgeting. She jerked her thumb toward the restaurant. "I didn't want to tell you inside with everyone."

"Are you sure?"

"She's due in July."

*"She?"* My voice didn't even sound like my own.

Sloan took a step closer to me. "Your father says it's a girl."

Her words punched me in the gut. "My *father?*"

Sloan's hands clamped over her mouth. Then she guided me over to a brick bench.

While I sat raking my fingers through my hair, she paced in front of me, wringing her hands. She was jabbering on about something, but I couldn't make any sense out of her words.

I finally held up a finger to stop her. "Are you really pregnant?"

"Yes. I'm sorry I didn't tell you sooner. Please don't be mad."

*Mad?*

The fog lifted from my brain. I jumped up and grabbed her cold hands, pulling them to my chest. "Sloan, I could never be mad about that." Tears burned my eyes. "I'm going to be a dad."

I blinked again.

*Knock.*

*Knock.*

*Knock-knock.*

*Knock...*

I waited, rocking back and forth on my heels in the warmth of the two Eden suns.

The door slowly opened.

Alice's hair was bubblegum pink. Her jaw dropped when she saw me, and she laughed. "Warren?" She ran outside and threw her arms around me.

I was finally home.

I blinked.

*You shouldn't do this.* I stared at the Jordans' house. I glanced back to make sure Azrael was OK. He was passed out cold on the front lawn, smoke rising from the burns on his wrist, and his open mouth collecting rainwater.

His heart was beating strong.

*Meh. He's fine.*

I looked at the house again.

*You're not supposed to be here,* my better sense told me.

*But they're right there,* I argued back.

My daughter was in that house.

Sloan was in that house.

*Just a peek. I'll stay across the spirit line. No one will even know I'm there...*

I slipped into the house unseen. Sloan and Nathan were on the sofa—*ugh*—talking in hushed voices I didn't dare listen in on. Because electronics can be problematic for spirits, as I passed by the baby monitor, I sent a wave of energy across it to power it *off.*

Then I crossed into the nursery.

"Appa?" None of the other syllables that followed made a damn bit of sense, but the word for Father in Katavukai was beautiful music to my dead ears.

I crept closer to the crib and saw Iliana kicking her feet as she lay on her back. She rolled onto her side and giggled when our eyes met.

OK, Alice's giggle was *second* best on any planet.

"Iliana?" I whispered.

"Appa," she said again.

I smiled.

"Appa." Someone was shaking me. "Appa, wake up!"

When I opened my eyes, Iliana was in my face.

A *grown* Iliana.

All my senses rushed back. Everything was so bright. And cold. And loud.

Holy shit, the *noise*.

Shouting.

Sirens.

Rotors.

A WKNC News helicopter was circling overhead.

My insides twisted and churned. I pulled my knees up to my chest and rolled onto my side, nearly blacking out again from the pain. The agony of healing rivaled that of getting shot.

I vomited blood all over the concrete.

Iliana's warm hands buzzed on my back, and the burning inside me eased. I focused on breathing in and out, and blood and fluid gurgled in my lungs. Finally, I rolled onto my back again, draping my forearm across my eyes. "I'm not dead?" I croaked out.

Iliana kissed my forehead. "No, you're not dead, thank the Father."

I peeked out from under my arm with one eye to look at her. "Were you hit?"

She shook her head. "I'm fine."

My lips were dry, and when I licked them, I tasted blood. "You used crystal water on me? I said I didn't want—"

Iliana patted her empty pockets. "I don't even have the crystal water."

"Then what the hell happened?"

Fury looked down at me. Tears had streamed through the dirt on her face. "Guess who's immune to hydrogen necroxide?" She leaned closer. "Angels who don't have *golden* blood."

Holy shit.

"I'm not Rh-null," I said, more to myself than anyone else.

I wasn't sure why the thought hadn't crossed my mind before. I'd been O negative when I was alive. No one had ever told me my blood type would change in the ever after.

I'd just assumed.

Gabriel offered a hand to help me sit up. When I did, something trickled down my chest and back. Metal slivers, fragments of the bullets that had struck me, fell from beneath my shirt. A few more were still slicing their way back out of my skin as my body repaired itself.

My father was out cold next to me. And the Morning Star was cuffed, chained, and gagged in the back of a Humvee. Reuel, Rogan, and Jett were all standing guard. Through the glass, I could see the Morning Star bleeding from his mouth and nose.

Profusely.

Apparently, the high-Z cuffs also limited his self-healing power.

Good.

The breeze hit the skin of my back in patches. I lifted my T-shirt's shoulder to inspect it. The back of the shirt was shredded. The front was not.

"None of the rounds that hit you exited." Fury ran her hand down the front of my torso. "You lost a *lot* of blood, but no one else was shot."

"You saved me." As Iliana stood, she pressed a kiss to my forehead.

"Then Fury bitch-slapped the Prince of Darkness with the butt of her rifle." Ionis was sitting on the hood of the SUV with his legs crossed. "It was epic."

"I'd better go help Dad," Iliana said, starting up the street.

Nathan was talking to the local police. "I guess this will be a legal nightmare to sort out." In our immediate vicinity, I counted over forty patrol officers, most of them in riot gear. The Claymore operators who remained were all in handcuffs.

Something felt off, but I couldn't put my finger on what it was.

"I heard they're sending in the big dogs from Washington," Fury said.

I was staring at the men in handcuffs. "How many soldiers would you say were here?"

Fury shrugged. "Maybe a thousand."

"Did you see any demons?"

She shook her head. "What are you thinking?"

"That this isn't over." I pushed myself up off the ground.

Nathan's conversation was escalating to an argument. The police wanted the Morning Star.

I launched into the air and closed the half a block between us with one powerful thrust of my wings. Terrified, the cops drew their weapons as I landed hard between Nathan and Iliana. "You won't touch him," I announced, lowering my wings.

All their guns were pointed at me. The man in front, who

was obviously in charge, gestured to Nathan. "He tells me Michael Claymore is responsible for what happened here today."

"And I'm telling you, you're not going to touch him. You and your men aren't capable of handling this." I took a step toward one of the officers, pressing my chest against the muzzle of his handgun. "Shoot me if you want, and I'll show you exactly how ill-equipped you are."

A ripple of energy floated between me and the group of cops. Then, reluctantly, the leader raised his hand, and his men lowered their weapons.

Iliana wiggled her fingers with a smile when I turned around. "There's no need for you to get shot again." She registered the worry on my face. "What's wrong?"

"We need to get out of the city. Only about half of Legion Nine was here, and *none* of the demons we fought last time showed up."

"Demons?" the cop asked.

We all ignored him.

"What do you want to do?" Nathan asked.

"We need to get back to Echo-5. Put some distance between us and civilians. How are the roads?"

"Unless a miracle has happened, most of them are still shut down. I had to ditch the Claymore car a few blocks away."

"What about the helicopter?"

"Grounded." He pointed at the cop.

I looked at the officer. "If you and your men want to be helpful, get all these humans off the streets and get our helicopter back in the air."

The man obviously didn't know what to think. It was completely against his training to let us leave, but you could see everything in him wanted us out of his city. I wasn't sure what the death toll of civilians had been thus far, but if I was right, that number was likely to climb.

I knew it.

He knew it too.

His eyes issued me a stern warning. "This isn't over."

"I'll give you an address to come find me."

Turning away, he clicked the radio on his shoulder. "One oh seven to EOC requesting all available units to begin moving civilians off the streets. And go ahead and release that Claymore helicopter..."

Iliana grabbed Nathan's sleeve. "Mom."

"What?" I asked.

Nathan pulled his hands back through his hair. "We radioed back to Echo-5 and told them the coast was clear. They were going to head this way."

I swore. "How did you call them?"

"Gabriel told Cassiel," he said.

"Gabriel!" I shouted.

He looked over.

"Call Cassiel back and tell her to get everyone at Echo-5 back inside the—"

*Kaboom!*

We whirled around, but the skyscrapers blocked our view in the direction of the explosion. The fighter jet I'd missed earlier roared past overhead, shaking the buildings.

I didn't need to see what it hit; the fear squeezing my heart told me.

Echo-5.

"Reuel, bring the Morning Star!" I screamed, and then I bolted into the air.

The Angels of Death descended with me over what was left of Echo-5. Iliana and Jett were right behind us.

Steel beams twisted up through the rubble toward the sky. A fire was burning somewhere beneath the partially collapsed floors. Everything from the front door to the back wall on the right side was completely gone.

The control room.

The office.

The entrance to the bunker.

The rest was barely standing.

My eyes searched the parking lot. The transport van was there. So were the cars I recognized.

Sloan, Adrianne, everyone else…

They were all still here, and dead bodies were everywhere, pulling at my attention like gravity.

Gabriel hovered beside me. "I can't make contact with Cassiel." He swallowed. "Or anyone."

Movement in the mountains drew my eyes. Camouflaged soldiers in gas masks—the rest of Legion Nine, I assumed— were coming through the woods like an army of ants.

I turned to the angels behind me. "Don't let them on this property!" I dove toward the building and landed beside what used to be the communal living room. I sent out my gift into the wreckage, searching for the living and the dead.

I climbed over the remains of a wall onto a pile of concrete chunks and drywall. Half of the second floor hung like a canopy over what was once a kitchen.

Someone was gasping.

An angel was pinned beneath part of the fallen wall. All I could see were legs. When I reached him and pushed off the broken sheet of high-Z metal, I saw the iron beam running through his midsection.

It was Egris, one of my angels who'd stayed behind. The

iron wouldn't kill him, but it wouldn't heal quickly. Iliana and Jett landed on top of what looked like a gun safe. "Help me get him out of here!" I called.

They flew across the room as something rumbled over my head. The remnants of the second floor crashed down on top of me. I shielded my head, but Egris and I were buried under the fragments of flooring and demolished furniture.

With adrenaline pumping through my veins and a guttural scream, I hurled the rubble off me.

Iliana and Jett started moving the rocks off Egris.

I heard more shifting. I looked up, but nothing major seemed to be collapsing. Searching the demolished ground floor, I realized the sound was coming from a massive pile with a mangled gym locker jutting out of it. The locker was wiggling just enough for me to notice.

"You got this?" I asked Jett.

He pulled a long piece of wood off Egris's face. "Got it!"

I sailed across the room and pushed the locker out of the pile. I plunged my hands in and began to dig, tossing pieces of steel and stone over my shoulder. I yanked out a computer monitor and threw it onto the lawn.

A small hand covered in blood and dust pushed through the hole it left behind.

Cassiel.

I grabbed her arm and pulled her out. She coughed, spewing chunks of dirt and gravel from her lungs as I held her upright.

"Where's Sloan?" I asked.

She coughed again and covered her mouth. Her head shook violently. "I don't know!"

Gabriel ran inside, and I passed her to him. He lifted her in his arms and carried her out of the building as I searched through more mounds of debris.

I found a piece of the metal armory cage that had been on the second floor, near the staff quarters. Beneath it, fresh death called to me. I shoveled through the rocks and metal with my hands until my fingers found another body.

I grabbed a fistful of their shirt and pulled them out. It was a Claymore uniform. The dead man was wearing handcuffs. His startled soul stared up at me, reluctant to leave his body behind.

Guns fired outside.

Out of the corner of my eye, I saw one of my angels get hit and fall. "Iliana!" I yelled.

They had finally dug out Egris and were pulling him off the iron spike. I reached in my pocket and pulled out the crystal water.

"Go. I've got him," Jett said to her.

She flew over and reached for the vial. I held it just out of her grasp. "Don't get hit," I said seriously.

"I won't." She extended her hand toward the battlefield, and the angel's limp body rose into the air.

I took a step back, stunned, as she pulled him to us and gently laid him at our feet. My mouth fell open. "Why the hell didn't we think of that earlier?"

She smiled and knelt down next to the wounded angel. "When have we ever had critically wounded angels to deal with before?"

Good point. Still…

"God, you're brilliant," I said, amazed as I went back to digging for another body. "Wait." I stopped digging and aimed my hand at the pile.

The body of another Claymore soldier rose through the rubble. I deposited him on top of the heap with ease.

Iliana chuckled as she opened the angel's mouth. "You're learning."

I pulled out another soldier.

And another.

And another, until finally, there were no more bodies buried under the building. "They aren't here!" I called to where Iliana was using her power to remove pieces from near the bunker entrance.

"I hear something over here!" she yelled back.

I flew over to join her, stopping midway because of the sound of a helicopter. I looked up and saw Anya on the outboard. She sent a shock wave of power down to the line of troops in the woods.

Behind the aircraft was a swarm of guardians. Suspended in their center, being toted in chains, was the Morning Star. With them, Reuel carried Azrael, whose body was limp in his arms.

Between the shots of the assault rifles, I heard what Iliana was talking about. Screaming inside the stairwell that led down below.

My whole body exhaled. "They're safe."

Iliana's face went slack. "We've been here for less than ten minutes. If you hadn't broken the elevator, they would have been in here when that rocket hit."

My stomach lurched. She was probably right.

Her ear turned toward the sky. "Do you hear—"

"Get down!" I screamed, diving over her.

*Boom!*

The ground shook with all the force of a ten-magnitude earthquake. The back wall completely collapsed, and more debris rained down on top of us.

But the explosion was far from a direct hit.

I sat up and looked back.

Azrael's hands were aimed at the sky behind the building.

When his eyes fell on me, he smiled.

# CHAPTER TWENTY-EIGHT

eat and smoke flooded the building as Iliana and I climbed out of the wreckage.

Azrael dropped his arms. "Didn't think I'd let you have all the fun, did you?"

I ran across the rocks, jumped over the wall, and hugged him.

He grasped a handful of the back of my shirt as his strong arms tightened around me. When I pulled back, tears sparkled in his eyes.

"Man, am I glad to see you," I said with a laugh.

"Looks like I got here just in time." He pointed over my shoulder.

I turned. The mountain was on fire.

"Fighter jet?" I asked.

"Coming to finish the job, looks like." He nodded toward the remnants of Echo-5. "Anybody hurt?"

"Nobody we know."

His crinkled eyes narrowed. "Is that…?" He was staring at Iliana, who was carefully picking her way across the wreckage.

She could have flown, but I imagined she was giving us a moment to ourselves.

"That's your granddaughter."

"God, she looks like Sloan."

"Right? She's amazing."

"She comes from good stock," he said with a grin.

I smirked. "Yeah. Yours."

"Exactly." He grabbed my shoulder. "Damn, it's good to have you back."

Our reunion ended as a group of soldiers climbed over the broken back wall. Azrael instinctively pulled me behind him before aiming his powerful hand at the men.

He blinked. "Claymore." General mode switched on. "Claymore, hold your fire!" Azrael climbed up on top of the broken wall.

Immediately, everything stopped. The men, and the angels, all stood at attention.

Well, almost all the men.

One who'd climbed over the back wall was still advancing. He had an angry sneer on a lopsided face. It was swollen and bruised, and his lips were the size of small continents. His mismatched eyes were narrowed, angry, and glued to me.

*Thacker.*

His commitment was impressive, and twisted. Especially considering the man he was so blindly devoted to had the power to heal him and didn't. His proximity to the Morning Star was probably the only reason he was vertical, as the reconstructive surgery alone would have been enough to level most mortals. This one, however, was still out for blood. *My* blood.

"Soldier, stand down!" Azrael boomed.

Thacker didn't listen. Moving his mouth as little as possible, he spoke calmly and quietly into his radio. "Red and green, you are clear to fire."

I should have known this asshole would be leading an attack.

Using my power, I thrust the barrel of his rifle up, smacking him in the already-messed-up face. He shrieked in pain through clenched teeth. Doubling over, he gave me enough time to rush in and tackle him.

"Incoming!" Azrael bellowed, searching the sky.

The soldiers following his orders dove under whatever they could find as mortars sailed through the air. One after another, Azrael and the other Angels of Death lobbed them back into the woods.

*Boom!*

*Boom!*

*Boom!*

"Iliana, we're going to need more rain!" I yelled as I yanked the rifle from Thacker's hands and slammed its stock into his wired-shut jaw.

Blood sprayed my face as I grabbed him by the throat and stood. I dangled him a foot off the ground.

*Pow!*

Thacker's head exploded. Something clinked around my feet as I dropped his body. His headless torso slumped sideways over what used to be the kitchen island. Laying at his feet was a knife.

I turned to look, and Fury raised up from behind her rifle, hidden by the half wall. I pointed at her. "I fucking love you, woman!"

"Warren, look out!" she screamed.

A mortar shell landed right behind me, catapulting me through the air and into the remains of the aboveground elevator shaft.

Dazed, I pulled myself from the rubble.

The blast had blown open the top of the bunker stairs. Iliana had fallen beside it. Above her, demons were descending from the sky.

Hundreds of them.

"Illy, you OK?" I called.

Suddenly alert, she patted her pockets. "I dropped it!" she shrieked. "I dropped the crystal water!" She crawled across the debris, frantically searching through the mess.

Orin landed hard on the debris in front of me.

"Oh, here we go." I pulled out my sword. "You tried to kill my daughter."

His smile was yellow. "And today, I won't fail." He pulled the final missing sword from a scabbard at his side.

*Shit.*

In Nulterra, I'd been able to channel my killing power through my sword, killing demons without even getting close. But my only sword-fighting skill was worthless here. Too many innocents were fighting close by.

Orin swung, and my helkrymite clashed with his.

I sliced low, and he jumped.

He jabbed. I slammed his blade sideways.

I swung at his head. He ducked.

He countered with his backhand. I dodged.

For all of about thirty seconds, I went straight Inigo Montoya on his ass. But it didn't last. The tip of Orin's sword sliced across my abdomen. It wasn't a fatal blow, but it shattered my focus.

Orin advanced. I backed up.

He swung. I jumped back.

He sliced. I retreated and tripped over something.

With a laugh, he swung with both hands, right at my face.

I ducked, dropped my sword, and grabbed Thacker's rifle at

my feet. Flipping it over with all the showmanship of a Silent Drill Marine, I shot Orin in the stomach at an angle straight through his heart.

His body collapsed like it no longer had bones.

I picked up my sword and sheathed it. "I've always been better with a gun anyway." Then I picked up Orin's sword and stepped over his rotting corpse.

The Father crawled out of the bunker hole. "Iliana!" he shouted, barely audible over the noise. She didn't hear him. She was battling a group of demons with Jett.

I shot four more angels out of the sky as I ran to him. "What's wrong?"

He grabbed my arm. "It's Adrianne. She heard Azrael's voice and was trying to get out when the bomb hit."

The bunker entrance was little more than a huge hole in the ground now. I brightened my wings to send light into the abyss.

Luca was standing closest to the top, but on the first landing below, Sloan was cradling Adrianne's bloody head in her lap. Sloan's healing light barely visible.

I touched my ear and turned away from the hole. "Iliana, Adrianne's going to die if you don't get over here."

Iliana's face whipped toward me, and she launched into the air in a perfect spiral that sent the two demons she was fighting onto their asses. When she reached us, she climbed down into the hole. I leaned inside again. "Everybody else OK?"

"We're fine," Sloan said, looking up at me.

I grabbed the blade of the sword I took from Orin and offered its hilt to Luca. "You know how to use one of these things?"

His eyes widened. "No."

"Me either." I leaned closer. "Just don't stick anybody we like."

He smiled. "Yes, sir."

Nathan ran over, panting. When I looked behind him, I saw a Claymore SUV with the driver's side door standing open. "Is Iliana in there?"

"Yeah, what's wrong?" I asked.

"We need crystal water."

I looked back down the hole. "Illy, did you find the vial?"

Light shined all around her. "Yes. It shattered."

I turned to Nathan. "It's gone."

He swore and threw his hands in the air.

"Who needs it?"

"Come on," he said and started back across the rubble.

We fought our way back to the vehicle parked on the lawn. When we jumped over the broken wall, I saw a fluff of white hair inside the car.

My stomach collapsed. "Oh no."

I hadn't even realized I'd frozen until Nathan pulled me forward. He ran around to the passenger's side of the car and opened the door.

He pulled Ionis out and laid him on the ground. "We were ambushed coming up the road. They got him through the windshield."

Black sludge oozed from Ionis's left lung. He was gasping and sputtering blood. His whole body was trembling.

I bent over him, and he lifted his hand. I wrapped mine around it and squeezed. His fingernails were a glittery royal blue.

He was trying to talk, but I couldn't understand him through the choking.

"Try to breathe, Ionis," I said.

"What's happening?" my father asked behind me.

"Az," Ionis gurgled.

Azrael dropped to the ground beside me and touched the messenger's cheek. The veins in Ionis's eye darkened as he fought to hang on.

Azrael spoke soft words of comfort in Katavukai, something I never dreamed in a million years I'd see.

With one more wet hiccup, Ionis's body went still. His hand released mine. And black trickled from the corners of his eyes as they stared lifelessly at the sky.

Rage pulsed through me.

The Father slowly approached Ionis's feet. "Oh no." His hands were over his heart.

Azrael touched two fingers to the black foam around the bullet hole. He rubbed it between his fingertips. "This is what we created."

"This is what *he* created." I whirled around.

A female prophet was using a keystone to release the Morning Star's cuffs while a pack of demons attacked Reuel like dogs.

Jumping to my feet, I threw everything I had at them. A wave of energy crashed like a tsunami, bowling the whole group over onto the grass.

But I was too late.

The Morning Star countered, blasting me backward into my father. Azrael pushed me forward, and we both advanced, side by side, as the demons regrouped. I tossed him my sword and shouldered my rifle.

Reuel grabbed two demons and slammed their skulls together with an audible *crack!* Azrael swung my sword and lopped off the head of a third. And I picked off the others, one by one, with my rifle.

Suddenly, a white fireball burst around the Morning Star,

consuming his body as he rose into the sky. Stunned, I froze and looked up, having never seen anything like it before.

Against the blue sky, it was clear why he was called the light of Eden. He looked exactly like his Eden sun. Hell, maybe this was his Eden sun.

Azrael drove my blade through the chest of the demon who'd freed the Morning Star. Then he, too, looked up as the surging white ball of energy sailed straight over our heads.

The light collided with the Father, a spectacular starburst of light and color. The two rolled across the ground as the light fizzled out, and when they stopped, the Morning Star held a dagger to the Father's throat.

I started forward, but Azrael's arm clotheslined my chest to stop me. "That knife is made of helkrymite."

"Impossible. Torman told us there were only seven swords."

"A demon lied? *Noooo.*"

"Cassiel verified he was telling the truth."

"Maybe he was. Does that look like a sword to you?"

*Damn it.*

The Morning Star dragged the Father back a few steps as everyone halted. "That's right. Now, maybe you listen to reason!"

All the fighting around Echo-5 slowly petered out. Cassiel, who'd been dragging injured angels out of the crossfire, side-stepped slowly over to stand beside me.

"Do you know what happens if I slit his throat?" the Morning Star asked, his eyes flickering with red.

"No. What happens?" I whispered toward Cassiel.

"The fabric of the universe unravels." Her breathing was shallow and quick, and her words were laced with panic. "We all disappear."

"If I don't walk out of here, none of us will. I'd rather be blinked out of existence than spend one more day in this mire of inferiority. And if I go, I'm taking every single being in Eden and on Earth with me."

He grabbed a fistful of the Father's white hair, yanking his head back. "So give me the Vitamorte, or I end *everything* now."

I looked toward the bunker. Iliana was climbing out. She held up her hands. "I'm here. I'm right here!"

Nathan's knees faltered. "No!" Reuel grabbed him to hold him up, and probably to hold him back.

With her hands raised high in the air, Iliana carefully crossed the rubble. No one else dared to move. Not even the demons to subdue her. The Morning Star was holding us all hostage now. Angels, humans, and the fallen alike.

"Please put the dagger down." Her voice was steady and calm as she climbed up on the broken wall. "Let this be over. I'll go with you, or you can kill me right here. No one else has to die."

"Get on your knees," he hissed.

Her hands still raised in surrender, Iliana slowly sank to her knees on the grass.

"Iliana, no!" Nathan cried.

She looked at him. "Dad, it's going to be OK."

Tears streamed down his face as he struggled against Reuel's hold.

The Morning Star's voice deepened. "Archangel, bring your sword."

At first, my ears didn't register that he was talking to me. *I* was the Archangel. But in that second, my only title that mattered was *Appa*.

When I didn't immediately move, he pressed the blade harder against the Father's throat.

Iliana turned to me. "Appa, it's okay. I'm ready."

I looked to the Father for help, but he only gave a slight nod.

Taking the sword from Azrael, I walked slowly toward my daughter with every intention of somehow driving the blade through the Morning Star's face. I stopped just behind her.

He cut his eyes at me. "I gave you the opportunity to join me, and now you'll forever wish you had listened."

"No!" voices screamed behind us.

Kane was holding Sloan.

Rogan was barely able to contain Jett.

"You should consider this a kindness, Archangel." The Morning Star raised his voice and swept his glowing eyes over the grounds. "May everyone say today that I am a benevolent god!"

No one clapped.

Or moved.

Or breathed.

Least of all me.

His eyes narrowed. "Or would you rather she be tortured?"

My hands were shaking uncontrollably.

"Warren," the Father said evenly.

I met his eyes, and peace washed over me.

Then he looked at Iliana. He held her gaze for a long moment before he finally said, "You know what you must do."

She bowed her head.

"What will it be, Warren?" the Morning Star asked.

The blade weighed a million pounds. I raised it, silently calculating if I could hurl it with enough precision to not kill us all by destroying the Father myself.

Then light exploded from Iliana. A searing beam across the lawn, straight through the Father's heart.

# CHAPTER TWENTY-NINE

The most brilliant light I'd ever seen on Earth or in Eden ruptured in the center of the field like a super-nova. The detonation blew me backward off my feet, and I scrambled against the powerful wind to right myself. Shielding my eyes against the blinding rays, I clawed my way across the grass back to Iliana.

When I reached her, I saw it. The light was bridged between Iliana and the center of the energy mass. Her feet were inches off the ground, her arms were outstretched, and her face was toward the sky, with her hair whipping in the wind.

Looking around, even Cassiel looked stunned, a miracle all by itself.

With a rumble that vibrated the ground, the light shot straight toward the sky, rippling the air in every direction as far as I could see.

Stars speckled the daytime sky, brightening until they each shone like the sun. One, directly above me, was pink.

Alice's star.

It was the auranos.

The light beam between Earth and Eden slowly transformed into a massive white moonstone staircase. At its top was the towering Eden Gate with its three arched doorways.

The outer arches were dim. The one on the left, which once led to Nulterra, now led to nowhere. The arch on the right was the door to my chamber in Reclusion. I doubted anyone had opened it in my absence.

But the ornate doors in the center, made of moonstone and pearl, were standing open. In their center was a silhouetted man, slowly descending the steps.

Honeysuckle and sea salt filled my nose as my eyes adjusted to the Eden sun. Every angel around me was kneeling, including every single member of the fallen, except the Morning Star. He was suspended in the air, frozen except for his eyes.

His eyes were on the figure coming toward us.

Iliana's feet settled on the ground. I grabbed her and pressed a kiss against her hair. Nathan threw his arms around both of us.

The rest of our family and friends crawled out of the bunker stairwell. Sloan stumbled as she ran across the rubble. Luca caught her around the waist, and Dr. Jordan was right behind them.

Adrianne was using her son as a crutch across the ruins. Her hair was matted with blood down the side of her face. Taiya walked with them, holding the hand of little Sloan.

"Azrael, go to your wife," a voice said from above.

Azrael stood and ran to the building.

"Daddy!" Little Sloan squealed, running to meet him.

He caught her in his arms and picked her up. Then he kissed his wife and hugged his son. Phillip's mouth was hanging open. "Whoa," he said, looking at the staircase.

Fury slipped under my arm. I smiled and kissed her forehead.

Then everyone gathered at the bottom of the stairs.

The man's face came into focus as he neared. It was the Father. No longer a withered old man, he'd been transformed to a younger version of Father John. The same small stature. The same unassuming frame. The same birthmark on his forehead, half of which was now covered with soft brown hair.

His eyes, too, were still his. Kind, compassionate, understanding.

He was smiling when he reached the bottom step. "Well done, kiddo," he said to Iliana with a wink.

Tears were glistening on her cheeks, but she covered her mouth as a rogue giggle slipped out. "How did you know I could do it?"

He leaned toward her. "Because I made you."

Iliana's head pulled back.

"I know the Morning Star likes to take credit for maneuvering your mom and dad together, but nothing happens under my nose that I'm oblivious to."

Sloan and I exchanged a glance. "You brought me and Sloan together?" I asked him.

"You were never a mistake, Warren." He looked at her. "And you were never created for evil, Sloan."

She nodded as tears spilled down her dirty cheeks.

Other spirits started down the stairs behind the Father. Angels *and* humans.

My mother, Nadine.

Ariel, the Archangel of Life.

Alice, my very best friend.

My wrinkled bulldog, Skittles, in Alice's arms.

And finally…

Sloan's mother, Audrey.

Sloan gasped and covered her mouth. "Mom?"

Audrey Jordan walked down to the bottom step, next to the Father, and reached for Sloan's hand. Crying, Sloan took it. "Sweetheart, I'm so proud of you," Audrey said.

Dr. Jordan put his hands on Sloan's shoulders, and she flinched. Then she looked back at his face and cried even harder. Both her parents embraced her.

Audrey looked over their heads and stretched her hands toward Iliana and Luca. "Hi, kids. I'm your Gran."

Iliana grabbed her fingers and squeezed them.

Then Audrey looked at me. "Thank you."

"I didn't do anything," I said.

"*Everything* was because of you."

My eyes burned, which made me the last human in the group to tear up. Nope, Luca wasn't crying either. But how many teenage boys would?

And neither was Audrey—because there are no tears in Eden. She looked at her husband. "Robert, are you ready to come home?"

Emotion choked him, and he nodded. Then he turned to Sloan and cupped her face in his hands. "Will you be okay?"

She covered his hands with hers. "I will be now."

When she released him, he stepped onto the bottom step, and the light of Eden washed over him. He inhaled like it was the first time in years, and he put his arms around his wife.

Behind them, Alice waved Skittles's paw. Alice's hair was a shade somewhere between flamingo and fruit punch. She squeezed past Dr. Jordan onto the bottom step.

I hugged her. "Sorry it's been a minute."

"A minute?" She held onto the back of my neck. "It's been a *bazillion* years."

I laughed. "I know. I'm sorry." I scratched Skittles behind

the ears and leaned over to let her lick my face. "Hey, girl. I missed you too."

Alice cleared her throat. When I looked up at her, she jerked her head toward Fury. "You gonna introduce me, or what?"

With a smile, I touched the small of Fury's back. "Alice, this is Fury. Fury, this is Alice."

The two shook hands. "It's nice to meet you, *finally*," Alice told her.

Fury looked up at me. "You talk about me?"

Alice pulled her hand closer. "*All* the time."

"What?" Nathan held up his hands. "You don't talk about me?"

Alice straightened. "Oh, he does. I'm pretty sure I know who everyone is."

She did a roll call, pointing around the group and successfully naming off all my closest friends. She guessed Nathan's parents because Nathan and his dad look so much alike, and she called out SF-12, even though she didn't know their names. The children, of course, she didn't know at all because they didn't exist the last time I saw her.

"Everyone," I said, "this is Alice and my dog—"

"*Our* dog," she corrected me.

"Yes. Our dog, Skittles."

"Hi, Skittles," Taiya said, waving.

Little Sloan tugged on Azrael sleeve. "Daddy, can I get down and play with the puppy?"

Azrael carried her forward. "You can pet the puppy, but the puppy can't come down and play."

She patted Skittles on the head. "Why not?"

"Because these friends don't live here anymore. See that step? That's as far as they can come."

Her little blonde head tilted to the side. "Like the hall-monitor line at recess?"

Azrael chuckled. "Something like that."

My mother was watching from the back of the group. "You have a beautiful family, Azrael."

"Thank you." He put his arm around Adrianne.

Had this been the real world, it might have been an awkward moment. But there was no sadness. No jealousy. No regrets.

At least not for my mother. Adrianne, however, looked a little wary. But, in her defense, she had just lived through a mortar strike.

"Nadine, this is my wife, Adrianne, and our kids, Sloan and Phillip."

"Hello, Adrianne," Mom said warmly.

Adrianne offered a small wave. "Hello."

"Who is that?" little Sloan asked.

"That's Warren's mommy," Azrael explained.

I heard Adrianne lean toward Sloan and whisper, "I had no idea she was so pretty."

Sloan laughed softly and rolled her eyes.

Ariel, the Archangel of Life, stepped down beside the Father and offered me a shimmering clear round bottle. "From the fountain of Zion."

I held it up against the light. "Crystal water."

"Almost a gallon of it. There should be plenty to heal the Earth for a time."

"Heal everyone on Earth?" Nathan blew out a sigh that puffed out his cheeks. "That's going to take a while."

Ariel shook her head. "No, it won't. Deposit it in four equal shares in the Pacific, Atlantic, Indian, and Arctic Oceans. Nature will do the rest."

I smiled sincerely. "Thank you."

This was twice Ariel had volunteered help after so adamantly refusing my pleas in Eden. She and I had almost come to blows after a heated argument in Zion over her passivity.

"You returned Fury's cuffs from the sea before we went to Nulterra. Now this. What's changed?" I asked, noting the guilt in her golden eyes.

She linked her fingers in front of her. "In Zion, you said that the chronicles of history would show that I chose to take a knee when the Angels of Life had the choice to fight. After I researched what *take a knee* meant, and learned more than I ever wanted to about American football"—we all laughed—"I decided we would not hide from this war."

Her eyes drifted toward Azrael. "Someone once asked for my help, and I denied them. I've regretted it every day since."

Ariel had been among the angels who refused to help Azrael protect me as a baby.

"Forgive me?" she asked.

My father's head tilted forward.

Movement up the staircase drew my eye. Someone else was coming down. I strained my eyes, but their face was silhouetted against the bright light behind them, and I couldn't make out their identity. Whoever it was had a petite frame, and they walked with a chipper bounce to their step.

I didn't know many people like that.

"Who is that?" Sloan asked, creating a visor with her hand to shield her eyes.

Reuel pushed through the center of the group. He lingered in front of me for a second, before pushing up through the center of the stairs. The woman's face came into view.

Nathan leaned against my arm. "Is that the chick from the bakery?"

I laughed as Reuel lifted her like a rag doll and hugged her. "Yeah, I think it is."

The Father turned back toward us. "It looks like Reuel is coming home. Anyone else?" He looked at me first.

"With your blessing, I'd like to stay." I smiled at my daughter. "I don't want to miss anything else if I can help it."

She laid her head in the crook of my neck.

The Father smiled. "I had a feeling you might say that."

"I'm going," Gabriel said. He looked across the lawn. "And I'm bringing Ionis home with me."

A hush fell over our group. "We're bringing all of our dead with us," the Father said.

"Is there any way to bring them back?" Nathan asked.

"I'm afraid there is not. The sacrifice they made here was great," the Father answered. Without another word, the bodies of the angels *and* demons who'd been struck down rose into the air and floated to the top of the moonstone steps.

"What do we do about the dead humans?" I asked.

The Father looked at the sun's placement in the sky, then looked at Iliana. "I think someone here has the ability to help them."

"You want me to bring them back?" she asked.

"I think all Azrael's men deserve a second chance."

I lifted a hand. "Not that Thacker guy though. I can't wait to inflict the final death on him." I looked all the way around me but didn't see his soul anywhere.

Fury chuckled beside me.

The Father turned to Jett and Rogan. "You both have done exactly what I asked you to do. Now that your job is finished, will you be returning home?"

Jett's eyes darted around the group. "Umm..."

"Sure, he's going home," I said, crossing my arms.

Nathan held up his thumb. "Yeah, Jett. Nice work. Time to go."

Iliana gave us both dirty looks. "I'd like to stay," Jett said.

But instead of Iliana, it was Fury he was looking at.

*Wow. This kid is good.*

The Father bowed his head. "I think that will be—"

"What in the Sam Hill is that?" Shannon shouted from the top of the bunker stairs.

She and Reese had stayed down below, but now she was staggering across what was left of the building. Her mouth was gaping, and her eyes were looking everywhere but her feet. She tripped over every rock and cranny she passed over.

All eyes turned toward Rogan.

He opened his mouth to speak, but Shannon beat him to it. "Nico, baby, are you okay?" She ran across the lawn toward us.

Again, we all looked at Rogan for his answer.

Annoyance was etched all over his face, but he sighed heavily as his earthly mother approached. "I'll stay," he said, shocking the shit out of us all. He pointed at Jett. "But you owe me, big time."

Jett laughed and slapped his best friend on the back.

"I believe that just leaves Cassiel," the father stretched on his toes to search the battlefield. "Where is she?"

"I'm here," Cassiel answered, behind me. She was on the ground, on her hands and knees, weeping. "I'm sorry."

"Why are you sorry?" The Father didn't have to ask; he would have already known.

"Because it was my fault the spirit line was destroyed."

I could have argued, but the Father beat me to it.

"We already discussed this," he said gently. "Cassiel, look at me."

She sat back on her heels, and Kathy handed her a tissue.

The Father looked at her kindly. "You did exactly as you were meant to. In the end, love always conquers evil."

She sniffed and dabbed her eyes.

Fury put her hand on my chest. "Go to her."

I lifted my eyebrows.

"I'm sure," she said.

I walked over and offered Cassiel my hand. She stared at it for a second before taking it. I pulled her off the ground and into my arms. "Thank you," I whispered against her hair.

The Father smiled at her. "So will you stay? I believe this planet suits you more than you believed."

She turned toward him, holding onto my waist. "My home is still in Eden, and I'm *so* ready to be back there, but I wish to not return until I've found Sandalphon."

"Oh yes…Sandalphon." The Father looked around like Sandalphon might wander out of the parking lot. He raised his hands, sending another shock wave of energy all around us that blew me and Cassiel back a step.

"What the hell was that?" Nathan asked, readjusting the ball cap on his head.

Cassiel looked toward the sky. "The spirit line."

With a thunderous *crack!* Sandalphon appeared between us and the building. He looked thinner and older, if it was possible. His clothes were the same as the day we'd been arrested, and he wasn't wearing any shoes.

Cassiel released me and ran to him, nearly toppling the old angel over.

"Iliana, do you have any strength left?" the Father asked.

"I'm tired, but I'm OK."

"Can you step up here with me?"

"Sure." Her foot was shaky as she stepped up beside him. Inside the light, she wobbled a bit. My mother steadied her with a hug.

"Now, how do you feel?" he asked.

Iliana's eyes were bright. "Amazing."

"Sandalphon." The Father gestured him forward.

It took a minute, but Sandalphon finally reached the stairs with Cassiel's help.

The Father extended a hand and pulled him into the light. Then he looked at Iliana. "You are the light of Eden. You have abilities beyond even what you know." His eyes slid toward Sandalphon.

Iliana's healing power glowed in her palms as she offered her hands to Sandalphon. When he took them, the light swelled and engulfed them both.

The light sparkled, twisting and swirling around them with every color of the rainbow. When the light show stopped, Iliana was holding the hands of a man I didn't even recognize.

Sandalphon had been transformed. The clock had been rewound, and this angel, who'd spent countless eons frozen as a decrepit senior citizen, was young again.

"Holy shit," Nathan said, echoing all my thoughts.

I started clapping, and everyone else joined in.

Sandalphon seemed unsure of what to think. He picked up his knees, one at a time, quite obviously amazed that the joints no longer ached. His white hair had turned black, and he must have grown three inches.

Cassiel stepped up beside him. She trailed her fingertips down his face. "Is it really you?"

He looked down at his foreign body. "To be honest, I'm not quite sure."

We all laughed, and she threw her arms around his neck.

Iliana came and stood beside me. "I think they look kinda cute together."

I chuckled and put my arm around her. "They certainly do."

Cassiel split a glance between me and the Father. "Wait till Metatron hears about this."

Metatron was another angel like Sandalphon, but the body he was trapped in was much, much older. When I'd met him in Eden, he'd been hoping that Iliana would have the power to put him out of his misery. Thankfully, now it wouldn't have to be by angel-assisted suicide.

"So what will you do now?" Sloan asked the Father.

"For now, I will leave this world in capable hands." He smiled at me. "We'll always be close by if we're needed, but something tells me, you'll all be just fine."

"What about my sister?" Fury asked.

The Father seemed surprised he hadn't thought of Anya. "That's a very good question. Anya, what will it be?"

Anya looked like a deer in the headlights. "Um, I really don't know."

"Well, I think I can speak for everyone when I say you sure as hell don't *need* the mantle of the Archangel. You were a total badass today," I said.

Anya blushed as everyone cheered.

Nathan looked over at me. "It's a damn good thing you went to Nulterra to find her. I heard she saved your ass out there."

I nodded. "A few times. There was no way we could have survived that battle without you, Anya. You saved all of us."

The group cheered again.

The Father turned his palms up. "The choice is yours. It's completely up to you."

Anya was weighing the decision. "Can I come back?"

"Of course," he said.

Anya looked at Fury with a hint of an excited grin. "It would be fun to fly."

Fury pulled her into a hug. "You've never needed wings to fly. Go, but don't stay gone too long."

Tears sparkled in Anya's eyes when she stepped back. "I promise." Anya walked up onto the steps, and she shuddered when she passed into the light. She rubbed her bare arms. "Goosebumps."

"I want to hear all about it," Fury said.

I looked down at her. "You know I've been there too?"

Nathan smirked. "Like the two of you ever *talk*."

Everyone laughed.

After that, we all said our goodbyes. I promised Alice I'd visit soon and asked her to look after Skittles.

"What do we do about him?" Iliana asked, pointing at the Morning Star, floating in the air. "We can't kill him. At least not until we're sure that all the Claymore troops have been healed."

"That could take years," Kane said.

The Father looked at the Morning Star. So much was loaded in that glance.

Anger.

Disappointment.

Love.

"You don't have to kill him at all," he finally said. "He created his own hell, and now he can spend the rest of eternity wallowing in it."

La Isla del Fuego.

---

*I saw the great sword come down from Eden,*
*having the key to the bottomless pit.*
*And he laid hold of the dragon*
*when a thousand years had expired.*

*The devil that deceived them*
*was cast into his lake of fire*
*and tormented day and night for ever and ever.*

---

"Secure him well, and take him through the spirit line," the Father said to Azrael.

Azrael bowed his head.

The Father stared at Az for a long moment. "Azrael, come here." He stretched out his hand.

Azrael looked at it and then looked at his kids and Adrianne. "Father, I'm mortal."

"Do you think I've forgotten?"

"I can't leave my family," Azrael clarified.

The Father reached farther. "There are some perks to being me. Come."

Azrael put his daughter down, and she immediately ran into Taiya's arms.

Azrael looked worried as he stood in front of the staircase, but he placed his hand in the Father's and stepped into the light.

His knees wobbled. I knew the feeling he was experiencing well. Absolute ecstasy.

The Father opened his palm, and the Morning Star's dagger materialized in it.

Azrael's smile faded.

"This took something from you," the Father said quietly.

Azrael didn't respond, but his shoulders withered enough to confirm the statement for all of us. I had no idea what the Father was talking about. There were never any memories in Azrael's blood stone about a dagger.

Holding the dagger by the blade, the Father offered it to Azrael.

Azrael took a step back.

"Do you trust me?" the Father asked.

Looking at him, Azrael took a deep breath, and with a reluctant swallow, he took the knife.

A surge of energy passed from the Father, through the dagger, and into Azrael's hand. A smoldering edge of energy burned all the way up his arm and neck and through his torso until it disappeared behind his back.

Light ruptured from behind Azrael's shoulders.

Wings.

Azrael crumpled to a knee in front of the Father as the wings spread wider than the Eden steps. He was crying, something I don't think I'd ever seen before.

The Father touched Azrael's head. "I love you, my son. Welcome back."

# CHAPTER THIRTY

*L*a Isla del Fuego was crawling with scientists—and *reporters*—when Azrael and I crossed the spirit line with our prisoner. We'd seen them from inside the breach, so we warped into a deserted edge of the jungle.

"I guess a surprise volcano is a bigger deal than we thought," I said, peeking out through an elephant-ear plant to count the humans present. *Nineteen.* "Do you remember being here at all?" I asked my father.

"Flashes. I've missed most of the past couple of decades," he answered.

I looked over my shoulder. "You and me both."

"What now?" he asked.

"Well, we can't exactly walk out there."

"Why not?"

"Because we're carrying a man wrapped up like a safety-yellow burrito."

"Then what do you want to do?"

I grinned back at him. "I kinda want to fly out there and say, 'Hark! Fear not!'"

With a laugh, he rolled his eyes. "We do *not* say that."

I straightened and turned around. "Then why don't you show me how it's done."

He smirked and drew the sword Reuel had given him before he returned to Eden. "Take notes, kid."

Without another word, Azrael launched straight up into the air. When he rose out of sight, I turned back to the Morning Star, who was sitting upright on the ground, confined to a military-grade restraint system.

His legs were wrapped in padding and secured with Velcro straps all the way up from his ankles to his hips. His wrists were cuffed in high-Z and chained to his ankles. His mouth was wrapped with about nineteen layers of duct tape.

I crossed my arms as I stood over him. "Bet you've seen him do this a million times."

The Morning Star just glared at me.

It was early in the morning in the Philippines, but the sky suddenly went dark. "Oh, here we go." I pushed apart the plants to look out toward the lake.

Azrael slowly descended from the sky. Like his clothes, his wings were solid black. He held the sword with both hands, straight up and down in front of him, as he lowered toward the lake of fire.

Everyone on the ground was either running away or pointing. One guy was filming it with his cell phone.

Azrael flipped the sword around, aiming the blade toward the crowd, and sent a ripple of golden sparks through his wings.

The gawkers took off then. All except the one man with his cell phone. Azrael dove toward him, and I'm pretty sure the man shit himself as he scrambled across the field.

Azrael landed a few feet from where I stood. "Why the hell would I say fear not?"

I laughed and lifted the Morning Star using my power. "You know that's gonna wind up on YouTube," I said as we walked toward the lake.

"Is YouTube still a thing?"

"Beats the hell out of me."

The sun was still covered in black, which was probably a good thing. Darkness could keep even the bravest of humans away. We climbed the hill where my empty-grave marker over-looked the lake.

"Why don't you let me take it from here?" I asked.

Demon or not, Azrael had raised Michael as his son.

"I helped start this. Now I'm going to finish it." He looked down at the Morning Star. "Any last words?"

The Morning Star mumbled furiously against the duct tape.

Az cupped a hand around his ear. "Nothing? Okay then." With a guttural scream, Azrael hurled the demon into his lake.

---

The sky was dark back in Asheville, but only because it was nighttime. The grounds of Echo-5, however, were lit up like the Fourth of July.

Red and blue emergency lights flashed everywhere as the entire property was overrun with official-looking vehicles. Only one of them I saw was marked Buncombe County Sher-iff. Most of the rest were unmarked. Some had acronyms I'd never even seen before.

Azrael and I were inside the breach, watching the chaos through the veil. "What the hell is all this?" I asked.

"I'll bet they've come for me." His tone was heavy and full of guilt.

"Maybe you should lie low for a while. Maybe even hide out in Eden until shit here blows over."

He shook his head. "I'm not running away. Michael was my responsibility. And the things he did, he did in my name. Maybe if I hadn't been such an arrogant prick, some of this could have be avoided."

"Az, this is serious. They'll take you to prison. Or they might just execute you and bury you at sea like Bin Laden."

"I know."

He crossed through the breach first with a thunderous boom. I followed him right into the center of the lawn.

All guns—a lot of them—turned in our direction.

Near the parking lot, Nathan was in handcuffs. So was everyone I could see wearing a Claymore uniform.

Sloan ran toward us, right into the line of fire. "Thank God you're back!"

"What's going on?" I asked, grabbing her and turning so I was between her and the guns.

"Every law-enforcement agency in America is here. Local, state, federal. They say a helicopter is on its way from Washington."

"Why is Nathan in handcuffs?" Azrael asked.

She rolled her eyes. "You know he can't keep his mouth shut."

A team of officers were having a frantic discussion in a huddle. Then, suddenly, they broke and stormed toward us. Gunmen, some with handguns, others with assault rifles, rushed Azrael and took him to the ground.

Another team escorted a man in a suit forward. "Are you Damon Claymore?"

Azrael didn't fight back as they cuffed him at gunpoint. He could easily break the restraints, but he didn't. "I am."

The man was searching the sky, probably trying to figure out where the hell we had come from and what the noise had been.

"Damon Claymore, you are under arrest for acts of domestic terror—"

*Whomp. Whomp. Whomp...*

Lights flashed in the sky as a helicopter approached. It was a big one, making the Claymore transporter parked on the lawn, look like a toy.

Soldiers cleared the field for the aircraft to land. In the dark, it looked a bit like Marine One.

The helicopter of the president of the United States.

*No way.*

The engine stopped, and as the rotors slowed, a whole new group of soldiers poured out of it.

Yep. Marines.

I didn't even know who was currently president.

A man walked down the steps, buttoning his suit jacket. He crossed the lawn toward us, but he didn't have the gait of a politician.

My eyes narrowed when he was close enough to see his face. "Enzo?"

"Hello, Warren."

"Holy shit." I'd never seen Enzo in anything but cargo pants. "Are you the president now?"

Enzo laughed. "No, not even close. But I am the head of Homeland Security, and I got word today that some of my old friends might have blown up the city of Asheville." He scowled at my dad. "Hi, *Damon*."

Sloan grabbed his arm, eliciting quick movements from the soldiers surrounding us. Enzo raised a hand to hold them off. "Enzo, you know who was responsible for this. It wasn't Az."

He patted her hand. "I know. Still, we need to take Mr. Claymore in. He has a lot to answer for."

"I'll go quietly," Azrael told him.

Adrianne and her kids came over. "What's happening? Why are you in handcuffs? Where are they taking you?"

"You're going away again?" Little Sloan asked.

Azrael got down on his knees in front of her. "Daddy has to go for a little while, but don't worry about me. I'll be just fine, and I'll be back before you know it."

"But we just got you back," she whined with the most pitiful face I'd ever seen.

"I'm sorry, sweetheart. I'll be back as soon as I can."

"Are you going to fly in that helicopter, or are you going to fly with your new wings?" The little girl flapped her arms.

He smiled. "Probably in the helicopter." He lowered his voice to a whisper. "This time."

She giggled.

He stood and kissed his wife. "I'll be OK."

"You'd better be, or I'll kill you," she said.

He smiled and kissed her again. Then he looked at his son. "I love you, Philip. Take care of your mother and sister."

"I will, Dad."

Enzo put his hand on my shoulder. "Don't worry. I'll get things sorted out."

I shook his hand. "It hasn't been the same, not having you around."

He lowered his voice. "You'd better be glad I've been exactly where I am."

"Absolutely."

"Where's Michael?"

"Dead. Sort of."

"Do you have a body?"

I shook my head.

"We're going to have to hang this on somebody."

"Just make sure it isn't Az."

"I'll do my best." Enzo looked at his men holding Azrael.

"Bring him with us." As they walked toward the helicopter, he shouted to the group guarding Nathan. "Let him go!"

Enzo and Az loaded into the helicopter with the Marines, and its engine started again.

Nathan was rubbing his wrists as he walked over to join us. "How the hell did we get that lucky?"

I looked toward the auranos, which was barely visible now, just past twilight. "I don't think luck had anything to do with it." I put my arm around Fury's shoulders. "You okay?"

"Yeah, are you?"

I pressed a kiss against her temple. "Baby, I'm better than I've ever been."

Smiling, she clutched the front of my shirt.

"It's done?" Nathan asked.

Adrianne was staring at me.

"We'll talk about it later," I said.

"No. Talk about it now." She looked at her son. "Philip, take your sister back to the bunker. Go in through the garage. The other entrance is too dangerous."

"Yes, ma'am." He reached for little Sloan's hand. "Come on. Let's go find Taiya."

When they were out of earshot, I nodded. "It's finished."

"Michael's dead?" Adrianne asked.

"Not exactly, but he's never coming back. The lake closed up before we left the island. It's not even there anymore."

"Where'd it go?" Nathan asked.

I lifted my shoulders. "Beats me. Hopefully, somewhere far, far away. Where is Iliana?"

"Dealing with Torman," Sloan said. "The Father asked her to strip him of his powers and set him free. He'll live out his days like a mortal."

"She can do that?" I asked, surprised.

"Apparently, she can do a lot of things," Nathan said as we

all started back toward the garage. "Kinda wish I'd stepped into that magical light myself."

"You will, someday," I said.

Sloan stopped as we neared the building, or what was left of it, anyway. "I can't believe it's gone."

"I know. Where the hell are we going to live?" Nathan asked.

Sloan looked up at him. "We'll never hear the end of it if we keep Luca in the bunker much longer. I've only been back for a day, and if I hear about connection speeds one more time, I might shove spikes in my ears."

"Speaking of connection speeds, what happened to my communication tower?" Nathan's hands were on his hips. "It was down when we got home yesterday, but there was so much shit going on I forgot to ask about it."

"Reuel did it," I said without further explanation. Thankfully, Reuel wasn't there to defend himself and incriminate me.

Nathan swore under his breath.

"What does it matter?" Sloan asked. "Echo-5 is gone. We have much bigger things to worry about."

"But all that power…"

"Nathan, it looked ridiculous," Adrianne said as we all started toward the garage again. "A thousand feet tall with only the top five percent covered with branches. It was never going to look like a real pine tree."

"You don't know that. The other trees would have caught up eventually."

"Not in your lifetime," she said.

"Not even in mine," I added with a laugh.

Fury looked up at me. "What will happen with your lifetime now?"

"As long as I stay here, I'll continue to age as a human. Then someday, hopefully you and I will go to Eden together."

The sound of paper crackling caught my ear. I looked across the group as Nathan shoveled a handful of candy into his mouth. Midchew, he stopped and looked at the wrapper. "Wait a second," he said around a mouthful.

"What?" Sloan asked him.

He turned the candy's label toward me. "Did you name your dog after me?"

I laughed.

He swallowed and pointed at me. "You did! You named your dog Skittles!"

"I did no such thing."

Fury leaned her head to the side. "The dog's name *is* Skittles."

"Reuel named her. Not me."

"Warren, there's no need to be embarrassed. You don't have to lie!" Nathan came over and threw his arms around me. "You love me! You really love me!"

Laughing, I pushed him away.

"You want some?" he asked, holding up the bag.

I turned over my palm. "I'd love some." My stomach rumbled as he poured the colorful candies into my hand. "I haven't eaten all day."

Fury plucked a green Skittle out of my hand. "Me either."

"I'm starving too," Adrianne said.

"You guys want to find some food?" Nathan asked.

Sloan raised her hand. "I hear Tupelo Honey survived the apocalypse. Anyone up for cheese grits?"

## A SLOAN MCNAMARA EPILOGUE

I knocked on the bedroom door *again.* "Nathan, what are you doing in there? Warren and Fury just pulled up the driveway."

Silence.

I banged harder. "Nathan!"

The door swung open so fast I jumped back a step. Then my eyes doubled as my husband racked a shotgun with one hand. I ran my hand down my face, shaking my head. "Absolutely not."

He stood there in nothing but a pair of tighty-whities and work boots. When he tried to pass me, I splayed my hand across his bare chest to stop him. "Oh hell no. You're not leaving this room until you put on some pants. And put the shotgun back in the safe." With both hands, I pushed him back inside. "What are you even trying to do here?"

"I'm going to scare him."

"You're scaring *me.*"

Nathan was attempting his stern-dad face. "That boy needs a healthy dose of fear if he's going out with my daughter."

I laughed and tilted my head toward the shotgun. "Is that thing even loaded?"

His mouth opened. Then he closed it. "That's beside the point."

I put my hands on his shoulders. "You are not allowed to embarrass her today. And this"—I let my eyes drift up and down—"is *embarrassing.*"

"This is me making a statement."

"Well…" I clapped my hands slowly. "Mission accomplished."

"Mom, Warren and Fury are here!" Luca called down the hallway.

I snapped my fingers at my husband. "Pants. Now."

Nathan caught my hand, pulled me to him, and twirled me under his arm.

"You're a crazy man," I said, laughing.

"You knew that when you married me."

"That I did." I walked to the bedroom door and pointed at him. "Don't make me regret it."

He winked. "Like you could ever regret all of this." He gestured down the length of his body.

I laughed as I walked out of our room. The end of the hall opened into the foyer of the living room/kitchen/dining room, and Luca was opening the front door.

My nose involuntarily scrunched when I saw Fury first on the other side of it. Bygones were definitely bygones, but she was still one of the most beautiful women I'd ever seen in real life. She wore suction-tight jeans with a black spaghetti-strap tank, an outfit I hadn't been able to pull off in…*ever.*

She smiled when she saw me—something I still wasn't used to—and she gave a small wave.

"You made it," I said, walking over as they came inside. I greeted her first with a hug.

Beside her, Warren had taken a departure from his nearly solid black wardrobe. He wore dark jeans and a navy T-shirt. His hair had grown long enough to tuck behind his ears in the couple of months they'd been back on Earth.

"For the house." He offered me a bottle of champagne as he pulled me in for a side hug and a kiss on the temple. "Love the new place."

I stepped back and looked around the tall, open living space. "Yeah, it's a bit of a work in progress, but we like it."

"It's not underground, so that's an improvement," he said.

"So true. Come on in. Luca, go tell your sister they're here."

"Yes, ma'am," my son replied.

"Where's Nate?" Warren asked.

I led them to the kitchen island, where I'd set out a few finger foods. "Hopefully getting dressed."

Fury laughed. "Hopefully?"

"Yeah." I rolled my eyes and put the champagne in the fridge. "Long story. One you definitely don't want to hear before dinner."

"Now, I must know," Warren said.

"Let's just say, he's being a bit overdramatic about Iliana's first date."

Fury squeezed Warren's bicep. "We don't know *anything* about that, do we?"

My head tilted. "Not you too."

Warren had the look Nathan gets when he thinks I'm being ridiculous. "I wasn't being dramatic."

Fury leaned against the bar. "I had to make him leave the sword at home."

I held up a hand. "You don't even want to know what I hopefully stopped."

"Men," Fury said with a smile.

"Where's Jett?" I asked.

"He's meeting us here," Warren said, shaking his head. "Probably stopping on the way to buy condoms."

"Warren!" I felt my cheeks flush with heat.

Fury backhanded his chest. "Stop it."

A door opened and closed behind them. Nathan walked out of the hallway, miraculously dressed in jeans and a black T-shirt. He always wore a double shoulder holster, but if I'd learned anything in seventeen years of marriage, it was to pick your battles. This one, he could have.

"I'll behave," he announced as he crossed the living room.

I laughed and shook my head.

Nathan shook hands with Warren and pulled him in for a one-armed hug. "Welcome back *again*. How's your dad?"

Warren slapped him on the back. "Glad to not be in prison."

Exonerating Azrael had been easier than Enzo had expected. The American government was happy to keep the whole thing as quiet as possible. They even went so far as to create a mythical enemy that the Claymore Army had so bravely defeated in Asheville.

"Azrael got some more good news right before we left," Fury said.

Nathan's brow lifted in question.

"The government is putting Enzo in charge of Claymore," Warren said.

Nathan's jaw went slack. "Shut up."

"That's amazing," I said.

"Yeah. They gave him a decent settlement too, despite *everything*."

"Are they still talking about moving back here?" I asked, hopefully, clasping my hands beneath my chin.

Warren nodded. "Fury and I are looking for a place of our own so they can move back to the mountain."

I excitedly clapped my hands together. Then I quickly

covered my mouth. "I mean, I'm really sorry you guys have to move again. I'm just—"

A wave of Fury's hand cut me off. "We always knew the move was temporary." She looked up at Warren. "Besides, I'm kinda looking forward to finding something that's *ours.*"

Looking at him, looking at her, it was clear: they really were perfect for each other. "Me too," he said with a smile.

"How does Jett feel about moving again?" I asked.

Fury shrugged. "He and Rogan are counting down the days until Rogan turns eighteen and they can get an apartment."

I laughed. "That's shockingly normal."

"I know," Fury agreed. "He'd move out now, but you know Shannon won't have it. She's hanging on every second that she can now that Rogan's back at home."

"Poor guy," I said.

"Poor nothing. I think they should both *stay* at home." Nathan wagged his finger between Fury and Warren. "That way there's two fully armed, responsible adults there to chaperone."

Fury grimaced. "But they're about to be adults, so…"

I shrugged. "And not to mention, Jett's already lived—"

Nathan's finger shot toward me. "You promised we weren't going to talk about that anymore. He's just a normal seventeen-year-old boy. That's what *you* said."

I chuckled and put my hands up in defense. "You're right. I take it back."

Nathan nudged Warren with his elbow. "So how are we going to play this? Good cop, bad cop?"

"I prefer outright threats," Warren said.

"Did you bring the sword?"

Warren jerked his head toward Fury. "She wouldn't let me."

I crossed my arms and looked at them both. "You want her to move in with Jett and Rogan? She's eighteen too, ya know?"

A deep crease formed between Nathan's eyebrows. "You and I have issues today, woman."

"Just trying to keep you from doing something all of us will regret, my dear." I lifted my wineglass and hid my mouth behind it. "As always."

Fury tried to stifle a laugh and failed.

Feet pounded the stairs on the other side of the house.

"There's my girl," Warren said, opening his arms.

Iliana ran to him, jumping into his arms. He twirled her all the way around before returning her to her feet. Holding her hands, he took in the full sight of her. "Wow, you look—"

"Too damn pretty." Nathan stepped over beside him and pointed toward the stairs. "Go change. Right now."

Iliana rolled her eyes. "Dad."

"You do look really pretty," Warren said quietly to her.

She smiled and did a twirl in the pink sundress. "Thanks. Mom picked it out."

Nathan whirled toward me, horrified. "You're responsible for this?"

"Paid for it with your credit card," I said with a wink.

He put his hands on his hips. "Issues," he said again.

"When did you get back?" Iliana asked Warren and Fury.

"We made a pit stop at the house but then came straight here." The corner of Warren's mouth tipped up. "Couldn't miss your first official date."

Iliana rocked back and forth on her heels. "You sure you're OK with it?"

Nathan opened his mouth to speak, but I gave him the *look.* Frustrated, his lips snapped shut.

"It's a little weird." Warren put his arm around Fury. "But Jett comes from good genes, so I can't object too much."

"And Jett really cares about you," Fury added with an approving nod. "Which is what matters most to all of us."

Nathan's mouth opened again.

"He jumped in front of a bullet to save her," I snapped to shut him up. "And if you don't simmer down, I'm going to let Iliana use her power to lock you in the bedroom."

Stunned, Nathan laughed along with everyone else. Then he zipped his lips closed and pretended to toss away a key.

Our daughter flashed me a grateful smile, then walked over to Nathan and cupped his face in her hands. "It's going to be all right, Dad."

He frowned but hugged her. "I just love you so much. No one will ever be good enough."

"I know." She kissed his cheek. "I love you too."

When she stepped away from him, I reached for his hand and pulled him to me. He pressed his lips against my hair, and I heard him sniff as he fought back tears. I put my arm around his waist—and felt another handgun tucked into his waistband.

The doorbell rang.

Nathan started forward, but I held onto the back of his shirt. I noticed Fury also had her finger hooked in Warren's back pocket.

Iliana went to the door. This child, who'd battled demons and saved mankind—for the first time in her eventful life— looked nervous. She blew out a shaky sigh as she reached for the door handle.

My heart fluttered for her.

Jett walked inside with a handful of wildflowers. Purple bee balm, pink swamp milkweed, goldenrod, and white wood astor. His face brightened when he saw her. "Hi."

"Hi." Iliana bit her lower lip.

"Oh. Here." Jett offered her the flowers. "These are for you."

"Guess we know why he was late," Fury whispered to Warren.

"Umm-hmm," Warren replied with a smirk.

Iliana held the bouquet to her nose. "Thank you. They're beautiful."

"So are you," he said quietly. His eyes darted nervously in our direction. His dark hair was neatly combed, and he was more dressed up than I'd ever seen him. He gave an awkward wave. "Hey, guys."

Nathan grunted.

"Hi, Jett." I walked over with my husband right on my heels and held my hands toward Iliana. "Can I put the flowers in some water for you?"

"Thanks, Mom," Iliana said, handing them to me.

"Are you ready to go?" Jett asked her.

When I turned back toward the kitchen, Nathan stepped in. "Just a minute."

*Oh boy.*

"Where are you two headed?" Nathan asked.

Jett looked like he was in front of a freight train. "Um…to the movies?"

"You don't sound so sure." Nathan crossed his arms.

"Yes, sir. To the movies." Jett swallowed hard. "And for pizza at the Mellow Mushroom."

"Pizza?" Warren walked slowly forward. His brow couldn't have been any more scrunched. "Is that what we're calling it now?"

Iliana covered her face. "Appa…"

Nathan elbowed him. "Do your light-ball thing."

"Dad!" Iliana shrieked.

Fury slapped Warren's arm as he conjured his power into his hand. "Hey! That's my son."

"Thank you, Fury," Iliana said.

Jett was standing a few inches behind her.

I put the flowers on the counter. "Ignore them. Illy, what time will you be home?"

"Midnight?" she asked.

"Eleven," Nathan corrected her.

"She's eighteen," I reminded him.

Nathan frowned.

"Eleven-thirty?" she asked with a hopeful smile.

He huffed. "Fine."

With an excited smile, she turned back to Jett. "Let's get out of here before he breaks out the high-Z cuffs."

Jett laughed and opened the door.

"Oh! Wait!" I pulled my phone from my back pocket.

"Mom…" Iliana groaned and rolled her eyes.

I put a hand on my hip. "I could've let your father come out here in his underwear with a shotgun."

Her face twisted. "Ew."

"Right? So smile like you mean it." I tapped the camera button on my screen and held up the phone.

Jett put an arm around her, and they both smiled as I snapped a photo. "Can we go now?" Iliana asked.

"Have fun," I said, tucking my phone back into my pocket.

"But not too much fun!" Warren shouted after them.

Iliana waved before closing the front door behind them. My husband dramatically crumpled over the counter, burying his face in his hands. "I hate it so much."

Walking behind him, I patted his back. "Come on. We'll drown your sorrows in a glass of champagne." I took the bottle out of the fridge. "Nathan? Want to do the honors?"

His face was buried in his hands. "I don't feel like celebrating."

I slipped the cold bottle under the front of his shirt.

"Whoa-ho-ho!" He bolted upright. "Holy shit, woman!"

Warren and Fury laughed.

I handed him the bottle. "Pop the cork. The sound of explosions always makes you feel better."

"Yeah, it does." He gripped the champagne by the neck, twisted off the metal cage around the cork, and pointed it away from us. With his thumbs he pressed, and the cork fired across the living room with a loud *pop!*

We all clapped, and I got four glasses down from the cabinet. Nathan poured them full and passed them around.

Fury lifted hers into the air. "To your new life, and hopefully, the beginning of a bit of peace and quiet for all of us."

"Amen to that," Nathan agreed.

Warren raised his glass, smiling at me. "And to our little girl, who's every bit as brave and beautiful as her mother."

I felt my cheeks flush.

Nathan clinked his glass with all of ours. "And to *all* of us. Who'd have thought it would take a bunch of humans to save the world?"

My arm froze midair as something deep and existential stirred inside me.

Warren must have registered the look on my face. "Sloan? You OK?"

A chill rippled my spine. "Do you think he knew?"

"Who knew what?" Nathan asked.

"The Father. He's the only being in existence with omniscient power," I said.

"What?" Fury asked.

I looked at Nathan. "Humans were created *after* the angels. And even the good ones, like Azrael, have never been happy they were made to take care of us. The Father never gave them a reason for it either."

Warren put his glass down and raked both hands through his black hair. "He always said omniscience was a curse. And he said, he was responsible for bringing me and Sloan together."

Fury touched his arm. "And if you hadn't jumped in front of

those Yahweh bullets, the hydrogen necroxide would have killed Iliana, and the Morning Star would have won."

"Fury's right," I said. "Warren, you're the only angel or human that could have saved her."

A hush fell over the room, all of us lost in thought, our minds traveling through time and between worlds. Everything finally made sense.

Everything.

The silence was shattered by the sound of Nathan's laughter. "Sloan, where's your phone?"

My head snapped back. "What? Why?"

"I need to call Azrael. You can bet your ass, he's *never* going to hear the end of this one."

**THANK YOU FOR READING!**

Please leave a review on your favorite eBook retailer's website! Reviews help indie authors like me find new readers and get advertising. If you enjoyed this book, please tell your friends!

**What's coming next?**

**DETACHED**

The Saphera Nyx Series - Book 1

*She wrongly inherited a destiny she doesn't want. Now, alone and in secret, Saphera Nyx must choose: either oust herself as a powerful spirit mage... or watch her city burn.*

**Want to be the first to know about its release?**

Sign up at

www.eliciahyder.com

JOIN
HYDERNATION
AUTHOR ELICIA HYDER
OFFICIAL FAN CLUB

# ALSO BY ELICIA HYDER

**Be brave. Be strong. Be badass.**

Roll into the exciting world of women's flat track roller derby, where the women are the heroes, and the men will make you weak in the kneepads.

A brand new romantic comedy series from Author Elicia Hyder.

# ALSO BY ELICIA HYDER

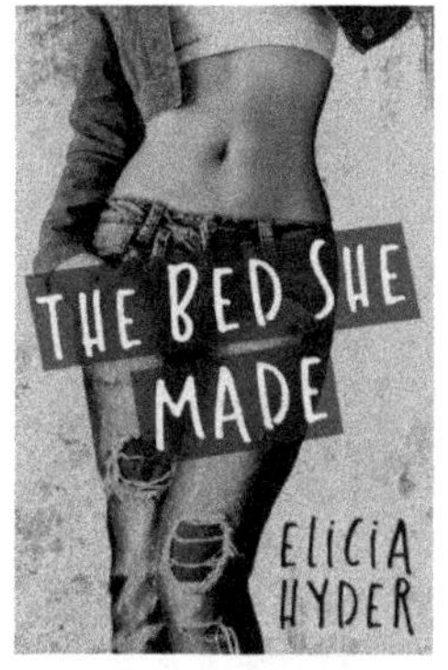

**The Bed She Made**

2015 Watty Award Winner for Best New
Adult Romance

*Journey Durant's father warned her that someday
she'd have to lie in the bed she made. But she
didn't believe him until her ex is released from
prison and he threatens to bring her troubled past
home with him.*

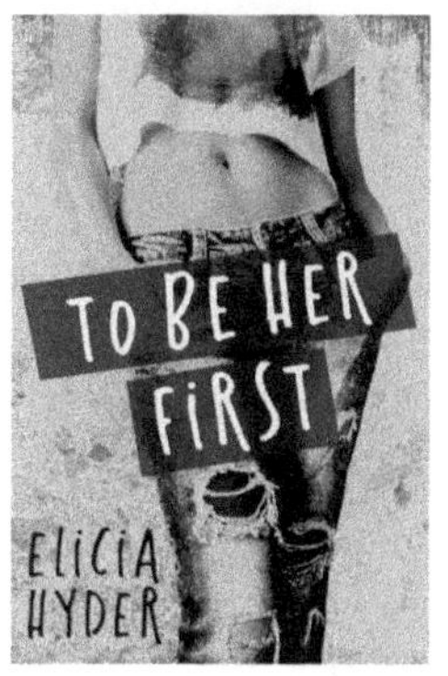

**To Be Her First**

The Young Adult Prequel to The Bed
She Made

*At sixteen, Journey Durant hasn't yet experienced
her first anything. No first boyfriend. No first
date. No first kiss. But that's all about to change.
Two boys at West Emerson High are vying for her
attention: the MVP quarterback and the school's
reigning bad boy.*

# ABOUT THE AUTHOR

In the dawning age of scrunchies and 'Hammer Pants', a small-town musician with big-city talent found out she was expecting her third child a staggering eleven years after her last one. From that moment on, Susie Waldrop referred to her daughter Elicia as a 'blessing' which is loosely translated as an accident, albeit a pleasant one.

In true youngest-sibling fashion, Elicia lived up to the birth order standard by being fun-loving, outgoing, self-centered, and rebellious throughout her formative years. She excelled academically—a feat her sister attributes to her being the only child who was breastfed—but abandoned her studies to live in a tent in the national forest with her dogs: a Rottweiler named

Bodhisattva and a Pit Bull named Sativa. The ensuing months were very hazy.

In the late 90's, during a stint in rehab, Elicia was approached by a prophet who said, "Someday you will write a book."

She was right.

Now a firm believer in the prophetic word, Elicia Hyder is a full-time writer and freelance editor living in middle Tennessee with her husband and five children. Eventually she did make it to college, and she studied literature and creative writing at the American Military University.

Her debut novel, **The Bed She Made**, is very loosely based on the stranger-than-fiction events of her life.

www.eliciahyder.com
elicia@eliciahyder.com

www.ingramcontent.com/pod-product-compliance
Lightning Source LLC
Chambersburg PA
CBHW071424190726
48292CB00001B/106